~ Shangri-La ~

ALSO BY ELEANOR COONEY AND DANIEL ALTIERI

*Court of the Lion:*
*A Novel of Eighth Century China*

*Deception:*
*A Novel of Murder and Madness in T'ang China*

# Shangri-La

## The Return to the World of *Lost Horizon*

~ ~

## Eleanor Cooney
## Daniel Altieri

William Morrow and Company, Inc.
NEW YORK

It is the policy of William Morrow and Company, Inc., and its imprints and affiliates, recognizing the importance of preserving what has been written, to print the books we publish on acid-free paper, and we exert our best efforts to that end.

Library of Congress Cataloging-in-Publication Data

Cooney, Eleanor.
    Shangri-la: the return to the world of *Lost Horizon* / by Eleanor Cooney and Daniel Altieri.
        p.    cm.
    ISBN 0-688-12872-6
    I. Altieri, Daniel.   II. Title.
    PS3553.05786S53   1996
    813'.54—dc20                                                                95-23492
                                                                                    CIP

*Printed in the United States of America*
FIRST EDITION

1   2   3   4   5   6   7   8   9   10
BOOK DESIGN BY LAURA HAMMOND HOUGH

For the people of Tibet
and
Tom Cooney

*there,*
*but for some discord*
*could i hear*
*the magnificent promise*
*begging to be saved . . .*

*born of ten thousand*
*years of eternity,*
*as time has caressed,*
*this ancient youth;*
*Shambala*
—WILLIAM JAMES KOVANDA

~ Shangri-La ~

# New York, 1966

They couldn't tell if he was Japanese or Chinese. He was old, and his nose was running, and he'd been standing in front of the locked gate outside the U.N. building for three hours, shivering and miserable. The guards had tried to explain that things were shut down for now, closed up for security reasons, that he could come back tomorrow. Now it was getting dark. People died on December nights on the streets of New York.

The two guards eyed the man from inside the warm shelter. He paced and pleaded, as if they were in control of things, as if they could just change their minds and let him in. A nut case, one of them had said. We're supposed to be on the lookout for nuts with bombs. But the other guard didn't agree that the old guy was a nut. Out of place, maybe, a little confused—but not a nut. They turned away, hoping that when they looked back he'd be gone, but he wasn't. The older of the two sighed heavily.

"I'm going out to talk to him."

His friend shrugged and rotated the toothpick in his mouth.

"Suit yourself."

The guard opened the heavy door and stepped out into the bitter wind. He went to the iron gate and pushed it open. The old man saw him and came forward hopefully. The guard shook his head, blocking the way squarely.

"No. I already told you," he said, holding up a hand as if to push the old man back and speaking loudly as people do when they think the one being addressed doesn't know English very well. "You can't come in here. You've gotta go home. Home!" he repeated.

"Home," the old man said, and his face crumpled as if he were going to cry.

"Yeah," the guard said. "Home! You got a home?"

A home, a hotel, something, the guard thought. The old guy didn't look like a bum, either, though his clothes were old and a little odd. A double-breasted suit like the ones you saw in old movies, expensive-looking but out-of-style cracked leather dress shoes, a homburg and an overcoat with a tattered fur collar. His face was gray, as if his gut hurt.

"You look kind of sick," the guard said. "You've gotta get out of this wind." Tears ran down the old man's face now. He looked so sad the guard was afraid he might start crying himself. The man was pulling papers out of his coat and holding them out.

"I want to go home," he said.

Airline tickets. The guard looked at them, looked at the old man.

"Airport?" he said loudly. "You want to go to the airport?" He shut the gate behind him, aware of his friend watching from a distance. He stepped to the curb and signaled. A cab cut away from the river of traffic and pulled up. Get this poor guy off the street, anyway.

The guard took a twenty from his own pocket. "Kennedy," he said to the wordless driver, put the old man in and slammed the door. He gave the rear fender a hopeful pat as the cab pulled away.

~

He could feel the cold creeping outward from his own bones. Even here, where it was warm. A bad sign, a very bad sign. The sickening speed of the ride had driven his illness deeper into him. Hurtling along, blood-red lights in front of them and brilliant white ones behind, his legs braced and his hands gripping the back of the driver's seat, he had opened his eyes long enough to peer out the window. Enormous aircraft, birds of prey in landing formation, moved ponderously through the glowing night sky directly over his head, lights winking like jewels, filling the world with their sound. He had expected to die at any moment.

Now he stood in the vast terminal and closed his eyes to the noise and motion of the chattering, garishly dressed people flowing around him and repeated the mantra for warmth and calm which had thus far sustained him. It took more time than usual, but eventually the muttered words soothed him. He opened his eyes and swayed. He felt a little better, the noise enveloping him slightly muffled, a faint heat rising in his thin old blood.

So. It was not so dreadful after all. A moment of panic, but it had passed. Now he knew what he must do. It was really very simple. He must find platform number twelve, and he must catch the late train to Shanghai. He pulled his gold watch from his pocket. He still had twenty minutes.

His friend Yang the porter would take care of him, would get him hot tea and dinner and arrange his bed. He approached a uniformed guard.

～

Hours later, tears streaming down his face again, he wandered the concourse. People's eyes slid over him as if he did not exist, and indeed he thought that perhaps he was a ghost after all. It was not merely cold which oozed from his bones now, but a darker mix of cold and sorrow. He spoke the words of his mantra out loud, his voice cracked and broken, the words mocking him like gibberish while people veered around him, their faces blank or harsh with contempt.

It was the pinging of finger cymbals which penetrated his haze of misery. He halted, lowering his voice to a whisper, and stared. He could do nothing about his tears, which flowed all on their own. But he scarcely noticed, because even as they flowed, they turned to tears of joy. His prayers had been heard. What was this in front of him?

Shaven heads, saffron robes, rhythmic chanting, the sweet ringing of tiny brass cymbals, ecstatic dancing.

". . . Hare Krishna, Hare Krishna, Krishna Krishna, Hare Hare . . ."

He approached, hands held out in front of him, tears flowing like rain.

～

They took the old man to their ashram, a run-down house in Jersey City. Back at the airport, he kept talking about Shambala, how he had to get back there, how he would die if he didn't get back there. They had listened sympathetically. They had agreed with him. Yeah, man, they said; we're all trying to get back to Shambala. Aren't we?

He was nameless. No ID, no wallet, no money, no nothing but some expired airline tickets to Calcutta. And he was sick. Very sick. They decided they would keep him at the ashram, feed him and nurse him until he got well enough to go home, wherever that was. They vowed that they would protect him from the cops and the hospitals. He'd wind up in Bellevue, or worse. He'd die.

He didn't get better, though. He got sicker and thinner and more and more out of it, ranting and crying and mumbling. And it happened so fast it was scary. A week after they brought him back to the ashram, he had shrunk and shriveled almost to nothing. They never left him alone, and they often gathered around his bed and chanted. It seemed to soothe him a little. Especially when he was ranting about "the thirteenth," whatever that meant. The thirteenth, he would say over and over. The thirteenth predicted all of this. All of this.

One evening when he'd been there almost two weeks, they had just finished chanting when he opened his eyes, looked at them, spoke clearly and lucidly, then rolled his eyes up into his head and died.

I came here to plead for the attention of the world, he said. If Tibet dies, the world dies.

## Autumn, 2007, Yunnan, a province
## in far western China

I don't think it would be immodest to say that I have a flair for writing. That last part pleases me. I'm almost sorry that no one will ever see it, but that's the way it has to be. Is it truth, or is it fiction? What makes fiction great is the truth in it. I would love to have shown that last part to our visitor, but of course I could not. Instead, he had to sit patiently by my father's bedside and decide for himself what was the truth and what was not.

The young man must have wanted to find my father very badly. He was writing his thesis, he said, on the legend of Shambala, the secret land that was supposed to exist somewhere in the remote Tibetan highlands. He had come all the way from England, from the Bodleian Library at Oxford. Our village is not an easy one to reach—so far west of anything, tucked into the folds of the foothills of the Kunlun Mountains. We are nearly to Tibet.

We live without electricity or communications, so he was the first to bring us the news: Tibet had been set free. The Chinese were withdrawing, pulling out troops and missiles and security police. Abandoning the high plateau at last. There was even a rumor, he said, that the Dalai Lama would soon return.

It was news I thought my father should hear, so, containing my fierce secret joy, I shouted it into his ear.

Damn the Tibetans, my father growled, starting up from his bed. Damn them!

I had not often seen my father display emotion, even during those terrible years of destruction. But now he pushed himself up strained and red-faced from his bed, quivering with anger. I struggled to arrange the pillows under him so he would not hit his head on the wall. There was no way to keep him down. Frail and aged as he was, over ninety, he became a fury with the memory. And the litany kept coming.

Damn their dark magic, their medieval corruption, their droning chants, their wretched music, their demons and spells. Damn their whole foul superstitious country!

He spat the last words out with such peculiar venom that our embarrassed guest, who had been striving to remain polite and impassive during the performance, winced with real fright. Sorry for the young man, I patted his hand to reassure him. Never mind, I said to him. Never mind. Then I held my father's shoulders, easing him down, soothing him with silly phrases and noises as if talking to a fretful baby, though the words in my mind were hard and clear.

Old man, I thought, you are living proof that it is very dangerous to make wishes. The genie who grants them is a harsh master, an ever-so-particular fellow. No doubt he is one of those many-armed and many-headed manifestations the Tibetans are so fond of depicting, an entity who knows the secret invisible parts of our souls and psyches the way an anatomist knows our bones and organs. When you address him, make sure your wording is precise, because he is vigilant. If there is any distance at all between your words and your wishes, he will show it to you.

My father, reading my thoughts, glared back at me. You've become like them, he said. You think like them.

And he was right. I had become quite Buddhist—though not in any formal way at all—in my attitude toward life, death, and fate.

Let him rest for a while before you talk to him, I said to the young man. He wants to talk. There are not many who are willing to listen. But let him rest for a while first. His mind is always clearer after he has slept. Come out to the courtyard. We'll have a meal and some tea.

What about you? the young man asked. Do you feel the way he does?

About Tibet? Oh, no. I smiled. My feelings are very different.

And I told him a bit of our story.

My father had been a career military man, first with the Kuomintang under Chiang Kai-shek. He had been a master cryptographer and translator in the war against the Japanese. But he changed his allegiance when the Revolution came and served in the People's Army of Liberation under Chairman Mao. The Kuomintang wanted him back, because he was the best there was at cracking a code, a genius, irreplaceable. Besides, they believed that they owned him. They had invested a lot of time and money in him; they had sent him, along with many of his colleagues, to New York City for an education. Tyrants are like that; they do not let go of you easily.

As for Father, party ideology, loyalty, and the like were secondary. He did what was prudent and expedient. When he saw that the Communist resistance was growing strong, hiding at first among the people, moving like a shadow through the hills and then rolling over the land like thunder, he knew that it was only a matter of time before the old regime would fall. He knew that a man of his talent could offer himself wherever he wanted to, and so he made the switch.

It was in the last year of the Revolution, 1948, when I was six and my brother eight, that we left our city home in Shanghai for a village in central China, to remove ourselves from the Kuomintang, who now had retribution on their minds. It was a fateful move for my brother. He had always been keen on anything military, the marching and the guns and the uniforms, but he'd been just a little child and could only play at it. Now, far away from the fascist government, in rural China with the Revolution sweeping the countryside, he was able to fully participate. Even the remotest villages had revolutionary youth groups, with marching and singing and drills—everything he had always admired. He took to it like the proverbial duck to water, absorbing the indoctrination during his most tender and formative years, shaping himself into a perfect cog for the great machine. As for me, I preferred to hide in the tall grass and build little pretend villages or watch the clouds.

Father watched the drills and the recitations with a bemused and detached air. I doubt that he fully approved, but he didn't have much time to contravene, because his duties called him away for months at a time. It was during one of his absences that there was an incident that hardened my brother, tempered him once and for all into what he was to become.

My father had been gone for six weeks, leaving Brother and me with our mother and her old parents. Soldiers came on horseback to our house, with loud voices and starched brown uniforms, sitting high in their saddles. They were KMT men who knew my father, had once been his comrades. Now they were members of the secret police. They had tracked my father to the village. When they could not find him, they interrogated my mother. Where was he and who was he with? They beat and kicked her, dragged her to the well by her hair and threatened to throw her in, but she would not talk. I remember dogs barking and chickens squawking, but no human sounds except for the grunts of the men as they pushed Mother against the bricks of the well again and again, knocking the air out of her.

Grandmother and Grandfather cowered, their hands over my mouth and Brother's, but Brother broke free and tried to attack the men. He was only a skinny little nine-year-old, and the men didn't even take him seriously enough to hit him. Instead, they seemed to find his efforts amusing, and when they had finished with Mother, leaving her in a groaning heap, they poked him, goaded him, and laughed.

Mother was never the same after the beating. She was pale and listless, and complained of a pain in her side for the rest of her life. The doctors could find nothing wrong, but she lived only another ten years, an invalid with a broken spirit. Her condition affected each of us. My father became a little more detached, staying away for longer and longer stretches. Brother became zealous, hard, and bitter as he entered adolescence, and I, being the one who mostly took care of her, developed a keen sense of other people's pain and sorrow, feeling them as if they were my own.

When my father was given the opportunity to go to Tibet, my mother had been dead for about eight years. My brother had joined the army before she died and was already an officer rising through the ranks. It was his life. I had gone to university in Shanghai, and then, like so many of my contemporaries—and since it seemed to be a family vocation—joined the army as well. Because of my superb education and no doubt because my father was now a general and my brother a second lieutenant, I found myself an officer by the time I was in my early twenties. I was a translator, and a good one. I enjoyed my work and was happy to be a part of the great changes. No one was hungry; everyone got an education. When the Cultural Revolution came in the mid-1960s and the head-bashing began, I was less happy. This was not what we had come all this way for, I thought, and so when my father received his assignment to Tibet, and invited my brother and me to come, I was eager to go. I wanted to get away from the madness.

Another reason I wanted to go was that I had been disappointed in love as well. There had been another young officer, handsome and smart. I had had a couple of little romances in college, and I wanted more. I was passionate, I wanted to know it all. But he stopped our lovemaking at the crucial point again and again, telling me that we had to save ourselves, that our union had to have the blessing of the Chairman and the Party, or else he could not participate. At first I thought he was joking. But then I came to understand that he meant it. For me, love was a private matter, belonging to the two hearts involved and to no one else. Even love is not immune to the madness, I thought. Let me get as far away from this as I can.

Tibet. I found the idea alluring anyway, even if I had not wanted to get away. The word had always been associated in my mind with the color blue. I had heard of the vast Tibetan skies, the silence and emptiness of the plains and mountains. Color always played a strong part in my associations. When I think of the day my mother was beaten, for instance, I see yellow—not the golden yellow of the sun, but the dull afternoon yellow of central China. On that day, the courtyard was hung with dry ocher husks of corn. The ground was parched and sallow, the light wan; even the sky, in my memory, was yellowish: the yellow of China, a hot, burned, used-up, and ailing place, an association I had never quite been able to shake off. When they said the word *Tibet* to me, I was ready to go. In my mind I saw not only the blue of the infinite skies but the clean frozen white of snow.

And so the three of us went. Our little military family—Brother, eager to get to the frontier, eager to assume command, to bring the message of the Revolution to the backward feudal Tibetans, by force if necessary; I, with my visions of space and quiet and reasonableness; and Father. What was it old Grandmother used to call him when he was absent from home for so long? A wild goose, a raven—her way of saying a profligate, a wayfarer. She would never have paid him the compliment of calling him a romantic.

Whatever he was, nobody owned his mind, of that I am certain. Who knew what his thoughts were? I tried to guess, watching him as he gazed pensively out the window of the airplane on our way to Tibet. And I got a clue: I saw a familiar expression on his face that I hadn't seen since he used to tell my brother and me, long ago when we were children, the tale of Peach Blossom Spring.

He had been a superb storyteller. He could hiss like a cat, growl like a bear, boast and swagger like a warrior, and scowl like a demon. But with this story, he took on a sly, conspiratorial demeanor. His eyes narrowed and his voice dropped as he drew us into the secret. Because that's what Peach Blossom Spring was—a secret land where a certain man—a fisherman—could go, where no one could ever find him. He had become lost one day and found the entrance to Peach Blossom Spring quite by accident. He poled his boat through a long tunnel of rock, the entrance a forbidding grotto hung thick with roots and vines, and found the secret land where it was always warm no matter what time of the year and green and full of the most beautiful flowers you could imagine. But mostly the valley was alive with peach trees—the sacred fruit of the immortals. Here, the simple fisherman was a king.

Father used to tell us a lot of stories, but that was the one we came back to again and again. We always wanted to hear the first part, the part about the secret tunnel hung with vines, told exactly the same way. But once we were in the land of peach blossoms, we demanded new tales. Father would sit and think for a few moments, constructing a plot, and then off we'd go.

Watching him gaze out the airplane window, I believed that he looked the way he used to look when he was dreaming up an adventure for the fisherman-king.

There is a Latin phrase—*rerum cogniscere causas*—"to understand the causes of things." Later, and for years to come, I would have ample time to try to understand everything that happened. And of course, to ponder the role of fate in our lives. A close companion of mine—someone the young girl on the airplane studying her father's face was destined to meet very soon—remarked once that we had two choices in the way we could look at fate: either it was brought about by the will of God or by the lunacy of man. Then he'd smile and say that maybe we had it all wrong. Maybe it was the will of man or the lunacy of God.

For my father, surely it was the lunacy of man.

And Brother? Well, my good friend was also fond of musical metaphors. He once said that life was like a composition for the piano. We have the melody, the notes, which represent the order of the events in our life. But the quality of that life lies in the expression, in the larger, unscored range of interpretation: tone quality, pianism, phrasing and pedal breaks, sostenuto and retard and the rest of it. Thence came the nuances, the depth and color, of our lives.

Applying that metaphor to my brother, I'd have to say that when he sat down at the piano of life, he, like the rest of us, had a passably good and fairly original composition in front of him. But he played it as if it were a march, a simple progression of predictably resolved chords banged out on the keyboard one right after the other.

~

As I said, the Englishman who sought us out must have wanted to find us very badly because by this time of the year it was cold and wet, the rough rutted roads barely passable by jeep or oxcart. The great mountains that stack up to the west collected the weather in thick dark storm clouds and gave it back to us in torrential rains. While so much of the world wants for water, we are at a loss to control it and are threatened on at least two sides by the promise of cascading falls and immense mud- and rockslides. That is why they have chosen the canyons beneath us for the hydroelectric project. But that is another part of my story.

My father was unusually lucid for our guest. It was as though something in him rallied for the final telling. So Tibet is free, he growled to our visitor when we went back in after his rest. Good riddance. Let the Tibetans have Tibet. I said nothing. Certainly I did not tell him of the quaint little prophecy I'd heard years before, and which I'd held in my heart for all these years—that Tibet, the land of snows, would be the Eden of the Third Millennium.

The young man spoke to my father. I searched you out, he said, because I heard an obscure rumor that you actually traveled to the hidden land of Shambala.

My father sat up in his bed, where he spent nearly

all of his days now, angry and animated, eager to talk. No one else ever really listened to him; in the forty-odd years we had been here, no one had regarded him as anything but a crazy old man. And they were not far from wrong.

Dutiful daughter that I am, I sat and listened to the story that my father told the young traveler. In a sense, it is true that my father searched for and found the hidden land. In another sense, he could not have been farther from it. I said nothing to contradict his story, sworn as I am to secrecy. It used to be difficult for me, but with the passage of so many years, I have become accustomed to holding the secret inside.

The young man solicitously placed a microphone next to my father's bed and switched on the tape recorder. The machine whirred while my father spoke.

"It was the spring of 1966. The Cultural Revolution—the eradication of the Four Olds: old thoughts, old actions, etc.—was gathering momentum. I, General Zhang, was involved but detached. I never believed that humanity had changed in any way, had become more noble. Already there was infighting within the factions of the old guard. And already, all across the country, things were running out of control. Children with knives and sticks, angry adolescents armed with rifles. Although the Chairman would hardly admit to any of this, insanity was surely the password for the day. We were murdering our own people by the thousands. And we were burying the soul of China.

"I, General Zhang, was summoned to an audience with the Chairman at his forbidden palace in Peking in the spring of 1966 to receive special orders. It was not so many years before that I had been decorated with many medals in the great war against the West in Korea. I had never met the Chairman and his colleagues, but I had heard, and by the early fifties believed, that they were strong, vigorous leaders of great integrity and vision. And I am sure that it had once been true. But by the spring of 1966 it seemed that they had fallen prey to the usual weaknesses of the human spirit.

"I was disgusted to find that the old men, these revered heroes of the Long March—Mao himself; his top general, Lin Piao; Mao's personal secretary and mouthpiece, Ch'en Po-ta; and the head of propaganda and the secret police, K'ang Sheng—had degenerated into sybarites and opium addicts. When I arrived, they were swimming about, fat, blubbery, and self-indulgent, in a heated pool. There were women, opium pipes, and pills lying about on cushions while Western dance-hall music played on a phonograph. It seemed to me that they were making a vacuous attempt at playing emperor. They complained to me about age and failing health and about the need to reclaim their life-essence. They offered me opium, the drug of the Revolution—a habit they had picked up to fight pain and sleeplessness on the Long March thirty years before, and one to which Mao had become increasingly addicted. It was the panacea for all of his little problems.

"I refused, of course. And sometimes I think, even now, that the leadership factions in China might well have been divided along the lines of addiction. But there was no mistaking who was in charge at that moment.

"I received my orders: I was to go to Tibet. Because I had earned the unlikely reputation as the modern-day Sun-tzu (author of *The Art of War*), part of my job was to play the role of the tactician behind enemy lines—specifically, to find a way to make the Tibetan people rally round the Panchen Lama. You see, the Chinese government had decreed the Panchen, the earthly Lama, the top religious leader ever since the Dalai Lama's flight to India during the revolt in 1959, seven years before. But as many will tell you, this supposed High Lama, this Panchen Lama, was already a quisling, our puppet. We needed his support in our conquest of the primitive and superstitious Tibetans. By then we had already appropriated the two largest provinces of Tibet—Hou-tsang and Kham—and proceeded to 'appropriate' the people and the resources of the rest of that land.

"Tibet was not so much an enemy as a thing, a place, a treasure trove needing to be completely picked clean, subdued and acquired. And I was to be military leader for that pillage. We left for Tibet. I was to be the chief of occupation, although that is not what they called it. My son and my daughter accompanied me. Both were rising young officers in the People's Liberation Army. These were to be exciting times for this little family. I did not know, of course, what my son and daughter were really made of—it took Tibet to reveal all of that. At home, my military prestige had acted as a sort of shield for my family. I myself was not so ideologically involved that I approved of or participated in the more brutal aspects of this Cultural Revolution, especially where young people were concerned. It was with a degree or two of detachment that I observed my son's and daughter's schoolmates acting out their mindless zealotry, turned loose from their ideological reeducation centers to run amok, dragging people into the streets, out of homes, shops, schools, trains, and buses, torturing and bludgeoning and murdering citizens for alleged crimes against the state.

"I was satisfied to leave China, to remove myself and my family from the locus of all this activity and to travel to the far frontier. It was a grand adventure, I thought. And there was the challenge of my assignment: to persuade the people of Tibet to replace the Dalai Lama in their hearts and minds with the Panchen Lama.

"One of the first things I did when we arrived was to instigate a series of propaganda broadcasts that would reach even the remotest areas by shortwave. I thought myself most clever. I had studied Tibetan myths in a superficial way, and I made use of a particular ancient legend of Shambala, a legend known to all Tibetans.

"In the broadcast I called the Panchen Lama the Future King of Shambala. According to their legends, this earthly Lama was, in fact, prophesied to emerge at such a time as all the foes of Tibet were defeated. I saw this as a way to begin to 'educate' the Tibetan people into believing that the Chinese were indeed on their side, and into giving their allegiance to the Panchen Lama, who was very much under our control. If we were successful in convincing them of this nonsense—that the Panchen Lama had indeed emerged as this Future King of Shambala—then it must be because we, the Chinese, had been successful in eradicating the foes of the Tibetan people: namely, the primitive repressive slaveries of their feudal monastic world. That was our logic and we bombarded them with broadcasts. We were relentless.

"By the autumn of 1966, the Chinese had arrived in Tibet with their vigor renewed by the Cultural Revolution. It was then that we began in earnest our methodical dismantling of the soul of that cursed place. That was when we began the destruction of nearly every monastery in Tibet. Six thousand in all, to be exact. The monastic cities were plundered and destroyed. Those monks who would not come around were tortured or killed, their sacred scriptures burned in massive towering bonfires as our Red Guard sought to destroy the perceived enemies of Mao's state. According to the more zealous of my compatriots, we were 'liberating' the Tibetan people from their age-old oppressive and archaic lamaist rule.

"Before long my duties expanded. Where I had been, as chief of occupation, involved solely with my broadcasts and related strategies, I was now ordered to oversee some of this systematic destruction. Again, I was not particularly caught up in the idealism, but I decided to make the very best of the situation. I quickly saw a way to exercise my prerogative and make a tidy profit in the process. With the help of K'ang Sheng, the head of Mao's secret police, and his ambitious little wife, I began a brisk but highly discreet export business. We dealt, of course, in superb rare antique Tibetan treasures, the likes of which the world had never seen. Collectors back home and in the capitals of Europe, I knew, would drool for these exotic items. I could discharge my duty, build my own collection—for I had quite an eye and a fondness for such things—and become a rich man at the same time.

"I made a considerable profit and hid my funds—as did all good high officials in the Communist party—in Swiss bank accounts. Those who would criticize me for my actions should remind themselves of this fact: We were, in a sense, doing the Tibetans a favor—every piece that I and my associates removed from the country was a piece that escaped certain destruction. They were fortunate that it was I who was leading some of these raids and not certain of my colleagues. I always made it a practice to remain one step ahead of the Red Guard activities. Often, I would arrive at a monastery a day or so before the soldiers, accompanied only by my son or daughter. I would appropriate particularly fine pieces of art and memorabilia before the mad adolescent soldiers arrived to destroy everything.

"Whenever possible, I would oversee the plunder myself to make certain that I did not miss any choice pieces. And I believe that my disastrous journey began with a specific incident.

"Far out on the central Tibetan plateau, a most desolate and dreary place, dry and rocky like most of that awful land, lies the town of Gyangtse—part secular, part monastic city. And like all their places, this too was a dry collection of sacred temples. In the midst of all this was the many-sided, nine-storied Kumbum temple. It was actually a collection of eighty so-called chapels, filled with sculptures, each of their walls covered with paintings of demons and saints and all of that.

"Because the place had so much that was interesting to us, we did not destroy it immediately. As we were exploring the big Kumbum temple we came across a bricked-up room inside the domelike affair at the very top. When we tore into it we found a mummified corpse hidden within. Some high lama or rimpoche or other; the Tibetans occasionally walled up one of their dead, decaying priests if he had been important enough in life. Indulging in a bit of morbid humor, I thought it clever of me to send the corpse back to Peking to the Chairman and his elderly friends as a 'gift,' along with some other priceless treasures. I thought it was a good joke, after all their complaining and whining about age and ill health. The old men in China would either have a laugh and destroy the damned thing or would put it in a glass case in one of their own private museums. But surely I did not expect what was to come. It did not cross my mind again, until . . .

"A few weeks later, I received a message by priority military transport, guarded and under great secrecy, from the Chairman and his friends. It came from out of the clear blue: Many thanks for the priceless treasure. Find the land of Shambala. Now we have proof that it exists. The dead priest spoke to us.

"I thought that they had smoked one pipe too many and had quite lost their minds. But there, included with their letter, was the first piece of what they called a 'treasure map'—the first, they said, of a series of clues which would ultimately lead me to the hidden land.

"I dismissed it, nearly forgot it. Of course the decrepit fools would get it into their heads that this mythic place was real—a place where, according to legend, the old could grow youthful again and live another two hundred years. I thought little more of it until one day a couple of weeks later, while looking at my upcoming itinerary, I noticed that among the monasteries slated next for destruction was the one that might possibly be indicated in the first clue that came with the letter from the old men in Peking.

"Since the monastery was nearby, and mostly to amuse myself, I went there ahead of the others. I was pleased to find this place to be particularly rich in treasures, and I removed many rare choice pieces for myself before allowing the place to be dynamited. But in the course of all of our work there—and there was much to do in the way of de-frocking monks and lamas and sending them out to work in our communes—I stumbled across what appeared to be a second clue. I knew that there have existed for centuries in Tibet myths and legends of Shambala which have included with them cryptic messages about the path to this secret, sacred land of theirs. A path to a place that is supposedly at once a state of mind and also physically real. Again, out of curiosity, and to amuse myself, I spent some time decoding this clue. I enjoyed the challenge, but it was one perfectly suited to me, the master cryptographer. Codes and ciphers simply fascinated me. It was an irresistible challenge.

"I unraveled the clue and went to what was indicated as the next monastery. Why not? I thought that perhaps I might find, as I had at the first, particularly rare treasures. I was not disappointed. I found some magnificent icon statues, with more gold and more detail than I had ever seen before—and lo and behold, what seemed to be yet another clue. Now I was truly caught up in the game—partly because the clues were challenging brainteasers, but mainly because they led me to finer and rarer treasures ripe for the taking.

"Each monastery and monastic city that we visited was reduced to a pile of rubble when we left. My son and daughter accompanied me on these 'visits,' which had taken us farther and farther into central Tibet, the desolate high plateau. My son did his part with great enthusiasm: He was an explosives expert and a zealous officer in the People's Liberation Army. My daughter had recently been appointed head of the Youth Committee for Cultural Revisionism. This was not because of her own achievements but because I would cover her mistakes for her. As time went on, I found that I had to cover for her more and more frequently.

"Although my daughter left China and came to Lhasa supposedly with the same enthusiasm as the rest of us, she began to exhibit a certain—shall we say—lack of hard determination. A couple of times, she talked me into sparing a fine old temple or chorten or a particularly fine statue or fresco or tanka. At other times, she intervened and saved the lives of some of the elderly lamas and rimpoches who would

surely have died if they had to give up their privileged exis-
tences to perform useful labor. Her actions annoyed me, but
she was very persuasive, and more than once she caused me
to capitulate. It was her brother, more than I, who was truly
angry with her at first.

"I found out later that the two of them fought about
her behavior a great deal behind my back. It was more than
just squabbling, I came to understand. Sometimes it was
heated and nearly violent, though to all outward appearances
they maintained the idealistic picture of good Chinese revolutionary youth.

"Then came a series of strange events on that high
desolate plain. The lofty Tibetan plateau is known as the
'Headache Mountains.' There is too little air. Shortness of
breath, a pounding heart, and migraines are common for the
unacclimated lowlander who ventures there. So are hallucinations and death. No one travels across those plains except
the nomads. The weather can change violently in seconds—
driving rains, hail as big as rocks, snow and sleet. The Chang
Tang is a ferocious place. Even we did not touch those
nomads as they glided past along the ridges like ghosts herd-
ing their yaks or collecting bricks of salt from their lakes.

"When one of my units reported by radio what they
had found, I thought they had ventured too high and too
far and were suffering some sort of delusion brought on
by oxygen deprivation. On a desolate road between distant
monasteries and nomadic encampments, a reconnoitering unit
of the People's Army intercepted what appeared to be a load
of contraband. And it was no hallucination. It was quite real.

"And very odd it was. All sorts of luxury Western
goods, along with some very unlikely technical and electronic
items: electric eyes, phonograph records. Instructional records

for the Western ballet for children! Where were such children to be found in Tibet? I wondered. The greasy, ignorant issue of the nomad, covered in yak skin? There was some hydraulic equipment, old airplane parts—nothing, mind you, of a military potential that could serve the Khamba rebels. There were also modern flush toilets, odd mirrored panels that we later learned were photoelectric cells or solar panels. There were cameras of all kinds, a movie projector, much blank film, and a large professional 35mm studio movie camera.

"This collection was indeed a puzzle, seeming to come from the direction of the Kunlun Mountains on the Chinese side of the Tibetan plateau and headed out toward one of the most desolate areas of Tibet, rather than toward the Gyangtse or Lhasa area, where there were still wealthy households—especially those of our collaborators. The drivers of the caravan had no information, because they only carried the goods a short distance before they were relieved, and so on. They did not know where the goods came from, where they were going, or where or when they would be relieved of their duties. They could only tell us where they had picked up the caravan. We believed them. It was obvious that their story was true.

"The contraband was appropriated and sent to my base camp outside Gyangtse. I, along with my son and daughter, examined the goods and concluded that they were bound for some outlaw chieftain or other. It was an odd and intriguing collection, we all agreed, but it just went to show the decadence of the wealthy criminal element which had thus far escaped Chinese authority. There were obviously more than just the elusive Khamba rebels still at large.

"Since I was in Tibet originally in the capacity of a propaganda minister, I decided to put the goods to use. Of course, I first picked out some of the choicer items for myself. Among the things that I selected was a Polaroid camera with instructions in Chinese, and many boxes of film. As for the rest of it, I displayed the various pieces, lecturing the soldiers and some primitive Tibetan villagers on the pitfalls of materialism. I vowed to find the person the goods were going to and make a clear example of him to everyone in that forsaken place.

"After the episode with the strange caravan, I concentrated on my game with the clues, continuing my treasure hunt. But this, too, now seemed to be taking me nowhere. After about the sixth or seventh clue, I was disappointed to arrive at a remote, shabby, impoverished little run-down hole of a monastery. The building was only a few grimy plank walls, its windows stuffed up with old smoke-soiled felts and sheep's wool. There was not even a wealth of livestock that I could see. And the yard, if you could call it that, was littered with the bones of animals, even more than was usual in Tibet.

"Aahh, Tibetans and their bones. They are under your feet and lying about wherever you walk. They are toys for children, the musical instruments of priests, the crockery of the housewife. Bones. Bones. Bones. The Tibetans live with these bleached and dried or carved and decorated memento mori every day of their lives, and are quite content to do so. At this particular little shabby monastery, you had to pick your way through the bones merely to reach the door.

"There were certainly no treasures here that I could see. I thought at first that I must have made an error with the last clue. This place was maintained by two ancient monks who seemed to have no idea at all of what was going on in the rest of Tibet. There were still such pockets, so vast and inaccessible is that land; even today, four decades later, I am sure there still are.

"There was a young boy on the premises, no older than ten or so, who, the old men told us, was the reincarnation of a late high lama. A tulku, a reborn, a god-king, as they called him. To me he looked like any other small grimy Tibetan boy wrapped in the tattered remains of the dead lama's robes. There were many such reincarnational claims made throughout Tibet, but when we sent these supposed tulkus off to the communes, they worked just like everyone else. What the Tibetans needed liberating from was their own vast web of superstition. But somehow here, in this place, it all seemed quite harmless, and so I indulged them, ignoring my son's urgings to raze the place summarily and be on our way. Would that I had. Would that I had. I told my son to be patient, that perhaps the old men were hiding some fantastic treasure which would put everything else we had so far found to shame.

"I admit that I was affected by this unprepossessing place. It was peaceful, lonely, and oddly refreshing. And I will be truthful. I had seen more than my share of the destruction that accompanied the new order of things, and I simply hadn't the stomach. The place just seemed altogether too shabby and pathetic to destroy. There was no library, no store of writings, no sacred texts.

"I decided then and there that I needed a small vacation. Over my son's vigorous objections, but with my daughter's too-quick approval, I sent the unit of soldiers accompanying us away, and settled in for a much-needed rest.

"I spent many hours in conversation with the old monks and, quite in spite of everything, became friends with them, and the boy in particular. I was charmed by their utter naïveté and innocence. I set up temporary headquarters at this monastery; my hosts were most generous. Of course, my son was alarmed by this incongruous friendship and continuously tried to lecture me on the folly and traitorousness of it—but since I was the highest in command in all of Tibet, who was there to question it?

"The boy was my particular friend, god-king or not, and I gave him presents. One was a little toy, a die-cast metal airplane. I was surprised at the expert way he handled the plane, narrowing his eyes and making the appropriate noises with his lips that children do when they are playing and imitating an engine.

"While I talked with the old monks, the child put on an extraordinary little display. He arranged some benches and other objects so that he had formed a sort of valley, with himself and the toy plane inside it and the high altar at one end. The toy was a model of a four-engine propeller troop carrier. The boy spun the propellers on the right-hand wing as he pivoted the aircraft around in the opposite direction, the typical action of a pilot maneuvering on the runway prior to takeoff. Then he taxied into position, revved his 'engines,' the pitch of his voice rising to a high whine, the distinct sound of aircraft engines racing with the brakes held fast, a trick of pilots on short airfields. Then he produced the sounds of sudden release, the aircraft leaping to flight speed and rising sharply on takeoff. When he had cleared the runway, he flipped the wheels into the bays, climbed, spiraled back down, the bank of his craft neither too much to slip and lose altitude nor too little to achieve his next highest concentric station. I understood what he was doing: He was attempting to reach altitude sufficient to clear the altar. How did he know all of this? The old men shrugged, and reminded me that their great teacher, reborn in this boy, had traveled in airplanes from time to time. Probably these were his memories, they said. I was accustomed to indulging them, so I merely smiled. But I wondered . . . and now, that is all I can manage for today. I'm tired. I must sleep."

~

Our young visitor leaves tomorrow, a little stunned, I fear. He spent a long week with my father in daily recording sessions. My father's story, especially the last part of it, was at least as startling to him as his news from the outside world was to us.

Today I walk alone without our guest. I am nearly over the ridge and will soon be on the path that leads down to the huge stone quarry; when I left the house my father was asleep and our young friend was sitting in the courtyard, entering his final notes into his pocket computer. It is a four-day walk to the nearest motorable road and he has made such a noble effort. I feel sorry for him. All that work, and all that distance traveled, and all he will have for his trouble—though mercifully, he does not know it—will be fragments of an incomplete tale. Alas, he is going to have to be satisfied. There were times when I wished I could tell him the rest. But I could not. I am, as I have said, sworn to secrecy.

I think about the news of Tibet that our young scholar has brought to us. I understand the worldly reasons why the long siege of that country is over. The foolish revolutionary zeal that made for aggression and war in our country has been replaced with the greed of capitalism—a small leap for those in power. It is really all the same thing. But what those in power have come to understand—those absurdly privileged sons and daughters and children-in-law of the Old Guard revolutionaries who are our leading capitalist mercenaries today—is that war is no longer waged for territory. It is a vast economic struggle for wealth and markets. To the rest of the world it seemed that Tibet was simply too expensive and useless for China to maintain. No longer profitable. But world opinion played a major part, too: China no longer stood alone. We would have lost the support of the entire world market if we had remained the oppressor of this quiet land of priests and nomads. Ostensibly, this appears the truth, the reason for my country's actions. But I know the real reason.

Yes, I am sworn to secrecy. But I have written a story, which my father will never know about and will never see. In fact, no one will ever see it but me. I have taken a risk by putting it on paper, but my heart and mind would have burst if I had not. It is only for myself; I read it, and it comforts my soul. There is no danger of anyone ever seeing it, though, because I have placed it where it will inevitably be destroyed.

You see, this quarry, and perhaps the entire valley with it, will soon be flooded to make way for a huge new hydroelectric plant. We are to have electricity at last in the far west, these Tibetan borderlands, the hinterlands of western Yunnan Province; and this progress is not a thought that I relish. My journal, where I have recorded all of my tale, is hidden in a lonely place at the bottom of this stone quarry. I come here to read it in peace and solitude; when I leave, I leave it where it is. Even as I sit now and read, I can hear the drone of heavy equipment nearby and the shouts of the men not far away. There are Canadian and American voices as well as Chinese; we are all one big happy working family now. . . .

I am serene in the knowledge that soon this valley, my journal, and the story it contains will be obliterated. There are only two other people who would remember any of the events I've described in these pages, and I do not know if either of them is alive or dead. One is the person to whom I gave my vow of secrecy, and the other is my brother. But his version would be a very different one from mine. And if he is alive, it is doubtful that there is any part of him left that the world would recognize.

# ~ 1 ~

## Spring, 1966

The radio man hugged himself for warmth, then rubbed his wool-mittened hand in squeaking circles on the windowpane. He crouched and squinted through the quickly fogging hole, listening to the crunch of footsteps on the path beneath him. He raised his eyes to the east. Distorted by the rippled glass, dark clouds glowered in the dawn light over the jagged wall of icy peaks soaring to the sky. The chill of night still embraced the shortwave shack anchored precariously to a tiny ledge several hundred feet above the valley floor. This was the only place where there was any reception from the outside. The night hours were optimum, though there had been even more static last night than usual. He had been in the shack since 2:00 A.M., and the fatigue of straining to hear and decipher was catching up with him. Opposite the wall of radio equipment, atlases, maps, ledgers, and log books, a potbellied stove valiantly cranked out heat. He turned his attention back to the tuner and minutely adjusted the dial, coaxing the faint voices out of the crackling void.

The door behind him opened. Without turning, he greeted his visitor.

"Morning, Lama. I almost gave up last night, but things are clearing a little now."

"Interference?" His visitor, shaking light snow from his clothes and boots, still a little winded from the climb, spoke with breath-saving economy.

"And how. Until just before you came up. Then . . . it was kind of like something shifted, just long enough. The angle, the atmospherics, something. I don't know. It's always a mystery to me. Of course, adjusting the antenna outside might have had something to do with it."

"That helped?"

"Yeah. For a few minutes. Long enough, anyway. Long enough to hear the bad news. It wasn't radio jingles I was hearing."

"I didn't think so. What are we hearing now?" He leaned forward intently.

"It's coming through again. Your timing's perfect, Lama. I wanted you to hear this. It's what I've been hearing all night." The radio man handed the other his headset. The lama put the apparatus on and concentrated for a few minutes through jabs of static before snatching them off his head.

"Ouch. Damn, but that's uncomfortable."

"We'll listen through the speakers." He turned up the gain and they both huddled close to the equipment.

"Where is it coming from this time?"

"Best as I can judge somewhere around the Gyangtse area. Not Lhasa. Propaganda radio now seems to be centered in Gyangtse. The Guanxi—you know, the plainclothes security police—still transmit from inside Lhasa, but this is different. Much heavier than what they were sending out a few months ago. You remember all that myth stuff. Tibetan legends and the rest of it. Remember we couldn't figure out what they were up to? Well, my guess is that they were trying to soften people up for what was coming next. Now it's plain old nationalist propaganda. From Gyangtse, I don't know why. Wait, it's clearing up again."

His hand reflexively adjusted the knob that turned the outside antenna in minute increments. Words, rapid and distant but distinct, crackled from the speaker: Whole phrases, spoken alternately in Tibetan and Chinese, bits and pieces from the writings of Chairman Mao emerging from the static, saying the same thing over and over: We will purify. We will correct wrongs and purify. We will destroy the Four Olds—old thought, old speech, old ways, old deeds. All must be destroyed . . . everything old . . . purified, purified, purified. . . .

~

"It's called the Cultural Revolution, and its defenders, the Red Guard," the lama said to his teatime companion. "Thousands of miles and high mountains are not sufficient to contain its vigor. In China proper, it means that if you are conceived as an enemy, someone possessed of old, bad, unrevolutionary thought or deed—and that is just about everybody—you are 'corrected.' "

" 'Corrected.' Oh, dear." His friend shook her head. "I don't think I like the sound of that at all."

"I myself prefer more direct language. Correction by defenestration, for instance, from the fourth floor. Or corrected with a fireplace log to the head, corrected with the butt end of a rifle. Corrected by rampaging adolescent schoolchildren. Your home burned down, your shop destroyed. Does it sound familiar? Have we seen this before?"

Wordlessly, his friend raised her delicate porcelain cup, sipped, and set it down again in its saucer with a tiny clatter. It was the only outward sign that her composure was even a little disturbed. The lama sighed.

"We've been listening to these damned bloody broadcasts for months now. The voices of Gyangtse and Lhasa. Those once-holy cities." He waited while she poured him more tea. When she proffered the sherry decanter he nodded acceptance.

"So. It's that lovely, innocent little word—purification—which alarms you. I was not unaware. I have been hearing things, too. This is no longer a mere military occupation."

"Ever since the Fourteenth Dalai Lama was forced to flee in 1959, I've known that any talk by the Chinese of a treaty of autonomy for Tibet was nothing more than a cruel ruse. Eighty thousand Tibetans died, crushed by the Chinese in the uprising that followed the Fourteenth's exile. And now this. I see no reason to expect mercy. Our country and everything in it is synonymous with 'old.' Old thoughts, old ways, old speech, old deeds. To them, if ever there was a festering nest of oldness which needed purifying, it is Tibet. And they are here, in Lhasa and Gyangtse, speaking that damned word over the airwaves. We know what 'purification' means in their own country. What will it mean here?"

He sighed and looked out past the veranda. "We have been drinking this tea without our old companion. He's been gone a long time. I very badly need to talk to him." He stood and bowed politely. "Madame," he said. It was part of their game. "We shall break off early. I have a bit of a trek before me, and I would like to be well on my way before dark. I think that it is time for me to invite our friend to come back to tea."

"Wasn't he rather emphatic about not wishing to be disturbed?"

"I don't expect to be greeted with a warm smile. But he's had two and a half months of meditation and solitude."

"Actually, it's closer to three."

"Yes. Well. Under the circumstances, then, I think I've been marvelously restrained. I do believe he'll forgive me." He paused for a moment before turning to leave. "Eighty thousand, Rose, and who knows how many more since then, while we've been safe and snug here in our valley."

~

At least he fervently hoped he'd be forgiven. He'd walked for the rest of the afternoon the day before, spent the night in a pleasant little hostel in an orchard in the central part of the valley, then continued on in the morning. The sun had been warm on his back most of the day as he crossed the rest of the valley floor. He stopped occasionally to rest and relax next to a stream or in the shade of a tree. With the warmth and the buzzing of insects, it had been tempting to drowse and dream, but he was on a schedule. He wanted to be at the retreat before nightfall.

He began the ascent of the steep rocky path and climbed steadily for an hour. With every switchback, he imagined he could feel Chang's irritation at the imminent disturbance. Very soon he was in the cool shadows of craggy overhangs and fancied that he was getting a small preview of the chilly reception he would soon be receiving. Or should I say icy blast? he muttered to himself as he clambered up the rough wooden ladder that took pilgrims the final ten feet or so of the journey to the bare ledge and the tiny wooden hut. Here I come, old chap, he whispered. I know it's fright-fully rude to drop by without sending a calling card first. I hope you haven't forgotten your exquisite manners.

Head and shoulders protruding over the rim of the ledge at the top of the ladder, he gazed at the closed door of the hut and saw instantly that things were not right. He felt no presence, angry or otherwise. The force field around a human, especially one such as his old friend, was a palpable thing. No. There was no one here. He was quite, quite alone.

He stood there on the ladder for a moment or two, wishing neither to continue up nor to climb back down. Finally he pulled himself up the rest of the way, approached the hut, and pushed the door open. He waited, holding his breath, while his eyes adjusted to the gloom. He looked at the small bed in the corner; no one, no corpse, nothing. The stillness and dustiness spoke eloquently: There had been no one here for months. He released his breath. There was a lamp on the table, and a box of matches. He lit the lamp. Tucked under the base of the lamp was an envelope with his name on it, in Chang's elegant handwriting.

He sat, opened the letter, and read:

My old friend—by the time you hold this letter in your hands, I shall most likely be dead. Because if you are reading it, it means that I will have failed in my mission. But I have no regrets for myself. Haven't I had a longer life than almost any man? No, my regrets are not for myself; they are for our world.

I think I once told you that we here in the valley received the incomparable honor, just a few years before your own arrival here, of a visit

from the Great Thirteenth Dalai Lama, invited by
Father Perrault. Knowing the possible riot of joy
his appearance would cause with the porters and
the people of the valley, and not wishing to draw
attention to himself, he arrived in the guise of a
humble pilgrim. A few of us, though, knew whom
we had in our presence. He spent many days in
private with Father Perrault. Apparently a rather
grim statement about what he saw for the future—you could call it a prophecy—had come to
Father Perrault's attention, causing him concern.
As you know, Father had his own disturbing visions of the future, and feeling that his long, long
years were soon to come to a close, wanted very
much to confer with the spiritual leader of our
country. You know what Father foresaw, but did
you know what the Thirteenth predicted? I know
the words by heart. I can write them with my
eyes closed. I tried—rather desperately tried, to
be quite frank—to relegate what he said to the
realm of poetic metaphor, a cautionary hyperbole.
But I fear now that his words were plain and
literal, meaning no more and no less than their
face value. And now, with what I've been hearing
on the wireless, I must acknowledge that his words
have a very specific meaning for us and our valley.
Here they are, my friend, though I had hoped I
would never have to say them to you:

".  .  . all the revered holders of the Faith
will disappear and become nameless. Monks and
their monasteries will be destroyed. The rule of

law will be weakened. The lands and property of
government officials will be seized. They themselves will be forced to serve their enemies or
wander the country like beggars. All beings will
be sunk in great hardship and overpowering fear;
the days and nights will drag on slowly in
suffering...."

The lama read for the next hour without lifting his
eyes from the page, until he came to Chang's closing words,
which caused his heart to drop like a stone:

> ... though I walk through the valley of
> the shadow of death, I will fear no evil ...

He read the letter through twice more before he finally folded it and put it back in its envelope with shaking
hands. He did a bit of calculation in his head, and the
equation had only one conclusion: Chang was dead, and had
been for many weeks. Of that there could be no doubt.

Full night had descended. For an instant he had a
vision, as if he were hovering weightless above the valley
floor, of the hut he sat in, clinging to the precipitous mountainside. A feeble light glowed in the one tiny window, and
a man sat at a table, very still, very lonely, and—this was
most obvious, from his posture and attitude—very indecisive
and very frightened.

He rose, blew out the lamp, felt his way to the ladder,
and started down in the dark. Steady, he whispered to himself. Steady, old man, steady. You don't want to break your
neck. Then you will be of no use to anyone.

He placed his feet on every rung with conscious care,

gripping the sides of the ladder with extra firmness for each step. He did not quite trust his legs, which were shaking in a way they hadn't for many, many years. At the bottom of the ladder he clicked on the small torch he had in his pocket and played the beam ahead of him on the steep rocky trail. The trail looked very different going down in the darkness than it had looked on the way up at twilight. It was reminding him of another time and place. Hadn't he been on a trail just like this one years before?

The torch cast its soft parabola a few feet ahead of him. The ground was hard-packed and strewn with pebbles and small chunks of stone, the way the surface of Mars or the moon was supposed to look. His thoughts jumped around like fleas. Calm yourself, he said sternly. What was this reminding him of? He swept the beam of light around the last hairpin turn at the bottom of the trail, and realized that he was unconsciously imitating the sweep of headlights on a tortuous mountain road. The beam passed over something round and dark to the side of the trail, and his heart contracted with fright before he could identify the object. A head, an ear. Shoulders. No, not a head, not shoulders: a rock, a branch. He stopped, squatted down, waited for his heart to slow. And he remembered.

France, 1916, forced nighttime retreat under advancing German fire. Hearts in our mouths, road steep and twisting and possibly mined, lorry engine straining and whining in low gear, jouncing, tooth-rattling descent, too fast for darkness and dangerous conditions, headlamps sweeping the dark woods with every turn. The driver's tense young frightened face in the lamps' reflected light. Around a turn, gasp of shock, brakes locking, lorry sliding sideways on gravel: a body in the road, head turned toward the lorry, eyes open and staring. No, not a body—half a body. Nothing from the waist down. Naked, uniform torn away. French? German? American? British? No way of knowing who or what he was. Only that he was a mother's son and torn in two.

We moved him to the side of the road, found the rest of him a little farther down. Drove on, legs weak, stomachs churning. Each man thinking, that could be me. That *was* me.

∼

"You've been pacing like a tiger I once saw at the London Zoo," she said, pouring him a third glass of sherry. "I'd have given anything to set it free. You must tell me what has happened, aside from Chang not being at his retreat."

He stood at the table, lifted the sherry glass and looked into the liquid amber. Very small comfort. He went to the balcony railing, turned, walked back, and sat down. He held his glass out for more. She raised her eyebrows only a little while she poured.

"Rose, do you ever think about England?" he asked abruptly.

"England! My goodness. England. Of course I think about England."

"I mean, do you ever think about what would have happened to you, what you might have become, had you gone back?"

"I know exactly what would have happened to me. I would be, right now, at this very moment, a lonely, shriveled little old thing living in a seedy but respectable bed-sitter in London, reading scripture from my tattered old Bible, singing hymns on Sunday in my cracked little voice. For years, I would have been helping in soup kitchens for the poor, leading drunks and riffraff in prayer, saving their souls; by now, I'd be the one receiving charity. Food baskets at my door and my name in the congregation's prayers when I was ailing. A little old Christian spinster, alone in my little room, washing out my worn but still serviceable smallclothes in my tiny sink, subsisting on tea and toast and the hope of being taken into the big, strong arms of the Lord on some glorious day."

"Well," he said, impressed. "I can see that you've given it a great deal of thought. I've thought about it, too, but my vision is less precise. I see a full range of possibilities. Including being one of those drunken riffraff in your soup kitchen."

"That's absurd."

"No more absurd than your vision of yourself."

"What else could I have become?" She waved a dismissive hand. "What other fate awaits a devout woman of no beauty? I use the word 'devout' euphemistically, of course. 'Narrow' would be a better choice, I think."

Her words startled him a little. No beauty? He looked at her. He had never thought of her as beautiful or unbeautiful; in more than thirty years of friendship, he had never looked at her with an appraising eye, any more than he had ever judged the looks of his schoolmates when he was a boy. They simply were what they were, the motley cast of characters who inhabited his world. Come to think of it, she rather resembled a schoolboy. Small, sturdy, ears that stuck out a bit, eyes a little close together but vividly blue. Her nostrils were sometimes rimmed with red like a boy's. He supposed he would have to concede that she was unbeautiful, insofar as he had never noticed her looks particularly and was now associating her with lower-form chaps with scabs on their knees.

Devout? Well, yes. She had once been most annoyingly devout. Like a halftrack in high gear. Viewing the world through one myopic lens. Addressing wise old lamas with patronizing condescension as if they were painted savages with bones in their noses. But thirty years in the valley had transformed her. She was now probably one of the foremost authorities anywhere on the religions of the world, and had learned Tibetan, Arabic, Sanskrit, and Hindi to facilitate her studies. She might have been narrow once, but now, in learning and breadth of vision, she was like a river that had overflowed its banks and spread itself farther than the eye could see.

"Perhaps you're right," he said. "Though I think you're being ungenerous with yourself. Now in my case, I believe almost anything I might come up with by way of speculation would be overgenerous. No, hear me out. I'm sure you remember a certain breed of gent who returned to England after a stint in the Foreign Service and spent the rest of his years pacing like that tiger you saw at the London Zoo. To those fellows, England was a cage. A green, cultivated cage of manners, convention, and stifling horizons. China, India, or Arabia was in their blood like a microbe. They prowled, they drank, often they made their own lives and the lives of anyone close to them miserable. Well, I think that I would have been one of those unfortunates in any case, even if I had simply been returning from Peking or Baskul. But I shudder to think what I might have become if I had wound up back in England after having been here."

"Yes," she said, nodding thoughtfully. "Yes. I see what you mean."

"And it very nearly happened. Had I not jumped ship when I did, they might have had me. Or suppose I had gone back without ever having recovered my memory? I would have been seething with mysterious feelings and emotions and a terrible sense of loss, but with no idea why. I think I probably would have gone mad, and I say that without exaggeration." He paused, thinking of his moment of unpleasant remembrance on the trail, triggered by Chang's letter and suggested by nothing more than a rock and a branch in the poor light. The recalled incident had been buried in his mind for fifty years, but unearthed itself bright and shiny and fresh as something from a time capsule. He wondered what else might be lurking in the darkness. "I believe I'm capable of going mad. I sometimes felt . . . well, a bit off balance when I went home after the war. I couldn't wait to leave again, to lose myself in some non-English world."

"Why is all of this on your mind?" she asked pointedly.

He sighed. "Because," he said at last, "I may have to leave the valley."

"What!" She fumbled with the crystal decanter. The top dropped to the floor with a heavy lead-glass thud and rolled under her chair. "Why?"

"Only temporarily," he said quickly. "It would not be like the last time. Nonetheless . . ." He raised his arms helplessly.

"Well." She gathered her composure. "I know you would not even consider it without an awfully good reason." She paused. "An awfully good reason."

"Chang was not in his retreat, as I believe I have

said. But this was." He handed her the letter. He rose, paced a little, and gazed at the far peaks while she read.

"Do sit still so that I can concentrate," she said.

"Quite," he replied apologetically and held himself still at the railing. He forced himself to practice serenity by watching the wind in the treetops at the edge of his garden. After a long time, he heard the paper rustle. He turned. She was looking at him steadily.

"So. The world may be on its way to kick down our door."

"Chang seemed quite convinced. Enough to cause him to do what he did."

"Are *you*? That is what's important."

"I don't know. I just don't know."

"Well," she said in a firm no-nonsense schoolteacherish tone for which he was grateful under the circumstances. "What we need to do is listen. Really listen. I want to hear some of these broadcasts for myself. Are you going up to the radio shack tonight?"

"Yes. Bryant says conditions will be good."

"Then I shall go with you. We'll listen together."

"I'm not at all sure I want to know the truth. If Chang was right, then there will be no choice for me. I'll have to leave."

"I know. But it wouldn't be like the last time."

"I hope not." He shook his head and managed a smile. "I'm a bit old for this sort of thing, don't you think?"

# ~ 2 ~

These people are like children, General Zhang thought, lighting a cigarette and securing it in his long ivory and silver cigarette holder. He offered the open silver case around. The old priests helped themselves happily, laughing and grinning as the general solemnly flicked his engraved lighter and held the flame for each of them. Blowing vigorous streams of smoke from their mouths and noses, they gathered round the one who held the square of magic paper in his hand, all of them staring intently as shadows slowly appeared on the glossy surface, shouting with joy as the shadows deepened and took definition, forming into images of themselves. The general could understand their amazement the first time or two he took their picture with the Polaroid. But this was the eighteenth or nineteenth picture, and he knew he could take another forty or fifty and produce a fresh miracle each time.

The only one who was unimpressed was the child. He had posed politely, then offered to take the general's picture, and did so quickly and competently. But the camera was not the thing that interested him. He could scarcely wait to get back to his toy airplane. While the general was busy with the old men, the child played nearby in the dirt, making a little runway, taking off, landing, and expertly making engine noises with his lips.

The old men would have happily gone on taking pictures and watching their images appear for the rest of the day and into the night. The general finally had to tell them that they would do more tomorrow, that he had to let the magic rest for a while.

He sat on a rock and smoked, watching the boy.

"You must have learned in another life how to use a camera," he joked.

"No," the child answered matter-of-factly. "The American taught me."

"The American?" Zhang asked. "What American?"

"The American I met in the valley."

Zhang laughed. "I'm afraid you're leaving me behind. What valley? What American?"

"I can show you," the child said. "Come with me." He took the general's hand and led him up the stone stairs to his quarters, an austere little room with a paneless window overlooking the desolate plateau. The boy opened a wooden box and took out a photograph. A Polaroid. The general took it and squinted at it. There was the boy, slightly younger, grinning, standing next to a tall Caucasian.

Zhang experienced an odd little jolt. Didn't he know this man?

"This is a fine photograph," he said to the child. "May I borrow it for a short while?"

~

In his own quarters, Zhang studied the picture with a magnifying glass. The faces of the boy and the man were not all that intrigued him. What were these strange buildings behind them? He could not see quite enough to classify them, but they did not resemble any monastic architecture he had seen so far in Tibet. No. They looked more like what he had seen in Egypt . . . except that there were also lofty towers, and the glint of the sun reflecting on glass. He had seen almost no glass in Tibet. Windows in Tibet were invariably open to the wind and rain, with nothing but a bit of tattered felt to stave off the elements.

The man and the boy in the photo stood in front of a technical installation of some sort. Just behind the man was an odd curved pipe.

A curved pipe. He felt something move and shift deep in the layers of his memory, like an animal burrowing. He studied the man's face intently, then put the glass down, astonished. A name had spoken itself in his mind—a name he had not said or even thought of for over thirty years.

Chalmers Bryant. Columbia University, New York City, 1935. Zhang, like many other members of the educated Chinese upper class, had attended graduate school at Columbia. There had been a program of guest lecturers, people who were not instructors in any official capacity, but who were involved in innovative independent projects. Some were outright mavericks. One such lecturer had been Chalmers Bryant, and his specialties had been mining and hydraulics. A lively and accessible lecturer, he had shown the students a series of drawings of a water system of his own invention, useful in remote areas, he had declared, because it would serve a dual purpose—it would provide water both for irrigation and for hydraulic power. At the time of the lectures, Zhang was certain, the system had never actually been built but was purely theoretical. The curved pipe in the strange photo had brought back the memory of those long-ago lecture diagrams.

And he was remembering something else now, too—something much more recent. The shipment of contraband intercepted by his men in the remote highlands had contained just such a curved pipe.

Zhang felt something else move into place in his brain. It was an old, familiar feeling, sharp and pleasant: the feeling of his finely honed mental equipment engaging to penetrate a cipher. It was a feeling he knew well and relished—but it was different this time. Usually, the order was reversed; he'd recognize that he had a code to crack, and would consciously call upon that highly trained part of his mind. This time, some deep part of him had recognized the cipher before his consciousness saw it.

He had cracked many codes in his time, including the ones that had led him to this place. But he had never before had the experience of *divining* that something hidden was presenting itself. There was simply no other word for it. What was divination but a word used to describe a process of the brain beyond its own consciousness? He sat very still, not wanting to disturb this strange new feeling. Yes, he was divining; and what this mysterious part of his mind was telling him was that the puzzle presented by the boy's photograph was the biggest, the most complex, the most challenging of his entire life. . . .

Darkness was descending. He turned up the smoking oil lamp, lit a cigarette, and picked up the magnifying glass. Something else whispered in his ear as well—something that told him, faintly ominously, that he must not fail.

There was no doubt. It was not a mere resemblance. The man in the photo was Chalmers Bryant, and the equipment behind him was Bryant's invention. And wait just a moment. Hadn't Zhang heard through his old acquaintances at Columbia just a couple of years after graduate school that Chalmers Bryant had disappeared? Yes. Vanished from the face of the earth—wanted by the law for some sort of illegal financial maneuvering involving other people's investments. Had the clever bastard managed to find refuge in a valley on the other side of the world?

What about the boy? He moved the glass so that it magnified the smile. The boy here at the monastery was no older than ten years. He had a gap between his front teeth. The child in the photograph was a trifle younger, perhaps eight years old. Old enough to have his permanent teeth in front. The teeth in the photo were gapped. He studied the picture for the next three hours. He could not escape the conclusion that the boy in the photo was the same boy who lived here at the monastery, and that the man was Chalmers Bryant. The problem was that the picture could not have been taken more than two years before, but Chalmers Bryant, a man who had been in his forties thirty years ago, stood there smiling, untouched by time.

~

The next morning, after the boy had finished his several hours of leading the old priests at prayer, he had gone straight to fetch his toy airplane and resumed his play.

Amazing, Zhang thought. The child made the transition from high priest reincarnate droning ancient prayers to small boy playing in the dirt in a matter of moments. The sun was shining in the high blue Tibetan sky, and the general's empirical Chinese mind was reasserting itself. Was it such a bad thing to set the boy free from this oppressive lamaist mumbo jumbo? He had seen other young "reincarnated" high lamas, lonely solemn children of five or six years decorated and exalted like little Buddhas on elaborate altars, babies shouldering a thousand-year-old burden when they should have been capturing bugs or helping to plow a field. But this child ... this one did his esoteric duty with such authority. And he did not seem to mind it in the least.

"So," Zhang said to the boy, who was banking the toy plane to bring it in for a landing. "Tell me a story. Tell me about the valley you went to. I have a special fondness for valleys. Perhaps I shall pay a visit to yours."

"I don't know where it is," the boy replied. "They carried me, and I was asleep a lot of the time."

"Asleep?" Zhang said, amused. "How could that be?"

"I was sick. They thought I might die. That's why they took me there. They told me there was a healer in the valley who could help me."

"You don't remember anything at all about getting there?"

"A little. It was a long, long, long trip. Sometimes I woke up. Whenever I did, there were different people carrying me and I saw snow and high mountains. Then the valley, where everything was green and there were big trees."

"Trees!" Zhang exclaimed. It was amazing that the child even knew what a tree was. There were a few stunted bushes here and there around the monastery, but one would scarcely call them trees. "A valley with trees. And you got well there?"

"Oh, yes. They saved me. I almost died, but they saved me."

Zhang leaned back against the cool stone wall and speculated. Meningitis? Encephalitis? Or just a simple fever? His own children had gone through childhood fevers frightening in their intensity, raging deliriums of mysterious origin that terrified him but which the doctors said were not truly life-threatening. How would ignorant priests know the difference? Or had the boy's life actually been in danger, and had he been saved by some healer in a strange valley, someone with advanced knowledge and abilities?

"There were some pretty buildings in the photograph," Zhang said. "They didn't look like regular buildings. Do you remember them?"

"Yes!" the boy said with enthusiasm. "They were big, and shiny, and there were a lot of them. Some of them were tall, but not as tall as the mountains all around the valley. They were really tall. They went all the way to the sky!"

"And . . . the American?" Zhang asked encouragingly. "Was he the one who saved you?"

"No. A doctor saved me. But the American was my good friend after I got well."

"Were there other Americans in the valley? Was the doctor an American? Or . . . English, perhaps?"

The boy became thoughtful at this question. "I don't know," he said. "There were other big people there. Big ones with light hair and round eyes. One of them was a lady. And there were people like us. People with black hair."

A lady? Americans or Europeans? Could the boy have been taken somewhere in India?

"Were you in another country?" he asked the child.

"I don't know. What is that?"

"Well," Zhang thought a moment. How to explain national borders to a child who knows nothing of it! "Could you understand their speech?"

"Sometimes. Sometimes I couldn't. But there were monks and rimpoches there who talked like me."

"And how did you get home when you got well? Did they carry you back the way you came?"

"No," the boy said, jumping to his feet with his toy plane in his hand angled sharply as if it had just made a steep takeoff in mountainous country. "I flew in an airplane!"

"Your friend the American," Zhang asked. "What was his name? What were you doing when that picture was taken?"

"Master Bar-Nard was his name," the boy said without guile or hesitation, banking his plane around imaginary peaks. "He was showing me some pipes he built to water the fields."

~

Later, as evening fell, Zhang took a long walk around the plateau. His mind hummed. Bryant, Barnard. An alias perhaps? A watering system! Airplanes! There had been airplane parts in the shipment of contraband.

Zhang had questioned the old men, of course, but they had been of little help. We don't know where the boy went, they said. He is a reincarnation of a very important man. He was very, very sick. The word got out that he would probably die. The next thing we knew, lamas came and took him away. They brought him back several months later well and strong. That is all we need to know.

Those old men affected Zhang in an odd way. Yes, they often seemed like children or naïfs—it was so easy to impress them with some bit of technological wonder like a cigarette lighter or a watch. But there were other times when he felt a subtle reversal of roles. This afternoon, for instance, when he had been asking them about the boy's journey, he had looked into their black ancient eyes and felt like a not-too-bright child for just a moment.

And there had been times when he had been half asleep in the early morning when the sound of the monks at prayer entered his consciousness. They achieved resonating bass notes so profound as to seem beyond the capability of the human larynx. His own father had had a deep voice, and when Zhang was small he enjoyed lulling himself to sleep to the low, reassuringly adult drone of his father's voice talking on the other side of the bedroom wall, the words unintelligible. Sometimes the monks' voices, deeper by half than his father's, cradled him in his half-sleep, and he felt that he was in the presence of a profoundly authoritative adultness such as he had never known.

Then of course, later, out in the sun with the priests while they laughed and grinned and shouted when he demonstrated his wind-up alarm clock, he was the grown-up again and they the children.

Zhang walked to the top of a small ridge. The shabby little monastery was glorified by the pink-gold light of the setting sun. Icy peaks stood cold and high in the distance, receiving the parting rays. He thought about night atop those peaks. Night on one of the planets in the outer ring of the solar system could not be darker, colder, or lonelier.

What if there was a valley—lush, green, and hidden—lying in the folds of those frozen crags? It was not impossible. These mountains produced their own weird weather systems; that he knew. Pressure vortexes, magnetic influences, inversions. Perhaps a pocket of teeming life, like something you see through a microscope when you look into a crack in a chunk of mineral. No, it was not impossible.

So far, the clues he had been following had been a

game, a challenge. But . . . hadn't they led him right to this spot, right to a small boy who chattered away about a valley where most unusual things went on?

And hadn't he seen a photograph of a place that should not exist, and a man who should have been old or in his grave by now?

Shambala. What if the foolish old men in Peking were right? If he continued to follow the clues—might he come upon the ultimate treasure trove? Might he find the secret of eternal youth? Was he not Zhang, who had yet to meet the code he could not crack?

# ~ 3 ~

"Very likely he didn't know where he was when he died. Probably he was wrapped in a protective shroud of delirium. He might even have thought he was here," the physician said.

"Here. Oh, Lord. Let's hope so. Let's fervently hope so." The lama felt the urge to rise and pace, but made himself sit still. "Of course, that would mean that he suffered badly before he reached that state of release. When the mental deterioration first set in, I mean. Lost and confused. Frightened."

The physician shrugged his shoulders in reluctant assent. Poor Chang, alone in that heartless city on his urgent, ill-fated mission. And in the winter, to boot. Each man was sure that his speculations were more dire than the other's. "Though that stage of it was probably mercifully brief," he offered. "The older one is when one leaves, and the longer one has been here, the quicker the deterioration. Once the time limit is passed, of course."

"Well. That's not terribly comforting, is it?"

The physician sighed. "I suppose not, if we're thinking of Chang. But as far as your case is concerned, there is some hope to be held out. Remember that there is a tremendous difference, depending on whether or not a person has exceeded the life expectancy he would have had on the outside. If Chang had never come here, he would have died of old age a long, long time ago. You, on the other hand, might easily still be alive if you had lived your life, say, in London." He shrugged again. "The worst that might happen—and I remind you that I am theorizing here—is that you would feel . . . well . . . a bit ill and ragged and then attain your true age. Catching up at an accelerated rate is a strain on the system, of course. . . ."

"Indeed," said the lama. "Don't forget that I've seen the effects with my own eyes."

"That's right. You have," the physician said with quiet sympathy.

"My true age, eh? And what if I was fated to die ten years ago? Longevity in my family is inconsistent at best. Perhaps I'll turn into a man ten years dead, or five, or only one. How very cheery."

"Yes. Well. Still," said the physician, "let's not forget that you've already proven that you have unusual vitality. You experienced dreadful hardship, both physical and emotional, the last time you left here. You survived. Others didn't."

"A fact I'm not altogether proud of."

"Rubbish. That may have been an appropriate statement in 1919. I can't tell you how many times I heard it said by virtually everyone who came back from the war. But the circumstances in 1933 were very different and you know it. You saved Lo-Tsen's life."

"Or destroyed it, depending on how you look at it."

"My dear boy, it is exasperating to hear you speak that way. You know that both of them—Lo-Tsen and the young fellow—what was his name?"

"Mallinson."

"You know that if not for you, both of them would have died."

"Or perhaps both of them might have lived if not for me. Mallinson did die. And Lo-Tsen is surely dead by now."

"No one short of God himself could have stopped that young man."

"Do you think so? A thousand times—no, ten thousand, twenty thousand times—I've thought that I might have been able to stop him. They could be here, now, alive and well."

"Sometimes I think the hardest thing about being human is our ability to torment ourselves endlessly with what might have been. It's the curse of our species. I'm certain that no water buffalo or caterpillar or mosquito ever inflicted such torture on itself. You realize, of course, that if you hadn't left, you would not have understood what you almost lost."

"How well I know that. When I returned, I vowed I would never leave again." He sighed heavily. "Of course, I'll have to break that vow if what Chang warned us of is true. But damn it, how do I know Chang wasn't suffering from some sort of delusion?" He paused and shook his head with a dry little laugh. "Listen to me. Years ago, I convinced myself to leave the valley. Now I am convincing myself not to."

"I don't wish to influence you one way or the other. But we should examine the facts objectively, if such a thing is possible. Here is what we do know—that the Chinese are out there in ever-increasing numbers. You yourself have heard their broadcasts. The question is not whether Chang was suffering from a delusion—I don't doubt that he heard what he said he heard, and I don't doubt that the Thirteenth spoke exclusively to him. The question is whether or not we take the Thirteenth at his word. If we do, then . . ."

"Chang obviously believed it with all his heart," the lama said gloomily. "Nothing else would have impelled him to leave here." He shook his head. He felt tears rising, something he had not experienced for decades. "And I am coming to realize something else. He did this for me, too. He hoped that he might be able to spare me having to leave. He left so that I might not have to. When I think of that old, old man making his decision, reaching inside himself for courage, packing his bags and all the rest of it, holding everything inside, alone, telling no one . . ."

"It certainly gives us an idea of the strength of his belief," the physician said quietly.

"I wish I had the same strength of belief," the lama said, bringing his hand down on the table. "If I did, I'd leave here in an instant. No vacillation, no looking back. I remember how it turned out the last time I experienced this sort of doubt. I was wrong. Dead wrong, and it was very nearly a fatal mistake for me. But this time—ah, yes, this time— there's the potential for a fatal mistake of much larger proportions. We're not speaking merely of my own very possible decline and demise, unappetizing to me though that is."

"No, we're not," the physician assented. "I can only offer you reassurance. Your health is excellent. The fact that you survived the rigors of that first trip out is a good indication to me that you would withstand the journey well. You must simply be sure not to be gone longer than ten days. That way you will be sure. Two weeks is the absolute limit, and then you'd be pushing it. I can give you elixirs that will help sustain you, and you'll of course have your exercises. . . ."

"*If* I *must* leave."

"Yes. Naturally. If."

"I certainly owe it to Chang."

"What you owe to Chang, my dear fellow, is to make the correct decision. The correct decision might very well be to stay right where you are."

"Damn. Where is a good oracle when you need one? I feel like bloody Hamlet."

"Yes. Well. Even he eventually made a decision, didn't he?"

"Indeed he did," the lama agreed. "And look what it cost him."

~

"Bryant, do you ever feel obligated?"

"Who to? Or, as you'd say it, to whom?"

Bryant and the lama were on their way down from the radio shack after a night of fruitless listening. Storms to the southeast had kept the reception maddeningly vague; unintelligible ghostly voices that sounded as if they were being broadcast from another planet emerged from the static from time to time, and that was the best they had done all night. The peaks high above them to the west were just receiving their first kiss of pink and gold light, but where the two men walked, it was still dark and chilly.

"I don't know. To the human race. To the universe. For what we have here."

"Well, sure I do. It's not every guy on the run from the law who finds a hideout as nice as this."

The lama laughed. "Hideout. That's a wonderful way to put it. It's a hideout for all of us in one way or another. But what I'm thinking of specifically is this gift of extra time.

I remember a colleague of mine back in India in the twenties, an older fellow, grieving over his wife who had just died. One evening when he was drunk, I stopped him from killing a tortoise. He was about to club it with a heavy stick for no reason at all except that he was angry that it would live for a couple of hundred years while his wife was dead at sixty-three. Damned bloody stupid pea-brained reptile, he said bitterly when I restrained him. It isn't fair. I agreed that it wasn't fair, but pointed out that it wasn't the tortoise's fault. Later I got to thinking: What would *I* do with an extra hundred years or so? Of course, it was nothing more than abstract speculation at the time, so I didn't carry the thought very far. How could I possibly have known that the question would someday become quite real?"

"Seems to me we'd want to avoid being a couple of pea-brained reptiles ourselves," said Bryant. "Not waste the gift."

"Exactly! In my case, it would mean becoming some-thing more than just my ordinary self living a long, long time. This place is a hideout for me, too. The ultimate hideout. Here I could cultivate my reclusive tendencies to perfection, about as far from England as I could get, and the world be damned. That's been the tradition here, of course, for centuries. An extended old age of profound study and meditation."

"Yeah. Well. It doesn't seem as if we can afford the luxury anymore, does it?"

"Scarcely. At least, not at the moment. And I can't say I wasn't warned."

"Well, I never had the privilege of meeting the old High Lama. But I gather he had some pretty serious things to say to you just before he died."

"That would be putting it mildly. He knew things were going to have to change. Chang told me once that the High Lama in his final years spent most of his waking hours in what he called clairvoyant meditation. And very talented at it he was, too. In one of my conversations with him up in that hot little room where he lived when he was much older than any tortoise has ever lived to be, he told me that he'd had a vision years and years before of the nations of the world strengthening in . . . how did he put it? 'Vulgar passions and the will to destroy.' He said he saw a time when machine power would multiply to the point where a single-weaponed man would have more power than the grandest army of old. And here was the part that gave me chills: He said that he saw a time, after they had filled the land and sea with ruin, when they would take to the air. He had this vision at least a hundred years before the most primitive experimental flying machines were first conceived of.

"He certainly had a way with words. I used to sit there in that room, which was kept almost as hot as a steam bath, listening to him speak in his matter-of-fact way, and feel cold little waves of apprehension. And he always referred to himself in the third person, which gave an odd removed quality to his pronouncements. His exact words were that he foresaw a time when men, 'exultant in the technique of homicide, would rage so hotly over the world that every precious thing would be in danger . . . the small, the delicate, the defenseless, all would be lost. . . .' These apocalyptic visions were heavily on his mind. He spoke of approaching Dark Ages that would cover the world in a 'single pall,' putting previous Dark Ages to shame. On my final visit with him, he talked of a 'storm' that he believed was coming. 'It will be such a one,' he said, 'as the world has not seen before.

There will be no safety by arms, no help from authority, no answer in science. It will rage till every flower of culture is trampled, and all human things are leveled in a vast chaos. . . .' "

The path they followed emerged from the cool shadows of overhanging rocks and into the warm morning sunshine just as he spoke these last words, but Bryant hunched his shoulders as if he'd been hit by a north wind.

"Brrrrr. Gives *me* chills just to hear you quote him," he said, " 'Exultant in the technique of homicide . . .' That's strong stuff."

"Rather. And I'd already seen some of that technique firsthand. And even by 1931, as I listened to the High Lama, it was becoming evident that the War to End All Wars had not quite done the job, that another chapter was coming up shortly."

"We were lucky to be able to sit that one out."

"We were indeed. And thanks to you, we were able to appreciate what we were missing."

Bryant had established radio contact outside of the valley by 1939, just in time for them to hear, ever so faintly, of the invasion of Poland by Germany. They had picked up a BBC broadcast on shortwave in the wee hours of an exceptionally clear night, and had huddled around the speaker in disbelief, straining to hear the tiny voice. In the months to come it had been peculiar to listen to the thin distant words crackling in on the airwaves from a million miles away, carrying news of a world under siege, while the skies over the valley remained blue and tranquil, the nights starry and serene. Bryant worked constantly in the next years to improve reception so that they followed the ghastly developments in ever-greater detail; by 1945 they missed little, including the deaths of Roosevelt and Hitler, the liberation of the death camps, and the bombing of Hiroshima.

"Talk about technique of homicide and raging hotly," Bryant remarked. "I guess he wasn't kidding."

"Yes. Old Lama Perrault's vision realized to an extent even he could not have imagined. And he had said that we could expect no mercy, but that we—here—could hope for neglect. Certainly it was neglect and not mercy that we experienced during the war. And when the war was over, I believed that it had been the storm Lama Perrault had warned me of, and that it had passed. For years I thought that it had, and allowed myself a secret sigh of relief. Because I had grasped the enormity of the job he assigned me when he made me his successor, which was to preside over the valley and its richness of art and learning, to preserve it and protect it. For years I had thought: Why on earth would he choose me, and not one of the older lamas who had been in the valley for years and years? Why not Father Briac, for instance? Perrault was a theologian, a profoundly wise and spiritual man. What was I? A clever boy, worldly to a fault, glib and facile, but when all was said and done, slightly damaged goods, and definitely on the run."

"Obviously he wanted a guy different from him," Bryant said.

"Precisely. Which meant that when he said he wanted me to protect this valley and everything in it, it might mean something a lot more than just presiding over it. When the war came, and seemed to be spreading everywhere on the globe, I knew there was the possibility that we might not be completely neglected. And I began to wonder if I would have to do something a bit more in the realm of the tangible. Mobilize an army, or . . . come up with some way of camouflaging the valley from the air. You remember."

"Right. You and I talked about things we might do. Painting the roofs of the buildings, replanting the fields on the valley floor so they wouldn't look cultivated. We even talked about seeding the clouds somehow to increase the usual cover. You bet I remember."

"So of course I was relieved that no planes ever appeared in our skies. The war came and went, and we were—as Perrault put it—neglected. I relaxed. Maybe what would be required of me would not be anything too awfully rigorous. Maybe I'd be able to just relax, and, well . . . catch up on my reading. I admit it. That was one of my first thoughts. How many times had I heard people express that wish? I was no different. Here I was, with vast amounts of time and a vast library . . . I think I mentioned my reclusive tendencies. Here was a chance to indulge them, to the fullest. But you know, Bryant, I don't think it's to be."

"Think maybe the storm's not quite over?"

"Well, it turns out that Father Perrault was not the only one having dire visions. While his were general, pertaining, it seemed, to the whole world, the Great Thirteenth Dalai Lama had a more . . . specific focus. His words seem to pertain to the fate of Tibet in particular. And . . . very possibly this valley. He and Perrault talked to each other about what they saw. Their conversation probably had something to do with Perrault's choice of a successor. No. The storm may not be over. And this time we may not be neglected."

The path in its descent put the swaying treetops at eye level. He gazed across the gently undulating greenery; it was easy to imagine that the branches moved under their own volition. He tipped his head to one side: Piano music drifted up from below the trees. In his mind, the notes rose as pretty little shiny black dots, arranging themselves in the early morning air like musical notations on a page. Chopin. Father Briac's offering to the new day. "And I might have to postpone catching up on my reading," he added.

The two men stood and listened for a few minutes.

"Nice," Bryant said, then yawned and stretched hugely. "Well, whatever's going to happen, it's not going to happen today. I think you ought to drop in on old Briac. It's been a while, hasn't it? Me, I'm bushed. I'm gonna saw some logs."

The lama stood where he was and listened to the music for a few more minutes after Bryant took his leave by a branch in the trail. Presently he spotted Bryant far below, lumbering down the steep path, pushing aside bushes and saplings with the unperturbed calm of a bear.

The lama continued on his way. He caught glimpses amid the greenery of the blue-tiled roofs of the lamasery complex. It was all he could see of the great buildings from here; sometimes he liked to stand below them looking up so that they resembled attractive blue-lidded ceramic boxes.

Now the path curved back into the dark shelter of the cliff face. He descended a set of carved mossy steps with water trickling down them from the many springs in the rock wall. Soon he was at the level of the trees and moving under the cover of their thick bowed limbs. The trees gave way to tall rhododendron bushes with extravagant pink and white blossoms; beyond them was the stone terrace outside Briac's music room. Music poured through the open French doors: no longer Chopin, but a glissade, then a fluid run that re-vealed little of the melody or composer. Then a fanfare, a grand loud flourish, open and violent, a discomforting arpeggio of broken notes. Schumann? Liszt? An unusual piece for the maestro's morning offering, he thought. As if the old man were answering the Chinese. He waited before presenting himself; he wanted to listen a while longer to Briac playing in solitude.

There was a long silence. Birds twittered and water trickled; he could imagine the old musician collecting himself, in front of him on the piano the usual sheaves of sheet music, brittle parchment yellowing with age—German, French, Italian—rarely consulted, all of it committed to memory many long years ago.

Then a new piece broke the stillness. Adagio, lento, marching almost. Fierce and powerful. It ended with strange chords trembling in the space above the stone terrace; slowly gathering strength and height, they became triumphal and unresolved, standing in his mind's eye in the soft morning air like a row of pillars. The lama could picture his colleague's large powerful hands with the extraordinary span holding down the keys of the long black piano, sending the notes of the final chords vibrating out to infinity. The old lama's mudra.

He waited until the last faint sounds had died away, then moved into Briac's line of vision, pausing just outside the French doors. The old man saw him, acknowledged him with his eyes, and started a new piece without looking down at the keys. He played several bars before speaking, and did not break his musical stride.

"Do you recognize it?" Briac asked. Without waiting for an answer, he continued. "Was anyone playing this before you left for the war?" He concentrated on his playing for a moment before lifting his head again. "The concert halls of London, perhaps? Performances around Oxford, maybe?" The younger man thought a moment. A preponderance of black keys. There could be no question.

"It's Debussy, right?"

" 'La Cathédrale Engloute'—'The Sunken Cathedral.' Such chords. They create a wonderful picture, don't you think? If we are to follow Debussy's thoughts, Saint Michel rises before us. Like a phoenix out of the ashes. Out of the water, so mysteriously. Listen to the build, the rise in this transition. Subtle, but . . ." He lowered his head and followed the shifting spread in his fingers as the chords progressed, ringing like bells. Now he formed the music with his shoulders, playing with renewed energy. The other listened transfixed until the final dying harmonics of the last note.

"An extraordinary composer, Debussy," he said.

"Debussy, Ravel, Stravinsky," Briac recited. "Music changed so completely after I left Europe. Revolutionary music filled the halls. At first, traditional audiences—disoriented, and feeling, I suppose, cheated—pelted the composers and the performers with eggs and rotten tomatoes. New tonal systems, discordant and strange. And the textures produced by the orchestras . . . the music was always there, but it took the generation after Chopin to realize it. These were the chords of the next generation. Your generation. A little before you, maybe. But certainly after my time and the salons to which I was privy. But we did begin to hear the first intimations of this newness in Mahler. Like the world tipping, waltzing out of sync . . ."

"An all-new Europe, rising out of the ashes of the old monarchies . . ."

"Yes. Your Europe, not mine, my dear boy," Briac interjected. "A new face for old problems, and a whole new school of modern diplomats with their white bow ties and formal tails and stiff collars and slicked-down hair leaning against the mantelpieces of the world, Lama, and hooking their thumbs into the pockets of a new world order."

"New world order indeed. It meant the end of the Great Game here in Tibet. The great powers of Europe— England, France, Germany, Russia—had to go home and tend to business there. No more vying for supremacy over one another with Tibet as the trophy."

"Exactly so. And now someone else has her eye on us. China is no longer happy with her role as 'benign and distant' courtly protector of Tibet. Mere tribute is no longer sufficient. The role no longer suits the waking dragon," the old man said. "This Cultural Revolution. This rampant . . . ideology—this is the right word?—means for Tibet just another round of the old Great Game of my time, with a new name. China is simply taking over from the old departed European colonialists. It is her turn now. Living a long time gives one a certain perspective on history."

"Well. It appears that the game is on. And that I, perforce, might be called onto the field."

The old man had stopped playing. He studied the younger lama.

"So it has come to that," he said after a while. "We have chosen a queer trade, have we not? Are you familiar with the Victorian humor of G. K. Chesterton?"

The younger lama laughed. "Of course. *The Club of Queer Trades.* How would you know about that? You never cease to amaze me. Members had to choose a profession, the odder or more unviable, impractical, or archaic the better, and make a go of it. At college, there was a time when we laughed very hard at that. Blind to the irony, of course. All of Europe was rumbling. What could have been more effete and useless and archaic at such a time than the life of the academician? University itself was a club of queer trades."

"And isn't that what we are here?" Briac asked. "Tucked away and secure, useless and removed? Decent enough, but quite out of it all the same? And out there, a fierce and predatory world. You are wondering what your role is. Do you remember in *Queer Trades* the 'Adventure and Romance Agency,' my dear boy?"

The younger man raised his head and laughed.

"My God, yes. How could I forget it? Where a poor bloke wishing to enliven his own colorless state of affairs pays dearly for something to 'waylay him and lead him splendidly astray.' That was the phrase," he mused. "Yes, indeed I do. He pays a sum to this arcane agency and their task is to surround him with startling and weird events, to sweep him away to opium dens and dangerous scandals and liaisons and international intrigues and such . . . the whole plot of his life worked out by a hired staff of clever novel writers."

"Well?" Briac watched him, eyes glittering.

"Yes. It sounds a little like my life, except that I didn't actually hire anyone to waylay me. And who, I'd like to know, is writing the plot?"

The old man began a courtly piece by Scarlatti. Under his skillful fingers the piano nearly mimicked the controlled, precious tones of a pedal harpsichord. "The question, dear boy, is: Are you ready for the Adventure and Romance Agency to abduct you from this life here?"

"Father," the other said after a while, "what sort of student was Lo-Tsen?" Unfazed by the abrupt change of subject, Briac played while he considered his answer.

"Ah. Wonderful, wonderful. A joy. But her playing was formal. The music of drawing rooms was what suited her. None of this stormy and expressive pounding of the keys for her. I think it takes a European to understand the Romantics, the Expressionists, the Impressionists . . . label them what you will. It is, after all, our special angst."

"I remember that she was always very much at home with Johann Sebastian. And Mozart . . ."

"Oh, and much before them. She was so good. A quick learner. Delicate. Fluid. Precise. But the interpretation was the drawing room. Controlled and restrained. Let us not forget that she was a princess. She came from another world, but it was a Baroque world after all. The salons of China were not so different from those of old Europe. I would say that she found in Bach, Mozart, Handel an expression for her carefully contained and—what is the word?—*sublimated* passion." He played a few more bars. "You have been thinking about her?"

"I have."

"More than usual?"

"Yes."

Father Briac ended the Scarlatti abruptly and switched to Mozart. "This was one of her favorites," he said. "She was particularly interested in Mozart. For many reasons. Not the least of which was the fact that he did what he did in a mere thirty-six years. She was fascinated by the brevity of his existence. She once told me that she thought a short life but an intense one was infinitely more desirable than a long and useless one."

"I wish I had done things differently," the younger lama said. "I wish . . . Oh, Lord. Mallinson put it very well indeed. The night we were arguing. He accused me of being cold-blooded, of admiring her as if she were an exhibit in a museum. He was right. He could not have been more right.

When I think of what was going on inside that girl . . . If I had just acted, everything would have been different. Not that it was the first time. I had a history of seizing up with diffidence and shyness around women I admired. In her case, she seemed so remote and untouchable anyway. . . ." He grunted with disgust. "Tell me, Father; will I ever outgrow my regrets?"

"Not entirely. But they will fade. They become . . . like museum pieces." He finished the Mozart sonata, started another, and played with dreamy concentration. The conversation was over.

# ~ 4 ~

## Near Gyangtse, a few weeks later

"It is an embarrassment, pure and simple," his son said with grave indignity. Behind them dust rose into the vast blue sky as a small disheveled string of Chinese soldiers ran across the ridge in morning exercise. "An embarrassment and a dishonor. Bad enough that you are my father. Have you forgotten that you are a general in the People's Liberation Army and Supreme Commander of the Autonomous Region forces?" This was not a question. It was a rhetorical pomposity the boy had picked up directly from his indoctrination commander. "A general," he repeated gratuitously. "This is proof of just how dangerous all of this is. If my own father can be seduced by the very feudal superstitions that we are eradicating . . ."

"I have heard you quite enough, First Son," Zhang interrupted. "I know where you stand. Although I owe you no explanation, I will give you one because I am a generous man," he said, with no generosity in his voice. "I will tell you once and for all that I am not, as you put it, 'seduced.' There is a puzzle here in front of us. Nothing more, nothing less. Surely nothing less. And I like a good puzzle." He held the Polaroid picture, which he had borrowed from the child, once more up to the light of the window.

"It is all foolish. All nonsense," the boy said. "So there is a snapshot of a man who looks like someone you once knew and some odd buildings. On that, and the testimony of a child, on the basis of a structure so flimsy that I am embarrassed to even think of it, you are ready to risk everything. I have told you what must be done. What would the Supreme Revolutionary Council think of these . . ."

"The Supreme Revolutionary Council does not think. That is not their job. They echo. They mimic. Like so many parrots and monkeys," General Zhang said with calm contempt. "The Supreme Revolutionary Council would destroy a treasure right under their righteous noses."

"I will pretend that I did not hear that," his son said, shocked at the sedition.

"You may pretend anything that you like. But as you have so earnestly reminded us all, I *am* the Supreme Commander of the Tibetan Autonomous Region." Zhang exhaled a long contemptuous plume of smoke and gazed at his son steadily. The youth gazed back defiantly for a moment, then lowered his eyes. So. There was still a shred of filial deference in the boy, Zhang noted. They hadn't quite rooted it all out.

"I have a logical mind," Zhang continued, taking momentary advantage of his son's submission. "I have given the matter a great deal of thought, and I can come up with no simple explanation for those buildings or the child's trip. But, of course, my son can. You say we are here in Tibet to end their feudal ways, to abolish serfdom and redistribute the land and to suppress the rebels who resist our efforts on their behalf. That is all well and good. But that is not the whole story, by any means. I say we are here to plumb its heart."

"Just because you have not thought of it does not mean that there is not a simple explanation. The buildings could be part of a . . . a false front, perhaps the facade of a World's Fair, Father. A cardboard movie set even. There are any number of explanations." Zhang raised an eyebrow and waited. "Part of a Western decadence that has grown unchecked while we have failed to be fervent and revolutionary enough in our efforts. We have been slack, and the cursed photograph is simply proof of that. And as for the child's purported trip, it is so purely typical of these people. You know yourself that they are forever creating such flights of fancy. Enchantment. Spells. Reincarnation. It is a sickness which we are here to cure." He shook his head. "They live in their minds. Nothing is real to them but what is in their minds."

Zhang looked at his son. The boy was steeped in the perennial folly of youth: the inability to see the world through anything but one particular lens. How limited. And how very tedious. He, Zhang, though a high-ranking officer in the People's Liberation Army, though present here in Tibet as an effective instrument of its ideology, kept his mind his own private property. He'd be damned if he'd let anyone into that inner sanctum to rearrange the furniture.

He laid the photograph on the table and leaned back in his chair. "If this is a movie set, or part of a World's Fair, or some other mysterious pocket of Western decadence, then are we not obligated to find it and cleanse it?"

The boy had no ready response to that one. He glared at his father, slammed his chair back, and strode to the door.

"You are soft on these degenerates, just like your daughter!" he flung back at Zhang before he left the room.

# Gyangtse

The narrow, dusty alleys between the monastic and secular cities of Gyangtse were alive with the buzzing of military motorbikes and the smell of poorly burned fuel from their noisy two-cycle engines. Beyond, over the broader main street, hung the acrid pall of diesel from jeeps and rumbling military transports.

He drives too fast, Sister thought, looking over at her brother. His jeep screeched around corners, nearly up on two tires as he negotiated the narrow streets and precipitous dirt trails. She knew that he got real pleasure out of scattering people and animals before him as he roared around corners or tore down the streets. He was arrogant and full of himself, she thought sadly, a combination of revolutionary fervor and privilege. A bad mix. And like most young soldiers raised on the Red Guard diet, he was wound up like a spring-driven automaton. She was beginning to dislike him. And not merely because of his evident bad qualities. No. The reason was Tibet itself.

She had come here, like her father and brother, full of purpose. They would help destroy a repressive feudal system, a medieval world of slaves and priests, and free the great mass of downtrodden and miserable people. But miserable people were not what she found. Instead, she saw beauty and peace on this great high plateau of Central Tibet—or what remained of beauty and peace. Her instructors back in Peking who trained her for her mission had failed to mention that the people who had labored under these rimpoches and their predecessors for generation upon generation had done so with great happiness in their hearts and a sense of benign wisdom from above. This may have run counter to Chinese Party doctrine, but it worked for the Tibetans.

She had also begun to feel acute embarrassment when she was out in public with her brother. It was not just the scoffing way he guffawed out loud. It was that he was her brother, that she was connected to him by blood. Because something was happening to her, something she could not talk about with anybody, something which she had never expected and which threw her into considerable turmoil. It had started to happen the moment she stepped off the plane in Lhasa. She was falling in love with Tibet.

It had started with the smells. Dark, smoky, earthy, zoological. If anyone had ever told her that for her the perfume of seduction would be a mix of rancid yak butter, dung, poorly cured hides, sweat, and the tang of urine, she would have dismissed him as insane. And if anyone had told her that the scent of food and flowers would blend harmoniously and appetizingly with those other smells, she would have been disgusted.

Smell and color had become inseparable in her brain. There were brown smells, yellow and scarlet smells, purple smells, blue smells. She saw noblewomen in the street dressed in their colorful, embroidered finest, wearing their wealth in gold jewelry on their ears, heads, and necks, their hair elaborately dressed and glistening with animal fat. She saw people in from the countryside, their garments stiff and shiny with filth, fingernails black with grime but faces and smiles radiant. Filth and brilliance, filth and brilliance. This land was a living work of art, and it was getting into her soul.

And she saw something else in the eyes of the people: pity for the Chinese invaders, and prayers that they be forgiven. Extraordinary.

It was no wonder poor Brother was looking worse and worse to her. A brother whom she had once loved. She gave him a sidelong glance now, watching him in her peripheral vision as she often did these days. Every self-satisfied look on his smooth face was the look of the conqueror. She hung on grimly to the door of the jeep as he negotiated a turn. He had lectured her angrily the few times she had managed to talk her father into sparing some lovely old building or painting or into showing a bit of mercy with old priests and monks flushed out of their monasteries by explosives. His manner toward her had been stern and cool ever since, and she had felt a sullen defiance growing in her, though she did her best to hide it. So far, she had not said a word about anything she felt.

~

That afternoon, she listened to the final broadcasts of the day before retiring to her tent. It was a large comfortable heated tent tucked up for windbreak against one of Gyangtse's secular city walls. Only weeks before, she had shared the tent with her brother and several members of her father's staff, an uncomfortable arrangement at best. Ever since they had commandeered the large central monastic chapel—the cathedral of Gyangtse, as it was called—she had had the tent to herself.

The center of its hard-packed floor was occupied with a long folding military desk on which she kept her records of area family names, monks and nuns, monastic landholdings and livestock, and maps and sketches to be used in the process of redistribution and "voluntary" communalization. A heavy metal gooseneck lamp was bent over a wooden crate and bench which served as a radio room. Her cot and minimal revolutionary necessities occupied the opposite wall beneath a canvas flap window.

Outside the door flap she heard the tiny rattle and screeching brakes of the cheaply made People's "Storm and Thunder" jeep. A canvas and metal door slammed shut and fell open again. Her brother's voice bellowed out greetings. It was a tone she knew well, the one he used to make himself more authoritative. This evening, he used it to accost his father as the general started his nightly walk across the town. She knew what it was that had her brother even more worked up than usual tonight, that gave his voice an extra decibel and made him slam the door to his jeep harder than he had yesterday. She knew, and so did the whole town. It was the captives, four old, very important high rimpoches, taken just today from their hiding place in the village, sniffed out by a small squadron led by her brother. Four old men; four very big feathers in her brother's cap. She had seen them, handcuffed, being led to the detainment area.

"Father," her brother said, just outside her tent. "I have had an inspiration. I know exactly what we must do."

There was a pause. She knew that her father was putting a cigarette in his holder. In the next moment she heard the flick of his lighter and smelled the pleasant fragrance of his freshly lit Balkan Sobranie. Her father's silence was tacit permission for her brother to continue.

"A public trial," he said. "Right here in Gyangtse. We will make an example of them in front of their own people!"

"Hm." A grunt from her father. A most eloquent grunt, she knew. It meant: Go on, I am listening, you young pup, though I am not going to give you the satisfaction of saying so just yet. They were moving slowly up the street now. She moved a little closer to the door flap. She wondered if her brother thought that she was inside the tent and wanted her to hear this exchange, or if he was being careless. Or maybe he didn't give a damn one way or the other whether she heard or not.

"An example, Father! We can show these people who their true oppressors are! Show them who keeps them illiterate and slaves to superstition! And," he said importantly, "show them that you, General Zhang, are as firm as a rock in your convictions."

Her brother had received his reward swiftly for capturing the old men. That same day, the People's Liberation Army Revolutionary Council had promoted him from second lieutenant to captain of the Gyangtse Division Autonomous Region forces. With every notch he rose, he became that much more unbearable.

There was another grunt from her father. She knew what that single syllable meant, too: I am still listening. Keep talking. But make it good. Damned good.

Brother's voice, earnest now, was absorbed by the buzz of a passing motorbike as he and the general moved out of range. She chanced a look through the tent flap: Brother was strutting like a little rooster behind his father, and Father walked determinedly ahead, trailing smoke like a locomotive. No matter that they were out of earshot now. She did not need to hear the rest of the conversation to know its outcome: Their walks and their postures told her everything she needed to know.

And already a plan was forming in her mind.

~

"Brother, I know that I have been lacking in my duties. I have been less than revolutionary," Sister said as she stood behind the soldiers' card table placed in the middle of the once-sacrosanct Gyangtse Cathedral of the Gelugpa sect. None of the soldiers could have been much more than seventeen, but they puffed on imported cigars and slapped their cards on the table like the cowhands they had seen in Western films. Instead of a saloon piano, their radio blared cheap popular Chinese music. "I am here to apologize to you and to all the members of my Youth Committee for Cultural Revisionism. I have been remiss."

The table of boys ignored her as she stumbled through her difficult apology. Brother laughed, loud and coarse, banged a card onto the table, and took another from the deck. One of the soldiers grabbed hold of Brother's arm and twisted it to look up his sleeve. Brother brushed him off and the table burst into a round of wild hoots of "Corrupt Yankee pig!" and "Running Imperial Dog card shark!"

"I am quite sincere, Brother," she persisted over the noise. "Last night I reread the works of the Chairman and realized that I have been inattentive and . . ." She struggled for a moment with the insincere words in her mouth. No one noticed. ". . . and guilty of incorrect thinking regarding these people."

While she was talking, there came from across the hall the sound of another beating in progress. She could hear a woman crying and the rhythmic lashing of the switch. The table of cardplayers continued their game except for one boy-soldier who leaned back in his chair, turned up the radio to drown out the noise, and took a deep lucky-hand suck of his cigar.

"Brother," she went on, "I know how to get the maximum propaganda value out of the trial and subsequent actions taken against these four high rimpoches." Her brother extinguished his cigar but still did not lift his eyes. "They will serve as a striking and unforgettable example to thousands of oppressors and oppressed ignorant alike in minutes." Her brother put his cards facedown on the table and looked up, raising a hand to quiet his rowdy comrades.

"You know about the hundreds and thousands of pilgrims on the road toward Gyangtse. Do you know why they come? Some from very far away?"

"They come for one of their yearly temple rituals," he said over his shoulder, not looking at her. He fanned out his cards and studied them. "We had not yet thought how we wished to deal with it." He closed his cards on the table.

"I know what to do," she said. "I know what will win you commendations from the People's Autonomous Region and from the Party itself in Peking."

He raised both hands for silence, and turned to look at her. She had his full attention now.

"It is not an ordinary temple ritual," she continued. "It is one of the major mystery play drama-dances for the whole of southeastern Tibet. It draws people and religious leaders by the thousands. That is why the four old priests who are now our prisoners were here in Gyangtse at this time. They were hoping that they could blend into the festival crowds."

~

Brother gloated with self-satisfaction during the next few days. The smells all around him, which usually made him gag, did not bother him now. He drove a little slower, became quieter, befitting the dignity of his new role. He was in his glory.

Father had relinquished total control of the upcoming

trial to him. And Brother, in turn, had relinquished the "artistic" control to his sister. In the following days Brother began, with his sister's help, a radio campaign.

Gyangtse Radio announced the capture of four "rebel" monks on the road between Shigatse and Gyangtse. The four rimpoches, the broadcast announced, had been planning on smuggling themselves out of the country to Dharmsala, India, and the exiled Dalai Lama.

As leaders of their respective sects and maintainers of feudal monastic establishments, these four would serve as high examples. The charges against them: unrevolutionary conduct, lamaist repression, and imposed serfdom. They were portrayed in the broadcasts as feudal overlords and suppressors of the new order. They were to be brought before the High Court of the People's Preparatory Committee for Autonomous Rule in Gyangtse, where they were to be held up as leaders of a backward and theocratic society, maintainers of a perverse monastic rule premeditatively working to keep 99 percent of the populace illiterate and superstitious.

For five days now the airwaves had crackled with the story, repeated several times each hour. Maximum saturation, Brother had called it importantly. Speaker horns blared the story from every street corner and rooftop. And always, just behind the spoken effulgence of metaphor and revolutionary hyperbole, was the musical accompaniment which was her brother's mark—martial music, tinny and blaring, meant to awe and inspire.

~

Crowds of devout pilgrims occupied the sagging balconies, roofs, and terraces of the four-story monastery building. This was to be Gyangtse's major festival dance, or *cham*, an event for which pilgrims from far and near had gathered by the thousands, filling the narrow roads around the town for many miles. Usually, their blissful, noisy anticipation filled the courtyard and rose to the stars. But tonight the crowd was slightly subdued. They were not sure what to make of the scene before them.

The stone terrace atop a wide flight of steps at one end of the big monastery's courtyard would serve as the stage for tonight's performance. But instead of the traditional prayer banners, bright red silks hung down from the scaffolding, and at center stage was a brazier holding a pyramid of bound texts six feet high. Behind and above the pile of books was an enormous portrait, printed on silk, of the avuncular moled face of Chairman Mao set against an exaggerated fairy landscape of clouds and mountains—certainly an unfamiliar deity to most of the people in the audience. And if the Tibetan crowd had been able to read the Chinese characters painted in broad black strokes on red silk hanging on either side of the portrait, they would have known that there was a name for tonight's performance: The Burning of the Books of Ignorance.

Recorded Tibetan music played through the speaker horns. When it was abruptly drowned out by Chinese music, the crowd fell silent. In the next instant, the stage burst with color and motion—but it was not the color that the experienced Tibetan audience had expected. There were no intricate brocade robes or masterful headdresses depicting animals, skulls, and demons. Instead, in a blinding whirl of great red silk ribbons and a crash of cymbals, eight rouged and pigtailed girls dressed in army greens and red leaped onto the stage.

Stunned for a moment, the Tibetan audience gaped at the bizarre spectacle: a whimsical ballet of rifle-toting pirouettes and stag leaps, countered on the other side of the stage by a rush of similarly weaponed male dancers, whose same rouged cheeks and painted lips were a peculiar contrast to their army fatigues. Sister had brought the dance troop all the way from Peking for this vivid display. It was a night of strangeness for both audience and performers—certainly the Tibetans had never seen or heard of a ballet of dancing soldiers, and certainly the dancers had never had the experience of being laughed at, which the Tibetans were starting to do, like incredulous children.

The speaker horns mounted on prayer-flag posts sent Brother's favorite martial music scratching and hissing into the gray overcast. With another burst of cymbals and drums, four Chinese dancers dressed in the robes of Tibetan high lamas inched furtively onto the stage, heads bowed and shoulders hunched as if in renunciation, one of them carrying a lighted torch. The laughter died abruptly at the sight of the "lamas." A young female dancer in green fatigues, spinning round and round on pointe shoes, her pigtails snapping in time to the twirling red streamers above her, came from the opposite direction and snatched the torch from the lama's hand. She stopped spinning abruptly when she reached the pyramid of books. The lamas dropped their heads to the stage as if in shame while the girl held the flaming torch menacingly close to the pile. Now the audience gasped.

The Chinese troops circulating among the Tibetans in the courtyard sang along with the patriotic ditties blaring from the speakers. Watching from the wings, Sister clenched her teeth, her pulses floating in anxiety. It could not work unless the timing was perfect. And if it did not work they were all doomed. She eyed the scattered groups of Chinese soldiers. They were in good spirits, enjoying the elaborate joke being played on the primitive, superstitious Tibetans. Armed with automatic weapons and happy in their arrogance, the soldiers' voices rose over those of the Tibetans, who now shouted and muttered in protest: Where was their mystery play? Where were their profound and intricate thousand-year-old dances?

The soldiers' rifles hung at their sides or loosely over their backs. Clearly, they suspected nothing. Even her own brother thought her substitution of a Red Guard ballet before the trial of the four rimpoches a masterly touch.

The recorded music became squeakily rhythmic. The relentlessly cheerful rosy-cheeked dancing soldiers leaped and spun around the stage. The repentant "lamas" pressed their foreheads to the floor; the girl frowned at them sternly and touched the torch to the pile of books. A column of flame and kerosene-scented smoke shot upward, drawing another collective gasp from the crowd. Sister cringed; the volumes were genuine, including priceless copies of the encyclopedic Tanjur and Kanjur. She had wanted to use props but feared arousing suspicion.

Now the "lamas" raised their faces from the floor and, wearing expressions of radiant joy and gratitude, joined in the song of Maoist enlightenment. Freed forever from their feudal and superstitious past, they tore off their robes, revealing green and red uniforms beneath. All were a great happy family now. Music blared from the speakers and the dancers whirled.

The singing voices rose: "How happy . . . How uplifting are the words of Mao Tse-tung. How joyous . . . how joyous are the people that he helps. . . . How wondrous . . . How wondrous . . ."

The four real rimpoches waited patiently in the wings to be escorted onto the stage for their forced roles in to-night's performance. Sister had told them nothing; there had been no way to speak to them directly. Under Brother's orders, they had been brought here directly from detention. Two armed guards flanked them. She had only a moment, she knew. The guards were singing along with the dancers and the soldiers in the audience. She walked in front of the old men, faced them for a moment, and spoke six Tibetan words which she had chosen and learned for just this mo-ment. They looked at her, startled, for perhaps a half second, then lowered their eyes in what she hoped was comprehension and assent. The soldiers beside them, still singing, were oblivious.

She gave a signal with a shaking hand. The banners painted with Chinese characters were lifted, revealing four giant *stoma*, the sacred Tibetan butter carvings, on high pedes-tals representing the traditional demons of "lust," "greed," "anger," and "fear." The carvings, painstakingly prepared for the original drama, had been seized by force from the artisans the day before. At the sight of the sacred carvings, the Ti-betan audience fell silent with astonishment and reverence.

The dancers lined up on either side of the stage area, singing and holding hands. Now it was time for the rim-poches to "perform." The old men were to go out in front of their own people and toss more sacred books into the brazier, making the fire roar higher still, causing the *stoma* to melt, obliterating the intricate designs—the flames of righ-teousness devouring the symbols of an old, dead past.

The soldiers prodded the rimpoches forward, but the heat made them stagger back. Already the butter carvings glistened and ran. There was no time left. In a moment when no one was looking in her direction, Sister slipped back behind the heavy canvas backdrop curtain and felt her way to a position just to the rear of one of the pedestals holding a butter carving. She uttered what sounded to her own ears like a prayer, and pushed with all her strength.

The *stoma* fell onto the brazier, toppling it. For a moment the carving lay facedown in the smoldering pile; in the next moment, flames roared heavenward as the butter ignited. Black smoke billowed, blue fire raced along rivulets of molten grease in every direction and climbed up the hanging silk banners and the portrait of the chairman.

The dancers and the soldiers leaped from the platform while the audience pushed back in panic. The four old men stood their ground. Sister put her head out from behind the backdrop, uttered another Tibetan word, and gestured frantically. They turned their faces, saw her, and moved their old bones in her direction with the alacrity of youth.

"Out, out, out!" she ordered in a hoarse whisper, directing them off the back of the platform to where they could circle back and join the crowds surging for the huge doors which were all around the periphery of the courtyard. Her heart pounded and her face burned as she dashed through the flames and leaped from the front of the stage.

∽

"I must assume that you did not know what was happening."

He stood over her, a cigarette dangling from his lips.

Sister did not move. She suppressed an urge to giggle. Brother, she knew, was imagining himself a Western bad guy in the movies. "Because it would be impossible to believe what they are saying and thinking about you. I know that it cannot be true." He was trying to entice her to talk, but she said nothing.

"If it were just up to me, I would dismiss it. Dismiss the entire incident as a negligent mistake. A failure of intelligence as to the treachery the Tibetans were conspiring. These statues of butter and all," he said with disdain. He sighed. "I myself thought the ballet a fine idea. You attempted to provide enlightenment for these ignorant savages, and bring them some culture. And you were trying to do Father a favor. His preoccupation with his . . . game of clues was making him look unrevolutionary. Soft on the Tibetans. The dance would have helped to remedy that impression in the eyes of his officers and troops, if it had been followed by the trial of the criminal priests as it was supposed to be."

He walked over to her radio desk and began to flip distractedly through the stacks of files she kept on area families. They were not in order; she had forged much of the material in favor of the peasants. The last thing she wanted was her brother looking through them. She began to rise, wondering how she could draw his attention away when she realized that his mind was elsewhere and he had not seen a thing. "As it was supposed to be," he repeated.

She looked away before his eyes returned to her. He patted the papers flat and walked in her direction again.

"You know that we lost radios and many important papers in the fire. I cannot do anything to defend you," he said harshly, changing his tactic. "It would not look right. Would it? Answer me. You will look at me. I outrank you now. I am a captain in charge of Gyangtse occupation because I am revolutionary and zealous and right-thinking. Because I follow the Chairman's words. And you are a threat to everything that we do here. Four of the highest priests in all Tibet were in our hands. In our hands, do you hear?" He leaned close. Spittle flew from his mouth with his words, but they only made her glad. This was the first she had heard that she had been successful. For the moment, her heart soared. Apparently she had not hidden her feelings very well, for Brother drew back, looking almost startled. "But don't worry," he added bitterly. "They cannot have gone very far, even with the help of those they beguile."

Now she spoke: "And what will happen to me, my brother? Captain?"

"You are most fortunate, Sister. You must thank your father and me. Father for putting the whole affair in my hands before he left and I for my broad-mindedness and fairness. I believe that the Revolutionary Council had voted for your execution on the spot."

"Of course. The glorious Revolutionary Council."

"Had it not been for our intercession, had it not been for the fact that your father is the highest in command, then you would have been worm's meat. Here. Shot on the spot, today."

"Well, I thank you for that, Brother," she said with genuine feeling. She supposed it was true. At least he had shown that much filial decency, a remnant of humanity.

"Whatever you wish. But I do not like your attitude. It is most unrevolutionary."

"Then I suppose that I shall have to change it."

"It shall be changed for you." He lit another cigarette and opened the door flap to look outside. "I believe that you can be salvaged. But you need discipline." He dropped the flap and turned back to face her. "Arrangements have been made. You will be flown back to Peking for reeducation. You will be reacquainted with right thinking."

Her heart gave a lurch of terror, though she did her best to contain it, like an explosive going off in an underground bunker. She turned an impassive face to her brother. "Of course, there is only one right way to think."

"You have been publicly denounced."

"Then I stand denounced, my brother."

"You do not take this seriously."

"No," she said. "No. You misunderstand me, my brother. I take it very seriously. More than you can know."

He leaned close, as if they were children again, conspiring mischief. Another tactical change. "Where are they?" he whispered.

"I don't know, Brother," she said, looking back at him, her expression open and imploring. "And that's the truth. I don't know where they are."

He searched her face intently for a moment or two longer, then grunted and left the tent.

∼

Outside Gyangtse, in a corral on the grassy plateau within a cluster of fences, farm buildings, and tents, four old men wrapped in rugs were hoisted off the backs of pack animals by a group of young farmers. The rugs were unrolled and the old men lifted to their feet and given hot butter tea and roasted barley.

"What of the girl who saved us?" the oldest of the

four asked as soon as he had taken a sip. "What is to become of her?"

"We know nothing more, Precious Ones," a young narrow-faced farmer said, his head bowed and his hands clasped in prayerful aspect. "We were given instructions to remove you from danger. We acted in the briefest space of time that we had."

"We are very grateful," another of the rimpoches said, lifting the salty steaming brew to his lips. "To you and your families." The farmers' wives and children hung a few paces back, faces creased with smiles of delight, in awe of the four august presences in their midst. The breath of the old men produced clouds of steam that mingled with the steam rising from the tea. The gray overcast had turned to granite but had not yet released its snow. "But our responsibility does not end here."

"We know nothing of the consequences, Precious Ones," the young farmer said, unclasping his hands and spreading them wide. "Our instructions were to remove you from harm."

"We must find out what has happened to her," the eldest rimpoche said. "After you have had some nourishment, you will go back to find out what you can. Whether she has been discovered or not. Then we will decide what can be done." He smiled. "You will be safe for the moment. They will not notice two or three more Tibetan farmers with their animals."

~

Brother allowed Sister to walk from her tent without the indignity of an armed escort. The people of Gyangtse, those capable of differentiating among their occupiers, had come to like her. They had found a place for their trampled feelings in her sympathies. Brother deemed it wise to draw as little attention as possible. She must go out without further incident.

She rode through town, Brother at the wheel of the jeep and two young men—the Guanxi plainclothes police escort—seated behind her. They bounced violently over the narrow dry rutted road between the crumbling whitewashed walls of Gyangtse. They had been driving for all of five minutes when Brother turned a blind corner and was confronted with a sight he plainly had not expected. A crowd of people were gathered around the tall military transport that was waiting to take them the long distance to the Lhasa airfield. Brother slammed on his brakes. The jeep squealed and slid sideways, nearly capsizing before shuddering to a stalled halt.

He cranked the engine over. Shifting into low and throwing his weight on the horn, he pressed the jeep slowly through the throngs. There was a commotion. Chinese soldiers were trying to push a crowd back, but they were outnumbered. It was obvious that this gathering had taken them by surprise. Brother's face was set and grim. He pushed forward, riding the clutch, engine whining and horn blaring. What was this ahead?

Tibetans, at least a hundred of them, milling about, blocking the far end of the alley where the transport waited. As they approached, Brother could see that they were not so much blocking the alley as surrounding something . . . or someone. The crowd swirled and surged around the jeep—not angry, not hostile, but excited, animated, shouting. The jeep inched closer; he caught a glimpse of bald heads and robes and cursed out loud. Damn! Some demonstration of monks. He'd scatter them. He revved the engine and pounded the horn.

The last few feet were like moving through deep mud. People surged and pressed before finally jumping out of the way. When the last of the crowd parted, Brother was so astonished by what he saw that he stalled the jeep again. Bald heads and brown robes—four heads, four robes. The escaped priests! He shot a look at Sister, but saw instantly that she was just as surprised as he. He turned back. The four old men were boldly walking right up to the jeep. He groped for his gun. The old bastards could be armed, could be hiding weapons under their robes.

But their hands were out in front of them, empty. They lined up between the jeep and the military transport that stood just beyond, engine idling, smelly black diesel smoke pouring from its raised exhaust stack.

The crowd tightened around the jeep as the four rimpoches approached. One of the old men raised a hand, and the crowd went quiet. Brother motioned to the two plainclothes police. They drew their weapons, eyes darting about nervously. Brother unsnapped his holster and raised the small sidearm into the air, but somehow the pewter-gray barrel of the pistol overhead made him no more confident.

The old man who had commanded the silence now lowered his hand and spoke.

"Chinaman soldier," he pronounced in his clear but hesitant Chinese. "We have come for the girl."

Brother lowered his pistol and pointed it at the monk. The old man clasped his hands in a gesture of prayer or conciliation. It could have been either. Sister sat rigid, not daring to breathe. The rimpoche gave her a quick smile of such warmth and brilliance that she felt an impulse to cry like a child. Brother took closer aim, the barrel only inches from the priest's face, his finger tensed around the trigger.

"Excuse me," the old man said, still smiling. "I did not choose my words very well. I should say, we have come on *behalf* of the girl. We have come to turn ourselves over to the authorities. To place ourselves, as it were, at your mercy for our perceived crimes."

Brother's face grew red and the veins of his forehead stood out. His finger tightened one more increment on the trigger. He spoke through his teeth.

"All four of you, now. On your knees." But his hand, comfortable with killing only from a distance, began to tremble.

"Down now, hands on your heads!" he shouted harshly, furious at his own lack of resolve. He swept the pistol in front of him menacingly. "The rest of you, move aside!" The crowd was making angry noises now. Brother shot his pistol into the air, the report reverberating from the whitewashed walls. He shot again. The noise subsided to anxious murmurs.

The four rimpoches obeyed, getting down on their old knees in the dirt. Sister nearly sobbed aloud. She felt overcome, not by fear or her brother's rashness or the awful confrontation but by something she could not name. Something flowed from these old men to her, something secret, something older than time, a steady current of strength like a sustained musical note, separating her from the squalor and danger. Her brother's red face and gun were far away and profoundly irrelevant. She looked around in awe. Where was she?

The rimpoches were on their knees, heads bowed,

praying now, under Brother's gun. Brother had them at his mercy, or so he thought. But in her strange state of heightened awareness she understood that in fact it was the other way around, and felt sad for him. There were a thousand reasons why her tears wanted to flow, reasons so much larger and older than just this moment, but she kept them in.

Brother raised the pistol and fired at the sky again.

"And stop the damned praying!" he bellowed.

They ceased praying. The old man next to the one who had been spokesman held up a hand and unfolded his fingers to reveal the beautiful image of a sacred conch tattooed in his right palm. Then he raised the other hand and opened it like a flower blooming, revealing an image of two eyes. They were only simple tattoos, but such was the artist's skill with a few lines that the eyes looked back at Brother as if they were alive. The others began to pray again, quietly.

"Put your hands down, old man. You give me the creeps," Brother ordered, brandishing the weapon. He heard his own voice losing force. "I'll shoot you. I swear that I will shoot the four of you if you are not silent. Now. And keep your heads down," he added. The drawing on the hand was disturbing enough, but not nearly so disturbing as the old priest's own eyes: altogether too alive and clear for his wrinkled old face.

"We know that the girl is to be taken away," the rimpoche said. "And if we cannot offer ourselves in her place, then we wish to accompany her. It is also our wish that what awaits her will await these frail old bodies as well. It is fitting."

"It is most fitting," Brother concurred.

He motioned to the two escorting police in the back of the jeep. "Put those four in the back of the truck with the troops, then. Since that is what they want. We will fly them back to Peking with my disgraced sister. And we will humiliate these old sorcerers in a great rally in the center of Tiananmen Square, making us heroes to the people."

The rimpoches climbed into the troop truck and the canvas flaps were fastened shut. Brother and Sister left the jeep and climbed into the cab of the truck next to the wordless driver, Sister in the middle.

It was a long ride to the airfield outside of Lhasa. Sister was sunk in pensive silence. Occasionally Brother was aware, in his peripheral vision, of her looking at him. If he turned his head to return the look, she averted her eyes. He felt peculiar in her sidelong gaze. He didn't feel anger or resentment emanating from her as he so often had before. It was something new and unsettling. The air around them felt different. He had known her since her birth, and now he didn't know her at all, and she seemed not to know him. She was studying him as if he were an interesting stranger on a bus or on the street.

He talked compulsively to fill the awkward void. By the time they were a few hours outside of Gyangtse, he had told her in at least twenty different ways why he had not ordered her execution on the spot and how he had sacrificed to spare her. He reminded her over and over how grateful she should be for the chance to be reeducated, to share in the Chairman's paternal mercies, to experience regrowth in the community of revolutionaries, to expunge the bourgeois evils from her being. He chain-smoked all the while, filling the cab with Maoist metaphors borne on stale cigarette breath, a droning litany punctuated by outbursts of programmed emotion. The peaks and valleys of his tirade perfectly matched the intermittently spine-jarring road beneath them.

Sister's head ached from the smoke and the rattle of her bones, but none of that bothered her as much as the effort she was making—unbelievable under the circumstances, but she could not help herself—to spare her brother's feelings. She felt a terrible pity for him, even love, and wanted to protect him from seeing himself as he really was. She did not hate him, could not hate him. It was as if she had shrugged off a shabby, dirty old coat when she left her old emotions behind. It had happened when the rimpoche smiled at her back in Gyangtse, and it was with her still. Such irony, she thought, to be sitting here listening to Brother go on and on about regrowth, reeducation, and expunging evil. Poor Brother. She felt the tears rise again, and had to look away from him.

She studied the endless bleak brown rocky landscape through the filthy windshield. Before them, the distant gray translucent mountains rose from the drab plains. The cab of the truck was separated from the rear compartment by a heavy canvas curtain, but she could feel the palpable presence of the old men riding with the soldiers. All was quiet in the rear; there was none of the usual bantering, arguing, or singing. She imagined the strange scene: callow young soldiers, some no older than seventeen, their ignorance almost perfect, silenced, uneasily eyeing the rimpoches, who had centuries in age between the four of them and wisdom enough for the whole world.

Fifty miles outside of Gyangtse, the sky hung threateningly low and gray. The air was heavy and dust no longer rose from under the tires. The landscape was changing as they approached the long straight shore of a lake. They went full circle around an outcropping of rocks and brush and passed the tumbled remains of an ancient chorten, desolately beautiful.

She had always thought old decaying things were strangely beautiful, but now, for the first time in her life, she understood why. In what was almost a visionary moment, she saw a universe of ascendant elementals in differing states of density, a world constantly materializing and dematerializing. Like thought, but so much slower—thus the illusion of solidity. And she knew that Brother saw nothing but a pile of crumbling stones and flaking gilt. He had stopped talking abruptly, and Sister wondered for a moment if he had read her thoughts.

But his attention was elsewhere. He was seeing something that Sister had not yet seen: in the distance, a line of soldiers and jeeps against the immense landscape.

The driver gripped the greasy steering wheel, grinding the gears as the truck bucked and shuddered, tires crunching over the carved prayer-stone shards of a fallen *mani* wall. Brother and Sister, bouncing mercilessly on the hard seats, held grimly to the dashboard. Whining in low gear, the truck rumbled down into a depression, and the horizon with its mirage disappeared.

Sister had seen the line of soldiers in the seconds before the truck went downhill. She stole a furtive look at Brother's profile, saw perplexity on his furrowed brow and understood his sudden silence next to her: The soldiers ahead were not at all what he had expected to see out here, and he did not know what it meant. Chinese soldiers lined up across a desert road could be there for a lot of reasons. They might simply be part of a straggling detachment with motor trouble—or they might be part of a confrontational road-block due to a sudden change in policy and command. Brother was aware of the quixotic nature of the politics out of Peking. The truck began its slow uphill climb, its old gears straining. At the top they would know.

It had been announced on all the radio channels that General Zhang's daughter was being transported to the airfield, a distance of just under a hundred statute miles from Gyangtse to the Lhasa area. It was doubtful that there had been time to report the capture of the four rimpoches. Perhaps it was only the general, back from one of his treasure hunts, rendezvousing with them before Sister was sent off. But that idea did little to please Brother either. He had wanted to be the one in command of this situation.

The truck came up out of the ravine. The soldiers were no mirage, and it was plain that this was no haphazard gathering. They were cordoned across the rocky trail two deep, and behind them were three vehicles, a handful of officers, and several plainclothes officials. Brother released a string of curses under his breath. It was a roadblock.

Sister could see him straightening his spine and putting on his best haughty manner as the truck ground to a halt in front of the armed soldiers. She knew that his plan was to question the authority of whoever was stopping them, but when two officers who outranked him stepped forward and came to the driver's window, she saw him wilt.

"What is this about?" he managed to say, leaning across Sister and speaking through the cracked vinyl of the zippered window.

The two did not respond. One of them walked to the rear of the truck. They could hear him pulling the canvas flaps aside to look in on the soldiers and prisoners. He came back around and grunted something to his colleague. They both examined the truck for a few more minutes, their boots crunching on the stony ground. One of them came around to Brother's window, and the other returned to the driver's side.

"Papers, please," he said politely. The driver fumbled with the pouch of well-worn papers that hung on his door.

Sister sat still and said nothing. The one standing at the passenger window said nothing. Brother was about to speak, but something in the man's manner stopped him. These were not men to be talked to.

The two walked to the front of the truck and studied the papers for a long time. Sister listened to the wind and the occasional restless scrape of soldiers' feet from the back. She heard brother's breath whistling in his nose, and felt sad for him because she knew he thought he was losing face and felt helpless to do anything about it. It was odd, and complicated, this feeling of knowing other people's thoughts. But these men studying the papers she could not read at all. They were blanks to her, complete ciphers.

The documents were quite routine, she knew, even if the cargo was not. They could be from the Border Affairs Office attached to a high echelon of the Military Police, or perhaps even top intelligence officers all the way from Peking. Their demeanor, whatever they were, was formidable. Brother could do nothing but sit there and look worried, and the driver rifled through his pouch in confusion, surrendering more scraps of officially stamped paper.

Each piece was removed from its dirty envelope, unfolded, passed back and forth across the bonnet of the truck, examined, and replaced. Some pieces were looked at more than once. One of the officers made notations in a little book. Sister could feel that the end of Brother's reserve was fast approaching.

After finishing with the papers and handing them back through the driver's window, the two exchanged significant looks and spoke in low important tones. One of the officers stepped around to Brother's window, opened the door, and motioned for him to step out.

"We have prisoners," Brother started to say angrily, but the other interrupted.

"Yes, Captain Zhang. We know. Congratulations. Peking is very pleased. Very pleased indeed." Then he smiled. "And we have special orders for you and your prisoners to accompany us."

Astonished, Brother hesitated for only a moment, then stepped down from the truck.

# ~ 5 ~

A lone pilgrim, oblivious to the roadblock, arms raised in his sooty robes, had been praying at the crumbled *mani* wall. Sister's gaze remained on him for a long time as they sped away from the lake. Long after he was out of sight, the image of the lone pilgrim remained in her consciousness.

Swirls of dust rose about the open jeep. Above them, the heavy sky still threatened, but now the wind had risen, snapping at their loose clothing. They drove in silence for an hour or so. Beside her, Brother gripped the bolted corner of the windshield, enduring the jolts in prideful silence. Just before they had climbed into the jeep, she had seen him hitch up his pants in a way that he did when he was feeling important. She was sure he was thinking about yet another promotion.

Weary of reading her Brother as if his skull were made of clear glass, Sister closed her eyes for a while. When she opened them again, the jeep was approaching a long dry airfield; moored at its side was an aircraft unlike any she had seen before.

Together she and her brother stared out through the

dusty windshield at the strange airplane. Moored with its bright red blocks and yellow ropes stretching and twisting in the wind, sitting back on its haunches with its nose pointed toward the sky, the craft seemed to her a beautiful mirage, a symbol from a dream trying to tell her something.

Sleek, shiny, and powerful in appearance, it was an older airplane, elegant and incongruously stylish against the bleak landscape. Its huge twin engine cowlings swept back from the leading edge of the wings in a racy prewar fashion. And the three-pronged tail gave it a distinctively amphibious look, like some sort of great silver air swimmer. It was as if someone had secreted a highly powered thirties aircraft in mint condition and had only recently taken it out for display, an extraordinary relic of an unknown museum, and had placed it, for maximum contrast, on this remote dirt runway.

Instinctively, searching for a clue, she looked to the four rimpoches crowded into the personnel carrier just ahead of the jeep. But they sat without speaking, their grimy-robed knees tucked up tightly in their arms.

A single bright red star on the plane's lower fuselage attested to its nationality as Chinese. There were no numbers or military insignia. There was an elaborate brachiation of vents and pipes underneath the engines as if they had been modified for high altitudes and mountain passes.

A private aircraft, perhaps? A very high official's luxury transport? A staff car for the air? Military Intelligence?

They had plenty of time to study and contemplate the craft while they sat a hundred feet away from it in the jeep next to the runway. At least ten minutes passed while a conference was conducted between officials and the driver of the personnel carrier containing the four Tibetans. They sat in silence, enduring the wind and the grit.

The four rimpoches were escorted from the carrier first. When they reached the bottom of the stairs, they prostrated themselves on the rocky ground, then climbed up stoically as if they had been flying all their lives. Then it was Brother's and Sister's turn to board. Brother was quiet and proud, plainly flattered that such an unusual and important-looking aircraft was to be his conveyance.

The long narrow cabin was surprising in its luxury. Far from the military drabness to which she was accustomed, its interior was hushed and fragrant. The mystery grew to tangible proportions. Sister's eyes ranged over the many incongruous details, returning often to the four old rimpoches seated in the tail section on a long fabric-covered couchlike seat, then to their guards and back to the plane's incongruous offerings. This was utterly unlike the spare luxury of Chinese high officialdom, where taste ran to ubiquitous ashtrays and square overstuffed chairs covered in white sheets. Nothing of that world was apparent. Here were details that spoke clearly of another age and atmosphere.

Seats, each upholstered in silk of a different pattern, were arranged so that passengers faced one another over exquisite little bamboo and rattan tables covered with lace and holding parchment-shaded lamps. The floors and aisles were carpeted in warm woolen Oriental patterns of blue and red complementing the tieback draperies at the windows; delicate wicker seats and cushions covered in patterned silks were placed here and there as an alternative to the regular seats. Since this was an aircraft and not a hotel lobby, everything was light in weight. But sumptuousness and luxury had not been compromised.

In the rear of the plane directly across from the old monks on a facing couch sat six Chinese soldiers. Their rigid, upright military postures, rifles grasped firmly between their knees, stocks resting on the floor, could not have been less appropriate to their surroundings had they been sitting in a flower garden.

Brother took his seat with comradely ease and turned to the officer who had escorted them on board and down the aisle to their seats. Sister sat down across from him.

"Well. I am most anxious to know to whom I owe this great honor. And who spared us the rest of the ride to Lhasa. I am certainly grateful for that."

"We can tell you nothing now, Captain Zhang."

"But . . ." he laughed self-consciously. ". . . I am the ranking officer for this escort. I need to know."

"Indeed. We are aware of that. And your record, Captain, speaks highly for you. But you must be patient." Though the man's tone was sympathetic, it was also authoritative, as if he were of much higher rank than his drab plateau wear revealed.

"This airplane . . ." Brother began again, tentatively.

"You must be patient, Captain. That is all I can say." The man's tone was polite and easy, but his air of quiet authority never wavered. It was plain that Brother was not going to penetrate that authority, that he was vastly outranked and was not going to be treated as a total equal.

"But I am a ranking member of the People's Revolutionary Council for the Autonomous Region. I am privy to any information," he said with a touch of peevishness that Sister knew too well.

"Perhaps. But then you of all people can understand the need for security in high-level matters. For surely, patience is as much a part of our training as military men as anything else." The man paused significantly. "Have you heard of the

Central External Liaison Department, Captain?" The man now fixed the boy sternly, the way the general used to look at him when he overstepped the bounds.

"Of course. Intelligence." Brother was plainly impressed.

"Very good, Captain. Then you should also know of the Cheng Pao K'o—Political Security Section."

"Certainly." But he wasn't so certain; that was clear in his voice.

"It is a matter of counterespionage," the man said coolly, leaning forward in a conspiratorial way.

"Problems within the occupation," Brother offered hopefully.

"Deep problems, yes," the man said, leaning back again. "And you," he added importantly, "will be a great help to us. But all this in good time when we are closer to China." The man looked at Brother for a few significant moments as if asking for his tacit understanding as a fellow officer. Brother nodded gravely in response.

"I understand."

"Excellent," the man said, and turned away. "I hope you will make yourself comfortable for now. You may obtain hot tea and biscuits after we are airborne, if you should wish. Ours is a long flight."

"But this plane . . ." Brother began, but the man seemed not to hear him and rose from his seat and went to the other end of the cabin. Sister saw a little flush of humiliation on Brother's cheeks, and willed him to keep silent. To her relief, he said no more, but settled a bit sullenly in his seat and looked fixedly out the small window at the bleak landscape.

One of the escorting soldiers moved down the aisle,

pulling down and fastening the opaque shades under the draperies. Then the stairs were folded up and the hatches were sealed shut and she could hear orders for the takeoff preparations being shouted from outside. Blocks and mooring ropes were released while the engines revved. She sensed that the winds had picked up considerably as the plane shuddered with more than the vibrations of its twin engines. But they could no longer see outside. Another security precaution, she supposed.

The craft was now in position. She could hear and feel the metal clunks as the control surfaces were tested. It must have been a difficult test, pointed into the wind as they must be, and the winds and dust were no doubt playing havoc with the rudders and ailerons. This would not be a comfortable takeoff. She did not like flying under the best of conditions. But what did any of it matter now? There was nothing to be done. You surrendered the flow of your adrenaline to a situation over which you had no control. And, clearly, she had had no control since Gyangtse; it was all in the hands of a higher authority now.

She felt the plane put its nose into the wind, pause for a moment like a cat settling onto its haunches before springing, then the thrust of the engines. They rolled forward, slowly and restrainedly at first and then accelerating suddenly as the pilot opened the throttle so that it felt as if they would be shaken apart by the ruts and rocks and clumps of grass that raced beneath their noisy wheels. They were like a great fat bird hopping and bouncing along the runway; for a moment the plane would be airborne, then it would bump back down onto the hard earth, engines at full throttle, the turbine whining beneath the roar.

Across the aisle, Brother sat firmly upright, jaw

clenched, white-knuckled hands gripping the armrests until she thought he might tear the delicate fabrics with his fingernails.

As they roared and bounced, she tried to remember just how much runway there was. She remembered boulders and scrub not far down the field. By now they were going much too fast to abort the takeoff. She had heard somewhere that the air on the high plateau was so thin it took a plane a lot longer to gain lift. She flicked her eyes at the others in their seats, but saw nothing in their closed expressions. She shut her eyes and let her mind go blank.

Then there was no more jarring, just an abrupt and eerie smoothness of motion as they parted company with the earth and went into a steep climb that pressed her back into her seat. They must have come through the low cloud ceiling already, for the angle of the light outside the translucent shades changed as they climbed and then rolled into a long steep bank, leaving the orb of the late sun somewhere below.

She studied the table lace hanging straight out into the aisle at an unreal angle. This was her only clue as to the direction of their bank, because her mind was unable to tell her what her body was experiencing. It felt as if they were drifting sideways at the same time that they climbed at an impossibly steep angle. The pressure of the tilt and her blind disorientation was dizzying. She felt she would be less uncomfortable if only she could see outside, but unfastening the shade would have attracted the soldiers' attention.

After what seemed a long, long time, they leveled off. The swimming feeling in her head subsided and her pounding heart began to slow. The altitude and the mountains that rise straight up out of this high plateau make takeoffs risky, she thought, but we have a skillful pilot. And that was her last thought before she fell asleep, her consciousness collapsing finally under the weight of the day's anxiety and uncertainty as if she had been struck by a heavy drug.

Her sleep was deep and dreamless, and she remembered nothing more until she found herself awake, the window shade pink with outside light and the imprint of fabric and wicker fresh and deep on her cheek. She wiped the spittle from the corners of her mouth. How long had she been out? She knew it had been hours. She had no memory of any dreams, but was aware, now, that the drone of the engines had followed her down into her sleep. And something, some change in the depth and pitch, was what had brought her awake.

Her eyes were open, but she had not yet fully sat up and looked around her. She held still and listened. Another sound had grown in and around the engine's roar, the way a vine intertwines with the leaves and branches of a tree. Overtones, deep and sonorous, almost below the level of hearing, made strange chords with the engine noise, moved under and around it. Then she knew what she was hearing: the four rimpoches in prayer, the discordant pitches and shifting resonances vibrating deep in the core of her spine, of her very being. It was doubtful that any of the old men had even seen an airplane as anything more than a distant toy in the sky. Surely none of them had ever flown in one.

She sat up and stretched her stiff, aching limbs. Then she saw Brother and felt a small shock.

He sat in exactly the same attitude as when she had closed her eyes and gone to sleep. She could see that he had not moved or closed his eyes all night. His gaze was fixed on the soldiers slumped against one another on their couch, their weapons lying in a careless heap on the red carpet at their feet.

He had been waiting for her to wake up; with her first motion in his peripheral vision, he turned, faced her, and raised his shade slowly while giving her an intense and significant look. She raised her own shade and looked out. Then they looked at each other. At first she could not comprehend what she saw.

He walked his fingers slowly down to his hip and began to unfasten the snaps of his holster. When the flap was open, he drew the pistol out slowly and held it against his lap, down and out of sight of the soldiers. His face frightened her; she had never seen such malevolence on his features before.

Then his expression changed to bewilderment as he lowered his gaze to the gun in his hand. When he looked up at her again his face was oddly blank; he raised the gun to the height of his chin and pointed it directly at her. Sister and brother locked eyes and her thoughts went white.

In the next instant, before she had time to utter a sound, he flipped the gun across the aisle and into her lap. It was a long moment before she understood that the weight that had landed on her legs was not that of a military regulation pistol. It was not that of any pistol she had ever touched. She picked it up and turned it around, her breath still caught in her chest. Now she understood Brother's expression. She exhaled. It was a toy: carved of wood and covered with thin plates of hammered tin for feel and color. They had been tricked. No. He had been tricked. She was no part of his plans. Yet for the briefest of moments there was a kinship, the old sibling connection rejoined.

"I never closed my eyes all night," Brother whispered with intensity, eyes black and dilated. "But I am not going to put up with this any longer. We have been tricked. Wherever we are going, it is neither to Xian nor Peking." This was what he had wanted her to see outside the window, and what her mind had refused to process for the moment: the white tractless glacial peaks below them, where there should have been the flat brownish plains of China, and the rising sun not in front of them, where it should have been, but behind them.

A sly look came across his face then. He stood up slowly, stretched, and moved nonchalantly into the aisle. Then, quick as a mongoose, he was upon the pile of rifles on the floor at the rear. He snatched one, the shoulder strap snagging in the heap, causing a clatter as he raised it.

The four rimpoches stopped their praying and began to giggle. The soldiers woke at the commotion; wiping the sleep from their eyes, they saw the spectacle before them, smiled, and raised their arms in mock surrender. The rimpoches doubled over in raucous amusement while Brother looked down at the rifle in his hands, stared for a moment, then broke it over his knee in rage. Another toy. All of them. Tin and wood. Parade rifles, painted to look like real weapons from a distance, nothing more. He looked around in helpless fury while the soldiers joined the rimpoches in the general hilarity.

Behind him, the cockpit door opened and the man who had first escorted them into the plane emerged.

"I knew the moment would be upon us soon, my friend. But I could not know when," the man said, walking slowly down the aisle, leaning first this way and then that to pull the shades up. When he reached Brother's seat he looked down at Sister. "I am too late to do him the honor of presenting our world to him," he said, indicating Brother's raised shade.

"Come back and sit down, my friend," he called to Brother in British-accented English. "We can experience some nasty turbulence above these peaks. They make their own weather systems. The bloody devil in them, you see." The man's tone was civil, cultured in its rhythms, so unlike the agitated hysteria typical of her ideological brethren. Here was the voice of a man educated in the West; his soothing manner reminded her of the tales of cultured warlords who would sit you down to tea before beheading you. But she sensed no menace in this man. That was not who he was.

Unlike poor Brother, she sensed no menace in any of this. Her inclination was to join in the laughter. She felt nearly giddy with relief: Wherever it was they were going, it was clearly not Peking—and that was quite all right with her.

Where were they? What mountains were those that pushed through the sea of clouds below? The Karakoram, the Himalayas, the Hindu Kush? Brother sank helplessly back into his seat and glared at her. It was plain that he believed her to be a conspirator with their captors.

This time, she avoided his eyes and stared down at the airplane's tiny shadow riding up and down over the range's sawtooth peaks.

~

By late morning, when Brother had finally dozed off, they began to lose altitude. The plane dropped down, down, and down again in a shuddering sequence, causing Sister's heart to race in panic. Brother came awake from his brief, fitful sleep and looked around as if he had forgotten for a second or two where he was. Instinctively, Sister looked to the soft-spoken officer, who sat nearby. His serene expression comforted her a little, until the plane bounced so severely that the engines' roar changed pitch and some of the little parchment shades jumped to the floor and rolled about the aisle. Still the officer's face remained calm; the rimpoches were stoic and the soldiers impassive. She turned her gaze to the window, and was distracted from her fear for a while by what she saw.

They had come down below the peaks of two mountains whose top halves vanished into thick clouds, and were maneuvering into the narrow passage between them. The plane banked severely so that on her side of the plane the mountain rode up in a massive heave of stone and ice. On Brother's side, the curtains hung out toward the aisle as the opposite peak vanished from view altogether, disappearing below the wing.

"Entering the valley is always a bit tricky," came the officer's voice. "But it is something that our pilot has done many times. We're in the best of hands." She nodded weakly, grateful for the reassurance.

Still tilted at a crazy angle, they dropped again, engines screaming as they fought a downdraft. Then they were through the gate, leveling off. The pilot repeated his virtuoso performance, taking them through a second, narrower gorge. Sister's ears popped ferociously, and she saw that they were approaching a level plateau.

The flaps were lowered, and beneath the cabin she felt the heavy mechanical rumble of the bays as they opened and the landing gear was cranked into place. Brother shouted at the officer in a panicked voice.

"I demand to know where in *hell* you are taking us!"

"Patience, Captain Zhang. And my apologies for the rough ride. One thing that I can tell you for certain, though, is that it is *not* to hell."

As they made their approach, Sister thought that the plane and everyone in it would vanish into the whiteness like a flake of snow. She saw nothing below them of human civilization, and it was not until they were almost on it that she saw a runway of sorts, of packed bare dirt. They touched down, rolled, and came to a smooth halt. The engines were cut. She sat, dazed, her head buzzing in the sudden absence of the engine's noise.

Sister, Brother, and the four rimpoches were given heavy parkas, mittens, and boots. Brother put his on angrily. This was a nicety he could not very well refuse; outside the windows was a sparkling, glacial world. One of the soldiers opened the door of the plane. Cold, clean air rushed in and filled the cabin; the stillness and silence after the interminable hours of noise and turbulence were as vast and deep as the sky. Sister imagined that her eyes and ears were open windows and that the wind blew through them unobstructed, clearing the dust from every corner of her mind, sweeping it empty and clean.

"Where are we?" her brother's voice demanded, breaking the spell. She opened her eyes. He was standing, facing the senior officer. "I demand to know who you are and why we have been taken here!"

"It will all be clear to you in time, Captain Zhang," the man said not unkindly. "You have my word." With that, he politely indicated the open door. "Please, Captain," he said.

They climbed down, their feet clanging on the metal

stairs in the stillness. Sister was almost euphoric. This was a place of such impossible beauty, so high, frozen, and glistening, that she felt as far from the seething streets of Peking and its grim reeducation center as it was possible to be without leaving the earth itself.

Someone shouted a greeting. She lowered her eyes from the great peaks and saw that a band of men had materialized and were coming toward them, sturdy mountain people dressed in furs and colorful rags. She had heard of such people—Sherpas! The senior officer raised an arm and joyously returned the greeting. The Sherpas prostrated themselves when they saw the four rimpoches, then rose and surrounded the little group, laughing and smiling, their faces brown and leathery, chattering happily with the officer in a dialect Sister had never heard before, the officer responding with ease and fluency. Brother's face was a mask of unease and suspicion.

Whatever they were talking about, it was obvious that Brother and Sister were the subject of the conversation. The officer spoke rapidly, gesturing in their direction. The head Sherpa listened intently, smiling all the while. His eyes met Sister's, and she could not help smiling back at him. There it was again. That smile that turned up at every juncture, first on one face and then on another, going directly into her soul, filling her with peace and reassurance. Brother returned the man's smile with a dark scowl. She wanted to take Brother's hand and soothe him, but she didn't.

Bundles were unloaded from the Sherpas' backs. Yak skins and heavy carpets were unrolled. The Sherpas began to wrap the four rimpoches; when they approached Brother, he pushed them away. His hand went reflexively for his nonexistent pistol.

"No. You will not touch me," he declared. "What is this?" he implored the officer. Sister saw fear in his eyes now, too.

"Captain. It is necessary. We have a long journey ahead of us, and it will be cold. Very, very cold. You will not survive without protection. Please."

"I'm not going anywhere!" he declared.

"You are going to stay here? Alone?" the officer asked pointedly.

"I . . . I . . ." Brother looked around helplessly. Behind him were the plane and the soldiers. Of course, they had no weapons, but neither did he, and there were many of them and only one of him. Around them were lofty frozen peaks and the icy wind. He had no choice. No choice at all. He allowed himself to be wrapped. Soon both he and Sister were inside snug cocoons of warmth.

"My apologies for this final necessity," the officer said when the Sherpas were finished. He produced a soft woolen scarf and approached Brother with the obvious intent of blindfolding him. Though tied and defenseless, Brother shook his head fiercely.

"No! I will not be humiliated!" he shouted. The Sherpas gazed at him with mild curiosity.

"Captain, Captain," the officer said in a kind voice. "This is not to humiliate you. It is for your protection, and for security. Nothing more. I give you my word." Again, Brother had no choice. Sister accepted her blindfold. There was more talk, and then, incredibly, Sister felt herself being lifted onto one of the Sherpas' backs. She heard objections from Brother, and knew he was being lifted, too, and felt sad for him again. He had expected promotions, medals, toasts. Instead, he got this.

~

The journey was a long, strange dream. The man carrying her was as sturdy as a mule, his feet as sure as a goat's. She became as familiar with the workings of his bones and muscles as if they were her own as he climbed, hour after hour. At first the Sherpas had talked among themselves, but eventually they fell silent as the weather deteriorated. She was warm inside her skins and rugs, but she knew that she wore a coating of snow and ice. Whatever Brother was thinking, he was keeping it to himself; for the first time in days, his thoughts were opaque to her, and she could only imagine what was going on in his mind. Sometimes she let her head rest on the Sherpa's shoulder and dozed, the man's steady plodding a constant rhythm beneath her, the wind filling her ears.

After many hours, she became aware of the grade growing gradually steeper and a subtle focusing of the Sherpa's concentration; she felt him choosing each step with even greater care and then using his hands as well as his feet as they climbed, placing them in what must have been carved niches. Though she could see nothing, she sensed an enormous emptiness to their right, and in her mind's eye saw a vast chasm, sheer, icy, bottomless. The man beneath her was her eyes and legs; she concentrated on balancing her weight to match his motions and on putting all her trust in him. She imagined the narrow treacherous ledge of ice their little band ascended, and was grateful for the scarf over her eyes. Now she understood what the officer had meant when he told Brother that the blindfolds were for their protection.

They climbed this way for another long hour before reaching what seemed to be a level spot with a bit of space where the Sherpas stopped for a rest and a consultation. She felt herself being lifted to the ground, where she sat like a bundled infant listening to the Sherpas' murmuring voices. She could hear Brother's breathing nearby; she spoke his name, but he did not answer. She knew that he blamed her for all of this.

After a brief rest, one of the Sherpas began what must have been a virtually vertical climb; she could hear his voice, responding to encouragement from his fellows, moving up and up, farther and farther from them, until the men on the ground became quiet and she knew they were watching him at a fair distance while he negotiated some especially treacherous span. She guessed that he was the strongest and most agile among them to be chosen for this particular feat; she could feel the suspense in their intent silence. Then there were exultant whoops; he had done it, whatever it was.

The Sherpas' voices were relaxed and happy now. They shouted jokes and banter up to their colleague and he shouted back down to them. She heard something plop heavily and with a clank to the ground, as if the man up above had lowered some sort of apparatus.

Now she was being lifted again. She felt a complicated body harness being buckled into place; a voice said something into her ear in a reassuring tone, and she was hoisted, dangling and twirling, into space.

A much clearer and more frightening picture of the wall the man had climbed presented itself to her. If she was hanging free, then he could only have negotiated some terrifying overhang. She saw a picture in her mind of a man, a speck against the huge whiteness, defying the laws of gravity and physics, crawling impossibly on the underside of some lip of ice as if he were a fly on an ornate piano leg.

She rose through the air in rhythmic pulls. The tension in the man's muscles traveled down the cable and spread along the infinite branching pathways of her own nerves and muscles; she was sure that she could feel the beating of his heart thrumming the taut cord in the pauses between pulls. Hanging breathlessly in infinite space, blind and helpless, she imagined the world and everything she had known receding beneath her as she ascended to some mythical place above the clouds.

Then she was there. Arms encircled her, pulled her in, and lowered her to the ground. The harness was unbuckled and she lay there, breathing in and out, waiting for her heart to slow.

One by one the others were brought up: the four rimpoches, Brother, and the other five Sherpas. The passengers were picked up again and carried another distance for about a half hour when the wind stopped abruptly and she heard the voices of the Sherpas echoing eerily. She was placed upon the ground and hands began to unwrap her from her rugs and skins. Then the blindfold was removed. She blinked as her eyes adjusted to seeing again, and then she gasped.

They had truly entered another world. They were in a vast cathedral of white and blue-green, with majestic frozen stalagmites for pillars and sheer glistening walls and waterfalls of ice. Time was the architect here, infinitely slow and patient, shaping graceful glassy downward-flowing curves and ripples over the centuries, indifferent to whether or not sentient eyes would ever look on the results.

She exhaled in wonder. Even the rimpoches were

awed, their heads thrown back and their mouths open as they gazed about in silence.

She remembered Brother then, and turned to find him. She hoped that they could at least share a moment of appreciation, however brief, removed from their conflicts and worldly concerns. He was behind her, unwrapped and with his blindfold removed. He glared straight ahead, as he might have done if they were in a bus station or a bunker, determined not to give the smallest shred of satisfaction to his captors. Or, she understood sadly, to her.

They rested for a while before the Sherpas rose and gestured for the others to follow them. Sister could see that the ice cave was in fact a tunnel with many twists and turns; the light grew poor as they walked, but ahead of them she could see patches of deep translucent bottle-green reflecting light from the other end. The rimpoches spoke among themselves in hushed tones. Sister understood a few words of their conversation. They were walking in a sacred place, but she would have known that anyway. Ahead of them, the Sherpas whooped and sang, enjoying the echoes. And soon there was another voice, not an echo of their own, hallooing in the distance. The Sherpas responded, hallooing back enthusiastically.

They rounded a turn, and there was a very tall man waving his arm, shouting greetings, striding toward them with a smile on his pleasant, heavy-featured face. A Westerner. No, not just a Westerner, but unbelievably, preposterously, an American. Sister had certainly never met one in person before, but she, like Brother, had seen plenty of American movies and recognized the broad nasal tones immediately, and knew that Brother did, too. Poor Brother, she thought for the thousandth time. Abducted, tricked, tied, denied the

honors and praise he believed were his due, and carried igno-
miniously to this strange cavern atop the world, only to come
face-to-face with his nemesis, the symbol of all that was
decadent and wrong as well as the object of his secret
adulation.

"You guys had me a little worried," the American
said in English, shaking hands with all of the Sherpas, who
enjoyed the little ceremony so much that they did it two or
three more times each. "That was some blizzard that blew
in. Christ, I was sure you'd lost your way or fell in a gorge
or some damned thing. But I should know better than to
worry. Eh?" He laughed and thumped the head Sherpa on
the shoulders while the man grinned with pride and delight.
"Here you go," the American said. "I know this is what
you've been waiting for." He produced a pack of British
cigarettes and handed them around to the Sherpas.

Brother was staring at the man. Sister looked from
Brother's face to the American's and back again while a most
peculiar feeling grew in her mind. Brother's thoughts were
plain to her again, as if radio interference had suddenly
cleared. Yes, she thought she recognized the American's face,
too. The man in the photograph. Father had shown it to
both of them. The man standing next to the boy, the American whom Father said he had known years before in New
York City.

"Hey, Your Holinesses," he said to the rimpoches.
"Am I glad to see you!" When it was obvious that the
four old men understood no English, he switched to Tibetan
effortlessly and repeated the greeting. More smiles, more delight. Except for Brother, whose face was pale and strained
and whose breathing had grown shallow. Unable to stop
herself any longer, Sister took his hand and held it tightly.

They used to hold hands sometimes when they were children, and he did not stop her now. When the American finished his greetings to the rimpoches, he turned to Brother and Sister and gave a courteous nod, then spoke in Chinese. "Welcome," he said simply. "I hope we can make you comfortable here."

"Thank you," Sister replied. "But I speak English."

"So you do, so you do!" the American said, impressed.

Sister gave Brother's hand an extra squeeze. This reawakened some awareness in him; he jerked his hand rudely out of hers and gave her a poisonous scowl. The man did not miss any of this. He looked at the pair curiously for a moment, then shrugged and turned to the Sherpas, addressing them in English again.

"Well," he said. "We'd better shake a leg. The lama's waiting for us." The slang term caused some hilarity. One of the Sherpas raised his leg and waggled it to and fro. She could see that the man and the Sherpas knew each other well, and that this was a regular game between them, his way of teaching them American idioms.

"Let's go," he said, and turned to lead the way. They rounded a bend and found themselves in a chamber of blasted rock containing a loading platform, an enormous wheel and other machinery, a steel cable, and a corrugated metal gondola, as if they were in the Swiss Alps and not these remote mountains at the top of the world.

Bowing graciously as if he were inviting them into a ballroom, the American gestured toward the door of the gondola.

"It took us twenty years to make the last mile a little easier," he said to Sister with obvious pride. "And we finished it just in time for our honored guests." Everyone climbed on except the Sherpas. "These guys won't ride on it, though. They don't trust it. They say they'd rather go on foot and take the old route. One of these days I'll get them to go for a little spin. It'll be a piece of cake. Right, fellas?" he said, stepping in after the others.

"A little spin," they chorused, laughing as if it were the funniest thing they'd ever heard. "A piece of cake!" The American slammed the door, secured it, and gave a signal to the head Sherpa. A motor hummed, machinery engaged, and the gondola moved forward with a jerk. They left the cave and sailed smoothly out over a deep valley of snow. The old rimpoches gazed down in fascination, while Sister thought that after the plane ride and being carried on the Sherpa's back and then hauled up like a sack of grain on a rope, she should have been prepared for anything. But she felt a giddy terror at this dizzy new perspective, the terrain falling away at sharp angles beneath them, minute details of the topography visible to the naked eye. This is what the eagle sees, she thought, thrilled and terrified, when he soars over his kingdom. She glanced at Brother; he stared resolutely down at his boots. The American was watching her, obviously enjoying her wonder.

"Not bad, eh?" he said with a smile.

"No," she said. "Not bad." He was regarding her with a mixture of reserve and curiosity, as if he was not quite sure who or what she was or if he should allow himself to like her.

"Who is the lama you spoke of?" she asked.

"You'll be meeting him soon. But don't worry. He's what I'd call a regular guy."

She was not quite sure of the meaning of that idiom,

but neglected to ask what it meant because they were fast approaching the ridge on the other side of the steep valley. They sailed above jagged, precipitous slabs of ice and rock, the rolling wheels on the cable above them making a frightening clunking noise as the mechanism passed over the support structure mounted at the highest point of the ridge. He saw her flinch and grip the handrail. Brother remained stolid, as if he preferred a plunge onto the rocks below to whatever lay ahead. The rimpoches looked at each other and laughed nervously.

"Nobody likes that sound, but it's perfectly normal," he said. "Makes you think the car's about to jump the cable. But it won't. I personally guarantee it. I engineered this thing myself, and I made it about three times as strong as it needs to be."

Did she dare ask him?

"What is your name?" she said. He paused for half a moment and considered.

"Some people call me Barnard."

"And you are American," she said, causing him to put his head back and laugh.

"I guess I was once," he answered.

He said no more, but looked at her, smiled, and watched her face the way someone does when he is anticipating a reaction. The monks behind her began to pray again. She shifted her focus from his face to the landscape below the gondola.

She knew there was no springtime at these elevations, but that is exactly what it looked like: the snow thinning and receding here and there on the steep slopes with tufts of new grass showing through. She looked at the American and saw that this was the moment he had not wanted to

miss: seeing her see the green grass. And his expression suggested that this was not all that she would be seeing.

They descended, the slope below them growing more
precipitous while the patches of green grew larger and more
frequent. She started to see flowers in the patches; then the
patches gradually gave way to meadows of grass and flowers,
the way it did when a traveler came down from the high
mountains to the lower elevations and passed from frozen
winter to full summer or even into the tropics in a matter
of hours. But of course, it was impossible for that to be
happening here. They had not gone down more than a hundred feet or so in altitude from an elevation of at least twenty
(fifteen? ten?) thousand feet. She could not see very far in
any direction around the gondola because of a fine mist, as
though they were passing through clouds, so the scenery
below unrolled itself mysteriously like a dream. At the moment when she saw the meadows of flowers give way to
cultivated rows of fruit trees, she heard one of the old rimpoches address his colleagues. He spoke his words formally,
as if he were quoting scripture or a prophecy.

"In times of trouble, the secret valleys will open themselves to the chosen ones," he said in a voice just above a
whisper. She heard murmurs of assent from the other old
men. She glanced at Brother. He looked stricken, like a man
trapped on a window ledge above a busy street. No—he
looked like a man riding the executioner's cart through the
city on his way to the guillotine. She wanted to comfort
him, but could not take her eyes from the unfolding scene
beneath them.

The fruit trees were in flower, in shades of delicate
white and pink, and beehives stood between the rows. The
smell of the blossoms rose and filled the metal gondola.

Still the American said nothing, just watched her with the same smile.

"Where are we?" she asked, her voice sounding thin to her own ears.

"Don't you know?" he replied.

As he spoke the gondola emerged from the fine mist into brilliant sunshine, and she saw the orchard give way to lush emerald cultivated terraces where shirtless farmers worked. The terraces descended like asymmetrical staircases for a giant into a valley like a huge bowl. Farther down, peeking out of the vegetation here and there and shimmering like mother-of-pearl, were buildings. She had seen Western science-fiction paperbacks with fantastic illustrations of cities on other planets; it was as if she were glimpsing one of those cities, but instead of sitting under a dome on a cold dark world in outer space, it sat under a blue sky, partly hidden by living green. A cloud of tiny yellow birds, startled by the gondola's approach, veered up and away past their window. She thought she might cry, though she had no idea why.

"Yes," she said. "I think I know." By now the rimpoches were praying, much the way they had when they were on the airplane, only now it sounded to her like a prayer of thanks for deliverance.

The gondola glided over treetops, so close that she could see the tender new leaves. Where it was springtime on the slopes above, here it was early summer. They rode down into the trees so that they were enveloped in green and glided for a few moments before the gondola came to a gentle halt.

This was no bare metal platform like the one in the ice cave above, but a marble terrace in a forest glen. Tangled vines grew along the railing and trailed across the expanse. Above them, the leaves made a canopy with beams of light angling through. Sister stepped out of the gondola, looking down at her army-booted foot on the striated marble, and thought that there should have been a dainty sandal on that foot, or even better, nothing at all. Brother put his own booted feet down in a crude and heedless way, the same way she had seen him do when he was treading on the sacred floor of a monastery after breaking down the door. He kept his eyes straight ahead, his face wearing the expression of the prisoner of war who tells his captors without words that he will not be broken. The rimpoches knelt, folding up their old bones nimbly, and kissed the cool marble as if they were returning home after a journey of a thousand years.

Sister gazed up to where the trees joined. When she looked down again, a group of fifteen or sixteen smiling, brightly dressed young people had materialized on the marble terrace. Boys and girls, younger than she by a few years, shy and happy-looking. The American spoke to them.

"Our guests have had one hell of a long day," he said in English. "They'd probably like to hit the hay for a while." The young people grinned and laughed the way the Sherpas had. Then Sister was surrounded by five or six of the young women, smiling, bowing, rustling and murmuring, and found herself gently compelled off the terrace and down a staircase. She looked back and saw Brother, taller by half a head than the young men who were similarly escorting him toward a different staircase. She knew that only she could see the fear in his otherwise blank face.

The staircase led to a stone-paved path through woods translucent with new green. There was birdsong and the sound of busy streams hidden in the foliage. The path became steeper until they were negotiating switchbacks; soon ferns grew taller than their heads and the air was cool with rising mist from a bigger stream she could hear below. No one spoke as they climbed down into the miniature river gorge; words would have been swallowed by the sound of the small waterfall they came to, pouring between over-hanging banks of dark green velvet moss, down in a silvery rush over glistening rocks and into a deep forest pool with a hollow roar. Clouds of insects hung peacefully in the air just above the furious white froth where the falling water boiled down.

They crossed the little gorge on a swaying rope-and-plank bridge suspended directly over the falls; she stood for a moment, enveloped by mist and the tranquil roar of the falls; she imagined the ages rising and declining while the water fell here, exactly as it was falling now, for thousands of years, making this music which her ear was now separating into a million component parts, its only audience the shafts of sunlight and the tall, still ferns.

The girls who escorted her waited patiently while she paused on the bridge. When she was ready, they started up the steep trail on the other side. The trail led to another paved pathway and then, abruptly, down an old, cracked, overgrown set of marble steps and onto another terrace, smaller than the first one, surrounded by a nearly tropical tangle of greenery not quite concealing the smooth white walls of a building attached to the terrace. A set of French doors stood open in a most inviting way; beyond the doors she glimpsed pillows, tapestries, and a beautiful canopied bed. Only then did it occur to her how tired she was. No, not tired; profoundly, quiveringly exhausted. From the moment she saw the bed she doubted that she could make it the few remaining steps across the terrace and through the doors.

~

The lama embraced each bony, musty-smelling old man in turn, marveling at the fact that they were, after all, composed of mortal skin and hair.

"I know we're not supposed to worry, but I did," he said to them. "It was a complicated business getting you here, let me assure you. Things would be a lot easier if we were all made of light and air, wouldn't they?" He sank into a chair and poured himself a brandy. Remembering his manners, he proffered the decanter, and to his surprise, the old men accepted. "You've earned it. And so have I," he remarked as he poured them each a snifter.

"Tell us, Lama," the eldest of the rimpoches began. "How did you know of our dilemma? Your intercession was an extraordinary feat. We are humbly grateful."

"Humbly grateful! What nonsense! I'm the one who's full of humble gratitude, or grateful humility, or whatever we're calling it. Mostly I'm grateful to the Chinese and their peculiar obsession with propagandizing. Did you know that they announced your so-called trial in advance on their radio broadcasts at least one hundred times? Saturation, they call it. And a grand thing it is, too, because it meant that the chances of one of the broadcasts getting through to me all the way up here were greatly increased. And it did. More than once. They told me where, when, and how, so I was able to dispatch my plane and some of my best people to intercede. I was never happy as a commander, but I'm getting better at it. Perhaps I missed my calling." He looked at his guests. "Each of you is a living, walking, breathing library.

And very nice fellows, as well. We couldn't just let them throw you on the great book-burning pyre, too. Here is your sanctuary in these times of trouble. If only we could save everybody," he remarked sadly. "But there are only a few whom we can allow to even know about this place."

"There have been troubled times before," one of the old men said with a shrug. "Terrible times."

"Yes, terrible," the lama agreed. "But not quite terrible enough to drive a man from this valley. A man who had lived here peacefully for more than a hundred years, mind you. He was a close friend of mine. His name was Chang, and he was no more and no less than a fine, learned old gentleman, or so I thought. My friend for more than thirty years—I thought I knew him, but I've only just learned what he was really made of. He lost his life for us. For all of us. For the world, really." The rimpoches waited while the lama took more brandy and gathered his thoughts.

"It was the Chinese who spoke to him—the same way that they spoke to me—with their infernal broadcasting. He was listening months ago, as we all were, when the Chinese were appropriating some of our legends and mythology for propaganda purposes. I heard them, too. They went on and on about Shambala and the Future King of Shambala, one of our oldest myths. It sounded to me as if the Chinese were trying to ingratiate themselves in some devious way, to convince Tibetans that the Panchen Lama—who is more or less controlled by the Chinese now—should take the place of the Dalai Lama in their minds and hearts. But their words had a special meaning for Chang. What he heard put a terrible fear into his old heart.

"But he kept it all to himself. The only reason I know what it was that moved him to leave here is that he left a letter for me in his meditation retreat, knowing that if I was there reading it, it would mean that I had come looking for him. And if I found the letter and not Chang himself, then it would mean that he had in all likelihood failed in his mission and would be dead. And that, I fear, is exactly the case. A horrible death, too, no doubt. You see, Chang left here—after telling me he was going on a meditation retreat on the other side of the valley—and somehow, God knows how he did it, went to New York City. Alone. He must have gone to India and caught a flight from there. Imagine. A man who was born decades before even the first crude flying machine was invented. His mission was to make an appeal at the United Nations on behalf of Tibet. I remember when we first heard the news on our radio at the end of the war that such a thing as the United Nations was coming into being. Chang was optimistic and excited at the very concept.

"And what would drive an old man—an old, old man—from his home, his sanctuary, out into a cruel hostile world scarcely recognizable to him? Something dire indeed.

"I am sure that you know that the Great Thirteenth once came to our valley, and that he had some gloomy words about the future of our country. I am sure that you are acquainted with his prophecy—he spoke of rampant destruction, hardship, overpowering fear, serving our enemies, and all the rest of it. But there was more to it. Something that the Thirteenth spoke to Chang about. Something rather frighteningly specific. He told Chang that when the Men of Han—the Chinese—spoke of the Future King of Shambala, it would be a sign that soon, very soon, one of them would find the key, would come to believe in Shambala as more than a mere legend, and would embark on a serious search for the hidden secret land. And if he should succeed in finding it . . ."

He looked around at the old men. He imagined that they knew what he was going to say.

"If he should succeed in finding it, then all will be lost. Tibet will be lost. Its secret soul will be destroyed, its beating heart stilled and cut out. Tibet has survived many onslaughts, but that is the ultimate violation, the one she will not survive. And if Tibet does not survive, then the rest of the world . . ." He shrugged. "Well. I don't have to tell you. If indeed there is a nucleus of hope for peace on this planet, it is in the profound knowledge of the human mind which is the special province of the thought and learning of this land.

"All of this brings us to the dilemma I face now. You see, the Thirteenth did not leave us empty-handed. There is a plan—an emergency plan, if you will. An ancient strategy. Similar ones have been around for centuries. I am sure you know what this sort of plan involves. There was a quote at the very end of Chang's letter. Are you gentlemen familiar with the twenty-third psalm of the Christian Bible?" He looked around at their faces. Learned scholars, all of them. They nodded.

"It was the favorite of Father Perrault. Well, Perrault and the Great Thirteenth agreed that the psalm was to be a signal, if you will, that the emergency plan was to be implemented. And a very appropriate signal it is, I might add."

" 'The valley of the shadow of death,' " one of the rimpoches said thoughtfully. "It brings to mind . . . certain references of our own. A land of shadows . . ." Then he looked at the lama comprehendingly. "Ah," he said gravely and sympathetically. "Very difficult . . . very dangerous. And not to be undertaken frivolously."

"No. Not a lark by any means," the lama remarked, looking around at their solemn faces. "And of course, I've been wondering why Chang kept all of this to himself for so many years, and I can only conclude that he never really expected it to happen. Not literally. Poor Chang. When the Thirteenth visited here and told him to beware of the Men of Han speaking certain words, there were certainly no short-wave radios in the valley yet. Chang must have believed that the Thirteenth was speaking in some metaphorical way, because how would we ever literally hear words spoken by the Chinese? I remember how disturbed he was after he spent a night up in the radio shack with Bryant a few months ago, when the propaganda broadcasts began. I was disturbed, too, but he was positively agitated. Now I know why. Imagine him hearing those Chinese voices, the voices of his own countrymen, crackling out of the void, speaking those very words he'd been warned of...." He shook his head. "And even when he believed the worst was happening, he still didn't speak, no doubt because he wished to spare me. He knew how reluctant I would be to leave this valley. So he tried to forestall the disaster he believed was coming by mustering his own limited strength and resources, and traveling to New York City. Oh, my. When I think of it . . . New York was a merciless city thirty-five years ago. I shudder to contemplate what it might be like now. And in the winter . . ." He shook his head.

"I will go if I must, of course. But naturally, I'd like to be sure. Simply knowing that the Chinese have uttered the name of the Future King, a rather popular legend in our land, is not enough for me. It was enough for Chang, but it's not enough for me. I'd rather not go blundering out there without the sure knowledge that some damned Chinese is actually searching for our valley. I am tortured by doubt, gentlemen. Exquisitely tortured. And it's not merely my own skin I'm concerned about, though I admit I'm rather fond of it. This plan can really be used only once. It's not to be wasted on false alarms."

"We can tell you this, Lama," the eldest rimpoche said after a moment. "The Men of Han are arriving in waves. They seem to multiply before our very eyes. They bring massive destruction. You would weep if you could have seen what we have seen. The invasion of the nineteen-fifties was quite bad enough, but that was a mere territorial invasion, a physical occupation, compared to what is happening today. These depredations are an attempt to destroy the very soul of Tibet."

"Tell me about the two young Chinese who were brought with you. A young man and a young woman, I believe."

"They are the son and daughter of a high-ranking Chinese general," the second rimpoche said. "It was unavoidable that they come with us. The daughter saved our lives, so we were obliged to save hers. She has done much to counteract the deeds of her people and her father."

"Really," the lama said thoughtfully. "She saved your lives? And how did it come to pass that her life needed saving?"

"It is doubtful that we would be here at all if not for her. She saved us with fire! At the risk of terrible danger to herself, she made a wall of fire at the festival which was to be our 'trial.' She had spoken to us in a stolen moment just before we were to go out and 'perform.' She said . . ." The old man turned to one of his colleagues. "What was it that she said?"

"She said in Tibetan: 'The fire will set you free.' Then there was terrible confusion and panic. A stampede. She directed us out the back and we joined the crowds. We went to a small monastery nearby, one invisible to the Chinese because of its smallness and drabness. Your people knew about it too; it was the first place they looked for us. They said you had sent for us, that we were to come to this valley for safety. We spent a day and a night at the monastery, hiding, waiting for the right moment to leave. We could hear the voices of the Chinese in the street, looking for us, broadcasting their threats through loudspeakers atop trucks, warning whoever harbored us that they were traitors and criminals and that they should turn us in if they expected any mercy. It was during that time that we heard the rumor— that the girl was a suspect as the perpetrator of the fire, that she was to be taken back to China for punishment. We could not allow that. We told your people we would not leave without her. And so a plan was devised," the old man said with a smile.

"Indeed it was!" the first rimpoche concurred. "Your people were extraordinary. So resourceful! We knew she was to be taken to Lhasa first, so we posted ourselves on the route we knew they would take. We turned ourselves in to her brother. Her own brother was escorting her to prison! Can you imagine such a thing? We knew of the young man's vanity. We counted on it, and we were right to do so. We knew that there was a possibility that he would simply shoot us, and it was a chance we were willing to take. But he didn't. He did what we thought he would do. He threw us on the back of the transport along with the girl. To take us back to Peking and help promote him to glory! It was impossible not to pity him."

"Did we say your people were resourceful?" another of the old men said. "That is scarcely the word. When they posed as Chinese officers along the road to Lhasa, we admit that there were a few moments when we believed that they really were what they pretended to be. And so, here we are. And the brother along with the sister. It would have been impossible to leave him behind without arousing suspicion."

"A difficult boy," the first rimpoche said. "But not hopeless. Not at all. If only he can wake from his trance."

"Hm," the lama said, thoughtful for a moment. He was remembering something he had heard once. Something to do with fire. "I'd very much like to meet this young woman," he said. "Do you think she would have any objections?"

## ~ 6 ~

Oh, Father, she thought. If you only knew.

It was late afternoon. The shadows had grown long while she slept. The same young women who had escorted her before had come and wakened her; she was invited to tea with the high lama, they said. Her army fatigues and boots had been removed; in their place was a silk robe and slippers. They led her from her room out through the French doors and down another staircase, the vegetation making a canopy of light and green over their heads as they descended. When they emerged, she found herself gazing up at a building that looked like the great-great-grandfather of all the monasteries her father and brother had helped reduce to rubble.

Its two great five-storied wings were set into the steep mountainside so that it overlooked the entire valley. A long, wide three-tiered staircase ascended to its massive front door. She and the young women climbed the white stone steps. At the top of the first tier was a terrace with wonderful strange statuary: dragons and gargoyles, stone beasts of both Asian and Occidental origin, keeping their vigil over the world below. The second tier had a smaller terrace, more welcoming, with marble benches, a fountain, and what looked to Sister like meteorites resting on pedestals here and there. The doors at the top of the third tier were of intricate bronze repoussé, flashing fire in the late sunlight; massive as they were, as tall as three men, one of the girls took hold of the handle with her delicate fingers and pulled it open effortlessly on its silent oiled hinges.

She had seen pictures of the interiors of the great cathedrals of Europe, so vast in height and space that you felt as if you were but a few inches tall. The interior she looked upon here was not quite of that scale, but the effect was similar. Over their heads, four open stories up, was a dome of leaded glass; below, to each side, was a curving staircase. The space between the two staircases was occupied by one of the strangest, most beautiful objects she had ever seen: a sphere of glass, six or seven feet in diameter, its surface carved with constellations, with the planets of the solar system, also made of glass of different colors, on articulated armatures within the larger sphere. The big sphere rested on legs of golden curling serpents and dragons.

They crossed the polished marble floor and climbed the left-hand staircase, giving her a chance to look more closely at the wondrous object. She could detect no seams in the glass, and the stars of the constellations were deeply etched into its surface. Passing closer to the sphere as she climbed, she heard the short whirs and clicks of its internal clockwork mechanism.

But she had little time to reflect on it, because soon they were at the top of the stairs and she was being escorted through what looked remarkably like a paneled English library. Doors opened onto a pavilion; her attention was distracted for a moment by what she saw beyond the railing;

parts of buildings peeking out of the vegetation, the same ones she had seen when she was riding in on the gondola. When she turned around again, her escorts had vanished, leaving her quite alone.

She stood and gazed out over the tender green tree-tops of the valley far below. The fragrant breeze filled the sleeves of her silk robe and lifted her loose hair. Water splashed in a nearby fountain, and birds sang and hopped about in the huge old tree whose branches dipped down close to the marble railing where her hand rested. A table was set for tea, with delicate china and flashing silver.

None of this is real, of course, she thought. In truth, I'm lying asleep on an iron cot in a detention center in Peking. With a gray blanket over me, green cement walls around me, and a gray cement floor beneath me. My poor mind has produced all of this to comfort itself. At any moment I'll be shaken awake, and my eyes will open to the pale cold dawn light showing through a grimy little window high up on the wall. A smiling, shiny young face, a young girl with pigtails and scrubbed skin, will invite me to rise to porridge and a cold bath and begin my glorious reeducation.

She looked down at her hand resting on the railing. Dreams dissolve as soon as you realize you're dreaming, she thought. This one will start disintegrating at any moment. Let me enjoy it for as long as possible.

"Hello! You've had a long journey!" came a man's voice from behind her, speaking in Chinese. The accent was flawless Peking. She turned, half expecting to see the pigtailed girl, since anything was possible in a dream.

Instead, she saw a man, another Westerner, in lama's robes. He looked about forty years old, with blue eyes and earnest, regular features that made her think of kindly forthright cowboys she had seen in the foreign movies she and Brother had been fond of when they were teenagers. He had a startled expression on his face that seemed to mirror her own surprise. She experienced a strange moment of thinking that she and her brother had been brought to a reeducation center of another sort, something at the highest level of secrecy, the West's answer to the People's Revolution. And this man would be its highest commander, the counterpart in rank of Chairman Mao. But nothing like the Chairman. He smiled diffidently and extended a hand.

"I speak English," she said, offering her own hand.

"Well. Yes. So you do, so you do," he said, then looked at her, still smiling, her hand in his, as if he couldn't think of anything else to say. The startled expression remained on his face; she liked that. It put her at ease. Jailers and inquisitors did not customarily wear a look of surprise; it tended to interfere with one's aura of implacable authority. This man projected anything but implacability. She thought that his brow bore the imprint of some perpetually unanswered question.

"Hugh Conway," he said then, giving her hand a couple of gentle shakes and letting it go, a modified version of the sort of handshake he would probably have given another man. "Some people around here insist on calling me 'Lama.' "

"My name is Ma Li. You're British?" she said with some surprise. "The other one was American."

"The other one. Oh, yes. Bryant. Yes, he's quite American, isn't he? It's been such a long time for both of us, though, that we scarcely think of being British or American or anything at all anymore."

"The man I spoke to said his name was Barnard. How many Americans do you have here?"

"Well, we have a few others, but he's the most visible one. Yes. He's been here a long time, but old habits die hard. Called himself Barnard, did he? Hm. Let's just say that Mr. Bryant has a rather colorful past. It's unlikely that the American authorities would still be looking for him, but I suppose he felt he needed to be cautious with a newcomer. A reflex, nothing more."

"How long *have* you been here?"

"Well, let me think. A good thirty-four, thirty-five years. Yes."

"You were brought here as a child, then?" she asked without guile. He looked perplexed, then laughed.

"Scarcely! I was quite a bit older than you are now, as a matter of fact. Very nearly old enough to be your father, actually."

The encounter was growing more peculiar by the moment. She had no doubt that he was telling the truth. Everything in his manner was truthful and artless, yet what he was telling her was impossible. He was putting his age close to seventy.

"And Mr. Bryant?" she asked.

"Much the same," he replied after a moment's consideration. "He's a few years my senior, but not many. He's quite a technical wizard. He's done marvelous things here. Really brought us into the twentieth century. Made radio contact possible, most notably, with boosters and transformers and such. With the world so complicated now, we really can't afford to be completely out of touch."

She was quiet for a time, and so was he. She was

remembering her emotions when she and Bryant and the monks had been descending into the valley in the gondola. When she had asked where they were, and Bryant had simply answered: Don't you know? And she had. She had felt no need for explanations. She had known in a part of her mind that was beyond the reach of words. She looked at him. He was watching her carefully.

"Why was I brought here?" was all she asked when she finally spoke.

He told her about the broadcasts and dispatching his people to intercede and bring the rimpoches to the valley, and how the old men had refused to be taken to safety without her. "They were showing their gratitude," he said. "And of course, when they told me about the fire you set, I was overwhelmed with curiosity. I simply had to meet you. I don't wish to burden your credulity. I imagine you've had quite enough for one day. But there are stories, myths, shall we say. Prophecies, actually," he said, a little embarrassed. "I don't always place a great deal of stock in prophecies," he added. "But sometimes they're . . . intriguing, to say the least. And you see, there is a story—a myth, whatever you want to call it—which is rather a fascinating one. Especially in light of what's happened recently. I'm sorry, I've quite forgotten my manners. Won't you sit down? We could have tea."

She sat. He poured hot, fragrant jasmine tea. She lifted the cup and felt the warmth of it in her hands and the steam rising to her nostrils, and contemplated the journey which had begun on the road to Lhasa when the convoy bound for Peking had been intercepted. Brother had certainly been fooled. Every detail had been flawless, right down to the buttons on the uniforms of the officers. But for her part, she remembered a strange absence of apprehension from that moment on, a peculiar calm that overcame her. At the time, she had attributed it to nature: She had heard that the gazelle in the jaws of the lion is released from its pain and terror in the final moments of its existence, a last little merciful provision, and she had thought that something similar was happening to her. It was not until they arrived at the airstrip and saw the impossibly elegant aircraft, looking like a symbol from a dream, something full of rich, urgent, but utterly obscure meaning, that her feeling of marching calmly to her doom had changed into something else.

"Yes. There are so many prophecies. It's often tempting to dismiss them as pure balderdash," he continued. "And some of them are just that. But . . . what are we to make of a prophecy—quite an old one, actually—which states that a woman will come along and use fire to help save the guardians of the true knowledge?" He shrugged. "You can understand why I had to meet you. Of course, prophecy or no prophecy, I'm delighted that I have." He smiled, then looked down at his hands, then fidgeted with his cup and saucer and looked out at the view.

She sipped her tea and tried to wrap her mind around the concept of herself as the fulfillment of a prophecy. She thought of her life: childhood, school, military training, all of it leading up to her presence at the festival and the moment she pushed the butter carving over.

"Whatever I did," she said, "I did of my own free will. I was not functioning under any sort of compulsion. Although of course my brother would disagree. He would say that my behavior was aberrant, that I was seduced. But I did what I did because of who I am, and that includes everything that I ever was."

"Your brother," Conway said thoughtfully. "I'll be

interested in meeting him. I'm going to try not to regard him as the personification of the enemy."

"But that's exactly what he is," she said, shaking her head. "You could not have a better example placed before you. You will learn everything you need to know about youth, idealism, folly, and personal ambition from him. He is like a recipe in a cookbook. The various ingredients are in perfect proportion in him, producing the pure but driven zealot you'll see before you. He is quite transparent. But my father . . . ah, my father is another story. His motives are far more complex, more mysterious, more his own."

"Yes," said Conway. "Tell me about your father. The old men mentioned him to me."

She shrugged. "He's your enemy as well. But understanding him is not quite so simple a matter as understanding someone like my brother. He's much older. He's lived through more, seen more, done more. He has a different sort of mind anyway, and always has. He and my brother argued a lot." She looked around and held out her hand to the valley beyond the pavilion rail. "They argued about this very place. Yes," she added thoughtfully. "It could only have been this place."

"Oh?" Conway said, alert. "What do you mean?"

"I told you that my father is hardly an example of pure revolutionary thinking. His mind goes where it wants to go. Believe it or not, he has come to believe that there is a place called Shambala. A hidden land. Not just a myth, a legend, but an actual place."

She paused. Conway was staring at her intently. She wondered if she should tell him the whole truth. She was reluctant, but supposed that she should. The look on his face made it plain that this was an important topic, to say the least. "Not only does he believe in it, but he's trying to find his way there. Or here, if this is the place he is looking for. He's a cryptographer. He thinks he's found a series of clues." She stopped talking. Now she was alarmed. She had obviously said something wrong; his shoulders had slumped while she was talking, and he leaned back in his chair with a look akin to despair on his face.

"A series of clues," he said tonelessly. "I'm sorry. Please. Go on."

She told him about the clues he had followed—the first one coming from Peking from the aging Chairman and his colleagues—as sort of a game, strictly to amuse himself, because he enjoyed cracking a good code and because they seemed to lead him to the best stores of treasures for his export business, and she told him how the clues had led to the shabby little monastery where the young boy resided. She told him about the shipment of contraband her father had intercepted, the Polaroid photograph, the boy's tale of his journey to a valley, and the most amazing part of it all— the American in the photo, unchanged by time. Apparently the very man who had escorted her down in the gondola.

"My father was not converted overnight," she said. "He gave it a lot of thought. He knew he could combine the search with his other duties. I don't know if his intent, if he succeeded, was to share his discovery with his superiors in Peking."

"God. I had hoped against hope that it wasn't true." He gave a dry little laugh. "What irony. What was I saying a few moments ago about prophecies?"

"What is it?" she asked, regretting that she had spoken. "What did I say? I am so sorry!"

"No, no, no, my dear. I am profoundly grateful that

you did. Prophecies may oftentimes be balderdash, but I'm up against it now. This is one which gives me no latitude. I can't afford to believe anything but that it is real. It's been a pleasant thirty-four years, but there comes a time in every man's life when he has to become serious. You could even say to grow up."

She waited. She knew that whatever he was going to tell her would be more than a match for her story about her father, the clues, and the legend of Shambala.

And it was. First there was the story about his old friend Chang leaving the valley to travel to New York City after hearing her father's broadcasts. Then there was the letter and the warning words of the Thirteenth Dalai Lama. And then there was his task.

"You've confirmed it for me, my dear, by telling me that your very own father is searching for our valley. You're quite right. This place and Shambala are one and the same. It's been called Shangri-La since before the High Lama who was my predecessor arrived here and . . . well, organized things. And now let me tell you what it all means for me, an old man who was hoping for some good years of peaceful contemplation. Damn. I haven't smoked for decades. This is the sort of moment when one wants a cigarette." He sighed heavily.

"It's rather like the fire extinguishers you see in hotels. You know—'In case of emergency, break glass.' Well, the moment has come for me to break the glass, so to speak. There is a plan, a contingency plan, prepared centuries ago for just this eventuality, and I am the one who must implement it. Your father is on a sort of treasure hunt. Following a series of clues, one leading to the next. The clues have been in place for centuries—nearly impenetrable, designed to let only the worthiest searcher through. Inherent in that, of course, was the risk of an unworthy but devilishly clever searcher getting through. Like your father. What I must do," he said, standing and going to the railing, "is divert him."

"Divert him?" she asked dubiously.

"Yes. With false clues. I must slip the key one into place. From there, if I'm successful, he'll progress to the rest of the false clues, which have been in place for centuries. The whole plan was devised hundreds of years ago."

"And where will the false clues lead him?"

"Down a false path. To a place which will discourage him from ever searching for Shambala again."

"Will he die there?" she asked quietly.

Conway thought for a moment. "Not necessarily. A death trap is not what it is. But I can tell you of a particular characteristic of the place the clues will lead him to. From what I've been told, a person's conscience is . . . awakened there. And then he must live with that for the rest of his life."

She thought for a moment. "In that case, my father may wish he were dead. But why is this task so perilous for you?"

"Well, you see, it's a bit tricky. Not only must I leave the valley, but I must allow your father's search to progress dangerously near to the final clue that would lead him here. I must place the false clue at the great Potala palace. He must choose the false one over the real one. I must do all of this, and succeed, and return to the valley within ten days. Fourteen at the absolute most, and that would be pushing it. Otherwise . . ."

"Otherwise?" she asked.

He sighed. "Do you know who Dorian Gray was? Well, never mind. Let's just say I'm something of a hothouse flower, and I must be back in my hothouse before two weeks are up, or else there will be . . . how shall I put it? some rather profound changes in my physical being. Suffice it to say that my life span has been extended here. My true years could catch up with me. Whatever infirmities I might have had, including death, if I had remained in the outside world, would catch up to me. Quickly. But that's the least of my worries. My fate is secondary. The job I have to do is what is important. Of course," he said, looking at her intently, "assuming that I'm not too late. Please tell me that he has not yet gone to the Potala. Please tell me that my vacillation has not cost us everything."

"He hasn't. But that was his next destination when I was taken off for reeducation. He was going to rendezvous with some other important officials in Lhasa. And they were going to decide the fate of the palace. They may dynamite it. I would not put it past them."

He had turned back to the railing. "Then I must leave tonight. There's no more time for deciding. I must prevent him from finding the real clue. And for God's sake, he can't be allowed to destroy the Potala. Tell me—have your countrymen no conscience at all? Have they even the smallest shred of a sense of going too far? Might they not stand in front of the Potala and say to themselves, no, I think not, not today?"

"Well," she said. "I am proof that such a thing is possible. Unless, of course, I'm just a pawn of prophecy." He turned back to her.

"I apologize. I know that it was your own will and conscience that made you do what you did. I know that in every war, there are people who defy the current and listen to their hearts. You are one of that glorious tribe. Don't think that because I have been in this valley for all these decades I am not aware of the war that swept the world twenty-five years ago. I made it my business to collect examples of people who did the right thing. But I also know that one of the prime strategies in war is to demoralize, and one of the best ways to demoralize is to destroy what's rare and irreplaceable. Like the Potala. Like this valley. It may be too late for both, but I must go."

"But why you?"

"It's my responsibility," he said simply. "I made a promise."

"Then you're going to have to take me along. In fact, I don't think you can do it without me," she said with finality. "If you're to succeed, you're going to have to get to my father. And no one knows my father better than I." She could see that his first instinct was to dismiss the suggestion as preposterous, dangerous, unthinkable. But the practicality of her words was inescapable. He looked at her for a long time, a trifle longer than was decorous for people who had just met. She felt a warm little wave of self-consciousness rise to her face before he finally spoke.

"But you only just got here," he said sadly. She merely shrugged in response.

"I'm here now. That's what counts." She had a peculiar sense of acceleration; their acquaintance was barely half an hour old, but they were already speaking in an intimate shorthand.

"Perhaps I can convince you to come back," he said ingenuously.

"Perhaps," she answered, looking at him reflectively, and thinking to herself, perhaps he could. Yes, perhaps he could. "What about you?" she said then. "How did you get

here? Did you follow a series of clues? Were you on some
sort of spiritual quest?"

"God, no," he laughed. "At least, not the first time.
My arrival here was something of an accident. Or so I
thought. I still haven't decided if it was an accident or not.
But we have a lot to do, and lots of time to talk later."

It had become evening. The valley below them was
dark while the sky above was still translucent. She stood and
joined him at the railing. The buildings she had noticed
before, the ones that made her think of science-fiction illustrations, had taken on an entirely different aspect now that
the sun had set: In daylight, they looked like opaque white
stone, windowless geometric structures like solid prisms.
Now, at night, light inside them showed through walls made
of marble that must have been sliced as thin as a piece of
bread and then etched from within with intricate designs, so
that the buildings looked like glowing jewel boxes among the
trees. Like a camera with its shutter open shooting a picture
on slow film, she looked long and hard at the glowing buildings, the lenses of her eyes steady and focused, taking it in
so that she would be sure to retain a clear image in her mind
forever. Conway stood beside her, and for a moment she
fancied that she could see into his mind the way she had
been able to see into Brother's. He was looking at the valley
much the way she was, and thinking, as she was, that he had
better make it a good look, because it might well be his last.

"What about my brother?" she asked at last. "What
will happen to him?"

"Poor fellow," said Conway. "It'll not go easy for
him. Incarcerated. Sentenced to peace, harmony, beauty, and
contemplation for the rest of his very long, very healthy life."

# ~ 7 ~

The radium dials of the plane's instrument panel glowed green in a ghostly way in the dark cockpit. Ghostly, too, was the motion of the co-pilot's controls in front of Conway, the pedals at his feet and the stick in front of him replicating the slightest motions of the pilot's controls. Ma Li sat behind Conway and the pilot and looked over their shoulders, fascinated. She had never been in the cockpit of a plane before. She found herself much less uneasy about the business of flying now that she had a hundred-and-eighty-degree view of the world outside and could see what the pilot was doing.

Conway was paying fierce attention to everything the pilot did, too, but for a different reason. In case of some sort of emergency, I want to know how to fly this machine myself, he told her. I know every peak between here and Lhasa, he said. I've memorized the relief maps, and I know every possible weather pattern. You might say it was part of my meditation over the last ten years or so, ever since I first smelled trouble and I knew that I might have to leave someday. I have made this flight in my mind a thousand times.

They had been airborne for two hours now. Though she could not see anything, she fancied that she could sense every icy peak and chasm in the blackness below, a detailed relief map of her own unfurling in her mind's eye. She thought of her father, and felt compassion for him. His children had vanished. He would be thinking that his son and daughter were dead. What was he going through, in his heart of hearts? He would be showing nothing at all on the outside, she was certain of that. And even though he had consented to sending her back to Peking, she still regretted causing him the pain she was sure he carried inside. And now she was going to assist in causing him more pain.

"Your father," Conway said gently, reading her mind. "I'm going to have to get to know him a bit if I'm to succeed."

She appreciated his tact. A more blunt way to put it would have been to say: Tell me everything about the bastard so that I can send him into a wilderness from which he might never return.

She sighed. "It is not difficult for me to imagine what he is doing right now. When my father received his assignment to Tibet, I remember that he was on the telephone right away to his friends in London, Paris, and New York— all of them dealers in art and antiques. He told them to stand by, that for the next few years he would be personally selecting for export the finest and rarest Tibetan pieces. He made elaborate arrangements for shipping and storage. I wish you could have seen him. He was on fire with anticipation. What brought him to Tibet was not ideology. It was his most unrevolutionary acquisitiveness."

She told him how her father coolly combined business with duty, always making sure the best pieces were removed from a library or monastery before the building was destroyed. "He justified his actions by saying that he was performing a service, that he was preserving the cultural heritage of Tibet by saving these rare pieces from certain destruction. He detested the word 'booty.' When Shambala became real for my father, I knew that he had visions of the priceless objects of beauty that he would find there, the absolute rarest of the rare, the oldest of the old, from the hidden land itself. His object was not only to become wealthy. He dreamed of the name such pieces would establish for him among his colleagues in the art and antique worlds. He wanted that distinction very badly. And now . . . I am sure that as a palliative to his grief, he is pursuing his 'hobby' with a vengeance. And not merely to distract himself. I am sure that he is punishing all of Tibet as well."

Conway was thoughtful for a while before he spoke.

"Your father is a connoisseur and a worldly man. When I was in the consular service, I learned fairly quickly that diplomacy does not only mean talking things through politely and reasonably. Sometimes it means getting the job done in the most practical way possible. Sometimes we must resort to certain—shall we say—time-honored traditions." He was quiet for a few moments. "Yes. Simple, effective, and most of all, highly practical."

~

They landed at dawn outside Lhasa at the same remote airstrip where she had first seen the plane. They were met by Tibetans in Chinese uniforms. And they had not arrived a moment too soon. Word was out, Conway's friends told them: General Zhang was due to arrive that night. They were driven, she and Conway reclining on the floor beneath burlap sacks, to a small compound of houses in the hills near the city. Conway produced stationery and a fountain pen, retired for a brief time, then dispatched one of the Tibetans into the city with a letter and some complicated instructions. Then, exhausted, they rested all day and the next night so that they could set out at dawn.

In the early light, Conway darkened his skin and hair, obscuring his Caucasian features with *todja,* the dark, greasy liniment Tibetans smeared on their faces for protection from the elements, and covered himself with the long hooded robe of a rural pilgrim.

Sister wore an embroidered hide tunic, authentically stiff with filth, and dressed her hair with grease and colorful scraps of cloth. She admired her murky reflection in the dirty glass of the truck window, and thought with deep satisfaction that her transformation was complete: It was the face of Tibet that looked back at her, a face as different from that of the scrubbed, pigtailed Chinese girl she had once been as a lotus is different from a daisy.

> To the Hon. General Zhang:
>
> It is a rare privilege to receive so distinguished a visitor to our city. In the interests of conciliation, I wish to extend an invitation to you to join me for tea tomorrow in the Museum of Atrocities at the Potala palace so that I may have the honor of personally escorting you and acquainting you with its many arcane treasures.
>
> Yours, Tenzin, curator

General Zhang pulled the canvas tent flap aside and gazed up at the great building, the onetime residence of the departed Dalai Lama. Of course, he could have whatever he wanted from it without an invitation. But he liked the civilized tone of the letter, the discreet, tacit language. Here was something that he had sorely missed in recent years. In the old days, you could sit down with your adversary as gentlemen and equals and come to terms. And after you did, you shared brandy and cigars and knew that you were participating in an old and honorable tradition. Bribery was a crude and inadequate word to describe such a transaction.

The Museum of Atrocities. The very name had tantalized him from the first time he heard it. There, placed on display by the Chinese, were relics of Tibet's feudal past—amputated hands, human thighbone trumpets, implements of torture, and the like. The cash value of some of these items on the black market would be incalculable, not to mention the prestige they would bring him. If he was reading between the lines correctly, the man who wrote the letter had access to the finest and rarest pieces, the ones that would have been hidden from the Chinese. Pieces he might never see if he were to simply exercise his prerogative.

Besides, he really did prefer to do things the civilized way if it was at all possible. The image of himself as a latter-day Genghis Khan was not one he particularly cared for; there was not, after all, much art to mere plundering. Any lout could break down a door.

He'd been planning a visit to the old palace, anyway. The last clue had strongly indicated the Potala as his next destination. How fortuitous and civilized to receive an invitation; he was sure that today's meeting would only facilitate locating the next clue somewhere within the enormous building. If he didn't know better, he'd be tempted to believe in destiny.

He replaced the curtain and went to his table to dash off a note of acceptance. He'd go by himself, of course. He had no intention of sharing such an opportunity with anyone. As a precaution, he worded his letter so that it was clear that though General Zhang would be arriving alone, his officers would know exactly where he was and with whom. And of course, his pistol would be in its holster inside the jacket of his dress uniform.

~

Conway had forgotten what a noisy, smelly place the outside world was. He and Ma Li had joined the throngs of pilgrims from all over Tibet making a circle around the Jokhang temple. Some simply walked and prayed, some crawled on their hands and knees, and others alternately walked and prostrated themselves, walked and prostrated themselves, blocks of wood strapped to their legs and hands. A lot of them, he knew, had traveled hundreds of miles this way, worshipful inchworms making their slow, painful way across the vast landscape of Tibet toward Lhasa.

Some of the travelers had matted hair and mad eyes; still others promenaded as if they were in a fashion parade, noblewomen and noblemen out for a stroll displaying their finery. There were children and animals, withered crones and fresh-faced youths, monks and farmers, all moving in a great clockwise circle, ignoring the armed and arrogant young Chinese soldiers who also moved in a circle, defiantly counterclockwise, against the flow.

Men of Han, Conway said to himself. You have arrived. The prophecies spoke of barbarians taking over the world and destroying the knowledge, and here you are. I know that barbarians come in many forms, and that the word is a relative term. We all take our turn at it at one time or another. One man's gentleman is another man's barbarian. There was a time when the Chinese were the protectors of Tibet against the barbarian hordes of the Mongols, but now it's all come round and it is you who are the invaders, you who trample the earth and soak it with blood. And walking at my side—I, an Englishman, the ultimate barbarian-gentleman—is one of your own. To her, you are now the enemy.

What he had not forgotten was how it felt to be one mere mortal in a crowd, vulnerable and exposed—to bullets, microbes, politics, war, hunger, the weather. Like riding a bicycle, he thought—it's something you never forget. His instincts for self-preservation were in place, he was glad to note. He put his head down and muttered prayers as two soldiers, arm in arm, their young faces scared and haughty, veered in his direction and brushed by him with only inches to spare. But Ma Li looked the soldiers boldly in the eye. Her audacity alarmed and impressed him; he knew that she had to look at them. How could she resist? Of course, her disguise was perfect, and not just because of the clothes and the dirt on her face. It was because she had truly become the Tibetan pilgrim she was playing. Conway had no doubt that her own brother would not recognize her now.

And her father? Well, that was a different story, Conway suspected. The man knew how to crack a code, that was certain. They would have to take care. A great deal of care.

They walked and prayed all morning. As the appointed hour approached, they made their way to a house on a side street in a part of the city that dwelt in the shadow of the great Potala.

~

It was most peculiar. It was like shopping for the ultimate Christmas gift for a man whom he had not even met.

Conway and the curator and an artisan monk stood in a cramped room at the end of a long corridor—a cave at the end of a tunnel, really—the ceiling so low that Conway had to stoop, deep underneath the palace. The beam of his torch played over objects of art and stacks of sacred texts. Even if they dynamite the palace, the curator had said, these things will be safe. When the dust settles and they have gone, we will dig them out.

Here were the rarest and oldest pieces, things beyond General Zhang's wildest fantasies. The light revealed gold temple carvings of elaborate and fearsome aspect, sacred dance masks, headdresses and embroidered silk robes, jewel-encrusted reliquaries, brocade tapestries of unimaginable complexity, furniture inlaid with gold and mother-of-pearl. Conway needed to select four or five pieces. They all had to be irresistible, but one piece would have to be just slightly more irresistible than the others. Like one of those magic tricks where the magician wagers that his subject will choose a certain card over the others.

He moved the beam slowly along the shelves, stopped, moved it back again and then up to the farthest corner near the ceiling. He held it steady there, and let his breath out slowly in a soft hiss of pure awe. There it was. It could not have been more perfect. The very soul of Tibet looked back at him. Terrible, beautiful, and best of all, something the general could easily pick up and carry under one arm.

He turned to the artisan monk, who was already rubbing his hands together thoughtfully. "We have an hour, perhaps less. Can you do it?"

∼

They're talking to each other at this very moment, Ma Li thought. My father is at a disadvantage, because he knows less about his adversary than his adversary knows about him. But it is only a slight disadvantage; he has might and momentum and eminent domain on his side. And he is not called a master cryptographer for nothing. Let's hope that Mr. Conway is a convincing actor.

You *are* acting, she had told him before he set out. Not lying. Acting. She had been impressed by his consternation at the prospect of having to lie, even for a noble cause. She had reminded him that life is a stage. You will be playing a fictional character, that is all. And you are doing it because you have to. *I'm* the one who's lying to him. I have to let him believe that I am dead. Part of me wants to run to him and say, Father, Father, look—I am alive, and so is your son.

She could picture her father reaching inside his dress-uniform jacket, his holster nestled securely against his chest, and pulling out his silver cigarette case. He'd offer a Sobranie to Conway, of course, and if Conway accepted, light it for him. Gentlemen, both of them. Her father's hair combed smooth. The smell of his English shaving soap, the creak of his polished leather belt.

She waited in the nondescript little house in the alley.

Her hosts were a pleasant Tibetan couple who had seemed to be expecting them and who also seemed to understand the gravity of the mission without asking a single question. She had been awed by the smoothly functioning network they seemed to be encountering at every turn, though she shouldn't have been. Conway had already told her that the valley had increased its communications with the outside world as the twentieth century grew more and more complicated.

We're like a country that realizes it can no longer afford a strict isolationist policy, he had said. Barnard has been the technological wizard who's hooked us up. He's even talking satellites now. Reminds us that the twenty-first century is looming just round the corner, and that if we thought the twentieth was complex, just wait. She had seen for herself that people outside of the valley were ready to respond and assist; how much they knew about the valley itself, or Conway, she could not tell—but what was definitely there was a powerful sense of solidarity. This was underground resistance of the sort you always see when a country is occupied by an invader, and Shangri-La was now an outpost of that resistance, a major nerve center, fully participating. She looked down at her grimy Tibetan dress. And so was she.

Conway had been gone for a couple of hours now. She had assisted him in the transformation from peripatetic to scholar, helping him wash the carefully applied dirt and grime from his face, hair, and hands. She had continued to talk about her father. He listened, attentive to every detail that might be useful to him in the deception he was about to perpetrate, managing all the while to convey his sympathy with her for having to betray her father. She had liked the way the skin on his forehead bunched into a whorl of concern while she talked; she knew it was just for her. Before he left, she held his hand in hers and carefully cleaned his fingernails, eradicating the last traces of the unwashed pilgrim. He had said that he would be gone for many hours, because he was going to wait until dark to make his way back down into the city. Darkness was an hour or so away. She was impatient for him to return, and not only because she wondered about the fate of her father, the Potala, Shangri-La, Tibet, and the world.

~

General Zhang leaned close to the glass. The hand was yellowish and the skin looked like parchment with a fine layer of fuzz or dust on the surface. As the tendons dried, they had contracted and pulled the fingers into a clawlike conformation. A bit of bone protruded from the wrist. The cut had been a fairly clean one; done, he guessed, with a heavy iron ax. Here and there around the hand he noted neat little piles of debris, perfect miniatures of the sandpiles one saw at construction sites or mines. Insects at work, boring within the hand, leaving tailings the way all miners do. The hand of a criminal, the card said.

In another case was a rectangle of rough, heavy wood several feet square with a hole in the center. Hinges opened the piece of wood so that it could be fitted around a man's neck, then closed and locked with an iron hasp. The collar of wood was just large enough that the person wearing it would be unable to reach his mouth with his hands, though he could hold the device up off his shoulders from time to time. Criminals would be sentenced to a certain amount of time in the collar. Any sort of rest or repose would be nearly impossible, and unless the man were fed by someone else, he would starve. Zhang looked closely at the neck-hole; it was smooth and worn, with a distinct patina. This one had seen a lot of use. He recalled a photograph he had seen once of a man wearing such a device. The wretched fellow had been squatting, hands supporting the collar, looking up at the camera with blank eyes, his hair long and tangled, as if he'd been wearing the thing for some time. Monks fed him, the inscription had said. Barley cakes and water.

And here was a femur, slender and graceful, intricately carved. The thighbone of a virgin, the card said. He straightened up and was startled to see in the glass the reflection of a man standing behind him. He must have been absorbed. He had heard nothing.

He contained his surprise. He did not turn right away, or flinch, or give any outward sign. Instead, he studied the femur for a moment or two longer and then spoke, in Chinese, still without turning.

"Interesting, don't you think—the significance of virginity in so many diverse cultures of the world?"

A throat cleared behind him, and a voice answered in British-accented English. "Oh, yes. Yes, yes. Fascinating indeed. Purity, and all that. And of course, the cult of the virgin attains its ultimate expression in Catholic doctrine. Or perhaps I should say its most *elaborate* expression."

"Certainly the notion of sacrifice is universal to all culture," Zhang answered in English, slowly turning, still showing no surprise, though his hand moved casually toward the vicinity of his shoulder holster. "And of course, a sacrifice must truly be a sacrifice. Otherwise there is no point."

He faced his companion and made a fast appraisal: Caucasian, tallish, younger than himself, cropped brown monkish hair, thick spectacles, a diffident smile, hands clasped in front of him. Tibetan clothing. Zhang lowered his hand from his shoulder holster: harmless and unarmed, too. That much was plain.

"We don't know for certain whether or not the virgin who once owned this thighbone was actually killed for this purpose. Some say yes, others say no, and that she wasn't necessarily a virgin. Or even a she, for that matter," the man said, his tone that of the scholar expounding enthusiastically, still smiling. "We'll never know."

"Not a virgin?" Zhang answered. "That sounds a trifle blasphemous, doesn't it? Of course, a forensic anthropologist could tell you the sex and age of the owner of this bone. Height, weight, state of health and nutrition, probable class, what sort of work he or she did physically. How long she was dead before the artist set to work." He eyed the man standing in front of him. He was not going to do anything so obvious as ask him who he was and what he was doing here. "I am General Zhang," he said, and waited. The man looked back at him curiously for a moment or two before answering.

"And I am Tenzin." Zhang expressed no surprise, but tipped his head inquisitively. The man laughed apologetically. "No, of course that has not always been my name. Middle-class people in Britain are not in the habit of giving their children Tibetan names. My given name is Hugh Conway. I am happy to meet you. And of course, you are wondering what I am doing here. An excellent question. I was a flier during the war. No doubt you have heard of the Hump?"

Zhang straightened up, impressed. The Hump was the popular World War II name for the pass over the Himalayas where Allied transport planes flew gasoline and later vast quantities of food, ammunition, and medicine into China after the Burma Road was destroyed by the Japanese. These flights were nothing less than a lifeline in the struggle against the enemy. It was a dangerous mission, and hundreds of Allied airmen had died doing it. Surviving fliers, some American and some British, had been accorded untouchable status within the borders of China—permanent guests, if they wished to be, their every material need looked after and exempt from political purges. Many of these Westerners had taken advantage of the offer and "retired" to China. This man appeared to be about the right age to be one of them. Nonetheless, Zhang saw no harm in a little bit of gentle probing.

"Ah. Persona grata status. Tell me," Zhang said, careful to put nothing in his voice that might influence the other's answer, "what was your opinion of the Goony Bird?"

"Oh, the Goony Bird. An absurd name for a beautiful plane. We were all unhappy when they replaced them with the C-46. Many more accidents after that, a lot of them on the ground. No, we weren't happy with our planes until they gave us the C-54. It was what the C-46 was trying to be. A four-engine DC-3, really. The Goony Bird had been a modified DC-3, of course, which was why we loved it so well. A dream to fly, really."

"Yes. Yes," Zhang nodded, "just so. Just exactly so. The Allies were fond of amusing nicknames for serious things, weren't they? I seem to recall an odd name they had for the place where the planes actually passed over the Hump . . ." He raised his brows questioningly, as if he couldn't quite remember the name. The man in front of him answered promptly.

"We called it the 'W,'" he laughed. "The sky with the crown of the Hump rising up in the middle looked just like the letter W. But I always liked to think that it stood for 'We're going to make it!'"

"Hm. So you accepted my country's invitation. But why choose a godforsaken place like Lhasa? Why not Shanghai, so much more like a Western city?"

"Your reputation precedes you, General. I know of your work to spare priceless art treasures from destruction. Like you, I appreciate what is old, rare, and fine. I did live in Peking for many years. But when Tibet was opened up, I saw it as an opportunity. I knew I was needed here. I was teaching English at the university in Peking. It was not difficult to use some of my contacts there to get me introductions in Tibet. I was especially interested in the collection here at the Potala. Officially, I am here making a scholarly inventory of the artifacts, documenting and researching. Personally, I am here because I love antiquities. When I heard that you were coming, I thought perhaps I might be of . . . assistance to you."

There it was, an offer, tacit and tantalizing. There would be time later to check on this person's credentials and veracity. Today, he'd let the man show him what he had. There was not a great deal of time to waste, since the fate of the vast old building they were in was uncertain. Built in the seventeenth century by the so-called Great Fifth Dalai Lama, it was sometimes referred to as the Buddhist Vatican. Some of Zhang's colleagues were emphatic and unequivocal about what should happen to the structure: If the Tibetans were going to be truly and thoroughly liberated from their repressive feudal lamaist past, then the Potala, the most tangible and visible symbol of that past, should be razed. Others advocating its destruction maintained that it was just another monastery, and as such deserved the same fate. Still others thought that the destruction of the Potala would foment a massive Tibetan uprising, and advocated letting the palace stand but converting it to secular use, perhaps using it as military headquarters. Others wanted to replace the Dalai Lama in the people's minds with the Chinese-controlled Panchen Lama, and install him in the palace.

Zhang himself was ambivalent. As a military strategist, he was inclined to agree that its power as a symbol of the past called for its destruction. As an appreciator of the old, the rare, and the fine, as his new acquaintance had characterized him, he confessed to himself a slight disinclination to reducing the vast old building, so rich in history, to a pile of rubble. As a father whose son and daughter had been swallowed up by the vast silent emptiness of sky and mountain that was Tibet, he often had an urge to smash everything in sight, the Potala included. He had decided to reserve judgment until after today's excursion. Now he was being offered a personal guided tour, as it were, by a knowledgeable individual keenly interested, as the letter had clearly stated, in conciliation—one of Zhang's favorite words in any language.

He gave a polite bow of his head to the Westerner in front of him. "I welcome your assistance, Mr. Conway," he said graciously.

"Very good, very good," the man said, rubbing his hands together happily. "Excellent. But first, some tea." He laughed. "And I do mean tea. Real tea, from Darjeeling. Not this dreadful rancid butter concoction the Tibetans call tea."

Zhang gave a small smile and nodded his acceptance. It was all part of the ritual. Tea first, brandy later.

~

Offering a bribe could be as delicate a procedure as cutting a diamond. You didn't want to be insultingly obvious; neither did you want to be so oblique as to fail to express your intent. What you offered had to be appropriate, because usually you had only one chance, and you had to see to it that all parties were able to maintain their gentlemanly veneer. And you especially had to avoid giving off the smallest whiff of shakiness. The world might very well depend on your success, but it was necessary to be casual, almost detached.

General Zhang was an excellent listener. Rather too good, Conway thought; preternaturally alert would be a better way to put it. Downright unnerving when you were pretending to be someone you're not. Conway had taken the general on a tour; the two men were now standing under some carved wooden ceiling beams supported by tall wooden pillars.

"No nails were used," Conway said. "Metal was thought to be too valuable to be used for nails, so the wood was precisely notched and fitted together. But then wood itself is a valuable commodity here in Tibet, because of course trees grow only in protected valleys at lower altitudes. The wood you see here had to be carried from great distances. And laboriously, too—without even the assistance of the wheel. The old Tibetans never used the wheel for travel—did you know that? The only wheel in this land was the prayer wheel. The reason for it was a prophecy that use of the wheel would destroy the social structure of the country. I find that rather fascinating. It wasn't that they hadn't discovered the wheel or didn't know what it could do. They knew all too well, and quite consciously rejected that efficiency and its subsequent effect."

"Deliberately chose to be backward, you mean?" said Zhang, a little roguishly, Conway thought.

"That depends very much on one's definition of backward, General," Conway replied with a smile. "Now here," he said, leading the general into a large chapel room, "are some rather marvelous images." Before them was a larger-than-life-sized gilded carving, intricately detailed, of a many-armed female deity with wise heavy eyes and a tiny smile. "Dharmavijaya," Conway said. "She represents the victory of the Dharma, the moral law of the Buddha, over the forces of darkness and ignorance that are always at work against ultimate liberation. Here she's in her Sambhoga-kaya form. Three heads, six arms. I'm sure she needs extra heads and arms to get the job done. Her smile reminds me of the Mona Lisa. And here," he said, leading the general to another image, "is Tara. She's sometimes compared to the Madonna. She's said to have been born from a tear of compassion wept by Avalokitesvara, the bodhisattva of compassion and mercy, when he looked down on the world and saw its suffering. See how her right foot is on the ground, as if she's about to rise and help all suffering beings. Next to her is Vajrasattva. The name means the Diamond Being. It refers to the nature of our true mind, the one hidden beneath the veil of our mundane consciousness, the pure principle which is in us and is restored to us in the moment of enlightenment."

"This principle is in everyone?" asked the general pointedly.

"It does seem a little difficult to accept, doesn't it? But yes. Apparently in everyone," Conway said with equal pointedness. He took a breath then, and plunged on. "This building has more than a thousand rooms. It took some fifty years to build. It is over three hundred years old. On the roof are the tombs of past Dalai Lamas. Not only is it a vast storehouse of art, it is a work of art in itself. It would be a shame, I think, to put dynamite to it."

Zhang shrugged. "Aren't all things transient and illusory anyway?" he said with the same prankishness of a few moments before.

"Perhaps," said Conway archly. "But the job of a curator is, after all, to postpone entropy as long as possible. I know that you, as a collector of antiques, appreciate the sentiment." Conway began walking again. "Which reminds me. In a couple of months' time I'm expecting the arrival for cataloging and safekeeping of some rather special items. Royal tomb art, said to date back to the time of Kublai Khan. Perhaps you'd be interested in seeing some of it," he finished in a casual tone.

He had timed it so that they arrived in a certain small room just as he spoke these last words. In the room was a table; on the table were the "gifts" Conway had selected earlier.

"Oh, yes," Conway said. "Here are some rather nice pieces. I'd be honored if you'd accept something. To commemorate our meeting. Of course, these are nothing special compared to the pieces I'm expecting." He rubbed his hands together like the aesthete he was playing. "But perhaps you'd care to . . . ?"

Zhang looked at Conway for a moment and then approached the table in an offhand way, though Conway could see his eyes focusing like the precision instruments they were. Conway felt certain that his pounding heart was making the front of his robe jump; he felt as if he were trying to outwit Professor Moriarty himself. Zhang had to believe that the choice he made was his choice, not his and Conway's.

Conway chatted on about symbology in Tibetan art and the ritual use of artifacts, scarcely aware of what he was saying, watching General Zhang, who circled around like a bird of prey in slow motion. There was a moment when he saw Zhang's shadow fall over the piece in question in a decisive sort of way; Zhang touched it ever so gently and looked up at Conway.

"Thank you," Zhang said. "You are most kind."

Conway smiled, not, he hoped, too radiantly. "Ah," he said with nonchalance. "Excellent choice. So. I will be expecting the other pieces in just a few weeks. Shall I have them brought here?" If I reward you, will you refrain from blowing up the palace anytime in the near future? he said in his mind.

"Thank you, yes," replied the general, another way, Conway was sure, of saying: Perhaps, but these pieces had better be damned good. "I'll be gone for a month or so on an expedition, but I'll be returning here when it's over. The timing should coincide."

Ah, Conway thought; an expedition to find the hidden land of Shambala, General? Actually, I sincerely doubt that you will be returning to Lhasa when it is over to collect the rest of your bribe. Not if I have been as clever as I hope I've been.

Conway smiled again, looking at the beautiful, grotesque object upon which the general's hand rested. Two birds with one stone, he said to himself. Two birds with one stone. "I'll be looking forward to your return. Would you care for more tea?"

"Thank you, yes," said Zhang, and pulled out his

silver case. "Cigarette?" he offered. Conway accepted. Brandy and cigars, tea and cigarettes. It meant the same thing: gentlemen coming to an agreement.

~

She waited for hours until fatigue and anxiety got the better of her and she decided to go and close her eyes for a while. She bade the couple good night and went to the small room where a comfortable palette awaited her. She lay in the dark for a long time, fully dressed, listening to the sound of truck engines in the distance. She knew that these were not personnel carriers she was hearing; they had the heavier, lower sound of munitions carriers. She had stood with Brother and Father often enough, listening to just that kind of truck. The kind of truck that carried explosives. The kind of truck that carried explosives toward old buildings. Carried explosives toward old defenseless buildings and left them a pile of rocks and dust. Rocks and dust and splintered beams . . . and sacred texts and prayer flags shredded and floating down to earth like snow or feathers . . .

~

Zhang exhaled a long plume of smoke and extinguished his cigarette. He finished the last of his tea, rose from his chair, and in the same motion tucked the silk-wrapped bundle beneath his arm.

"Thank you so much for the very informative tour, Mr. Conway," he said. "You have been most helpful."

Conway rose. "It's been a pleasure. Please allow me to escort you. It's easy to get lost here."

"Mazes are my specialty," Zhang replied. "And I don't wish to keep you any longer."

There was the smallest moment of hesitation as Conway grasped his meaning: Get lost. I want to look around without you breathing down my neck. Zhang watched him closely. Wandering around alone was exactly what Conway did not want General Zhang to do.

"It's I who will escort you, Mr. Conway. We will say good night."

"Of course, General."

Zhang picked up an oil lamp with his free hand. "I'll need this."

"We are at your service," Conway said, unhappy but resigned.

They walked. "Tell me, Mr. Conway," Zhang said. "What is at the core of your appreciation of Tibetan religious art? Do you not think it's a manifestation of a system seething with superstition?" It sounded to Conway as if Zhang were testing the Party line on him.

"I find it profoundly compelling," he answered truthfully. "I think they've done a magnificent job of portraying the deepest aspects of the human mind, conscious and subconscious, in all its mysterious complexity. The art has too much integrity to be dismissed as anything less. When they talk about attaining perfection, it's not in the limited sense that you find in other religions—being rewarded for your dubious virtues, getting into Heaven, or Valhalla, or some such place. It has to do with perfecting the one trait that makes us truly human—conscious compassion."

"And is there room in this world for compassion?" Zhang asked. He had stopped walking, and stood holding the oil lamp high, looking at some designs painted on the walls of the corridor.

Conway was not sure if Zhang was asking such a monumental philosophical question ingenuously. Maybe the man enjoyed a good debate. Maybe he was just amusing himself. Or maybe it was a question he had asked himself more than once. Perhaps he was thinking of his son and daughter.

But Conway's answer stuck in his throat when he happened to glance up and see what was painted on the ceiling directly over Zhang's head. He flicked his eyes down just as Zhang moved the lamp so that he was looking at Conway's face instead of the wall murals. He did not think that Zhang had seen the motion of his eyes, but he imagined little telltale trails of leftover light like the ones you could see for a tenth of a second if you waved a red-hot ember in the dark. He held the general's gaze.

"Introducing compassion into this cruel world," he answered, "would make it a different world. Rather like introducing the wheel into Tibet."

The general smiled a slow smile.

"Very good, Mr. Conway. And so, good night. We will see each other in a few weeks' time." He stood where he was, holding the lamp, his bundle under his other arm, plainly waiting for Conway to leave. Conway had no choice but to bow and say good night. As he bent low, he saw in his mind Vajrapani, the fierce and wrathful deity who was the defender of the Dharma, with his snarling face and his headdress rimmed with human skulls.

Om mani padme hum. Vajrapani, defend us now, he implored silently.

Don't let him look up.

~

She awakened to someone sitting down very gently on her sleeping mat. She opened her eyes in the dark, but did not move or speak. She lay still and listened to him breathing. In through the nose. Out through pursed lips. It was as eloquent as speech: Hard work. Relief. Guarded optimism. Tension dissipating. On his clothes, the bouquet of Sobranies. Like smelling her father. On an impulse, she groped around and took his hand. His hand relaxed into hers as if it had been looking for hers at the same time. The skin was warm and dry, pleasant and familiar-feeling.

"Your father is what we call a formidable chap," he said at last.

"Did it come down to brandy and cigars?"

"It did. Tea and cigarettes, anyway."

"Have you saved the Potala?"

"I think so."

"And Shangri-La?"

"I hope so."

"Tell me what happened."

He pressed the flesh of her palm with his thumb.

He rustled about. A match flared, startling her; he lit a cigarette. One of her father's. His face in the momentary light looked tense and animated. He blew out the match and she felt him relax a little. "I believe I have effectively introduced the idea of not reducing the Potala to rubble. But we both know the decision is not entirely up to him. He's a man with a lot of influence, but not exactly God in this matter. He has, I'm sure, superiors to convince. We shall have to wait and see. As for the other matter . . ."

She waited, still holding his hand.

"I succeeded in tempting him. He chose as I hoped he would. My little gift was irresistible. It served two purposes. It was a sort of pre-bribe offering—an hors d'oeuvre before the main course—and it was the vehicle for the false clue. When I left him, it was in his hand. But . . ." She saw the cigarette end glow and heard him exhale.

"But what?"

"But quite by accident, we came within inches—actually, a foot or so—of the real clue. The one that would eventually lead him straight on to Shangri-La. He was standing right under it when I left him. I don't often pray, but I did this time."

She could feel curiosity emanating from her like a radio wave, though she said nothing. Certainly her father had never told her anything at all about the clues. All she knew was that it began when the letter with the puzzle in it arrived from the Chairman and his friends, and her father retired with it to his tent to amuse himself. He had emerged a few hours later with a smug smile on his face, and the course of their lives was changed forever.

Conway let go of her hand and stroked her hair in the dark. "You've made a terrible sacrifice. Don't think I'm not aware of it. You helped me deceive your own father. In return, I owe it to you to tell you everything. Besides," he said simply, "I trust you. How could I not, after what you've done?"

She held her breath. He put out the cigarette.

"What your father received at the beginning was a chart of the stars, and a bit of verse saying that this was the way to Shambala. The chart was of constellations and so forth. Not Orion's Belt or the Big Dipper; Tibetans have their particular constellations. They're the same stars we all look at, naturally, but they've imposed their own pictures on them. When the old men in Peking sent the chart to your father, they probably didn't even recognize it as a chart of the stars, but knew that Zhang the master cryptographer would figure it out, whatever it was.

"And figure it out he did. Sometimes simplicity is the hardest disguise to penetrate, but nothing is too complicated or too simple for your father. Tibetan mythology is full of references to Shambala being on another planet; there is a particular constellation associated with the sector of the sky where that planet is supposed to be. He took that constellation, lifted it out of the star chart, made a diagram of it, and laid it over a map of Tibet. He adjusted the scale until he had three stars lying precisely on top of three very old, very well-known monasteries. Two would not have been enough; three gave him a solid geometric basis. With the three stars planted firmly over the three monasteries, he then marked the map of Tibet with points, a point for each star in the constellation. He surmised that if he went to the latitude and longitude of each point, he would find another monastery. And another clue telling him which monastery to go to next.

"Of course, he had to decide where to start, and how to proceed. He saw that one of the stars in his triangle corresponded to a monastery he had already destroyed. Presumably, the clue had been destroyed along with it. That left two in the triangle. Assuming that the second clue was in one of those other two buildings—and that was only an assumption—he had a fifty-fifty chance of proceeding to the right one. So he chose one, and went there. I'm surmising all of this from what I know of the nature of the clues."

"You're quite right. I remember him arguing with my brother. He was enjoying the challenge, saw it as a diverting excursion, but my brother said we were making a pointless trip to a place not on our schedule. But my father insisted. Now I know why. This was before he took the search seriously. He was still just entertaining himself, curious to see if his calculations were correct."

"Once he was there," Conway continued, "he had to find something that would tell which 'star' in the constellation he should proceed to next. He couldn't just proceed at random. Your father guessed correctly that not every star in the constellation would represent a monastery. A searcher would have to follow an exact order. Even if he accidentally stumbled onto a clue at a monastery, it would be meaningless unless he had proceeded in the correct order.

"You see, what he was looking for, and what he found in the places he visited, was some sort of pictorial representation of the constellation. It would be something different in each place. It could be in the form of a tapestry with demon eyes positioned like the stars, it could be a relief pattern hammered into a silver vessel, it could be a pattern carved in a wooden lintel. that sort of thing. An alert searcher would recognize it when he saw it. And he would know which point represented the monastery he was standing in, and he would study the other points to see which ones were emphasized in some way—a bigger, brighter eye, a deeper, more elaborate cut in a carving. And here's the devilishly clever fail-safe which assures that only a diligent searcher who has proceeded in the correct order would know where to go next: Imagine yourself standing in monastery A, looking at a pictorial representation of the Shambala constellation. You've found not one, but two 'stars' with obvious emphasis—monasteries B and C. How do you know whether it's B or C that you're to head off to next? Well, if you've arrived where you are by proceeding in the proper order, then you'll recognize that one of the 'stars' represents a place where you have already been. You'll know that it's the other emphasized 'star' that represents your next destination. And off you'll go."

"So. That's how he found himself at the monastery with the young boy," Ma Li said, remembering. "That was when the game ceased to be a mere amusement. How well I recall the change in his attitude. And how well I recall my brother's anger and consternation."

"I remember that child," Conway said. "He needed surgery. He would have died without it. One of the prices we've paid in increasing our communication with the outside world is a slight loss of security. We took a chance. The boy was never instructed to keep it a secret; his guardians believed that would be too much like lying. They figured that if he ever talked about it, it would just sound like a child's fancy. The odds against someone like your father coming along and finding the boy were very, very high. But find him he did."

"He did. And so here we are, you and I. And there *you* were. When you left my father, he held the false clue in his hand."

"Yes. Cradled lovingly. An old artisan monk had helped me. Just hours before the appointed meeting time with your father, we engraved the constellation on the piece, just so, making it look like part of the decorative pattern that was already there. Oh, it was a damned bloody marvelous job, considering that we were pressed for time. The artisan is a genius, no doubt about it. He knew what was at stake, though of course not all the details. Nor did he want to know. He followed my instructions, and the results were beautiful. Beautiful enough, I hoped, to take your father in. And it would have been in the bag had he not then made known his wish to browse unattended. I knew the real clue was an integral part of the building, something I could not remove or alter. But I didn't know exactly where it was, and since we'd been pressed for time, I hadn't located it yet. With a thousand rooms, I thought the odds were with me that it wasn't anywhere nearby. But it was. And your father went and stood right under it."

"My God," she said. "What was it?"

"It was simple and lovely. A ceiling mural. Of birds, positioned like the stars in the constellation. Two of them with plumage just a little bit more elaborate than in the others. In a tree, in the land where Amitabha Buddha dwells. The Western Paradise. That was when I prayed. I could only hope that my gift would distract him from looking up."

She found his other hand, held both of them now. "But . . . what exactly was this object with which you hoped to bewitch my father?"

"Oh," he said, laughing, shaking his head. "Oh. You've never seen anything like it. Never. Not even your father, in his wildest dreams of plunder, has seen anything like it."

~

The yellow light of Zhang's tent lantern cast a buttery glow that deepened the rich ocher burnish of ancient bone. Intricate tendrils of silver twined sinuously up to grasp the inverted cranium like a vine growing around a rock. The tendrils and the skull sat atop a column of repoussé silver that rose from a base of taloned demon feet, also silver, claws relaxed and in repose, but alive and ready.

The skull's upper teeth had been replaced with perfect replicas in gold, and the hole at the base of the skull had been rimmed with gold. Zhang lit a Sobranie and poured brandy into the hole. He raised the goblet, made a silent toast to the man whose skull this had once been centuries before, put his lips to the rim of gold, and drank.

Alas, poor Padma, or Gompo, or Thondup, or whatever your name was, I knew you well. And I will know you better. I am planning on getting a little bit drunk tonight, and you are going to assist me. And you are going to assist me in another way, too. You are going to help extract payment from this godforsaken barbaric wasteland for the loss of my son and daughter.

He thought of their faces when they were children, he thought of a plane going down, and he thought about the search parties he had dispatched. Then, soldierlike, he put it out of his mind and returned to the task at hand. Yes, you will assist me. But first, a little business.

He drained the last of the brandy from the skull and laid it with infinite care on its side on the tabletop. He turned up the lamp, smoothed a piece of paper before him, and copied the pattern made by delicate marks incised in the bony arch of the skull's palate, carefully noting the two that were deeper and just a bit wider than the others. When he was finished, he set the goblet on its base so that the empty eye sockets were on a level with his own eyes. Upside down, the vacant holes slanted upward ever so slightly, giving them an impish, almost jolly look. Zhang stared for a few moments into the sockets: pools of the same black night where stars hung and comets soared. What are *you* looking at, he muttered, turning the skull decisively away so that the sockets gazed at the tent wall instead of at him. Then he reached for his bottle.

~

Conway and Ma Li listened to the engines of the munitions trucks for the next day and night. The engines were never turned off; they just idled for days at a time, filling the air with their acrid stink. The trucks had been clustered on the streets below the palace since the convoy had arrived a week before, soldiers lounging about waiting for their orders. Sleepless, Conway and Ma Li lay close together all night for warmth, talking and listening. We can't leave until we know where your father is going and until we know what is to happen to the Potala, Conway said. And the engines just idled and idled and idled.

Why was I allowed to leave the valley? she asked. They lay flat on their backs in the dark under one blanket, the smell of diesel in the room with them. You knew me for five minutes. Technically, I was your enemy. You told me secrets you haven't even told other lamas. I've seen the valley. I know it's real, but I wasn't kept there, like my brother. Why?

Well, I knew who you were, he said. The starter of fires and all that. Remember?

No, I am serious. No balderdash about prophecies.

He squeezed her hand under the covers. No, I promise, no balderdash. The same thing happened to me over thirty years ago. The man who was High Lama of Shangri-La just . . . knew me. An ability he developed, he told me, with mental discipline and all. I've been studying too, of course, but not for nearly as long. And I'm nowhere near as talented. But . . . well . . . with you, I just knew that I knew.

I wish this were fifty years ago, she said then. A hundred years. I wish I could know it as it was. The old city of Lhasa. No jeeps, no motorbikes, no soldiers, no munitions carriers, no telephones. Just the city and the silent Tibetan night sky full of Tibetan stars.

He was still for a while, listening to the truck engines, caressing her fingers in a delicate, pensive circular motion.

I think that someday it will be that way again, he said.

~

Early in the morning, they heard the sound of gears laboriously engaging and orders being shouted. The convoy of munitions trucks, laden with explosives, moved out, away from the palace, through the city streets and away until they were heard no more.

And on the same day, Conway's contacts reported to him. General Zhang was leaving the city with his troops. And which direction was he traveling in? Conway asked.

He was taking the road that heads directly north, they told him. With that, Conway turned to Ma Li and put his arms around her. That's where we wanted him to go, he whispered. I guess he never looked up after I left him alone in the palace.

~ 8 ~

The Valley of the Blue Moon
spread out far beneath their terrace, green and hushed. Karakal, a dazzling white pyramid of Euclidean proportion,
loomed above the western floor of the immense narrow geologic rift. Light reflected off Karakal's granite peaks and
sprawling ice fields cast a glow over the valley's lush verdancy
and the lamasery's blue-tiled roofs.

The quiet rhythms of life went on as usual. But with
nightfall the entire valley below the cliffs returned to its
anxious vigil: Droning prayers rose from the halls and meditation rooms, white pennants waved in the soft night breezes,
sending their prayer heavenward: Om mani padme hum—
Hail to the Jewel in the Lotus. The huge ornate cylinders of
prayer wheels spun ceaselessly, centrifuges flinging entreaties
to the four winds as the steep walls of the surrounding
mountains reverberated with the boom of the drums, the wail
of the conch shells and oboes, and echoed the ancient,
mournful blasts of the great nine-foot thungchen trumpets,
all petitioning the universe for one thing only: the safe return
of Conway.

~

It was late morning and they were playing a Schubert quartet in the open pavilion in the courtyard amphitheater beneath Conway's drawing room.

At least Bryant assumed it was Schubert. It didn't sound like Mozart to him; he'd come to know Mozart's pristine clarity. Nor was there the ardent fanfare that he had come to recognize in some Beethoven and nearly all of Schumann. Here was the brooding, somber, dark, and romantic voice before the lieder. Cello and violin seemed to seduce and pull plaintive answers from the piano instead of making a bold pronouncement of their comings.

In the midst of a stock scandal, Bryant had left New York and Palm Springs far behind in the era of Swing and at the time had little musical ear for anything else. But because of Conway, he had learned to recognize some things and had even grown to appreciate them.

If he had given it much thought, it would have seemed that his ear was quite refined lately. But he did not think about it; he was simply more vulnerable than usual to the effects of the music because of the worrisome absence of his good friend. He was altogether unaccustomed to the intensity of his feelings these last days.

With the music rising from below, he spoke to Miss Brinklow, who sat across the tea table from him.

"My God. We fiddle like Nero while Rome burns."

"That is hardly what I'd call fiddling, Chalmers," she said with good humor. "And this is hardly Rome."

"I stand corrected. A poor metaphor."

"A poorer simile."

"Maybe. But I still can't help feeling like that."

"It's the same for all of us, I'm sure," she said, and poured him more tea. "The Chinese boy still won't join us?"

Bryant snorted at the impossibility of this suggestion and spooned his sugar aggressively. He remembered the first time he'd laid eyes on the soldier with the angry, frightened eyes. And how he'd felt trouble. The boy was profoundly annoying, and Bryant was not very proud of his feelings. There was this peculiar sense that Bryant had in his presence—that he was face-to-face with a single component part of a vast organism, a part that was never meant to be separated from the whole. Rather like meeting up with a drone bee or a soldier ant alone and far from its nest and its specific function as part of a much larger smoothly running machine. It made the boy bitter and surly, strange, bristly and isolated. The fierce unbending purposefulness of insects always came to mind when he met up with him, and if he thought about him, he could just about see a pair of antennae, mandibles, and compound eyes instead of a head.

Not much had bothered Bryant over the last thirty years or so, but this kid was truly getting to him. The mere fact of his own annoyance bothered him deeply, too. Where was his compassion? What had he learned in his years in the valley?

"At least we have the good news of the Potala's being spared, then, don't we?" Miss Brinklow said brightly. "Isn't that what you heard on your radio? There has not been any change in that news, now, has there? Nothing today?"

"No, simply that Premier Chou En-lai had issued an order to spare it. A great symbol of Sino-Tibetan cooperation. Doesn't that beat all? That's the last I heard."

"I hope it's not one of their dreadful ruses. You

know—first they appease you, give you words of assurance, and then *Boom!* They blow it up behind your back. Behind the world's back. Like their treaties. Nasty business. Everything around us, all this great art," she said, taking in the room, the terrace, the courtyard below, and the music rising from it. "So very fragile, isn't it? All of it. All of our greatest achievements."

"You sound just like Conway, Miss Brinklow."

"I do, don't I? Well, it's not surprising. He's in here, you know." She tapped her chest over her heart and then unrolled a table napkin from its delicate jade ring. "I can't help thinking like that now. It's trying for all of us, isn't it?"

"We wait, I guess. That's all we can do. What else is there? What else do we have?"

"Much hope," she stated, slipping the tea cozy from the hot kettle.

A light breeze rose up from the valley floor and whispered through the branches surrounding the drawing-room terrace, setting off the music of the hanging wind chimes. Diatonics and pentatonics. Its effect with the Schubert was sublime, even if the composer had not considered it. A tremolo, a string ostentato, a tensely quiet passage leading to a burst of chimes. Restrained and pagan all at once, like the Daphnean explosion of Ravel. When the big concert Steinway entered the piece again, it was to the sheer rhapsody of harmonics. The music was greeted with the enthusiastic and unsolicited response of the Tibetan music students who were seated in the amphitheater around the quartet. They clapped and sent up gasps and ululations of approval. The Tibetans were sincere and excited about their art. So much different from the restrained and silent Western audience that dares not cough or clear a throat. Miss Brinklow always told

Conway that watching the Tibetans respond to Western music caused her to hear it differently. To listen like a child all over again, as if for the very first time. Conway had said that the Tibetans probably did hear things in the music that Westerners could not imagine, so different were the tonalities to which they were accustomed.

In the remaining minutes of their tea, the music suddenly changed, dominated now by the hammering of the pedal harpsichord, but Bryant had hardly noticed its historic regression. The pavilion filled with the courtly rhythms of Scarlatti and Corelli. Had he been listening closely he might even have guessed the vibrant Mannheim School Italians. But his thoughts had closed around him, shutting out everything else.

"My goodness, Chalmers, did you hear that? That had to be simply one of the most beautiful moments in music I have ever experienced."

Bryant nodded distractedly.

"You know," he said, "I've been thinking of Mallinson a lot lately. Sad to say, I've hardly given that poor boy much more than a moment's thought over the years. But he's popping up all the time in my head now. Maybe it's this Chinese boy we have here. He reminds me a lot of Mallinson."

"What was the word our good lama used before he left the valley? Truculent. That was it. The boy is as hostile and truculent as Mallinson was. Suspicious of everything."

"A wonder he hasn't tried to beat up on us. All that anger."

" 'Anger blows out the lamp of the mind.' I heard that in school when I was a girl. I never forgot it. I don't remember who said it, or even if I ever knew. But that image is so clear, isn't it? I suppose it's a matter of time whether innate human goodness wins out over the demon they have implanted in him."

Bryant rolled his eyes in exasperation and was about to pick up his cup when Miss Brinklow startled him with renewed authority and determination.

"I suggest that *we* visit *him*. Since he will not come to us, we shall do the polite thing. All of his training—well, it is rather like a religion with him, isn't it? I think that I understand something of this. When we first came here, I didn't see the Tibetans for what they were. To me, they were just more of the world's great crowd of heathen brethren waiting to be reformed. Awakened to the one true faith. I was at least as blind and sectarian as he is now. Wouldn't you say, Chalmers, that this is just what the boy is about— full of that very same missionary zeal? And if I could grow beyond that, then there is also hope for him."

"Yes. It's very much like religion. But I fear it might run even deeper. He's been honed, like a machine part. And he's as hard as steel."

"Goodness. In that case, I think I shall let you go alone these first few times. Man to man, if you'll excuse the expression."

Bryant merely grunted as he rose from his chair.

～

The boy had requested a room high above the valley floor, in one of the buildings added to the original lamasery complex. A room from which, he had announced loudly, he would be the first to observe the arrival of Chinese troops over the valley's forbidding passes.

Many of these new and modern buildings seemed suspended from the cliff face. They had been inspired by the most daring aspects of Western and Oriental architectural design. Almost all had been erected since the late 1930s, during the period of high energy that followed Conway's first return. There had been much celebration in the valley, but at the same time, looming clouds of war had been gathering over the rest of the world. There had been a feverish desire to celebrate all that was new and Western while preserving what was old and venerable. The Modernist Movement had reached even here.

There was a hint of Egyptian temple building in the crisp Deco lines and a whiff of things almost Babylonian or Persian in the stepped and tiered gardens. Several of the newer buildings spanned the lacy mountain rivulets on magnificent stone arches. In the springtime these rivulets turned into torrents and generated enough electricity to keep the newer structures brightly lighted. Wood, because of its rarity—the lamasery had protected the conifer forests of the valley and foothills—had been used minimally for decorative features rather than for structure. Glass and tile were used lavishly to contrast with the predominance of carved stone and concrete. The effect of all of this added construction was to give this end of the lamasery and its outbuildings a stylish but almost fortresslike appearance. An architectural oxymoron: a citadel of well-manicured and pleasing proportion climbing up the steep east wall. The boy enjoyed a secret fantasy that he was looking at a Chinese stronghold, albeit a most surpassingly beautiful one. But that was just one of the games he played as he looked out the rear windows. Another was to assess the buildings with the eye of a demolitions expert.

At night, everything changed. What he saw in the ravine below after dark was odd and unnerving. Purely geometrical shapes of thin etched marble and colored glass filled the forest with an eerie glow, transforming the view below into a piece of abstract art that had nothing to do with its appearance during the day. Art. The whole wretched place was a celebration of the useless, the abstract, the decadent. Old dynastic China had had the same sybaritic and self-centered devotion to useless aesthetics, lavish encrustations growing one upon the other down through the centuries, extravagant and parasitical. The place needed an unsentimental cleaning out, like any nest of vermin, and the wealth distributed. He knew the seductive power of art. Gazing out on these buildings at night, he could feel the pull.

For days he had moved restlessly back and forth in his room, rarely leaving, spending most of his time staring out the broad window that looked out over the valley. Though he was free to come and go as he pleased, and had been invited to do so by the American and others, he refused. He treated himself as a prisoner. He had spartanized the room as best he could, tossing every heretical book from the shelves and pushing out the door every object of decadent beauty.

He watched streamers of mist coil and snake through the evergreen forests that rose along the steep foothills. It was not difficult to imagine that these mists were telltale smoke from the campfires of an oncoming army.

∼

Bryant found the room and knocked on the door. He heard the bolt being moved back. The boy pulled the door open, then rudely turned his back and walked to the single chair and sat. There was nothing in the room now but the chair, a bed, a desk, and a reading lamp. He had even rolled up the carpets and tossed them in a heap in the corridor. A door led from the room to a comfortable Western-style tiled bathroom, a luxury the boy could not expunge, though Bryant figured the boy was using the bathroom, because he could see a wet towel on the floor. Bryant knew the fixtures well, their labels speaking of such distant places as Pittsburgh, Cleveland, and Akron, all of them towns whose streets he had walked at one time or another years ago. He had engineered most of the plumbing for the newer buildings himself, a difficult task considering the lamasery's cliff-face geography.

The boy was eating at the desk. Rice and broth. It was all he ever asked for. His posture, even while he ate, was defiantly crisp and military.

"May I come in?"

"You are already in, Mr. Bryant."

"Well, it's not the greeting that I'm used to around here. But it'll do. At least your English is better than my Chinese."

"We're all required to learn English."

"Yeah. Military Intelligence and all that." Bryant laughed. "Now there's a scary thought for you. Military Intelligence."

"Since the liberation of Korea," the boy said stiffly, "all ranking officers within certain foreign divisions are required to learn the language."

"Well, hell, that's good, I guess. Maybe we all need to talk it out. I've learned a little Tibetan myself, and some Hindi. Enough to get by when I'm working with the locals," he said conversationally. Bryant looked at the boy's meal. "You can get yourself something a little more appetizing than that, you know. We grow everything here."

"This is sufficient. It is what I asked for. It is military staples."

"But we're not military, son." He looked around the room with a frown and half-smile. "I guess that would explain your style of decor, huh? Hell, when I was young in the States I never wanted anything to do with those military folks. Kept as far away as possible. Oil and water, in my case. Government regulation and I don't mix too well."

"So I hear," the boy remarked drily.

Bryant smiled. "So you've heard a little bit about my checkered past, eh? Well, it's no secret around here. It's true. There were some federal agents just itching to get their hands on me when the stock market went bad, but that's another story."

"One I should like to hear. In detail. But let me explain something to you, Mr. Bryant. The People's Liberation Army is not just 'the military.' It is a way of life. A state of mind whose object is the liberation of feudally oppressed peoples."

"Yeah. You folks have been leaving your 'state of mind' all over this godforsaken country."

The boy ignored Bryant's comment. "In any case, I do not wish to change my diet. I will be returning to my division soon. Indulging in rich foods now would create a difficulty of adjustment later."

"Well, about that . . ."

"You mentioned Hindi spoken in the valley, Mr. Bryant?" the boy interrupted. "Does this mean that we are somewhere in India? Over the border? Kashmir, perhaps?"

"Well, where the borders are exactly has never been clear to me. The damn borders keep changing with all the messing around going on out there. I've seen a dozen geophysical maps and the mountains just seem to confuse everything. Hundreds of miles of these huge peaks all around us. So much of the Kunlun and Karakoram Ranges are virtually unexplored."

"And why is it so warm here?"

"A lot to do with thermodynamics and some geothermals. That's my prepared answer," Bryant said, glad for a normal question he could answer without politics or antagonisms. The boy lifted an eyebrow and put his chopsticks down. He rose and went to the window. "It has to do with the nature of these mountains and the angle of the sun," Bryant continued. "It's even warmer in winter for us down here. You see, the valley is below the level that would normally be considered ground level out here—a mile or two—well, lower than that even. A profound geologic rift. That's why the peaks seem so extraordinarily high around us. Karakal, that big pyramid looming over us, is only twenty-eight thousand feet, but it seems much higher than Everest because of our unique vantage." The boy stared at the big mountain. Clouds hid the jagged summit and thick bands of mist rose on its sheer flanks as whirlwinds of powder danced up and down the impossibly high snowfields.

"You see those plumes of snow rising off the peak? The snows blow perpetually up there and the winds are notorious. The summit of our mountain is permanently in the jet streams. Just like Everest. Head in the Clouds, Conway always says." The boy listened attentively.

"As for the valley, our air heats up and then is pretty much trapped by the unusual topography. If you were to fly a plane over the valley, you'd have a hard time finding it. We seem to be almost always obscured by a thick cloud cover, but it's still bright and warm down here. A wind shadow of sorts. Probably a phenomenon unique in the whole world. But go up only a few hundred feet and the change is drastic. Go up a few thousand, brutal. Hell, you know about that. They covered your eyes, but not to keep you from seeing anything. There's nothing to see, no clues or landmarks, just mountain peaks forever, and sickening drops. They did it for two reasons—to keep from scaring you to death, and to keep your eyeballs from freezing. Lowlanders can't generate the heat that these Sherpas can. Some almost supernatural ability they have.

"The airplane has to land on the plateau," he went on. "That's almost two and a half miles above those trees down there. This is a sheltered valley. It allows for the efforts of the mind rather than the constant sweat of the brow."

The boy regarded Bryant. "My father saw a picture of a man taken in the last couple of years. He swore that he had known that man in New York thirty years ago, but that the man had not aged. I saw the photograph. The man looks exactly like you. Tell me, Mr. Bryant, are you that man?"

Bryant shrugged. "I can't deny it. Yeah, I knew your dad."

"So you are at least seventy years old," the boy remarked appraisingly. "Yet you appear to be in your forties. How is this done?"

Bryant shrugged again. "Well, we do age, actually, just slower. And we don't seem to suffer decrepitude, no matter how old we get. Just about everyone here gets the blessing of dying in their sleep, peacefully. How it all happens, I don't really know. Of course it's peaceful here, and the food and air and water are untainted, but it's more than just that. I personally think it's some kind of beneficial radiation that actually changes the blood and the metabolism." He stroked his chin and studied the boy as if reassessing him. "Conway's got quite the way with words. What was it he once said? Oh yeah. 'Time is like some balked monster, waiting outside the valley to pounce on the slackers who have managed to evade him longer than they should.' "

"And do you think this is right?" the boy asked coldly. "To enjoy the privilege of an extended life span while the rest of the world must obey the usual laws of nature? How do you justify this in your mind? Are you doing anything for the human race that would warrant all these extra years of health and productivity?"

Bryant sighed. "Those are very good questions. The fact is, I don't justify it. It's what fate dished out to me, so I'm sure not going to fight it. I will say this, I've reformed. I'm a better man than I once was. But you know, son, you're going to have to ask those same questions of yourself. This is your home now, and is going to be for a long, long, long time."

"There is another route to this valley, is there not?" the boy asked abruptly. "A trade route. I do not believe that all of these luxuries—grand pianos and fancy plumbing and such—were hauled through the air on a rope and carried on the backs of Sherpas. There has to be another way in. And that means another way out."

Bryant considered for a moment. "Maybe there is, maybe there isn't. If there is, I can guarantee that you will never find it." He stood abruptly. "Okay. I didn't have to come up here. I've tried to make friends, but you just won't have it." The boy started to speak, but Bryant held up a hand. "You're plain rude. I'm going to try to understand, and be patient with you. But . . .

"Enough small talk. You're stewing in your juices up here in your self-imposed prison cell. You're coming with me now. I'm going to take you around, show you the ropes, give you a little tour way down in our valley. And before you say any more, I'm going to lay it on the table. You're not going to find a way out. You might as well get used to it. Get it over with. Go ahead and be as angry and as fervent as you want. It's irrelevant here. Our Sherpas—those who visit us—have a tradition that goes back for centuries. They're the only ones who know the way. And even with their help most of us could never make it. The extremes and the winds would scare the pants off Sir Edmund Hillary. That's it in a nutshell." He opened the door. "C'mon, kid. Where's your sense of adventure? Didn't you like to explore when you were a boy? I have a feeling you might even change your mind. People do change here. Believe me, I've seen it."

But deep down Bryant wasn't so certain about this one. He thought of something Conway had once said: that the air in this valley somehow put your past life into focus so you saw all the seminal events of your meager life before Shangri-La through the tightening lens of a telescope. But now he wondered if there would be anything for this boy to see. As much as Bryant wanted not to believe it, to extend the gracious benefit of the doubt, it seemed as if the young officer was intractable.

The boy walked resignedly in front of Bryant and took a jacket from the hook by the door.

"Mallinson," Bryant said, thinking out loud. "By God, but you do remind me a lot of Mallinson."

"What?"

"Forget it. I'll explain it some other time."

~

They passed through a forest of immense rhododendron, the trees a mass of red, white, violet, purple, blue, and every conceivable shade in between. The stone pathway was littered with the fallen sticky remains of the heavy-scented flowers. Bryant had just pointed out a complex of low stone buildings shaded in the half light at the edge of a fruit orchard, saying that the buildings were a center for the study of Buddhist and Tantric thought, ethics, the evolution of the soul and the latest in Western quantum physics and higher mathematics.

He had explained that many great minds were lured by highly secret invitation to come to Shangri-La to teach and study. A lot of them were people who had researched and taught for decades and who found themselves approaching the end of their useful lives or were about to be turned out to pasture. Often quite old, sometimes in poor health, their families gone or scattered, they would receive discreet invitations. These invitations, Bryant explained, gave nothing away at first but only referred obliquely to a well-funded private foundation. The invitations came as beautifully hand-calligraphed cards. If the recipient showed any interest, more was revealed to him or her, gradually describing, with a little more detail each time, as the epistolary correspondence ensued, an institution that would offer the recipient tenure for his or her final days—days that could now be spent any way the person might wish—including undisturbed study, writing, or contemplation of the potential of the human mind, free of the struggle for survival those final years might otherwise entail.

If the person was still interested, arrangements were made to meet the guest in India. This was how the valley had attracted some of the world's best talent at the point in their lives when their knowledge and training were just beginning to ripen—usually the age of decrepitude and death. Theoreticians, scientists, thinkers, theologians, artists, musicians, writers—once they arrived and learned that their productive years were to be extended as much as a century, they tended not to change their minds and want to go back.

"And how did you get here?" the boy wanted to know. "Surely you didn't receive a hand-calligraphed invitation."

"No. You're right. I didn't. Recruitment methods change with the times. Time was, they used to bring in parties of explorers lost in the mountains when they wanted 'fresh blood,' so to speak. People from all different countries. The way we got here was a little different. Four of us arrived here together. Conway, Miss Brinklow, Mallinson, and me. Flew out of a place called Baskul, in India, during an uprising. Conway and Mallinson were with the British Consular Service. I was just—well, I was traveling. Thought we were being evacuated to what's now Pakistan, but we turned out to have a different pilot from the one we expected. He had other plans. Flew in a different direction completely and crash-landed not far from here.

"We expected to die, but instead old Chang came along—as if he knew we were arriving—and invited us to Shangri-La. It became pretty clear later on that it was Conway they wanted. The rest of us were incidental. Old Father Perrault, the guy who pretty much founded this lamasery, knew he was going to die and wanted a successor, it seems. He had some kind of powers. As if he knew Conway was out there, and brought him here on that plane to take his place. Which he did, eventually, but it was a rocky road for him. Mallinson never could adjust to the idea of staying here. An angry kid. Talked Conway into leaving with him. It's a long story, but Conway did leave—and came back almost a year later, alone. Mallinson didn't survive.

"The three of us have been here ever since. We've all changed. People mellow out here. Miss Brinklow was a missionary back then; she was all set to convert the heathen Tibetans. Thought she'd have the lamas singing hymns and saying the Lord's Prayer before too long. She gave that up a long time ago. Now she's content to study languages so she can do her own research on comparative religion. No more Bible-thumping for her. Even changed her name from Roberta to Rose. She thought it had a softer sound. Me, I make my amends for my past."

They held continuing seminars on world affairs and politics, Bryant explained to the boy. Even with spotty radio reception, they had managed to stay surprisingly current. The destruction of Tibet and all that it meant was, naturally, the most prevalent topic on people's tongues these days. And we have a perpetual meditation for world peace, he added, continuous and unbroken for over twenty years now, ever since the world war of the forties.

"I'm not what you would call a profound thinker," Bryant told the boy, "but I've done a lot of work these last thirty-four years on the technical side of things. Radio communication, transportation, and the like. Made it easier for some of these people to get here. So I figure that's my contribution. My justification for being here." He stopped and watched the boy. "Give yourself time," he said. "Even you could learn to like it here."

Captain Zhang did not respond, but gazed down at the buildings, his thoughts unreadable. Bryant was unaccustomed to people who did not at least respond politely in a conversation, so he pushed on.

"But I pay attention to some of the stuff they talk about here," he said. "There's one class I'm particularly interested in—it's all about the nature of human good and evil. What they're trying to pin down is whether or not evil exists as an absolute, or if it's relative. They compare the major religions of the world, and they look at examples of what we think of as psychosis. The ideas they're throwing around right now have to do with the notion of damaged souls," he said, waxing enthusiastic. He stopped and cleared his throat.

"And of course, we've got all kinds of study going on of Buddhist thought and scripture. Those old rimpoches who came in with you are walking treasure troves of knowledge." Knowledge that you people are doing your best to wipe out, he thought, watching the boy's impassive profile. Bryant knew that the boy's concepts of good and evil had been much simplified by Chinese Revolutionary thinking. How convenient it must be, he reflected, to have such complexities all neatly broken down.

The boy had let Bryant go on for quite some time. Bryant knew that he was merely being a good soldier, allowing the American to fulfill his duty as escort. They emerged from the dappled, fragrant shade of an orchard and were just ascending the steep stone steps of an arched bridge that spanned the rocky stream that ran the valley's length when the boy turned to him and spoke.

"You know, don't you, that my father is searching for this valley. Actively searching. And he will probably find it."

"Knowing your dad, I'm sure he'll give it a hell of a shot. But then our lama's no slouch, either," Bryant said tersely. "Your father was a brilliant man when I knew him. Quite a mind for languages and mathematics. What he wouldn't give for the libraries in this valley."

"My father served the Kuomintang as a cryptographer. He broke everything the Japanese could send and nearly everything the American imperialists would use much later on the Korean Peninsula. But we do not talk about those days. The valiant war with America later, of course. But we do not talk of my father's work for the Kuomintang fascists."

"Well, the way I see all that fascist stuff is that it's mostly six of one, a half dozen of another. General Chiang Kaishek or the Japanese, right? Take your pick."

"Pick?"

"Choice. American slang."

"We did, ultimately, take our 'pick'—with the Revolution. All enemies of the people were thrown out."

"It just seems such a shame," Bryant mused to himself. "Such a shame."

"And what is the shame, Mr. Bryant? That you are not in agreement with the politics of the Cultural Revolution?"

"Well, that too, of course. I guess I'm just not a joiner. Didn't even join the damned Boy Scouts when I was a kid. Too many oaths and uniforms. It just wasn't my cup of tea. Even then, it seemed too much like surrendering your soul." He leaned on the railing and looked down at the swirling water. "No. I meant that it's a shame that you have to give up your self, your uniqueness."

"And what of the consequences of the cult of individualism, Mr. Bryant? Too much freedom destroys the world. Your capitalism is the ultimate expression of individual freedom without concern for others, is it not?"

"Well . . . maybe so. It's not my capitalism anymore, but I can't deny that a lot of greedy bastards ran rampant with it, me included. I'll grant you that."

" 'Greedy bastards,' " the boy enunciated pointedly. "How well you put it. I shall have to remember that phrase."

Bryant watched the youth stepping up onto the bridge. Who was he? Suppose this very same kid had grown up in, say, Columbus, Ohio. Who would he have been then? He was a hard one to read. Bryant didn't have a lot of faith in his own ability to assess character in a stranger. He hadn't understood the girl when he first saw her in the cave. He had often disliked people on sight, only to find out later how wrong he was. He had learned to take his own first impressions with a grain of salt. But he thought he was picking up something here from the boy, something that was quite at odds with what he was saying. It was almost as if the younger man were testing his words the way your foot tested the bottom of a lake before you walked in to bathe. Was this young soldier hearing the echo of his own words bouncing back to him from the sheer walls of the mountains around the valley and from the walls of the great buildings, and were they perhaps not ringing so true? Was he experiencing the first small fissures in the ideological marble?

"Surrender yourself to a greater good," the boy said. "That is what you do not understand, Mr. Bryant. We surrender ourselves to the greater good of the people."

"The good of the people, yes. But how can you say that what's going on out there in the rest of Tibet is for the good of the people, for Christ's sake? Excuse my language. I'm not a religious person. But, hell, the good of the people! That's crazy!"

"We are here to liberate people from old ways, old thoughts and deeds that bring about their own oppression through ignorance. The good is not always easy to see at first."

"Well, Tibet is sure as hell full of everything old. What you see out there is old and grimy, greasy and worn. There's no denying it," Bryant said with an expansive gesture, taking in the world beyond the mountains. "Hell, all of this earthly existence is something of a game with these Tibetans. But it's primitive in appearance only. Watch out for what's beneath the soot and rancid butter grease, son. Because what's out there beyond this valley is surely not ignorance. That's one thing I would bet on, if I were still a gambling man. 'There may be gold powder sprinkled in the humblest cup of tea.' That's a saying they have."

"We bring the Cultural Revolution for the good of the people," the boy repeated, as if Bryant had perhaps not heard him. "To rid them of their archaic ways." As he spoke, the boy scuffed his military issue boot along the delicate carved slats of the railing, reminding Bryant of a child carelessly dragging a stick along a picket fence.

"I hear the word 'good' bandied around a lot," Bryant replied after a moment. "And you have accomplished a lot of good. Your first Revolution in 1949 was a superb effort; you fed the starving masses and dethroned the warlords and petty tyrants who brought so much pain to your people. But somehow you lost touch with your objective. I think your Chairman Mao said that politics is war without blood. If that's true, son, then what's going on out there? Because there's sure as hell plenty of blood being spilled. As Conway would say, it isn't just a debate at the Oxford Union anymore." He shook his head sadly. "Hell ... maybe evil *is* an absolute.

"Did you ever study the French Revolution? Now there's an object lesson for you. Keep a revolution around long enough and it all goes sour. The good guys become the villains. Like Robespierre and Stalin. The same thing could happen to your Chairman. It always seems to come around to that. It's some sort of cycle they can't seem to avoid. They lose it, they get greedy, they get corrupted, they start to behave just like the tyrants they overthrew. And it *is* happening to you. There's no 'good of the people' in this new Cultural Revolution of yours. It brings out the worst in folks. Thugs and bullies have license to run amok. Young kids who don't know any better are running around with baseball bats and dynamite, out of control. You're a scared and angry people, taking what you think you want but not what is yours."

"Then you do not understand either our geography or our history. I shall have to give you a proper lesson sometime soon."

"Yes, well, maybe so," Bryant conceded.

"Yes. Maybe so, Mr. Bryant," the boy said archly. "And when we take this place, then you shall have an object lesson as well."

"But why? Seems to me this is your kind of place. What you've got here is a great experiment in human cooperation. Everyone shares. No one rules. Everyone has enough." He managed a smile and took in the boy from top to bottom like a tailor addressing his challenge.

"I see no sharing," the boy said, "beyond the confines of your elite enclave, which is what this is. You haven't shown me how your so-called 'work' in this valley benefits the world. If no one ever leaves here, then what possible good could any of your precious knowledge be doing for humanity?"

"You're a hard one, aren't you?" Bryant said, shaking his head. "Well, it's not strictly true that no one ever leaves. There are some pretty advanced people here in Tibet who actually do come and go. The knowledge they carry is what you might call . . . rarefied. These people have been studying the human mind for centuries, and they know a thing or two. I like to think of this valley as a storehouse of that knowledge, and also of a lot of fine culture and art. Fragile things that need to be guarded from a harsh world. They're safe here. It's as if . . ." Bryant had never really articulated these thoughts before, but it was coming together for him as he spoke. "It's as if we have what's needed here to re-seed the world with beauty, wisdom, art, and knowledge if the worst ever happens out there, if everything gets wiped out."

"A rationale for elitism," the boy said tersely, "and a system of superstitious oppression. Nothing more."

"Did I say you were hard?" Bryant said. "I take it back. You're impenetrable. They ought to name some kind of rock after you. What I want to know is how your father, so brilliant and rational, could have been seduced by the Party line. How could he participate in the destruction of this country?" Bryant shook his head and removed a pack of cigarettes from his pocket. He thought perhaps he had allowed his own feelings to show too much, and a gesture of appeasement was definitely in order. He tapped one free and offered it to the boy, who accepted it, somewhat to Bryant's surprise. "I don't smoke much myself. I mostly keep them for the Sherpas."

"My father was not, as you put it, 'seduced,'" the boy said after a moment's thought, blowing out a long plume of smoke from his Sobranie. "Not by the Revolution, at any rate. My father never had—how do you say?—much stomach for ideology and politics. And there is a part of him that is not purely rational."

"Then you acknowledge that there are other things to interest a man," Bryant remarked. The boy ignored this, inhaling his smoke thoughtfully and leaning out over the stream.

"My father was a military man first."

"Was?"

"Is. My father *is* a military man first. As I said, it is not ideology but the challenge of strategy and tactic that captivates him, Mr. Bryant. He was obsessed with finding this place. It was the ultimate puzzle, the challenge of his career. It was an embarrassment to me and to others. I believed that he was a foolish romantic on a futile quest. What am I to think now?" he said, gazing out over the valley. "He was right. What am I to think?" He turned and faced Bryant. "But be warned. My father rarely fails."

"We're plenty worried, you can bet your life on that. The man I knew back in New York so long ago was brilliant. A mind for puzzles and languages without peer. If anyone can find this place, he can."

"Mr. Bryant, what are those steps and terraces up there, and what are all those people doing with . . . nets?"

"Glad you asked. Despite all my blabbing, the music and art and high thought are not my business. That's my business, up there. My latest bit of hydraulic engineering. I started mining for gold up there a long time ago. Jack-of-all-trades, they call me. Even the Tibetans have learned the idiom, only they point and laugh when they say it. But I dabble. I read and study, and I figure things out. I may not be a technical wizard, but these good folks are always able to make sense of my drawings and schemes."

"Schemes, Mr. Bryant?"

"Bet you never thought you'd see a good old-style North American salmon run—complete with locks and ladders, invigorating runs and breeding tanks. It still takes protein to run a body properly here. Well, some bodies." He shrugged. "I can't do without it. Conway's become like the rest of them—so spiritual, you know, hardly physical at times. Sometimes I even think he could almost live on flowers and air and sit on a stem of barley without bending it. That's something the Tibetans say of their magicians. Tantric magic, demon strength, levitation, and all that."

"Mr. Bryant, why do you go on so? It is irrelevant to me. Magicians. Levitation. Our own people were oppressed for centuries by such . . . what is your term? Mumbo jumbo. But we threw it off. We freed ourselves. I have one purpose, and one purpose only: to leave this place."

"Sorry. I forgot." He paused while the boy pulled nonchalantly on his cigarette, studying the view with a kind of practiced indifference. From where they stood it was possible to take in the mountain and the entire magnificent complex of the lamasery perched high above on its cliffs: the staggered rooflines, the towers and balconies, the windows both clear and colored rising three and four stories, the stepped tiers of stone and the levels of hanging gardens that softened the whole and brought it back into the earth. The lamasery's milk-blue roofs contrasted it with the tremendous gray rock bastions above, pillars of stone tenuously supporting a world of inconceivable mass and height.

They stepped down from the ornamental bridge and labored up the steep slope toward Bryant's hatchery.

"There is one thing that does interest me, though. How did your soldiers manage to relieve me of my weapon aboard the airplane? I did not allow myself to sleep, at least not before the incident. When did they take my pistol and replace it with the toy?"

"A toy?" Bryant smiled broadly and shook his head at this information. "Is that what happened?" He laughed. "They probably didn't replace anything, Captain Zhang."

"What do you mean? I saw it. A toy." He was breathing hard from the climb and his growing irritation. "A crude child's toy of wood and tin."

"Is that what you saw?" Bryant said, still smiling with obvious delight.

"Mr. Bryant," the youth said, stopping and planting his feet, bending over with his hands on his knees, catching his breath. "I have been patient. Most patient. I have allowed you to lead me around this place at some length." He exhaled in exasperation. "But I will not be made to look foolish. It was not a hallucination. My sister . . . also . . . saw . . . the . . . toy gun."

"Did she tell you what she saw?"

"*I threw the gun to her.* It weighed nothing. It landed in her lap."

"But was it a light toy gun that landed in her lap?"

"What are you saying, Mr. Bryant? That I did not know what I saw? That I am crazy? Suffering delusions? I can assure you that I am not and that I was suffering nothing at the time. And my sister saw the toy gun, too. And the rifles piled on the floor. I could tell by her reaction."

"What I am saying, Captain Zhang, is not that you didn't see a toy gun. Or that your sister didn't. But she might have seen something quite different. After all, you were her captor. Am I right on this?" The boy looked Bryant squarely in the eye and crushed his cigarette disdainfully beneath his boot. "Captain," Bryant continued, "when we enter certain realms in this land, we lay ourselves open to potent magic."

"Magic. Magic, Mr. Bryant?"

"The four rimpoches who were on that plane are not ordinary men. One of those old guys is a highly revered Naljorpa. A magician. A practitioner of Tantric magic. Some of it goes back a very long way to ancient Bon traditions."

"What rubbish," the boy said, a trifle uneasily, Bryant thought.

"I told you, they know the human mind. Don't you see? It's all in the *perception* of things. People have the wrong idea about what 'magic' is. It's not the manipulation of matter. They didn't do anything to your gun. There were no rays coming from their eyes, or anything like that. They just kind of . . . well . . . made you *see* it differently. I'd be very curious to know what your sister saw." He put his hands on his hips and shook his head. "If ever there was a meat-and-potatoes kind of guy, it's me. But if I've learned anything at all in my years here, it's that we create the world through our senses. I've seen things here that have made me toss aside my concepts of reality. You know how these people put it? Reality—the phenomenal world—is like the sound of a bell, Captain. It's perceived but it may not be kept. All things are equally perishable, existing somewhere only in the senses of the observers. And your senses can be tinkered with. That's it. That's as much as I understand."

The boy did not speak for a moment. He and the American stood and looked at each other.

"Fascinating," he said at last, causing Bryant to raise his brows questioningly. "Fascinating that even you—capitalist, crass materialist, and criminal that you are—are susceptible to the seductions of superstition and irrationality, capable of talking nonsense just like these Tibetans. I will concede that it is seductive indeed. We Chinese have fought this sort of thing, and the oppression it inevitably leads to, many, many times throughout our long history, Mr. Bryant. But I know what is real. And what is real is that we shall take this place, too."

They were halfway up the hill to the hatchery. Bryant shrugged, and started walking again.

"Not if we can help it," he said with a smile. For Bryant, it was just an ordinary smile, the smile of good manners. But to the young captain it was the chilling smile of an old, old enemy.

~

"I don't know. That kid makes me nervous."

"Oh, surely it's not as bad as all that!"

"It's as bad as all that. Worse, maybe. Christ, I've never seen anything—animal, vegetable, or mineral—as hard as that kid. Excuse my French. He scares me."

"You're exaggerating again, I'm sure."

"No, Rose. I'm telling you the God's honest truth. He scares me. Here, let me give you a hand."

It was the day after Bryant's walk through the valley with young Captain Zhang. He and Miss Brinklow were climbing to the radio shack, a trek she did not often make, and Bryant was gallantly pulling her up the wooden ladder.

"It's as if—how can I put it?—as if what the old Thirteenth warned us about in that prophecy has already come true. About the Men of Han finding this place and everything being wrecked because of it. I mean, he's here. Now. He's found it. Maybe it's too late for us already. Too late for the world."

"Chalmers!" Miss Brinklow said sharply, pausing on the ladder. "Stop that this minute. You're like a cat with a mirror. You're scaring yourself. It's nonsense. He's only one man. One boy, actually."

"The prophecy said just one of them would do it."

"Yes. But he's not the one. He's all alone. He has no army. He's ineffectual. What can he possibly do?"

"He's determined to find a way out of here, and I wouldn't put it past him to do it. He'd find his way back here then—and he wouldn't come back alone, I guarantee. Or maybe he doesn't need to go get an army. Maybe it's just his presence here. Like a—a cancer cell. I feel as if we ought to lock him up. Or something."

"Chalmers!" she exclaimed, genuinely shocked now. "Do you hear what you're saying? Lock him up! If we were to do that, then I guarantee you it would be the first step toward the destruction of everything we are. Everything this valley holds dear! It would truly be the beginning of the end. We cannot violate our principles in order to preserve them. It simply doesn't work! You know that!"

He stared down at her. She gazed back up at him

fiercely, her feet planted on the ladder. She was a plain little woman, but her eyes sometimes blazed like a pair of head-lights. He sighed.

"Yeah. I do know that. You're right. It's just that . . . goddamnit, that kid's in here while Conway's out there. It's all wrong. It's been more than a week since Conway left. He's more than halfway through his maximum time. His absolute maximum time. He's already pushing it. I'm getting really jumpy. Where is he? What's keeping him? Why hasn't he sent even one radio message, like he promised he'd try to?"

" 'Try,' Chalmers. That's what he said. That he'd *try*—to find a radio, to get to it, to get a chance to use it. To get through the awful weather and interference if he did find one. God knows the situation he's in. We can only imagine." Miss Brinklow's eyes softened a little then, as if she'd turned down the dimmer switch. "As for what's keeping him, well . . . I can think of only one thing aside from death or imprisonment that would stop him from coming right back."

Bryant looked back at her blankly for a long moment before he comprehended. Then he shook his head emphatically. "No," he said. "Nope. Uh-uh. Not him." He pulled on her arm, hauling her up to the next rung. "Come on. It's windy up here."

# ~ 9 ~

She had awakened him in the middle of the night in their tiny room in the rear of a monastery behind the Jokhang temple in Lhasa. She hadn't spoken or shaken him; she had simply lighted the lamp and was looking at him when he opened his eyes.

"You're sweating," she whispered. His hand went to his face reflexively.

"It's warm in here," he whispered back.

"No, it isn't. It's actually cool." They looked at each other.

"No," he declared. "It's warm." He pulled her close. "And I was having a rather boring nightmare. Classic stuff. Leaden legs, blurry eyes, the whole bit. All the hackneyed details. Right down to some nameless, faceless thing chasing me. I'm embarrassed to even tell you about it. Most unoriginal."

Her hand on his forehead was not just the tender touch of a lover. It was that, of course, but it was also an exquisitely sensitive instrument measuring heat, moisture, and minute galvanic variations. It took all of his training and concentration to keep the sweats and trembles within bounds.

Nothing he had ever done in his life—not surviving the Great War, not struggling over a mountain pass in a blizzard with his face frozen—had been as difficult.

This was their ninth day at the monastery. They had retreated there on the day her father had left Lhasa; Conway had wanted to wait a day or two to make sure General Zhang was really and truly gone. We have plenty of time, he told her. I am still well within my allotted limit.

Now, many days later, he was running out of time. He was running out of time, sick in body and soul, and trying to hide it from her. In a few days, he might never see her again.

A week before, after they had made love for the first time, she had been sunk in pensive silence for a while. He, in uncharted territory, said nothing, merely waited. What do I know about women? he asked himself. He rummaged through his memory, thinking of his mother, his sisters, Miss Brinklow, for God's sake—the only women he had known at all well. Then she spoke.

My father. What will happen to him? Where is he going?

I can tell you only what you already know, he had said, and this is all I know: He'll follow the clues. They'll lead him away from Shangri-La, geographically and in every other way.

Will he die?

The idea is not necessarily for the searcher to die, he had said, offering what reassurance he could muster. I believe the idea is that the searcher survive, and return to the world, and spread the word that Shangri-La is a terrible place, a place to be avoided at all costs. Of course, from what I know, it's a dangerous journey, not a garden party by any stretch. The physical part he'll probably survive, if he's tough. And careful. As for the condition he'll be in psychically . . . well, all I know is that it will depend on what is in his heart and his conscience. He will be deciding his own fate.

That is not much comfort to me, she had said, and fell silent again. After a minute or two she spoke. It may be hard for you to understand. I deplore what he has done. I know that he would have allowed me to be sent back to Peking for "reeducation." I know that he has been a destroyer and an opportunist of the worst sort. But . . .

But he is your father, Conway said.

Yes. He is my father.

Conway had known what she was going to say next. It was like the tiny interval when you place the gramophone needle on a record and hear a faint ghostly echo of the music that's about to play. He heard her words before she even spoke, and he experienced it all: despair, heartbreak, bitterness, resignation, acceptance.

I can't go back with you, she said. I must be there to help my father when he returns. If he returns. He has no one else. Certainly he does not have my brother, and the rest of his family is dead. I am the only one. If what you say is true, that his conscience will determine what he finds there, then . . . I have no choice. He's going to need me.

Conway had known about the powerful filial sense of the Chinese. Abandoning an aged parent in difficulty would be unthinkable. No matter how reprehensible the parent might be—she simply wouldn't do it. And of course, though she had not said it, he knew that she felt partly responsible for sending her father on his journey. Partly responsible? There was no polite way around it: In her mind, she was responsible, never mind how good the reasons were for doing it.

I have nothing but admiration for you, he had said. I'd stay with you, but I fear you'd have nothing but a handful of dust instead of a lover before too long.

Plaintively, she asked him how much time they would have together if she were to go back to Shangri-La with him. He considered, then told her he wasn't sure just how long. She pressed him: how long? Reluctantly, he told her: a long time. A long time? she had asked. Fifty years? Seventy-five? A hundred? A long time, he said again, and put his fingers on her mouth. Let's not talk about it. Why torment ourselves? We're here now. We'll make the next few days the equivalent of a century.

The physician had told Conway what to expect if he stayed out too long. It would be little things causing trouble at first—digestive upsets, headaches, poor stamina. Then perhaps weakness and insomnia along with a general feeling of debilitation. Your bones might start to ache, the physician had said, and you might start to have unpleasant dreams when you do sleep. You might progress to fevers and chills next, as the serious aging compensation begins to set in. After that . . . well, probably you will begin to see definite signs on your face and body of accelerating senescence. Irreversible, we assume, though arrestable if you get back here in time. If not, well . . . rapid deterioration according to your particular genetic heritage. Stroke, infarction, aneurism, metabolic collapse, delirium, dementia. Death.

The fevers and chills had started yesterday. The ache in his bones had begun a few days before. Instead of insomnia, he had found himself unable to stay awake for more than a few hours at a time. So far, he had hidden it from her. Their precious few days together had been glorious, almost enough to make him forget. The weather had been sweet, the sun streaming in their tiny window each morning. She would rise and go out to get their provisions for the day, for they had decided that she in her Tibetan guise would be far less conspicuous than he. While she was gone, he would call on every shred of inner discipline that he possessed, repeating his mantras for calm, peace, and health and dealing out the precious drops of the elixirs the physician had given him.

That morning, just before he expected her to return, he examined his face in the small beaten-metal mirror on the wall over their washbasin. The image was blurry and distorted, but there was no mistaking a certain deepening of the hollows and shadows of the planes of his face, like looking at a relief map.

So, this was how it was. Love had eluded him all his life. Father Perrault had told him three decades ago that after five years in the valley, all past attachments and passions would fade. But he had had no particular attachments or passions, either for people or work or anything else. Then he had left the valley and nearly lost it forever. When he did find his way back, he had quite literally kissed the ground, pressing his lips to the earth of the Valley of the Blue Moon and vowing never to leave again, so it was not as though he had any ambivalence about leaving the world behind him. His attachment and passion was for the valley itself.

Certainly he had believed that there was no one in the outside world who would mourn his absence. There had been a few questionable episodes in his past that veered in the direction of love, including a brief engagement, and he had believed that he loved Lo-Tsen, who had left Shangri-La with him and young Mallinson the first time decades before. The debauched lechering he had indulged in along with everyone else during the Great War was certainly not love. But now it was here. These few days were it, the love of a lifetime compressed, as inversely short as his life had been long, like a karmic debt for his unnaturally extended years, and shortly he would be forced to leave it behind. And he was struggling to be Romeo and Valentino—unaccustomed roles for him under the best of circumstances—while in the teeth of exponentially accelerating decrepitude. He had to laugh.

Cheer up, old boy, he had said to his funhouse reflection. It's your honeymoon.

~

He had indeed been having a nightmare when she woke him up to tell him he was sweating, though it was scarcely the tried-and-true old standard he had said it was. There had been no leaden legs, no nameless faceless thing. What he had encountered was far worse. He had not known that his mind contained such horrors.

Going to bed earlier that evening, he had noticed that the ache in his bones had intensified just a bit, as if someone had cranked a control knob up one or two increments. When he was drifting off after their lovemaking, just entering the phantasmagorical zone one passes through on the way to sleep, a picture formed in his mind of his own skeleton, faintly greenish against a dark background, like a medical radiograph, the vivid details and contours defined not by light but by pain. The throb in his bones followed him down into his sleep, and in the dream that ensued, his skeleton was an entity separate from himself, a fearsome, alien thing determined to escape the dying flesh that encased it, snarling and angry at having been detained in a larval state inside the skin, the pain an announcement of its gathering intent. That was when she had lighted the lamp and pulled him up out of the nightmare.

When they went back to sleep, he was careful to arrange himself so that if she woke first in the morning she would see only the back of his head. What he did not want her to see was his slack, ancient face unconscious and helpless, ragged snores escaping from his open drooling mouth. Not a pretty picture, old fellow, he said to himself, taking a furtive drink in the dark from one of the little bottles the physician had given him and which he kept tucked away under the bedding. Not the recommended way to cause a fair maid's heart to go pit-a-pat. Unless of course from pure terror at the sight.

When he woke the next morning, his hand moved to his mouth to make sure all was in order. His teeth had been aching, and he felt them now, testing for looseness. He had had another dream after they went back to sleep, not exactly a nightmare, but sufficiently unpleasant: He dreamed that they were talking, having a lovers' conversation, and that he realized that his teeth were as loose as a fistful of dominoes, ready to come out in his hand. In the dream, he strove to hold his teeth in his jaw while maintaining a jaunty and debonair demeanor.

His teeth were, in fact, slightly loose. But not so loose that they would fall out today. And what was all of this if not the ultimate exercise in living for the moment? Perhaps his teeth would fall out tomorrow. The devil take them. For now, they were still rooted in his head. The sun streamed through the window. He turned to her and gave her his most radiant smile.

"Good morning," he said.

She had not been quite quick enough. He caught the expression of concern on her brow just before it vanished. He pretended he had not seen it. She smiled back at him, warmly, lovingly, as if the two of them were in the finest suite at the best hotel in old Shanghai, with not a care in the world.

"Our friends are here," she said. He rose, doing his best imitation of a seventeen-year-old getting out of bed. He had read somewhere that people endeavoring to appear younger than their years usually make the mistake of bustling about briskly. How wrong they were, the author had said. Youth is languid and loose-limbed. It had been a book of satirical humor, but there was real truth in that statement, which stood Conway in good stead now. Stretch, yawn, rise, take your time, stroll to the window.

Outside, a pair of ravens swooped and cawed, passing by right at the level of Conway's eyes, the whooshing of their enormous wings plain to his ears. He and Ma Li admired these outlaws of the air, loved to watch them from their tiny window as they went about their complex business. They were perfect creatures, he thought, watching one of them stretch its wings into a long lazy glide. There were ravens in the valley, and they had always been a delight and a solace to him when he watched them from the window of the lamasery. Insolent, arrogant scavengers, blue-black and as big as geese when you saw one close up. Indifferent to the human society below them except to the extent that it yielded choice refuse; birds that buried their dead and held their treetop council, strutting and arguing over the entrails of a carcass, fully sentient, their adolescent offspring screeching for attention and their share of the day's banquet.

He leaned farther out the narrow window and looked down to the market courtyard at the bottom of the hill, where a group of Chinese soldiers passed in and out of his line of sight between the high walls. They seemed to be teasing someone, the victim just out of view. One of the soldiers clutched what appeared to be a small animal in his arms, turning evasively this way and that in a childish game of you-can't-have-it.

There was jeering and catcalling and the usual arrogance of the occupier. They could just as easily have been Mongol or British. Any bully of the moment would do. But there didn't seem to be any real violence going on in the square below today, and for that he was grateful. So far, all their days there had been peaceful. When she went out this morning, as she did every morning, he would watch her from the window until she disappeared around the corner.

∼

It was miraculous. She had got her hands on a bottle of brandy, along with their usual fare of tea, butter, eggs, and barley cakes.

"Beautiful, clever girl!" he exclaimed, kissing her and taking the bottle from her hands. "How . . . ?"

She shrugged. "Some things are eternal, and you find them wherever you go. The sun, the moon, the stars, and the black market."

He blew the dust from the bottle; the label was French. He had been thinking about a drink. He was glad that he had neglected to ask the physician before he left the valley about the effects of alcohol on someone in his condition. No doubt it was contraindicated. But he could feel, in advance, before he even pulled the cork, the warmth traveling down his gullet, blooming in his stomach like a flower, and spreading deliciously out to his limbs and up to his head. It would take very little, he knew. He remembered how one small drink of sherry affected his aged aunties when he was a boy, how quickly they became giddy and their hats went askew.

It only took him a second or two to weigh the losses against the gains. He pulled the cork. A drop or two would soothe him, loosen his tongue, promote the intimacy he had missed out on most of his life. They didn't have years, the way most lovers did, to discover everything about each other. They barely had days. Hours. He poured two cups, raised his in a toast.

"Eat something first," she said firmly, and produced her next surprise, a can of Norwegian sardines and a minuscule glass jar of Black Sea caviar. "The oil will be good."

"Your ingenuity takes my breath away," he said, and put his arms around her. "I haven't tasted caviar for almost forty years."

"You have a fever," she said, drawing back from the embrace and assessing him with a clinical eye.

"It's nothing," he said. "Nothing at all. Like a little hangover. Not that you would know anything about hangovers, of course."

"What makes you so certain?" she said with a smile and a hint of a challenge.

"You? Hung over? I refuse to believe it," he declared. "Me, of course. It was an almost constant condition at a certain time in my life. The Oxford days. Stumbling across the green at Christ Church at dawn and such. I don't think I ever woke up feeling well. Then later, in the consular days and at Government House, it was practically obligatory. I was certainly not the worst of them. I kept myself on an even keel most of the time. But there were some chaps in the diplomatic service who were simply disguised drunks, if you know what I mean. I think a lot of them joined just for the endless rounds of parties and affairs. No, the only time my drinking was out of control was during the war years. The only way to bear it was to get blind, stinking mad drunk whenever I could. Oh, my dear, you would not have loved me then. No, indeed. I killed and lechered in great style. I did what everyone else did, the great crazed millions, just as the creators of war intended." He looked at her. "No, I can't believe that you have ever been drunk. Have you?" She laughed and took a healthy drink of brandy.

"You forget that I was a student in Shanghai. I was not much different from the rest of the human race." She laughed. "We even waxed poetic. Weren't the Chinese the original poetic waxers? You can read Chinese poetry from twelve centuries ago about getting drunk and contemplating the moon and such. And you can read even older poetry about the horrors of war, words you'll swear were written yesterday."

He shook his head, remembering. "Dying in a war is ghastly. Surviving can be ghastly in its own way. War means the abuse of every emotion, and if you survive, then everything, and I mean everything, survives with you. Your noble deeds and emotions as well as your not-so-noble ones. I told Father Perrault when I first got to Shangri-La three decades ago that the Great War had exhausted my passions, left me bored and fretful and with the feeling that I was living a lie. You see, it's common for those of us who did survive to believe that the best of us did not make it back. That was precisely how I felt. Certainly it affected my ability to love. Who was I to love or be loved when better men than I lay in mass graves at Flanders, Verdun, the Marne, Belleau Wood?"

"And who are you to love or be loved now? Isn't this a war right here in Tibet? Aren't people dying all around us?" she said, stroking his cheek.

"I've come a long way. Or maybe I've gone back a long way. I don't know. I'm not asking questions. But the siege, for me, is over." He took another drink and kissed her.

"Father Perrault," she mused. "The High Lama. Your predecessor. You told me how all of you got there, on the plane out of Baskul, and how you loved it but your friend Mallinson hated it. You've told me that you left once, long ago, but you never told me why."

He looked at her. He had decided in advance to limit himself to four swallows of brandy. He had already had two. He doubted that two more would be enough to get him through this. He took a third. "You're going to think I'm a fool," he said.

"Never," she said.

"It was . . . a complicated moment." He laughed. "It seems that I have a policy never to leave Shangri-La unless I'm in the company of a beautiful young Chinese woman. In fact, I would not have left at all if it weren't for her."

"Oh? And who was she? Should I be jealous?"

"No. First, because what I felt for her was only something I mistook for love. Now I know better. Second, because she didn't love me anyway, she loved young Mallinson. And third, when you hear her sad story, you will feel only sorrow for her."

He looked at his cup and the fourth swallow of brandy. He did not drink it, but swirled it as brandy is supposed to be swirled so that it sends up its vapors, so conducive to reflection and conjuring, which rise and enter the nose and brain and seep under even the most tightly closed door in the mind.

"I think I told you that the four of us—I, Mallinson, Miss Brinklow, and Bryant—had been in Shangri-La for a couple of months. One by one, all of us, with the exception of Mallinson, decided that there was no particular urgency about getting back to the outside world. Bryant, of course, was only too happy to have stumbled into such a pleasant place where the federal agents would be unlikely to follow, and Miss Brinklow was still filled with missionary zeal to convert the heathen, though I think I recall a certain dreaminess making its first appearance in her eyes right about then. Poor Mallinson. To him, it was as though there was a contagion passing among us, causing us to abandon reason, to go slack before his very eyes. It must have been like a bad dream to him.

"And it would have been, except for Lo-Tsen. Mallinson and I had both noticed her. She was lovely, but remote, untouchable, virtually silent, expressing herself only on the keyboard of a clavichord or piano. Chang had told me that she had arrived in the valley forty-seven years before, at the age of eighteen. She had been of royal Manchu stock, and had been on her way to Kashgar to meet the man she was betrothed to when her carriers got lost in the mountains. She had been brought to the valley and had been there ever since.

"Chang had made an allusion to the fact that she had been . . . how did he put it? '. . . more than averagely reluctant to accept the situation.' Those were his words. But the magic five years had done their job, so he told me, of stilling the passions, of putting her past life in perspective. And watching her from afar, as I often did, it seemed that he was right. She was utterly composed and self-contained. It was difficult to accept that she was in fact sixty-five years old, because she was as fresh and youthful as a teenager.

"In the meantime, Father Perrault died, but not before anointing me as his successor. Mallinson was always accusing me of losing my reason, of being seduced by the place. And in a way, he was quite right. Why would the High Lama choose a whippersnapper from His Majesty's Consular Service to take his place? I wrestled with questions of fate that had never occurred to me before. I was more than a little preoccupied.

"Mallinson never gave up on the idea of leaving. Chang had told us that it would be quite impossible for him to leave without guides. Imagine my shock when Mallinson came to me one night to tell me that he was getting out, that guides were waiting up in the mountains to take him, and most shocking of all, that Lo-Tsen had not only arranged it, but was going with him, was out there with the porters, in the mountains beyond the valley, right now, waiting for him. And he wanted me to come. He begged, he implored.

"I, of course, was shocked to learn that Lo-Tsen was leaving. I hadn't yet told Mallinson the full truth about Shangri-La, that it was a repository not only of the best knowledge of all the world but a pocket of anomaly where the means to extend human life to twice its normal span and more was practiced regularly. I blurted out that Lo-Tsen couldn't possibly leave, not without disintegrating like a preserved flower when the bell jar is abruptly removed. Then, of course, I was obliged to tell him everything. He had thought during our entire stay that I was cracked, for falling under the spell of the place, as he put it, for not sharing his urgency about getting out. Now he was convinced that I was quite mad. We argued. He still tried to convince me to come. He flung it at me that he had been warned about me before he came to work with me at Baskul, that they had told him that ever since I'd been blown up in the war I'd been not quite right, and that now he saw that it was true.

"He left, in fury and despair, alone. But he was back in a few hours, almost in tears, telling me that he hadn't the nerve to make the traverse by himself to get to where the porters were waiting, and again begging me to come. I'm young, he said, and so is Lo-Tsen. We have our lives ahead of us. Doesn't that mean anything to you? I reminded him that she was not young. We argued again, and I must give Mallinson credit—he took himself in hand, and, as calmly and rationally as he could under the circumstances and given his state of mind, challenged me point by point, lambasting me for my credulousness, asking me to tell him what empirical evidence I had to support anything Chang or Father Perrault had told me, pointing out that I would never have believed a story like this if I had heard it in a monastery in England, that I was seduced by these tales simply because I was in Tibet and so forth. He likened the valley to a spider's web, with a lot of wizened old men lying in wait to pounce on anyone who passed by.

"He argued compellingly, but I was unmoved until he delivered the coup de grace: He told me that he and Lo-Tsen were in love, and that he knew, absolutely knew, that she was really and truly young. He knew, because, he told me, they had been intimate.

"These words brought everything crashing down for me. Not because I was jealous, but because it made a lie out of everything Chang had told me. That she had undergone the transformation, that her past life had receded, that she was content to be there. That her passions had been stilled. I remember thinking that a dream had dissolved, the way all-too-lovely things did at the first touch of reality. Whoever or whatever Lo-Tsen was, Chang was wrong about her, or he was lying about her. She was willing to risk everything to leave the valley. Mallinson, with the knowledge of a lover, was sure that she was only a young thing, and was desperate to leave with her, and unless I helped, he would not be able to do it. Was anything more deserving than youth and love? At that moment, I did not think so. And I knew I was incapable of refusing him.

"In the next moment, I agreed to leave with him. You have never seen a man more possessed by joy, relief, and gratitude than poor Mallinson.

"We left. We trekked for many hours until we found the Sherpas and Lo-Tsen. No doubt she had given up hope, for I have never seen such a look of love and relief on a girl's face as when she saw Mallinson at last.

"I could not have known at that moment that their love story was to be an even shorter one than yours and mine. Nor could I have known that the next days and weeks would bring me more sorrow than anything I saw or experienced in the war. The mind, miraculous mechanism that it is, has its way of disconnecting us from our pain. I was to lose for a while all memory of those dark days. And when

I regained it, I thought nothing could save me from the grief and regret it brought with it. Nothing."

He stopped, sighed, and gazed out the window at the low gray sky. He still held the cup with its teaspoon of brandy. "But let me jump ahead a bit, to the weeks before my memory returned. I think you'll get a more vivid picture of my experience if I relate it to you as I lived it.

"It's interesting to learn just how thin and insubstantial is the layer of consciousness that gives continuity and organization to our memories, forming it into what we call our lives, our histories. If you've ever had the experience of dozing off in an inappropriate situation—at a play, for instance, or in a roomful of people having a conversation, you know with what ease the fabric disintegrates and you simply pass into another world.

"In those weeks before my memory returned, I seemed to be inhabiting another world. And with good reason; I was in the grip of a fever, another casualty of an epidemic. Moving in and out of delirium, I came to understand that I was in a hospital bed, in a ward, and that the kindly attendants changing my sweat-soaked sheets and sponging my brow were French nuns. I learned that I was in a mission hospital in Chungkiang, with no memory of how I had got there. I had a powerful sense of having come through something terrible, but I simply could not get a grip on it, exactly like trying to remember a dream that has slipped away. The fabric of my life had disintegrated.

"And then one day while I am lying there dozing, my physical health slowly returning under the excellent care of the nuns, I think that perhaps I am dreaming and delirious again, for I hear a British voice—male—approaching, speaking French with the Mother Superior. The voice stops at my bed, says good afternoon in English, and I open my eyes: The chap standing over me gazes in astonishment. He looks utterly familiar, but again, I cannot get a grip on where I might have seen him before or anything about the circumstances of our acquaintance. I can do nothing but return his greeting, politely and pleasantly, while he stares, a great turmoil evident in his eyes. The next thing I know, he drops to one knee by the bed and says, 'Conway! It's me! Rutherford! You're alive! Good God, man, look at you!' or some such.

"He and the doctor and the Mother Superior had an excited consultation then. He told them that he knew me, that he was a friend of mine, that we had gone to school together, and that I had plainly lost my memory. I accepted this; I did feel that I knew the man and could trust him, even if I could not place him, and what he said made perfect sense. I decided to put myself in his hands when he offered to take me home. I certainly had nothing better planned for myself, and I hoped that perhaps when he got me 'home,' wherever that might be, I might regain my past.

"When I was strong enough to travel, we left Chungkiang, sailed down the Yangtze all the way to Nanking, took the train to Shanghai and got on a Japanese liner bound for San Francisco. The journey to the ship from Chungkiang had been full of peculiar moments when I felt as if I were just about to remember. The smells and sounds of China were second nature to me, prodding memories forward but not quite all the way out into the light, like something moving around behind a curtain in my brain. I spoke the language fluently. Whoever I was, I had lived here, I knew it, it was part of me.

"And Rutherford continued to fill me in on what he knew of my life. He said we had gone to Oxford together, Balliol College, that I had been something of an achiever, winning prizes in rowing and such, that I was an accomplished musician, that I had shown all sorts of promise until I had gone off to the war. He said I'd had a bad time of it, came home, did a spell at Oxford as a don of sorts, then, with my fluency in Oriental languages, joined the Consular Service and went east in the early twenties and lived in various places around the Orient, especially China. That was the last he knew of me, he said, until he found me at the hospital in Chungkiang. I remember listening to it all politely, dispassionately, the way one would listen to interesting stories about a distant acquaintance. And occasionally something he said would cause something to shift around behind that curtain in my mind, but then I would gaze out across the water or out the train window and feel whatever it was slipping away.

"The ship made a stop at Yokohama. One of the passengers we picked up was a famous pianist named Sieveking, and we were lucky enough to have him as our dinner companion. He was fresh from concert appearances in Tokyo and Yokohama, and was headed for a tour in America and then on to Havana and the Presidential Palace in Mexico City for a special performance. We got on wonderfully, he and I. You have to understand that my loss of memory didn't affect my ability to speak, or my manners or education. I mean I didn't feel as though I were just thrown into the middle of society without a clue, like a man from Mars. I was able to sit at dinner and converse with Sieveking in his native German and I could remember all sorts of normal things, books and music and all. I just couldn't quite recall . . . who I was or where I had been.

"Sieveking was a charming fellow, and he loved to play. It was not at all difficult for Rutherford and some others to prevail upon him to give a concert on board the ship. No rest for the wicked or talented, you know. He agreed, and on the appointed evening went belowdecks to check on the condition of the ship's piano. I followed him discreetly. He hammered out some Brahms and Scarlatti, testing the action of the keys, warming up. I was listening just inside the door, and he saw me. He gave me a smile while he played—a few measures of Liszt, a wild flourish of a Schumann Fantasy, just for my pleasure. A little private joke, a sort of connection between us without words. He was really an extraordinary pianist. Then, without its even seeming like a memory coming back, I felt my fingers twitching as the master played, and I knew that I, too, played the piano.

"Well, it's after dinner now, and Rutherford and I return to our cabins to freshen up for Sieveking's concert. We have a drink in Rutherford's cabin and I'm still hearing little bits of the music Sieveking was practicing, but I don't give it much more thought.

"Sieveking gives a good concert. Scarlatti, Brahms, the usual repertoire. He even does a little Debussy, beautiful dreamy stuff. But it's the Chopin that gets to me. Something's moving around again in my mind, and it's a melancholy feeling, something bittersweet that goes beyond the emotion in the music. Like languishing in the aftermath of a dream where you were so much in love with some wonderful person that when you awaken all you can do is pine. It's an uneasy sense of loss, a feeling that something both extraordinarily wonderful and extraordinarily sad has slipped away from me. And I'm seeing pictures in my mind of some remote and beautiful place. And again, my hands are twitching, my fingers telling me they want to play.

"At the end of the concert Sieveking's admirers press him into a long series of encores. He does mostly Chopin because that's his real specialty. And all these feelings of loss and regret are threatening to overwhelm me, as if I am hearing the love song of someone I have jilted terribly.

"After the last of his encores, he leaves the piano and moves toward the door followed by a bunch of admirers. I am unable to resist. I slip onto the bench and touch my fingers to the ivories the great man has just warmed. The static friction of his shoe is still alive on the pedal brass. The glistening black and white keys look stark and definite and full of intent. I begin to play.

"I don't even think about what I am playing. It simply flows out of me, and the feelings I described earlier, of loss and regret, are eased while I play. Meanwhile, people are drifting back, listening with interest, murmuring among themselves, though I am scarcely aware of them. I finish the piece, and sit there, a little stunned, when I hear a sudden burst of applause and someone crying Bravo, bravo! It's none other than Sieveking himself. My dear boy, he says, that was extraordinary. What was it?

"At first I can only tell him that I don't know. But I can see that the master is excited, and for his sake I make an effort to remember. Then the answer pops into my head, and I speak the name out loud: Chopin, I say. Yes. Chopin. Impossible, Sieveking says. But it is Chopin, I say, feeling suddenly tired and impatient, raising my voice a little. I know it's Chopin. Why must I argue?

"Sieveking sees my state of mind, and tries to soothe

me. I know everything Chopin wrote, he says, and he didn't write that, although it sounds just like him. I concentrate for a moment, making a supreme effort, a little embarrassed at my outburst. It's an unpublished piece, I say then. I learned it from a man I met who was once a student of Chopin. And here's another one, I say, watching my hands move over the keys, the music flowing out of my brain freely.

"When I finished the second piece, I glanced up and saw Rutherford looking at me with a solicitous and perplexed expression, while Sieveking looked as if he were about to burst at the seams. Chopin died in 1849, he said. If you knew a man who was a student of his, you must have been very, very young and the man very, very old. I thought a moment. Yes, I affirmed, the man was very, very old. My next thoughts I kept to myself, for I knew then that I had not been young, that the meeting had been recent, only a few months before.

"There was a lot of excited arguing. Sieveking didn't know what to make of my story, but he wanted me to record these pieces as soon as we got to the States. I agreed, mostly because I was anxious to get out of there. The great sadness was welling up again, threatening to swallow me, and I needed some air. Because I was remembering. That the man who had taught me the Chopin was Alphonse Briac, one of the old lamas in the Valley of the Blue Moon, and that he had been elderly indeed—nearly one hundred and twenty years old.

"I retired to my cabin. I lay in the dark, reviewing my whole life, like watching a tattered newsreel. And when I got to the part where I saw Shangri-La, and Father Perrault, and Lo-Tsen, and Mallinson, I let out a great cry of anguish, for now I knew what it was I had lost, and what had caused my mind to shut down like an overheated engine. I went and woke up Rutherford and told him everything. He was wonderfully patient and encouraging. He was a writer, you know, and so he knew how to listen and could absorb every detail. I believe we talked all night. I remember the hot tropical sun on our heads and my exhaustion when I was finished. But I had made my decision hours before. I knew what I had to do. I was sorry about it, because Rutherford had been so decent to me, but I had no choice. I knew I must find my way back, or die trying."

Outside their window, the light had climbed so that the clifflike walls of the Potala turned gold. Ma Li listened to Conway's story without a word, scarcely daring to move or take a breath for fear of disturbing the spontaneous flow of his narrative.

"When we docked at Honolulu the next midnight, I took a change of clothes and a little money, slipped out of my cabin while Rutherford was sleeping, and walked down the gangplank. Within an hour I was aboard another vessel, this one just a trifle less luxurious than the liner I had forsaken. I had signed on as an able-bodied seaman aboard a banana boat bound for the South Seas. The captain, a huge Polynesian, was apparently accustomed to taking on questionable footloose types like myself without identification or credentials, for he asked no questions when I gave him a nom de guerre. Before the night was over we had left Honolulu behind and I was in the upper bunk of a tiny cabin which I shared with a most agreeable Filipino chap who spoke no English and was not overly awed at having a tall haggard Brit barge into his quarters in the middle of the night.

"I worked my way from Honolulu to Fiji to Singapore to Bangkok as a crewman aboard tramp freighters and such. It took nearly three months, during which time I squirreled away my less-than-princely pay. I kept my mouth shut, did my work, and let the tropic sun bake me until I was nearly as brown as my fellow sailors. I enjoyed watching my whiteness disappear, took comfort in being among Asian faces and voices. It eased my terrible sorrow a little, made me feel that I was being absorbed back into the world I had so rashly forsaken.

"When we reached Bangkok, I took my accumulated earnings and converted most of them into a bank draft made out to Rutherford. I wanted to pay him back the money I knew he'd spent on me. I enclosed a letter, thanking him and reassuring him that I was alive and well and telling him that by the time he received it I would be on my way to the northwest and not to try to trace me, for I would be long gone.

"I was lean, hard, and very brown when I set out. I headed north, traversing Thailand by train and lorry. I steered clear of Burma, though it would have been a more direct route, because the British were still very much present there. I wanted to avoid my countrymen in case some well-intentioned sort, having heard through the old-boy network that I was cracked and had jumped ship in Honolulu, should try to catch me and ship me back to England in a straitjacket. I crossed into French Indochina and made my way from there to the mountainous tribal areas of southern China in Yunnan Province. I found my way to the Yangtze near the city of Li-chiang and followed it north, sometimes by boat and raft and sometimes, where it was impassable, on foot. After the river leaves Yunnan, it forms the border between Szechuan and Tibet, traveling north through territory as desolate and remote as the moon, which suited me perfectly. I left the river and began heading west in an empty spot about forty miles north of Yunnan—no border patrol, no officials, no questions. I squeezed out a salty tear or two of gratitude when I finally placed my very dirty and calloused foot on Tibetan soil, but the fact was that I still had at least as far to go—and much harder miles they would be, I knew—as the distance I had traversed since leaving my last freighter in Bangkok. Then I heaved a great sigh.

"Because at this point I had only one clue. I knew that Shangri-La lay somewhere in the extreme northwest corner of Tibet, in the shadow of a mountain almost as high as Everest: Karakal. That was what the residents of Shangri-La called it. I didn't know if it was on any map or even had an official name, but there was a chance that once I made my way to the region that the name Karakal would mean something. It seemed like little more than a wild and slim hope as I stood there on the edge of Tibet with the plains stretching away before me, but it was all I had. It had been more than six months since I had taken my leave of Rutherford in Honolulu the previous November, and the worst of the winter would have passed in the Tibetan highlands. I made my way to the northwest to pick up the rocky, tortuous road that travels twelve hundred miles along the edge of the plateau from one end of Tibet to the other.

"I joined up with nomads. I told them I was on a pilgrimage, which was certainly not a lie, a quest, that I wanted to study the sacred books and scriptural esoterica of distant monasteries. I would travel a certain distance with this or that trading caravan or family, and they would pass me on to the next with a friendly word. Lively children, obstreperous pack animals, wives with their elaborate headdresses, marriageable daughters giving me the eye, smelly felt tents—I crossed the plateau, in about two months' time, in the company of these hardy, cheerful people, everyone so greasy and dirty but so happy, until I reached the far north-west corner of the plateau. I'm sure you've heard the tired old saw 'So near and yet so far.' The phrase never had more meaning for me than when I stood gazing at that place where the world changed, where the Kunluns and the Karakoram Range loomed against the deep blue sky. It was August of 1932."

Ma Li interrupted him then, telling him that she wasn't going to let him go on until he took some nourishment. She had more surprises: foil-wrapped cheeses and Swiss chocolate. He still held the cup of brandy in his hand. She had watched him raise it to his lips a dozen times during his narrative, but always he lowered it without touching it.

"Now what, I asked myself? I was standing there looking at one of the most mysterious and inaccessible mountain ranges in the world, immense walls of white going up into the clouds. I felt about as significant as a flea, and with no more idea of where to begin than a flea might have. I turned to my nomad friend, the head of the last family group I'd traveled with, and asked him if he knew of a peak called Karakal. He laughed, and said he did, but everyone knew that it was a place that existed up here—and he pointed to his head—in dreams and in stories that you told to children.

"Ah, well, I'd like to know more about those stories, I said. Can you direct me to a monastery where I can rest and study? He smiled, and said he thought he knew of a monastery in the foothills about a day's ride from where we were. He recruited his eldest son to take me there while the rest of the family camped and rested.

"At this first monastery I rested for a day or two, and when I mentioned Karakal, I was sent on, with guides, to another monastery higher up, and another after that. I stayed a day or two in each one before being passed along to the next. In each place I would ask about Karakal, and got in response all sorts of fascinating tales and legends, none of them very consistent. But the name always drew a strong response, and I'd find myself sent along to the next place, where, my informants would tell me, they might know more. And so off I'd go. At least I was moving in what felt like a decisive way. My departure would be announced to the peaks and snowfields by a fanfare of conch shells and long thungchen trumpets. Sometimes after leaving one monastery we'd be met on some high rocky pass by a contingent from the next, for all the world as if they'd telephoned ahead. Sometimes my 'tour guides' would be carrying a sedan chair, though I never availed myself of it. I can tell you that at those head-pounding heights, where every millimeter of strength was drained from my trembling muscles, many was the time I wanted nothing more than to be carried. But I endured, though I knew they could have done it without difficulty. Their hardiness and endurance seemed scarcely human sometimes.

"Thus I progress for many weeks. I experience my moments of doubt, of course, when it seems as if I'm just wandering pointlessly. I never mention the name Shangri-La. Something inside constrains me; I feel as if I am walking an exceedingly delicate line, that Karakal is my code word, that I should not overstep. Certainly it's the word that results in motion and seems to give direction to my odyssey. Life up to that point had taught me that the path of least resistance worked best for me—particularly when I lacked a better plan.

"It's been weeks of trudging in the mountains. I'm well acclimated now, and I've met some colorful characters along the way, and I'm starting to wonder if this will be how I spend the rest of my life, when I arrive at a place where my magic word is greeted without any particular recognition. But the lama invites me to look at sacred texts. Seems to want me to. I oblige him, though I am scarcely able to read them, but he is eager. You've seen such books—thick parchment pages bound between wooden slats. Of course you have."

Ma Li nodded sadly. Indeed, she knew what Tibetan sacred books looked like. She had seen her brother pile them up and burn them often enough.

"I turn the pages of one such volume, and what do I find but dried pressed flowers. Edelweiss, to be specific. My heart leaps quietly in my chest. Nothing at all grows at this altitude in the frozen rocky ground around this lamasery, let alone an alpine flower. I don't say anything. I merely turn and smile. The lama smiles back. Shrugging is not part of their physical vocabulary, but I could have sworn that's what he did. And he sent me on to another lamasery.

"There I discover not only pressed flowers but the dried peels of fruit. These little austral signs increase as I move along, and I am starting to notice the wind chimes. Each lamasery has its wind chimes, and in each place they play a different little melody. Not a melody exactly, but the chimes play a distinct set of notes randomly. I begin to notice a musical progression in the relation between the sets of notes the different lamaseries use. There had been wind chimes in Shangri-La, and I strive to remember the notes they played. I am beginning to believe that the musical progression I am hearing now as I travel from lamasery to lamasery will lead naturally to the notes of the wind chimes of Shangri-La. The flowers, the fruit peels, the wind chimes—I start to believe that I was intended to see and hear these things. I want to believe.

"Breathing the rarefied air all these weeks and absorbing the atmosphere in the lamaseries has definitely affected me. I feel as if they know who I am when I arrive at each new place, that they've been expecting me. It's in the air. As if there are psychic eddies swirling about, and I'm the rock in the stream. And from what I knew, it was possible. I knew that certain high lamas had psychic abilities, startling prescience. It wasn't just a vague sort of feeling about things that they had—rather, they'd developed their native intuitions into a sort of radar. They . . ."

"And do you have this ability, Mr. Conway?" Ma Li interrupted. That was her pet name for him. Mr. Conway. It had never sounded so good to him.

"My predecessor, Father Perrault, possessed it," he answered her seriously. "As for myself . . . perhaps I haven't been as assiduous. I've concentrated more on secular matters in the valley, and increasingly, with world affairs, pressures from the outside, which, in this modern age, cannot be ignored even in our cloistered world. That seems to suit my talents more than discipline and contemplation. I am a keeper of the valley's tradition. More the diplomat, I guess, which of course is what I used to be. The title 'high lama' doesn't automatically confer these abilities on one." He laughed. "Of course, I haven't been there very long. Not compared to Perrault, anyway. Maybe it will come to me eventually. But he was a spiritual type, a contemplative, to begin with. He was a Capuchin monk searching for remnants of Nestorian Christianity when he stumbled upon our valley. He lived there for the rest of his very long life, building it into what you saw, and he gradually let go of his single-minded Christianity and started to study with the Tibetan masters early on. Yes. He had 'it,' that radar. I know it for a fact."

"And how long was Perrault there?" she asked. She knew he didn't want to answer that question. He had avoided telling her how much time they might have had together in the valley. "Never mind," she said when he just looked at her sadly. "A very long time. Go on."

"He had it," Conway continued. "And so, it seemed, did the lamas I met in the last part of my journey.

"I've been trekking for weeks, five or six, when my guides and I reach a place like a shining pinnacle. We'd heard its wind chimes long before we saw the bright strings of prayer flags against the sky. This wonderful little monastery sits like a blazing white citadel on top of the most commanding ridge you could imagine. It is at least three or four stories high, with beautifully ornate woodwork around the windows and little painted balconies stacked up along the side. Not in the usual advanced state of entropy. And the view: A sea of mountains and clouds and rock formations and an occasional stunted, twisted tree like the plates in a hundred-year-old book of fairy tales. Beauty not of this earth. As in Shangri-La, I had continually to remind myself that it was still our earth, but not one that many men would ever know. And the melody that sang out from that place—the melody we heard before we ever saw a building—that was another thing . . .

"In those high breezes the notes of the chimes are beautiful beyond description. Somehow they have bridged the aesthetic and tonal gaps between our Western musical system and theirs. Which causes me to think in my fevered brain that this place is some sort of milestone in my journey. I am received most graciously by old lamas and younger monks and novices. I had been treated well everywhere along the way. But this was different. It seems absurd to say it, but I felt like the Prodigal Son returning.

"There are three old anchorites in particular. High lamas, rimpoches, I don't know. That was never clear. And one of them was especially old. Amazingly ancient. Even though these mountain people are often weatherbeaten and leathery by the age of forty, and look like Methuselahs at sixty, I could tell that this man was really advanced—a bag of bones, light as a bird, frail as porcelain. More than half in the other world. One eye blind and milky, the other black and shiny as a piece of coal, and not a tooth in his head, but with that sly, sententious look of the prankster. And I could imagine that each year as the fire in his old body dimmed, that one black eye just shone more brightly. Grinning and chortling as if all of life was just one big joke. A man who should have died ages ago. I thought at first that he was senile, and humored him a bit, I'm afraid."

Ma Li was watching Conway and thinking that the sickness was in remission while he told his story. He was on his feet, gesticulating like a dancer, revitalized by his tale, feeding off the strength of his narrative. Was this Conway's *Thousand and One Nights,* his *Scheherezade?* Keep talking, my love, she thought. Perhaps if you do, the time for us to part, possibly forever, will never come.

"They took us to an uncharacteristically clean interior. It was a large central hall with tall windows that looked out on the splendid mountain scenery. The high rarefied light lent the impression of a clerestory to that open hall. The walls and beams were draped with rugs and bright flags. There was the usual altar affair and the ubiquitous pillows and in the corner a large piece of furniture draped in tattered heavy fabric. And the incense—did I neglect to mention that the air was thick with sickly sweet incense? If the windows had not been open I would have keeled over on the spot.

"We had arrived early in the day. My guides were fed and housed in a considerably smaller and less ornate outbuilding that seemed to be used only for incoming Sherpas. They don't mind this lack of democracy. In their world, some are chosen for this and others for that. It's simply the way they think. They are guides and bearers and they are delighted to handle important and holy personages—they consider it an honor to shuttle them joyfully on their ascended monastic pilgrimages.

"I rested before the evening meal. The monks provided me with a small chamber off the main hall, with a sleeping mat and a surprisingly clean rug to cover myself with. It is now several hours later and there are tall shadows stretching through my window and outside the most heavenly purple light on the mountains. But before I am even fully awake and up and ready to join my hosts in the main hall, I am met at the door by a deferential young novice carrying, of all things, a silver tea set and a cup and saucer like something out of my old aunties' cupboard. The china was mismatched and chipped, and I remember thinking, a little ungraciously, that my aunts would have sent the silver back to the kitchen for a good polish.

"I don't think that there will actually be tea in the pot. I expect some sort of rancid butter concoction and am quite prepared to drink it, already bracing myself for this little act of diplomacy. Imagine my shock when he pours me tea. Actual tea—fragrant, hot, perfectly brewed and steeped to satisfy the most discriminating tea parlor palate. And perfect little sugar and cream servers as well. No doubt the white stuff in the creamer is yak milk, which I don't think my aunts ever served in their parlor, but that's quite all right. I ask no questions.

"I am wondering about all of this and gratefully sipping my tea when I hear a bell just outside my door. A sound out of my former life: a little tinkling dinner bell. 'Dinner is served, Mr. Conway,' a voice says, in English, with painstaking deliberation, as if the speaker had memorized this alien phrase and practiced it over and over for just this occasion."

"I go to the main hall. Seated around a low table on pillows are my hosts, the three older monks, including the ancient one. I see that there are plates and cutlery on the table, again mismatched and chipped and with the forks and knives not quite in their proper places. But it's close enough. And the smells! You can imagine how I have been eating for the better part of a year now. What's wafting under my nose at this moment makes me wonder if I'm in a lamasery in Tibet or standing outside the kitchen door of the finest restaurant in London. I swear that I am smelling roast lamb. Tibetan Buddhists will eat meat when the occasion calls for it, always of course with apologies to the animal's spirit for taking its life and thanks to it for its flesh.

"It's a splendid meal, served Western style with the meat in the center of the platter and vegetables—none that I recognized particularly, roots and leaves of some kind, but they were tasty and spicy and did quite well substituting for potatoes, carrots, and onions—arranged around it. Everything is done to perfection. They even have fresh mint leaves to go with the lamb, and a carafe of dry red wine. More mysteries. I thank my hosts profusely and eat and drink like the half-starved animal that I am while they laugh and laugh with delight. I guess my manners weren't too atrocious, at least not by their standards.

"After dinner they offer me a cigarette, some elegant Russian brand. Very stale, as if it's been sitting in a can since the turn of the century, but delicious. While we are enjoying our postprandial smoke and I am still thanking them profusely and they are still shaking and chortling with pleasure, the ancient lama gets up, springs up, actually, agile as a boy, makes his way over to the draped thing in the corner, and yanks off the cloth like a stage magician. The only thing lacking was a drumroll.

"There was a piano under there. I couldn't have been more surprised if it had been a coach-and-four. An old pianoforte, with open scroll and filigree work and with an ancient ball-and-claw bench tucked under it. Looks as if it had been a fine drawing-room instrument once upon a time in the last century. Dusty and broken down, but still noble. Pieces of veneer and floral marquetry peeling off in the bone-dry air. The folding music stand is still intact, but half the curlicue fret work is broken away. The keys—genuine old ivory—are yellow and cracked like your grandfather's teeth, and the fold-down cover is missing.

"I put my cigarette out in an ashtray with the name of a Bombay hotel on it that's been placed in front of me. Now the old man motions for me to join him. He is ebullient. He is standing over the keyboard picking out little tunes with his index finger like a child, off-key little ululations coming from his raspy throat. I'm still in shock, but I go over to it and join the old man, while the others stay seated. They're all watching, faces full of amusement and digging at the remains of the lamb with their fingers.

"The old man starts to hammer out a beautiful little

étude that's vaguely recognizable. I pull out the bench for him, but he waves it away. He'll have nothing to do with sitting Occidental-style, I guess. I expect he's never used a proper chair in his life.

"He plays this strange little melody until it dawns on me that it's composed of the notes from the wind chimes which I first heard when we were approaching the monastery. I improvise a variation on his little theme to let him know that I'm on to him. He looks up at me with his one black eye and gives me a toothless grin. I grin back. I wonder if they applaud up here. I clap my hands for him, and the others join in, and he's bowing and bobbing in a marvelously funny burlesque of a concert pianist. Soon we are all applauding each other and laughing. It is a wonderfully innocent moment, transcending all barriers of language and culture.

"Then my ancient friend pulls the bench back for me and motions me to sit and play something. The first thing that comes to my mind is the Briac Chopin. So I begin one of the unknown pieces, a lovely nocturne. I haven't played for months and months, of course, so I'm a little rusty at first, but I warm up to it. It is then that I notice that the action and the tuning on that handsome old beast have been perfectly maintained. Another mystery.

"I manage to get through about half of the composition when I stop and the monks begin to applaud me. The piece is not one of the ones I played on the ship for Sieveking, and I am having trouble remembering the rest of it. I'm staring at the keys when the old man moves behind me, leans over with his arms resting on my shoulders, and attacks the rest of the piece as if he were Paderewski himself. Playing with only the first two fingers of each hand, he finishes it. He has completed the work from the exact measure where I left off. I am struck as dumb as if I were carved from stone. He, too, knows Father Briac's Chopin manuscripts . . ."

Conway looked at his cup, raised it, and finished off the brandy. The rest of the story was quick and simple. He had passed the test. The next lamasery he was sent to was Shangri-La. He was home. He found out later that it had been Chang, anticipating his possible return, who had put out the word among the high initiates of the lamaseries in the region after his departure from Shangri-La with Mallinson and Lo-Tsen: Watch for an Englishman with the name Kara-kal on his tongue. If he is the right one, send him on. The last lamasery had been an outpost of sorts, on the route of the trade caravans bringing goods to Shangri-La, and taking a few things out as well. Before Conway was sent on, the ancient piano-playing lama had presented him with a perfect ripe mango. . . .

~

All the vials of concoctions that the physician gave him, all the extracts and serums made from rare roots and leaves and ancient formulae could not have given Conway the strength that the telling of his tale had given him. But now Ma Li could see the deep lines on his sallow face draw tighter. He rubbed his chest and stomach, and she could feel his pain.

Time! There was not enough time.

They rested for the remainder of the day. He slept deeply while she watched him. His breathing was so light and shallow at times that she leaned close to look for a pulse in his neck. When he woke toward evening she could see that for the briefest of moments he was still in his dream, whatever it might have been, and didn't know where he was.

In the next moment, he was there with her. He smiled.

"It's not fair for you to watch me when I'm asleep. It puts me at a terrible disadvantage."

"What about me?" she said, stroking his face. "When you're asleep, you're not with me. You're far, far away, and I can't follow."

"Not so far, not so far. Just around the corner. Besides, we old fellows need our rest."

"You didn't tell me all of your story," she said seriously then. "You didn't tell me what it was that you remembered after the concert on the ship. The part of your life you lost after you left Shangri-La."

He was quiet for a moment.

"Give me one more drink of brandy," he said, "and I'll tell you."

It was late afternoon now. They could hear the noise of a diesel engine idling in the distance, no doubt a Chinese troop carrier. They had both noticed an increase in activity the last two days or so, as if a fresh wave of soldiers had arrived in the city, but neither had said anything to the other.

"I told you that Lo-Tsen and Mallinson were in love. And they managed to be in love despite the fact that they had no language in common. Occasionally I found myself in the odd position of interpreter." He paused again, remembering. When he resumed his narrative, he spoke quietly and rapidly, his words tumbling over one another so that Ma Li saw the events he described as if she were watching an old film where the action is jerky and speeded up.

"The weather was dreadful. Snow in the high country, then rain and sleet at the lower levels. We trekked for days and days, helplessly following our guides. Mallinson wanted to cross over into India, which was so close, but Lo-Tsen wanted to return to her home in China. He argued, but she was adamant, and he capitulated. We came down out of the mountains and began to cross the Tibetan plateau. We'd all been bundled up, of course, so when we hit the plateau and the weather improved we shed some of our heavy skins and such. But Lo-Tsen kept herself wrapped up. She told Mallinson that now that they were betrothed, he shouldn't see her face until they could be properly married. In China.

"He complained a little, but I reminded him that she was, after all, royalty. I was uneasy about her behavior, but kept it to myself. We acquired ponies, and traveled for weeks. She grew less and less communicative. Mallinson became confused and upset, believing that she didn't love him anymore. Again I intervened. She comes from a different world, I told him, a world she wants to rejoin. In her world a man and a woman are often perfect strangers when they marry. The bridegroom lifts a veil on the wedding night and sees his bride's face for the first time. You have already been intimate. She is trying to reestablish some of that propriety. Go along with it. You will be proving your love.

"He did his best, though I could see it was a strain. We were halfway across Tibet, near Gyangtse, when one morning she called out feebly from her tent that she needed water. These were her first words to him in weeks. He took water to the tent. She would not let him in. The sound of her voice made him afraid that she was ill. He begged and argued. Pleaded for her to let him look at her.

"Finally he wouldn't take no for an answer. He

pushed his way in. There were murmurs of distress from her, his voice low and pleading, a few moments of silence, and then he backed out of the tent, his face white with shock. Good God, man, what is it? I said. He could only point at the tent. I bent over and peered into the darkness. Lo-Tsen was not there. In her place was a woman who might have been her great-grandmother. Crying, pulling the cloth back over her face.

"Mallinson and I could not speak. We stared at each other. Lo-Tsen sobbed inside the tent. The nomads we were traveling with stood back and watched. The wind ruffled our hair.

"Then he went berserk. Jumped me, knocked me to the ground, shouting that it was all my fault. I knew there was no logic to it, that he had simply snapped, so I overpowered him and held him down while he ranted.

"He wore himself out quickly. Then he was grasping my jacket with a new fervency. She's ill, that's all, he said. She's caught some dreadful disease. We'll get help. We'll find a cure. You have to help me. Please, Conway, help me!

"Of course, my own mind was reeling. I was in shock no less than he. What had we done? What had I lost? I shouted into his face that we had to turn around and go back. Back into those mountains, he said? Are you insane? She'll die. No. We need a doctor, he said. A proper doctor, not some witch doctor shaking a stick over her. He went and spoke to her through the tent. No, she did not want to go back. Yes, she wanted to find a doctor.

"India, he said. We must go down into India. Darjeeling is almost directly south of here. There'll be doctors. Hospitals.

"I was wild with grief and regret and despair. I

wanted to turn around and start walking back to Shangri-La right then. But I didn't. I could not bring myself to abandon them. Whatever delusion Lo-Tsen was suffering from that made her think she could leave the valley and keep her youth, and that now allowed her to think a doctor could give it back to her, I could only feel compassion for her. And God knows I couldn't blame poor Mallinson. And I could see that they could not possibly make the rest of the journey without my help. The poor boy was unraveling, and she was turning into an old woman. I said I would accompany them to Darjeeling, but that after that I was going to leave them and try to find my way back—though it seemed as hopeless as finding my way back into a dream.

"We traveled south. Lo-Tsen grew older before our eyes, much older than the sixty-five I calculated her age to be. We never made it to India. We stumbled into Bhutan by mistake. Anti-British feeling was endemic there, and Mallinson got high-handed with some tribesmen we encountered. They responded by running him through with a sharpened stick right before Lo-Tsen's eyes. It took him half an hour to die. I talked them out of giving us the same treatment, though just barely. They let us go. We crossed back into Tibet. Lo-Tsen was broken; she said she just wanted to go home. Would I please, please get her back to her home in China.

"Of course, I could not refuse her. She had no one but me. With a heavy heart and with the vision of Shangri-La growing ever fainter behind me, we trekked the rest of the way into China. Somewhere in western Szechuan I caught the contagion that was raging through the province up from Yunnan and Indochina, some tropical bug that drove my temperature up to a hundred and six, I am sure. Dengue fever, most likely. We lodged with farmers along the way, Lo-Tsen mopping my blazing forehead and forcing sips of water down my throat. I went in and out of lucidity; one of the last clear moments I recall was asking her why she didn't catch the fever, too. She said that she was immune: She had had the same fever in the great epidemic of the 1860s. But you were a baby then. How could you have survived? I asked her. No. I was a very young woman, she said. I was not eighteen when I got to Shangri-La, as everyone thought. I was well over thirty. My family had lied about my age to my betrothed. That is why I look like an eighty-year-old woman now, she said, because that is what I am.

"She got me on a train to Chungkiang, where she turned me over to the nuns at the French Mission Hospital. She bade me farewell, said she could get home by herself from here, that I was in good hands. She thanked me, kissed me, and was gone. She was still beautiful, never mind how old she was. I sank down into my fever and slept for days, but before I did I heard the nuns and the doctor discussing the old woman who had brought me in. How sturdy and courageous she was, though she was old, most old.

"When I woke from my long sleep days later, I did not know who I was or where I had been. My mind had contrived to release me from my grief and regret. And that was how Rutherford found me—innocent as a newborn babe."

He was standing near the window when he finished his story. A beam of late afternoon light slanted into the room. She did not speak; she knew that for the moment he was far away. She put her hand to her own smooth young cheek and thought of Lo-Tsen. She wondered if the Manchu princess had been traveling with a mirror. No doubt she had

had a small one in her hastily packed belongings, the kind you carry in your evening bag, just big enough to let you discreetly check your eyes and lips. It was not difficult to imagine her kneeling in her tent on the windswept plateau, anxiously scanning a few square inches of her face at a time in the dim light.

What could her thoughts have been? Had she known that she would wilt and shrivel? Had her preserved youth and long years in the valley been a static prison for her, one she would escape at any cost? Or had she actually believed that she could take that youth and freshness with her? It was certainly possible that she had been a little mad. A young woman on her way to be married finds herself waylaid in a lonely forty-seven-year time warp. Who was to say what had happened deep in her mind?

An air horn sounded nearby, startling both Ma Li and Conway. He turned to glance out the window, and the light caught his face in such a way that the fatigue and illness, which had been smoothed and softened while he was under the spell of his own tale, were starkly revealed, his features and the color and texture of his skin distorted like a manic Expressionist painter's vision of decay and decrepitude. The effect lasted no longer than two or three heartbeats, receding as soon as he withdrew his face from the shaft of light. But she had seen it. She jumped to her feet in a panic.

"You have to go back. Today. Now. We have no more time." She moved briskly, gathering up their meager belongings. She did not look at him. She did not want to see the sadness in his eyes, did not want to lose her momentum and resolve. Her military training served her well in this moment. Move quickly. Do what you know you must do. Sentiment exists in some other world.

He was quiet. He did not interfere. She felt him looking at her while she worked.

"Tonight," she said, still avoiding his eyes. "This is the perfect time. The soldiers will be drunk or asleep. And don't tell me that you feel fine, because I know it isn't true." She yanked the sleeping mat back on the side where he slept, revealing his cache of bottles. "You thought I didn't know about these. Little bits and pieces of Shangri-La," she said, holding a blue-green bottle of pellets up to the light. "Probably sugar pills. Or bat dung," she joked, trying for a little lightheartedness. Still he was quiet. She fussed with her things for a few more minutes. There was pitifully little to do. They carried almost nothing with them. This was it—the material remnants of their life together, their household, their kingdom—a few odds and ends that could be stuffed into a bag in a matter of minutes. No pianos, no books, no silverware, no photos in ornate frames of children, distant summers, or long-dead pets. She kept her head down. She had thought she could outdistance it, but it was right behind her now, breathing hard, pounding the earth. It would be on her in the next moment.

She felt his hand on her shoulder.

"I have a better idea," he said. "Let's wait until dawn. I want to wait for the stars to come out tonight. I'm going to show you the Shambala constellation. I'm going to show you which star is Shangri-La."

∿

They could smell the smoke of a smoldering campfire near the airstrip outside of the city. They had been walking for two hours, and the sun was just sending its first rays over the eastern horizon. They wore the same clothes they had been wearing when they entered the city nearly two weeks before. Ma Li was trying hard to keep her rising alarm at bay; they had slept only an hour or two, and when Conway awoke, he looked as if he had lost another ten years and for a few terrible moments he did not seem to know where he was. He shook it off quickly, and they were on their way, but she cursed herself for not insisting that they leave last night. She had a powerful sense of the exponential progression of time now; minutes were years, hours were decades. His walk was a little slow, a little stiff, as if he were in pain but making a mighty effort to hide it.

And something else was wrong. There had been no response to Conway's coded message that the time had come for him to leave. He was supposed to be met and escorted from the city, but no one had appeared, and so they had no choice but to begin walking, Conway using the last of his strength and with no idea of what they would find. The military presence had grown like a fungus.

They had passed army vehicles, trucks, and troop carriers everywhere in the city as they walked the predawn streets; occasionally they passed a truck with a soldier asleep in the front seat, feet protruding out the window, snoring to the accompaniment of Chinese popular music playing on a radio. As they passed one truck, Conway caught a few words of the lyrics of a song: Oh, my most sweet and revolutionary apple blossom, I renounce all others for you. My worldly goods are few and threadbare, and I renounce them too for you.

They had tiptoed past. The cab of the truck was bathed in a faint greenish light from the portable radio on the seat; the soldier looked no older than seventeen or eighteen; his sleeping face was as smooth and guileless as a baby's, and his rifle lay cradled in his arms.

The smell of smoke grew stronger as they approached the airstrip. They could see the silhouette of the plane in the dawn light. And there was the outline of a tent, which they had expected and hoped for. But there was another shape as well, one they had not even allowed themselves to consider: a military truck, parked at a careless angle as if whoever drove it there was not on official duty but possibly sleeping off a drunk before reporting back to headquarters. And a radio was playing. Quietly, barely audible. Chinese popular tunes.

The plane was tethered about thirty paces from the parked truck. The tent was right next to the truck. Where was Tensing, their pilot?

"Damn and double damn. Wait a moment," Conway whispered to her. Stealthily, he passed the truck, glancing inside it on his way by, and approached the tent. She watched him lift the flap, look inside for a moment, and then ever so gently replace the flap. He was back at her side in a moment, his face blank and grim.

"I'm afraid we have visitors," he said. "Two in the tent. One in the truck. And there's no sign of Tensing." Her heart began to hammer. They had been aware during their time in the city of an increase in the Chinese presence, but only peripherally; they had felt secure in their hiding place, and had been so intent on one another that they had not really grasped the extent of the occupation. And all of them so young. An army of children.

"Well. It's plain what I'm going to have to do," he said. She grasped his hand, which was hot and clammy, and felt tremors running along his bones at intervals like a pulsing electrical current. She had felt the same thing once before in her life, in the hand of an elderly relative in terrible pain from cancer. She saw fine beads of sweat on his forehead, though the morning was chilly.

"You can't," she whispered frantically.

"Perhaps not, but it's what I'm going to do," he answered tersely. "Now help me, there's a good girl. The moorings. And the blocks. I know the tank was full when we left it. Let's hope the gods are with us. If there are any. I'm afraid I'm going to have to ask you to do it. I'm all in for the moment." She looked at him. He was breathing hard from the effort he had just made. His skin looked as if a lightning storm raged just beneath the surface.

In the next moment she was moving across the open space between their cover and the airplane. The craft seemed enormous when she was in the shadow of the wings. She kicked the wooden blocks away from the tires. She went to the tail of the plane and undid the mooring rope there, then came back and fumbled with the rope attached to one of the wings. The tip of the wing was very high off the ground, way beyond the reach of her outstretched arms. She had to pull hard on the rope, which made a loud thrumming noise as it passed through the ring. There was no way to do it quietly, and the sound filled her ears.

"Halt!" came a shout from behind her. She did not turn immediately but finished pulling the rope through. When she did turn, she saw a very young Chinese soldier, hair tousled and face rosy with sleep, looking like a child who has wandered from bed into his parents' party. The difference was that this child pointed a rifle at her.

"Halt!" he shouted again. "Identify yourself!"

She wound the rope with elaborate care as if she were

coiling up a garden hose. Options tumbled through her mind. Two more soldiers, rumpled and dazed and fumbling with their weapons, emerged from the tent. They were privates; she outranked them all considerably. At least, she once had.

"Good morning," she said, still winding the rope. Then she placed the rope on the ground, straightened up, and saluted the soldiers crisply. "At ease," she said then. "And perhaps you can explain why you were sleeping on guard duty." She lifted her nose as if she were sniffing the air. "I smell alcohol." The astonished soldiers stared at the Tibetan woman speaking perfect Chinese. "I shall have to report you, of course," she continued. "I am well acquainted with how it is to be on duty in a foreign place far from your home. You feel that you're on the frontier. The tendency is to let discipline relax. However, you woke quickly, and I shall include that fact in my report to Colonel Kuo," she said, naming a colleague of her father's.

A name the soldier evidently knew, for he lowered his gun a few centimeters. She could hear the other two murmuring to one another. "First Lieutenant Zhang," she introduced herself sternly. "In charge of cultural affairs and special liaisons. You. Private." She turned and addressed one of the soldiers who had emerged from the tent. "Assist me. The rope." She indicated the other wing.

Immobilized by confusion, the youths stared at her, weapons only half raised. "SHALL I BE FORCED TO ADD DISOBEDIENCE TO AN OFFICER TO MY RE-PORT?" she said, projecting her voice in a most unladylike way. "DO YOU WISH TO BE RESPONSIBLE FOR THE FAILURE OF AN INTELLIGENCE MISSION?"

The soldier she had addressed came hesitantly forward. "Untie the rope," she ordered in her most peremptory tone. She turned toward Conway, whom the soldiers had not seen yet. "Major," she said, addressing him by the rank he had held fifty years before. "We have assistance."

Conway stood up from behind the clump of bushes, startling the soldiers badly, and not just with the suddenness of his appearance. Haggard and hooded, he looked like a figure out of some medieval tale of retribution. Even she felt a mild shock. Had he aged in just the few minutes since she had last looked at him? He walked toward her, stiffly, his face in shadow. The astonished soldiers followed him with their gazes, the one with the rifle forgetting his weapon for the moment. When Conway was closer, she saw that his features were set in pain, his eyes not quite focused.

"Soldier!" she said sharply to the youth who had started toward her. "The rope!"

The private, still watching Conway, moved toward the place where the mooring line was tied. He knelt and began to undo the knot. Conway shuffled closer. Ma Li put her hand on the door of the plane, then realized she was unfamiliar with the mechanism that opened it and dropped her hand. The soldier with the rifle raised it again and pointed it directly at them, his face churning with confusion. Conway came to the door, reached up weakly, and released the catch. The door came down like a folding bed, making a staircase to the ground. Conway put a foot on the first step. The soldier aiming the rifle came a few steps closer.

"You must identify yourselves!" he said. Conway turned to look at him for a moment, then turned away and put a foot on the next step. The soldier she had ordered to untie the rope stood still, the rope halfway through the ring, the rest of it hanging slack in his hands. The third soldier, the other one from the tent, had done nothing. He still stood exactly where she had first seen him. The radio in the truck played absurdly: The granaries are full, but not as full as my heart with love for my little soldier.

The one with the rifle had an almost pleading expression now. "Identify yourselves!" he repeated, his voice rising. She turned and gave him a smile.

"Too long away from home, eh?" she said. "Too long away from your girl. Yes. It has been a long time for me, too. I'm not sure that all these love songs are good for morale. Like songs about water when you're in the desert. Not altogether healthy."

She was aware of Conway advancing a few more steps up the ladder, heavily, feet scraping, breathing hard, while she spoke. She moved closer to the soldier with the rifle. "But of course, there are remedies for a lucky few." She put a hand on her hip suggestively, cocking her head to one side. "You are young. I like them young. How old are you?"

The rifle was pointed at Conway, but the soldier, mouth ajar, was looking at Ma Li now. "How old are you?" she coaxed. "I need to know. For my official report. That is," she said, looking him up and down, "if I decide to make one out at all. How old?"

"Eighteen," he whispered. Mentally, she counted Conway's steps behind her. He had to be close to the top.

"Eighteen," she said. "Half boy, half man. So much to experience yet. Smooth and young. Malleable. Eager to learn," she went on mindlessly, not daring to turn to check Conway's progress. My revolutionary dove, together we will fly into the great future, sang the voice on the radio. Together we will fly. She heard Conway reach the top step.

"Ma Li, come with me," she heard him say in English. Still smiling, she turned away from the youth and looked at Conway standing in the door of the plane.

"You know that I can't," she answered. "And don't make me cry in front of these soldiers," she added in a flat voice as if they were discussing weather patterns and flying conditions.

"You can," he said.

"No, I can't."

"Please," he said, mustering a last bit of strength into his voice.

"No."

"Then I'll wait for you. Make your star chart. Put it on a map. Remember the name Karakal. Find a radio. I'll be listening. Ma Li to Govanda, Ma Li to Govanda. If you're close enough, I'll hear you. I'll come and fetch you."

"How long will you listen?" she said, her throat constricting.

"Twenty years. Thirty. Forty. Until I hear from you."

She turned to the soldier holding the rope. "Finish your job. Do as you are told." He yanked the rope the rest of the way through the ring. There were several moments of silence. Then she heard Conway pull the door shut, the metal groaning mournfully, the mechanism of the latch clicking into place with finality. She looked at the youth holding the rifle. "A young man needs a teacher," she said, barely paying attention to what she was saying. She heard the plane's engines cough and fail, cough and fail, then catch with a roar.

She turned and went to the place beneath the pilot's window. Conway opened it and looked down at her. His face was pale and strained with illness.

"Can you do this?" she screamed through her cupped hands. "How long has it been since you've flown a plane?"

He hesitated. "I've never flown a plane," he shouted back. "Not actually."

"What?" She put her hands on the fuselage in a panic, as if she could hold the plane back.

"But lots of practice. A flight simulator. Brought in by Bryant a few years ago. Just like the real thing."

She could think of nothing to say to this. She held her desperate hands on the smooth cold skin of the plane for a few moments while they looked into each other's eyes. Then she dropped her hands with resignation and backed away from the plane. She watched the window snap shut, saw him blow her a kiss.

The throttle roared. The soldiers stepped back out of the way, too, and the craft began to lumber down the runway. It gathered speed, bouncing and roaring, then left the ground smoothly enough. She saw the wings dip from side to side, Conway telling her all was well. It was an astonished group that stood on the ground, Ma Li and the three young Chinese soldiers, watching the elegant DC-3 become a droning speck that finally disappeared into the clouds.

She watched the empty sky for a while before she turned and faced her soldiers.

# ~ 10 ~

They moved in and out of the circle of light, strange shapes and stranger movements like phantoms against the flickering fire. They were General Zhang's soldiers. They spoke softly among themselves as he knew they did all the time now, their heads bowed conspiratorially, murmuring. He didn't always know what they were saying, but the words "crazy" and "mad" and "dangerous" separated themselves from the sub rosa litany.

As the days on the plateau stretched into weeks, Zhang chose now and again to walk back to his tent in the evenings in a purposeful diagonal that took him through clusters of soldiers eating and talking. Lately, whenever he approached a group, the animated hum of conversation would drop to a droning whisper, a sound not unlike the wretched chanting of monks. And when he moved closer, the whispers gave way to silence. There was only the sullen clatter of their mess kits as he walked by.

~

The winds chilled the huddled soldiers and buffeted the tight circle of trucks and rattled the dry grass of the northern

solitudes. These were the final grayish-pink moments of twilight, the dying light closing on the endless expanse and the
low rocky hills. Inside the circle of vehicles, the soldiers
struggled with their first fires of the evening, tossing hunks
of damp wood from the backs of the trucks, wood that they
had carried for hundreds of miles. Days of frustration with
their meager, stubborn fuel supply caused them to play a
dangerous game. Goading each other with shouts and jeers,
they rushed forward and splashed gasoline on the smoldering
logs, dodging the fire as it lashed back, sending flames and
embers skyward.

This game of flame-dodging was the sole pastime left
to the troops, and they did it only when they believed the
general wasn't looking. Zhang had ordered a ban on all card
and board games. Any dice tossed or mah-jongg tiles laid
out would be construed as tantamount to an act of treason.

He had given no explanation to the men, but it was
his belief that games and frivolity would cloud their minds,
corrupt them in some way, weaken them for the final push.
He had a vision of himself and his soldiers preparing themselves with monkish asperity for what had, in his mind, taken
the shape of a mystical quest. But the men were chafing under
the discipline; they had traveled four hundred miles across
the Tibetan plateau, and with every desolate mile they grew
increasingly sulky and morose, like Columbus's crew when
they believed that they were going to sail off the edge of
the earth.

The general had grown irritable too. For the last
several days, his moods had swung violently. Sometimes he
was infused with a sense of purpose and destiny that made
him feel almost holy; at other times he felt merely raw,
irascible, and edgy, swaying on the brink of nervous exhaus-

tion, his actions and decisions Draconian and arbitrary. He never really slept; the corners of his mouth sagged and dark puffy bags grew under his eyes. His characteristic brisk purposeful walk, his trademark in Gyangtse, had become furtive and obsessive, exhaustion molding his face like a stroke.

The men learned to stay out of his way like children avoiding a bad-tempered, unpredictable father. It was not that they were afraid of hardship. They were well equipped for that, and willing. It was not that. It was the increasing vagueness of their mission. It was not as if what they were doing was a logical part of an actual campaign. The more empty the landscape grew, the more resentful and uneasy they became.

They had been nearly three weeks out on the great expanse of the Tibetan plateau, heading north from one tiny ancient monastic village to the next. Some days travel was good, but on other days ice and deep rutted tracks made truck passage slow and treacherous.

It was the time of year that did not even see passing caravans of nomads and herdsmen. The general and his men were approaching the vast redoubt of the Kunlun Mountains that spanned the borders between China and the northernmost provinces of Tibet. They were drawing closer to where the Silk Road, the ancient trade highway that ran for two thousand miles east and west connecting India and China, traveled a high route over mountain passes. Zhang knew that there was a legend about a hidden valley along that trade route, and when his clues pointed him in the direction of the Silk Road and the Kunluns, he was exultant. Nothing was going to stop him now.

The journey had already drained three of the convoy's five fuel-tanker trucks, and the general had ordered them left behind, with their crews, in a way that spoke soberly to the soldiers. He abandoned men and equipment on the empty road, minimally armed, radios all but useless, with no indication that he would return. It seemed as if he were forsaking everything he had known.

~

On the evening of the eighteenth day, after many hours of holing up in his tent, going over his maps and papers, General Zhang had just extinguished the gas lantern that hung from the center pole. His pupils had begun to dilate, adjusting to the soft orange glow of his kerosene heater. That was when he noticed an odd light showing beneath the edge of the rear window flap. He lifted the cloth and peered out into the night.

There was a light in the abandoned hermit's shack on the hill behind them. He decided to call his aide-de-camp, who always remained on call until it was certain that the general was asleep.

The aide's task, usually predictable, had recently become difficult. Of late, staying awake until his superior slept was a problem: The general never slept anymore. He was awake for half the night, cloistered in his tent, lantern burning.

Zhang called the man's name and waited the usual amount of time it took for the major to bundle up.

The aide had his own tent not far from the general's, but it was not nearly so warm. The quartermaster had not allowed for a second kerosene heater to be packed in their stores. But it was not terribly frigid this evening—in fact it was warmish compared to the last few nights—and it should not have taken much time for the man to pull on his long underwear and trundle over to the general's tent.

Zhang waited. Usually the man called out an acknowledgment when the general summoned him. Perhaps Zhang had not shouted loudly enough.

But there was little wind tonight, and their tents were not so far apart. Zhang stood motionless, testing the still air around him for evidence that the silence had been disturbed. He believed that he had called out, thought he could sense the reverberation of his own voice in his head.

Or was he mistaken? He held his breath. The camp was quiet, and he could hear the soft thudding of his heart in his chest. Then he remembered the light under the rear flap of his tent. Instead of calling for his aide again, he lifted the flap a second time and studied the hill and the now darkened silhouette of the abandoned hermit's shack.

The light was gone. Who could have been up there?

They had already questioned the villagers before they pitched camp. They were told that the shack, about a hundred feet up the sloping rocks above the camp, was part of an ancient hermitage, and had been vacant for nearly twenty years. After the death of the old religious hermit who had been there as long as anyone could remember, the villagers had kept the shack empty, regarding it as something of a shrine.

But the general had seen a light. He had watched the soft yellow glow of a lantern or a candle showing through the ragged shreds of window felt, watched it moving about, as if someone carried it back and forth, the light showing through the cracks between the boards.

Was it one of his men? Had there been perhaps an illegal card game in the shack? Was someone taking refuge there? He was about to call for his aide again when he realized that he'd forgotten the man's name. He stood with his lungs inflated and his mouth open preparatory to calling out his aide's name, which he had uttered at least a thousand times, but it was gone. Well, "Major" would do. The loss of memory was only momentary, he was sure. A result of stress and exhaustion. At least he'd remembered the man's rank. He could remember the faces and names of nearly everyone else, the remaining number of trucks in the convoy, the last readings on the maps.

It was, after all, a difficult journey. An odyssey, really. And they were close. Very close now. He could feel it. The clues were dovetailing. Soon he would be able to make it up to his men for all the hardship he had put them through. They understood his need for discipline. Didn't they? Was it excessive? In any case, he would share the prize with them. He would arrange for them to have secreted wealth, too. Surely they deserved that; they had trusted him. He would offer them the best of everything that they found. The first pickings, of course.

Zhang was at the front of his tent again by the door flap. All was quiet outside. He was about to raise the canvas and call his aide when he thought he heard—or felt, he was not sure which—an exhalation of breath behind him, inside the tent with him. He pivoted, quite expecting to find someone standing there, never mind that there was no possible way anyone could have entered the tent.

There was no one, but the feeling persisted. He went to the rear of the tent and lifted the window flap. There was the light in the shack again. It seemed brighter now, as if it had been turned up—an oil lamp? The light moved around as it had before. And the shack was bigger, too, than he had first thought. It had several rooms, and more windows than he had first noticed. He watched the light dim at one window and go bright at another, as if it had passed through a door in a wall.

This called for an investigation.

～

He knew he was nearly up to the shack, but from this point on the path he was unable to see it because of the steep slope ahead of him. The winter air of the high plateau was unseasonably still and warm. He stood and looked down: The dying campfires gave just enough light to define the outlines of the trucks and the figure of a lone soldier walking out onto the grassland to relieve himself. Zhang turned and continued his climb.

Then he was over the rise. The beam of his torch swept along the rocks and came to rest on the door of the old hermit's retreat. It was a surprisingly ornate doorway for so rustic a structure, its weathered lintels and brackets show-ing the faded remains of elaborately painted detail such as he had seen at wealthy monasteries. A conceit of the artisan, perhaps? No doubt some foolishly superstitious notion on the part of the carpenter that his religious efforts would win him some sort of heavenly merit, Zhang reflected with scorn. The lamplight moved again and seemed now to be shining directly out at him through the gaps around the doorframe.

"Hello, who is inside?" Zhang asked loudly, first in Chinese, then in his faltering Tibetan. "Hello. I am General Zhang of the People's Liberation Army of the People's Re-public of China and the Autonomous Region of Tibet." The stream of words, hollow and pompous-sounding to his own ears even as he said them, hung irrelevantly in the black night air. He shook his head, embarrassed at himself. He waited a long moment, his blood pounding in his temples. There was no reply.

He lowered the scanning beam of his torch. He was twisting the lens, widening its focus, when someone answered—a very old voice, in flawless Chinese.

"Please come in from the night, General Zhang of the People's Liberation Army of the People's Republic of China and the Autonomous Region of Tibet."

The tone startled Zhang. It was calm and assured, as if rehearsed. Outside, Zhang collected himself. He raised his torch, noticed that the light had gone dim and orange. Damn. The batteries were new. He tapped it on his palm. The light brightened for a second before dimming to orange again and then extinguishing altogether. He tapped it again, then whacked it hard with the back of his hand. Nothing. The only light in the world now was the lantern glow leaking through the cracks in the wood. He threw the torch down the slope with disgust and pushed the door in.

The light in the room was not what he had expected. There seemed to be no single source, no lamp being carried about. The room was bathed in an even light, with no dark corners or shadows, as if everything had been dipped in a luminous liquid. The place was almost festive. The walls and ceilings were hung with colorful fabric and strings of prayer flags and sacred tankas.

In the front of the room along the eastern wall on a low platform sat an ugly little old man with big ears, draped in faded monkish clothing amid a confused pile of old rugs and cushions. He was eating, noisily, and scarcely took notice of his visitor now that he was inside. He glanced up from his repast and managed a grunt, but that was all. He sipped from a bowl of something very hot. Zhang could see steam rising. Probably that ubiquitously dreadful Tibetan concoction of rancid butter tea, he reflected.

Zhang waited. He felt oddly patient, even serene. The monk would speak when he was ready.

The room was comfortably warm. There were two small braziers full of glowing coals. On the western wall was a small altar covered with a delicate scarf on which some musical instruments rested. Zhang recognized a conch and an oboe hautboy and a skull clapper with a strong resemblance to his Potala skull goblet. To the right of the instruments, silver repoussé offering dishes to the tutelary deities had been set out, filled with the obligatory water and grains and roasted barley meal and placed beneath a small gilded statuette of some deity or other.

The figurine rested on a little shelf also containing a foot-high golden chorten set with jewels. There were rows of unlit candles. Behind the altar and icon shelf hung an elaborate circular mandala. In the adjoining wall was a doorway draped in fabric, light glowing through it from the room beyond. Sleeping quarters? A library or meditation room? He had a sense of many more rooms beyond the one behind the curtain. He found himself studying his surroundings in a way not at all like himself, with unusual passivity and attention to detail.

"Do you think this old man lives well?" Mildly startled, Zhang turned back to the old man, who was sliding his emptied bowl onto a stand beneath the brazier. "It is a good place on the rocks. More splendid than one would imagine from the humble exterior. I am right?"

"It is . . . surprising," Zhang conceded.

"But not as splendid as what you are looking for?"

"I was told this shack was empty."

The old man shrugged. "Does it look empty to you?"

"Where is the light that I saw moving about from outside?"

The old man shrugged. "What does it matter? You see me, do you not? And the altar and the pretty flags and the painted silks? And I am seeing you, General. Quite clearly. And I must add . . ."

"But where is the light coming from, old monk?"

"But where is the soldier going to, old general?" There was a coy gleam in the hermit's eyes.

"What are you saying, monk?" Zhang asked, feeling suddenly defensive.

The old man sighed and shook his head. "Oh, General, General, General. Such a coquette you are. And in that uniform! All right, all right. You and your men are simply . . . sightseeing! Yes. Yes. Camping. Picnicking. It's all very jolly. That's why you won't let them play cards, eh?"

"I . . ."

"Wait!" the old man said. "Something's coming in!" He raised a hand to his ear and made a pantomime of twisting a knob. At the same time he emitted squawks and high-pitched noises like a radio being tuned. Then he did a perfect imitation of a faint, distant electronic voice emerging from the static and interference. "People of Tibet! All your foes have been defeated! Your true leader is among you! He is the Future King of Shambala . . . !" A wave of static cut the voice off. The old man twisted the imaginary knob a little more. He shrugged. "Lost it," he said, and grinned. Zhang stared, stupefied.

"I know what you're looking for," the old man said,

waggling his finger at Zhang as if he were addressing a mischievous child. "Am I right? But such quests don't agree with you, Chinaman. I must say you're looking terrible." Zhang could not even manage a denial. "But many men are looking for Shambala, General. There's no need to hide it! All through history. The ancient sacred books indicate a magical place: A state of mind? A real place? A place that only the enlightened can reach? A place that is hidden, accessible only through arcane clues, a valley hidden deep between the sheerest mountains? A place that opens itself up as a refuge to the worthy before hiding itself again? Like a crack in a rock that seals itself up. Yes, General. But *your* Shambala is called . . . Shangri-La."

For a moment the name buzzed in the air. It sounded familiar. But everything else did, too, as if he were passing through a veritable cloud of déjà vu. The name, himself standing here, the hermit, the moment, all of it. Familiar and strange all at once.

Was the old monk offering affirmation that he was near his goal? What was this word, Shangri-La? The strange-sounding name rolled around in his head and came to rest upon his tongue. He whispered it, cautiously, testing it first. Then he spoke just above a whisper. "Shangri-La . . ." How lush and strange it sounded.

"I think you should see it before you go any farther, General Zhang. Perhaps you will not find it to your taste after all. Yes. Do you buy something from a merchant before examining it?"

Zhang felt tired. He rubbed his eyes for a few long moments, feeling as if he were actually taking a little nap while he did it, eyes luxuriously closed. He had a hard time opening them again. It was just like the feeling he'd had a few times in his life when he was trapped in a dream in the early morning, unable to force his eyelids apart.

When he was able to open his eyes, he was no longer in the shack but standing on a grassy slope a few hundred feet up on the rim of a valley. He could smell the sun-drenched air, a fragrance of wild flowers and new grasses, hot and redolent with the lost summers of his childhood. He felt the gentle fingers of a breeze on his shoulders, caressing the hair on his neck.

He turned around and gazed up the slope toward a stand of trees and towering white peaks beyond. A small herd of gazelles bounded down the hillside, their feet touching only air. They stopped a hundred yards below the general and began to graze unconcernedly along the footpath, lifting their heads, jaws moving from side to side, pricking their ears from time to time, their large black liquid eyes gazing out over the lush green valley.

He could hear the old man's voice, but he couldn't see him. It was as if the monk stood just behind him, speaking quietly over his shoulder and into his ear.

"Do you see the gazelles, General Zhang, and how they come right to the footpath and do not run from you? No one hunts them here."

"Where on earth is *here*?"

"It's what you are looking for, General. But allow me to show you more. . . ."

"Where is this place, how did I . . ."

"Come, General. Let me show you more."

Zhang had no intention of going farther, but he was unable to resist and found himself turning around, once again against his will, to face the mountains. He was sinking, or the mountain walls were rising about him, the craggy summits of jagged rock and ice and lofty snagged clouds were falling away and rising above him at the same time. He was dropping into the valley! And evening dark was settling upon him. He was out of control, and he definitely did not like it. . . .

∼

General Zhang stood on wide marble stairs just below a set of huge bronze doors. On either side of the stairs were magnificent marble carvings and delicate wrought-iron work. There were deer, lion, crane and tortoise, dragons and demons, Chinese and Tibetan iconography peaceably shoulder to shoulder. The stairs ascended toward the bronze door in three broad even flights separated by terracelike landings, each a serene resting place with rails, a fountain, and a tiled pool. The air was warm and scented with flowers, which grew in profusion in stepped gardens along the hillside, encircled by two vast wings of the building.

He stood in the middle of the staircase looking down. It was as if an hour or more of evening had passed in the few minutes he had been standing there. Already the first stars were visible in the darkening purple sky. As the light faded, he noticed something else: a peculiar glow showing through the greenery around the foot of the huge staircase. He wasn't at all sure what he was looking at, and though it was beautiful, he was not sure he liked it.

In a few moments it had become even darker and the glowing phenomenon brighter and more distinct. The stairway, the fountains, and the building all faded in importance. There was only the brightening ravine. In the odd light, the branches of trees became a web of interstice and silhouette. He did not want to look, but he could not help himself. He felt slightly dizzy. His breathing was rapid. The soft breezes cooled his damp skin, causing him to shiver. And the voice in his ear implored him: Look now! Look into the trees! This is Shangri-La!

They were buildings, but he did not feel that they were habitations. These were seamless, solid geometric shapes, like a forest of jewels—cubes and hexagons and cylindrical towers—composed of some translucent material etched on the inside with intricate designs like sandblasted patterns on crystal. It was not like standing in the dark and looking at the warm inviting glow of firelight in a window. Watching these shapes, he felt chilled and vulnerable and utterly ill-equipped to understand what was in front of him, as if he were looking at an alien installation, a colonization from another world, the soulless compound eyes of enormous in-sects. His heart pounded, and he imagined he could hear the sinister hum of machinery from within the glowing shapes.

And now he heard the sound of a thousand wind chimes....

"Enough!" he shouted, and dropped to the ground. He felt dry bristly grass against his chest through the fabric of his shirt. "Enough!"

"Then enough it is, General Zhang," said the old man's voice, and Zhang was raising his head from the wooden floor of the altar room of the shack. The monk had not moved. He was still seated comfortably among his pillows and rugs and sipping from his bowl of hot butter tea.

Zhang would have broken down the walls to get out of there. It was as if the infinite space of sky and plateau outside were crushing in upon the meager space within the hermitage. He turned toward the door and remembered his pistol. He felt down along his hip for the leather case and the heavy weight of his Russian-made Kalashnikov. I should kill the old sorcerer, he thought, closing his hand on the weapon's butt. Then the monk spoke again: It was that same voice that had come from nowhere and everywhere in that mountain valley only seconds before.

"All our actions, General, and all our thoughts, flow like water, their springs buried deep in the mysteries of the past. Everything we do and every consequence is what our sages call the 'force of old actions.' Once you turn down these dark corridors, you don't know what you'll find because you do not know where you've been. Be careful, General, as you approach the . . ."

Zhang did not wait for the old man to finish his nonsense. God, how he wanted to put the old bastard out of his misery—but he wanted out of there even more. He did not even take the time to shoot him.

～

Zhang had not intended any of what happened in the wee hours of that morning. It had simply happened. He went over the sequence of events again and again. He approached every minute of the night before from different angles, replaying everything in his mind. And each time he reached the same inevitable conclusion: For the good of their mission— a mission that would ultimately be beneficial, he told himself, not only to the People's Liberation Army but to the People's Republic of China, although he no more believed in that than he believed in the existence of a beneficent God. But he knew he did what had to be done. Given the tension of the situation, anything else would have resulted in outright mutiny.

No. He had had no choice in the matter: In his

reports, the major's death would be recorded as a casualty, an unfortunate accident, no more. Which, in a sense, it had been. His explanation would fall into place when the time came. There was no need even to rehearse it. For the hundredth time this morning he went over the events of just a few hours ago.

After the bizarre experience in the hermit's hut—an experience he discounted as something to do with mind-altering drugs or hypnotic suggestion—Zhang had stumbled down the hill to the camp. He immediately proceeded to wake up his aide. This time he did not call out to him but went directly to the man's tent.

The major had been sleeping soundly for the first time in days, perhaps due to the unusually comfortable warmth of the evening. When Zhang shook the poor man out of his sleep, he told him only that something strange had happened on the hill by the old shack, something that might be of significance to their mission. But the exact nature of that mission was still a mystery to everyone, including the aide, whom he ordered to dress and to accompany him first to the village by jeep.

The major had a working ability with spoken Tibetan, much better than the general's. Zhang wanted to talk to a farmer named Tsondup who had innocently and good-naturedly offered his services when the convoy had arrived the day before. Tsondup was the one who had told them about the abandoned shack and who knew something about the hermit who had lived there for so long. And he had been patient with the major's halting Tibetan. They found his hut and woke him—rather, his dog woke the whole village as the general and his aide approached.

And though they had got him out of bed in the dead

of night, when Tsondup recognized the Chinese officers at his door he was cheerful and cooperative. The general didn't say anything about his experience on the hill. He merely informed him that he, Tsondup, had been temporarily recruited into the service of the Chinese army. The major assured him that he would be able to return to his family and animals in a few hours.

It was between 3:00 and 4:00 A.M. when they climbed the hillside to the shack. Empty for fifteen or twenty years, Tsondup said again and again. The general did not respond. He hadn't even told his aide anything about the purpose of this predawn expedition. It was plain that the aide was apprehensive; while the villager chattered away innocently, the major didn't speak at all except to translate for the general.

When they were nearly to the hermit's hut the general told them how he had seen a light in the hut as he was getting ready to retire. He said he had gone up to investigate, and had been surprised to find it not only inhabited but lavishly well appointed. He said nothing about the peculiar experience of finding himself in a strange valley, which would have been embarrassing to relate, but thought to himself that returning with two companions might somehow make him less vulnerable to the old man's trickery, the hypnotism or projected hallucinations or whatever they were.

The shack was dark when they reached it. He whispered to the two men to watch out, that the hermit was a sly old dog, to keep an eye on him.

He put his hand on the door and it swung inward on utter blackness with no resistance at all. The air inside smelled parched and deserted, ancient and dusty. Like a tomb, he thought, and switched on his torch.

The thin shaft of light revealed rotting beams and a

littered mud floor. No brightly lighted chambers, no colored banners, no tankas, no altars, no pillows. Nothing. And most of all, no old man. And it was plain that it had been many long years since anyone at all except birds and rodents had set foot here. Zhang felt the bristly hairs on the back of his neck rise, and a thin chill walk up his spine. The aide and the farmer said nothing, as if this was exactly what they expected. Their silence enraged him. They had never believed a word of what he had told them.

While they stood looking at the heap of rubbish and the rocky uphill slope showing through a gaping hole in the rear wall of the shack, the fullness of their conspiracy entered his gut like a spike. Hadn't everyone been whispering behind his back about his crazy secret obsession? The situation had become too risky. His men were on the brink of mutiny already. Now word would spread that the general was suffering delusions. What he had to do was clear. There was a good wind up now. He extracted a cigarette from the packet in the breast of his jacket. Then, patting and rifling his pockets for his missing lighter, he reached down and in one smooth premeditated motion released his pistol from the leather holster at his hip, took aim, and shot the poor Tibetan farmer and the faithful major before either had time to register any reaction.

~

He knew where they were going. It was all making sense. Everything was right. The last clue had taken them northwest of Lhasa vertically across the Tibetan plateau toward the Kunluns and the Silk Road. He went over his calculations a hundred times until he was satisfied. He saw where they were pointing him, and exulted. Legend and reality were becoming one.

He repacked the back of his personnel carrier that morning with a renewed determination, rolling his notes and papers, his precious cipherings, in heavy felt and stuffed them down deep behind the metal-framed seat. He had had no sleep at all, but everything that had happened on the hill last night was behind him now. Events had been unfortunate but expedient. He felt surprisingly refreshed, and for the moment possessed the calm certainty that he held the world in his arms.

He rewrapped the Potala skull goblet in a protective layer of thick felt, rolled it carefully back up into his duffel bag, and pushed it down behind the seat with his papers. He was ready.

For those few to whom a detailed explanation might be necessary, his story was simple: A quick but tragic end had befallen his aide. Having gone up the hill with him the night before to investigate the shack for reasons of security, the man fell to his death. The poor major slipped from the narrow path on some loose shale and plummeted into a gorge which lay on the far side of the hill. His body was unrecoverable. As for the farmer, no explanation was necessary. In the scheme of things, the death of one more Tibetan was scarcely worth the trouble of making a report.

I fired my pistol into the air, Zhang whispered to himself, rehearsing his tale. But no help came because a fierce and sudden wind had risen, buffeting the camp so that no one could hear the shots. We went alone, and we didn't tell anyone else where we were going. A mistake I much regret.

⁓

The caravan of trucks and soldiers set off again. The general settled deep into the broken springs of the troop carrier's seat and never gave another thought to the empty seat next to him.

They had gone only another forty or fifty kilometers across the grassy trails with the foothills of the Kunlun Mountains rising like a gray wall ahead of them. Every number, every azimuth, every note pointed their way through a narrow mountain pass which began in the saddle of low hills ahead. The contour maps on his lap verified that much. But beyond that point, they were not very accurate. The canyons and mountains beyond the hills were not well charted.

Zhang was about to remove another map from its packet to verify their direction with the compass when he heard the horns sounding and saw the headlamps of the troop carriers flashing behind his vehicle. His driver immediately stopped and at the general's command began to turn around. They bounced over the rutted earth off the trail and pulled up to the first carrier in the line. By now all the trucks were stopped in a long row. And there was nothing but the sound of engines idling in the silence.

"What's happening back there, soldier?" the general called up to the driver as men climbed down from the transports. There was shouting at the rear of the convoy. The commotion was coming from somewhere behind the weapons carrier.

"Sir, one of the fuel-tanker trucks broke an axle."

"Abandon it," Zhang said tersely. Their destination could not be much farther. Besides, the map pointed to deep canyon lands ahead. They would be forced to abandon the trucks and set out on foot very soon in any case. "Top off the tanks in the convoy and see if the other tanker truck has any capacity left." Zhang looked up and down the convoy line from his window and was just about to pull his head back inside when the driver responded.

"Sir, we had better do that fast. The petrol's pouring out."

"What?"

"Sir, a tank was punctured when the axle broke. They're trying to stop it up, but ... Sir?" the man said, taken aback by a sudden look of shock and pity on Zhang's face.

It was an instant of cinematic clarity. Just like the evening before in the hermit's cabin, he could see and hear everything. First the earsplitting thunder of the explosion, then the awful screams of soldiers who had been standing too near at the moment that the convoy was bathed in a brutal swirling miasma of heat and light.

"Sir?"

Zhang looked up and down. For a heartbeat, the aftermath of the vision held, then wavered as if distorted by rippled glass before vanishing altogether.

Nothing had happened. The convoy was undisturbed.

Zhang leaped from the car. "Have everyone move away from the tanker. Now! Everyone! Everything as far away as possible. Move!"

Then he was in his seat, the driver looking down at him, still waiting for him to say something. His words, which he thought he had shouted, were still in his mouth, formative pressures against his tongue and teeth, not yet uttered. It was exactly like the moment when he had raised his head from the floor of the hut. He grabbed for the door handle. He would get out.

"Sir?" the lorry driver tried once more to break in on the general's troubled silence.

Then, as if time had stuttered, from behind and all around, the air cracked with light and explosion. The grassy stretches reverberated. Screams shattered his ears. The tanker truck had gone up just as he had seen it only a moment before. And even before the screams had subsided, he saw a clear vision of himself pushing forward, with only half the convoy, draining the fuel from the remaining trucks and leaving half the men to nurse the injured and bury the dead and wait out the long days until assistance arrived.

He could think only of Shambala, and how his dream had given it a name.

# ～ 11 ～

## Peking city limits, early spring, 1967

The train halted abruptly, hurl-
ing Lieutenant Colonel Huang Ho-she rudely onto Sister.
They toppled to the floor, and for moments the two lay
compromised, distant cousins sprawled in a tangle of arms
and legs in the littered aisle of a Peking coach car. The
hissing rush of steam from the great black locomotive ahead
was like the long constricted breath of the monster closing
around them. Ma Li struggled to get up, pushing at the heavy
forearm lying across her chest.

"I am sorry, Little Cousin," the lieutenant said, holding her firmly to the floor as angry voices rose outside the
car. "Stay down low. If you want to stay alive, that is."

The lieutenant leaned over and took hold of the general's arm, pulling him off his seat and down onto the floor
with them. Outside, the jeers and shouts grew louder. Cadres
of Red Guard youth were rallying to the accompaniment of
bullhorns and accordion music, and now, bright red armbands
flashing, had begun a human roundup. Loudspeakers played
martial music to the constant chronicling of heroes and enemies of the state.

General Zhang crouched on the filthy coach floor a

few feet from his daughter. He was unconcerned with what was happening outside, like an autistic child in his own world. He did not even seem to mind being yanked rudely to the floor by the lieutenant colonel. Getting his attention these days meant grabbing his shoulder, shaking him, and speaking forcefully into his one good ear.

He had been in a hospital east of Peking ever since his return from Tibet a few months before. The doctors finally released him, saying that he had at least calmed down enough so that Sister could take him home. With the help of her cousin the lieutenant colonel, Ma Li had chosen a remote village in a distant western province for them to go and live in, as far away from the center of government and the reach of ideology as she could get. And close to the Tibetan border. That was her little gift to herself. She had vowed to stay with Father for the rest of his life, and the doctors had said that he was in excellent physical health. She knew that she might be an old lady before her obligation to him was fulfilled. When it came time for her to set out for Tibet, she did not want it to be too far away. When they boarded the train the day before, she told herself that this was the first leg of her journey back to Shangri-La.

For most of the trip the general had sat staring out the window, though it was unlikely that he focused on anything outside. Sometimes he talked to himself in a soft voice: arguments, orders to his men, warnings, reprimands, encouragement . . . sometimes he wept and remonstrated, his voice high, faint, and strangled as if he were dredging up his worst regrets and reliving them. She listened sometimes, but felt quite shut out from whatever drama was playing itself out in the privacy of his mind.

The night before, a hundred miles out of Peking, she

had been half asleep in the seat behind her father. He was awake, looking into the opaque blackness beyond the train window, talking, in a voice just above a whisper. She had been dozing, not paying close attention, when a word he spoke brought her to full wakefulness. She was not entirely sure, once her eyes were open, whether she had dreamed the word or whether her father had actually spoken it, but it was many hours before she could go back to sleep: Shangri-La. She thought he had said Shangri-La.

Lieutenant Colonel Huang was one of the few connections in the army that she and Father could still trust without reservation. A distant cousin, Huang was orphaned when his family tried to escape from Shanghai during the Japanese occupation; he had been boarded with an elderly aunt and occasionally with them during his schooling.

And now, with so many peculiar rumors on the military grapevine, the lieutenant colonel had sought them out when he heard of the general's return from Tibet. He caught up with them, surprising them at the hospital. You are going to need an escort when he leaves here, he had said. The political climate is not good. I will go with you. When the time came, knowing that they must pass through Peking, he had contacted a friend on the police force, who had promised his assistance in case there should be trouble. It was the lieutenant colonel's way of repaying old kindnesses.

The first thud was a stone cracking the window a yard above their heads. Was it intended for them? Then came a volley of eggs, hurled with force against the thick window glass. The glass ran thick with yellow yolk, and now something else. Blood. Pig blood, most likely: the Cultural Revolution's universal symbol for the bourgeois parasite.

When the pelting ceased, Huang released Ma Li with

a cautionary finger pressed to his lips. He rose to his knees, bringing his head up just high enough over the seats to peek out at the crowd around the platforms and on the tracks.

"Quite a greeting. This is the world of chaos you return to," he said.

Sister tried to raise her head to see for herself, but Huang pushed it back down. "I would keep my head down. And keep your father still, unless you want to get us all shot." Feet tramped by them at eye level as the car emptied.

The train lurched forward, hissing and groaning. A cloud of hot steam enveloped the car and the train came to another violent stop, still alongside the platform. They could not have made more than a halting seventy-five feet or so inching forward past the obstacles on the tracks. Just in front of the big black locomotive a group of placarded, dunce-capped old men and women were being herded along by a gang of adolescent Red Guards. They stumbled along the tracks wearing around their necks crude hand-calligraphed advertisements of their "crimes."

A knot of white-jacketed policemen forced their way through the crowd and pushed aboard the train. Five officers noisily entered the empty coach car. One of the policemen caught Huang's eye as he and Sister and the general huddled low in the aisle. The officer quickly averted his eyes. He dispatched his comrades, telling them to search the forward cars.

Lieutenant Colonel Huang recognized his friend. He had been right to plan ahead. They would not get through the dangerous maze of Peking's anarchy without help. With the other police officers moving forward of their car, Huang's friend looked carefully about him before approaching the three in the aisle.

"Ho-she . . . Lieutenant Colonel Huang Ho-she. It is good to see you still alive. Even though it has only been a few days. We learn to take nothing for granted now," he whispered. "But we haven't much time. They are looking for the general. They heard that he boarded this train somewhere east of the city. I told them they were mistaken, that he had left by another route days ago. We are lucky that they do not have a picture of him. There are new *dazibao*, public denunciation posters, up all over the city, and the general's name is high on the list."

"What!" Sister exclaimed. "But why?"

"It comes from the very top," the policeman whispered. "The rumor is that he failed to deliver something that was promised to the Chairman. That makes him a traitor. An enemy of the state. He has been declared a fascist with old leanings. Things are not good. Not good. Last night crowds of Red Guards stormed Zhongnanhai's Gates of Magic Light. They've seized the Old Palace Headquarters, looking for 'corrupt old leadership.' That is the current battle cry, and I am afraid your father has been put in that category. The Chairman and his heir, Lin Piao, have fled to their luxurious Huangchou retreat while their Red Guard henchmen do their dirty work up here. And now I must go. I have already talked to you for far too long. Stay down."

He straightened up and hurried to join his comrades before they suspected anything.

Huang pushed himself up so that he was eye level with the window. His friend had been right. Posters were everywhere, rattling in the breeze, fresh new paper naming fresh new enemies covering over the old, tattered ones.

He lowered himself down again. "We will simply stay

down until the train moves beyond the city. And we must be careful, too. Our proximity to the general will contaminate us by association as enemies of the state."

She knew it was true. A great violent purge was under way. Old leaders, their wives and children, left to the tender mercies of the Red Guard under the "leadership" of the Chairman's wife, his head of propaganda and secret police, K'ang Sheng, and his secretary, C'hen Po-ta. She crouched on the dirty floor, her heart hammering, and concentrated on the footprints and flattened cigarette butts inches from her nose. Had she ever stood on the pavilion in the Valley of the Blue Moon and smelled the perfumed breeze?

There was another lurch. Huang's police friend must have done some fancy talking outside. They were moving again, and this time the train did not stop.

They relaxed as the train gathered speed. They climbed back into their seats when they were sure they had left the crowd and the placards behind. Huang sighed. "What happened to him out there? You have never told me. What do they mean, he did not deliver? All I heard was that they found him wandering about in some godforsaken wasteland with only a few of his men and no weapons. They were incoherent. They couldn't tell us anything. All they could do was weep. No one knows anything at all." He shook his head, watching her impassive face. "What happened? Tell me. Anything."

Sister studied her father's face for a moment before turning to her cousin. "I have no idea." She shook her head. "Absolutely no idea. Do you think he tells me? I can assure you he does not." Then she turned and looked out the window at the flat gray city outskirts rushing by.

# Huangchou: the same day

"So. No one knows anything." Ch'en Po-ta's voice was nervous and high-pitched with anger and suspicion. K'ang Sheng turned and faced the window of the Huangchou retreat, hiding the angry flush on his cheeks. "You tell me that no one knows anything," Ch'en Po-ta went on. "You expect me to believe that? Eh?"

"I don't care what you believe, Secretary Minister Ch'en Po-ta," K'ang Sheng said and spun around. "Perhaps it is that the Chairman once again cannot relieve his bowels. It makes him testy and difficult. He is not rational."

"That statement could cost you your life. And have you branded a counterrevolutionary, and every member of your family in the process," Ch'en Po-ta taunted. "We are in a crisis for power. A crisis for power," he enunciated.

"It doesn't matter *what* one says anymore, does it, Master Po-ta? Anything can brand one a traitor in our Great Proletarian Cultural Revolution. We who did our part in stirring up the nests of Red Guard bees might now be stung ourselves. You too."

"Let us not change the subject. What of the Chairman's Shambala? Am I to simply dismiss it as part of his addiction? The opium speaking? The morphine monkey on his back? Eh? How convenient. Or is there something else? What do you know, and what are you hiding?"

"He is a crazy old fool, Ch'en Po-ta. This Shambala business is the last straw," K'ang Sheng sputtered and threw up his hands. "He pushes this country into a hole, right to the brink, with his maniacal wife and his Red Guards and with us. Oh, yes, we help him. Let us not pretend that we don't. You and I. And while our Red Guards tear old leaders from their homes and beat them with sticks, Successor Lin Piao goes into his states of delirium. The morphine monkey is on Lin Piao's back as well: The sounds of the streets become too strident for his ears, the daylight too bright for his eyes. And the Chairman, with him, sits back on his cushioned toilet and both of them are seeking, like men obsessed, a fountain of youth. That is *all* it is and you are a gullible fool like them if you think there is anything more."

K'ang Sheng leaned forward emphatically while he spoke, his face so close that his dry acidic breath warmed the hairs on Ch'en Po-ta's chin. "A dying Chairman wants his youth, and his heir apparent wants the power of renewal. Think of it, Master Po-ta. Form the picture in your mind. Shambala." He spat the word out with disgust. "Is there nothing more pathetic? They cannot let go of the reins of power. They want after some foolish notion of immortality. A magic land, a paradise of restoration—something they saw in an opium dream, no doubt." He scrutinized Ch'en Po-ta then, twitching his nostrils in an appraising way. "And you, Mr. Secretary. What am I smelling? Are you beginning to smell like a sour old man yourself? Is it your vanity? Are you in on the madness, too?"

"Feh! What nonsense. My interest is purely tactical. And by the way, I still don't believe you, K'ang Sheng. What of the millions you and your wife have salted away from the plunder of Tibet—the art and treasures? You, not I, are the one who would have reason to withhold the truth of a hidden land. Imagine the wealth in that hidden valley. The mythic beauty. The mythic *riches*. What have *you* learned of this Shambala? What have *you* learned of this top-secret search, I would like to know?" Ch'en Po-ta narrowed his eyes. "You can lie to others, but not to me. You have hidden everything.

What happened to the general. What of this Zhang, our general of occupation? Eh? There are reports that he returned, alone, barely coherent. But from where?"

"He was not alone. There were a few soldiers with him," K'ang Sheng said with a dismissive wave of his hand, and Ch'en Po-ta thought that his colleague now seemed to tremble with the effort of his lies. He was so very unconvincing as he continued. "They were not paraded through the streets. They were too crazy and pathetic. There was no secret land, there were no riches. The rumor is that they were captured and tortured, brutally, by Khamba rebels in the far northwestern foothills and only a few escaped. And those who did could tell us nothing more. That is what we know, Mr. Secretary," K'ang Sheng declared and turned away.

Ch'en Po-ta seized K'ang Sheng's shoulder and aggressively pulled him around to face him. "Liar." He leaned close to K'ang Sheng and breathed on him the way K'ang Sheng himself had done moments earlier. "Why do I not believe you? Perhaps because you make such a valiant effort to sound sincere."

K'ang Sheng pulled away indignantly. "You are the liar, Ch'en Po-ta. You fabricate all of this. You exploit rumormongering to create a political issue."

Ch'en Po-ta snorted. "I know about the long secret hours you have spent with the Chairman and Lin Piao. I know that our General Zhang did not appear in Peking. He did not show up with his daughter and his lieutenant. He was not on the train because he has come down here to you and Mao, instead. Eh? Where are you hiding him?"

"You are a crazy man, Ch'en Po-ta. You have become as crazy as they. You are deluded. You have spent too much time believing your own lies. There is no secret land. There is no Shambala. There was no search. And there is no General Zhang here."

"He is here and you are lying," Ch'en Po-ta said, stabbing the air with his finger. "And furthermore, he has brought you the secret maps." Ch'en Po-ta lowered his finger and leveled his coldest, most lizardlike stare at the head of Mao's secret police. K'ang Sheng stared back.

"You are the liar, Ch'en Po-ta."

"No, K'ang Sheng, it is you."

## Yunnan Province, 2007

My father died yesterday, quickly, quietly, and without a struggle.

Finally he had someone besides his daughter to listen to him; someone who had come a long way to hear *him*, his tale, and nothing else. Someone with an open mind. Someone who did not judge or jeer. It was the first time that I had heard the entire story from beginning to end. Up to now, I had had to be satisfied with pieced-together fragments. So when he spoke at last to the young man, he was really speaking to me.

Listening to him, it was a bit like being a child again, hearing one of his stories of ancient Chinese warriors and magical quests. But this time, it was no nursery tale.

My father's death was merciful when it came. I was reminded of the legendary warriors of his tales who fought their way through the underworlds of demon kings and horrendous ghosts to finally lay down their swords. Sometimes nature grants us mercy.

~

The young scholar left me a portable solar-powered tape player and a copy of the tape he had made. I listen to it again, wanting to hear the tale of my father's journey to the other hidden land one more time. He is gone, but his voice, lucid and strong, fills my little room:

~

"I knew that the explosion of the truck was an obstacle thrown in my path by the gods. And I came through the inferno like a vessel fired in a kiln—set, hardened, tempered. Nothing was going to stop me. I took the increasing difficulties as a sign that I was almost there. I knew the mythical tales of searchers undergoing punishing tribulations before entering Paradise. I knew of the tests of wit, the convoluted and deadly riddles, the encounters with ferocious beasts that stood before the gates of heavenly places. It all seemed right to me. I was twice as determined as before, and though the men were on the verge of mutiny, I brought the whip down on their backs. Some of you will have no choice but to stay right here, I told them. The rest must come with me.

"But first I lightened my load. I reduced our cumbersome caravan to three vehicles: mine, the remaining tanker truck, and a single troop carrier. The rest I abandoned. A select handful of my best soldiers rode in the troop carrier. As for weapons, aside from what my soldiers carried I abandoned everything except one mounted machine gun and a rocket launcher. We scavenged the other carrier for tires and parts that we might need later. We moved with alacrity and efficiency. I was thankful for the explosion. It had cost some lives, but we were a lean, tight, galvanized unit that finally moved out toward the foothills that lay ahead.

"We were just south of the rocky ground of Lake Yaxier. We had passed Takenake, Jituo, and Lazhulong. The winds that had muffled my gunshots on the hill the night before had subsided so that we experienced again a peculiar warmth and stillness.

"In a sense, we were exactly like Columbus and his men approaching the limit of the known world. There was no indication on our maps of what lay beyond the next foothill ridge: The large-scale maps simply showed the usual geologic folds and creases with no specific details. The small-scale relief maps simply stopped at about this point. We were about to enter unsurveyed territory, as so much of the Kunluns are, and the feeling was very much like approaching the edge of the earth.

"We drove the trucks as far as we could, abandoning them on the side of a trail on a steep ridge. We were now some fifty miles northwest of Lazhulong as the crow flies. We bartered for pack animals with some nomads and loaded the beasts' wide backs with the heaviest of the equipment. There were now twenty-five of us altogether, carrying on our own backs what we could manage of the rest of the weapons, ammunition, radio equipment, charts, maps, food, and supplies.

"We were now at least three ridges in from the flat of the plateau, each of these foothills higher than the last. The mountains still loomed like a white wall far in the distance. I assumed that another plateau lay between the low hills and the mountains, and I decided to reconnoiter. I took the rucksack, containing both the Potala skull goblet and my notes and clues, two compasses, and a complex ship's sextant with which I had become quite competent at shooting the endless night skies, hoisted it onto my shoulders, and began to climb. I did not trust these things to anyone else. My newly appointed aide carried the weapons and ammunition for the two of us.

"By the time we reached the top of the ridge, we were aware of the inadequacies of our maps. Instead of another plateau, we were shocked to find a vast, forbidding canyon land stretching before us to the horizon, with the mountains in the far distance.

"In China, my people have a long tradition of observing the behavior of animals as a way of foretelling the immediate future. The restlessness of geese and sheep, deer and fox, horse and cow, dog and cat can warn us of an impending earthquake, hurricane, tornado, a sneak attack by an invading army or the presence of spirits. This was why I had the yaks shot when they balked, white-eyed with terror, refusing to climb the trail to the top of the ridge so that we could descend into the canyon. Many of the men had come from peasant backgrounds, and the animals' fear was infecting them. I could not allow it. I had the equipment moved from their backs first; then I ordered my aide to draw his pistol and put them out of their misery. He did, but what happened next was even worse for the men to see than the recalcitrant pack animals.

"I had chosen this man to be my new aide because he was the oldest and most experienced, and the highest-ranking officer next to the late lieutenant. Imagine my reaction when this officer, whom I knew to be manly and an experienced soldier, dropped to his knees after he had shot the last animal, his face crumpling like an infant's, and fell weeping upon the carcass.

"I ordered him to stand up immediately, but he merely raised his red, wet face to me, blubbering about a buffalo that had belonged to his family years ago, that he had loved the animal, that his father had killed it when it injured itself, that he, a small boy, had hidden his grief, because to the rest of the family the animal was no more than a farm implement, that he had had to eat the flesh of his friend because of course the family was not going to waste the meat. Now, all these years later, on that desolate ridge, his pistol still warm in his hand and another animal dead at his feet, his grief erupted.

"I drew my pistol. My hand twitched with the desire to put a bullet in the back of his head and leave him there with the yaks, but the eyes of all the men were on us. Instead, I fired the gun into the air, shocking him into silence, then ordered him to his feet with a firm kick.

"As we began our descent down the steep hill, I took a final compass reading because the walls of the canyon would eventually block out our lines of sight. We thought we would mark out the prominent features in the canyon, noting their locations and directions since our maps were now useless. I decided that there must be some heavy iron deposits in the canyon walls, because the compass needle spun uselessly as we descended. Very well. I still had the sun in the sky to guide me.

"No one talked as we descended into the canyon. The tall, solemn rock formations, shaped by wind and water of vanished centuries, discouraged conversation. We were entirely on foot now, carrying only food, gear, rifles and pistols.

The rocket launcher had been jettisoned along with the vehicles long before; making my way down the steep, rocky trail just after the incident with the yaks, I remembered how I had looked back over my shoulder at the abandoned equipment and felt something akin to pity for it; I remembered thinking that the headlights of the trucks looked like the eyes of a dog that has been ordered by its master to stay behind.

"Get a grip, I told myself. You too are slipping. This is exactly what they train out of you in boot camp: flabby, wallowing, self-indulgent womanish sentiment. I stopped then and, in full view of the men, took off my boots, scooped up a handful of gravel, put it in the boots, put the boots back on my feet, and yanked the laces tight. I stood up. The men stared at me; I looked fiercely into the eyes of each of them before turning and resolutely resuming the descent.

"We walked in silence for several hours. My feet became numb, though I could feel my socks moist with blood inside my boots. Good, I thought. A little mortification of the flesh is what I need. And I knew that I had made an impression on the men. Their customary silence had a new and refreshing quality: They had been cleansed of their sullenness once and for all.

"We kept the sun to our left, though it disappeared from view as the afternoon wore on and we descended to the canyon floor. Now we walked through long purple shadows and pockets of chilled air like the breath of a basement or a tomb. The rock formations far above us took on the aspect of huge heads tilted toward the sky in various attitudes of attentiveness, as if they were listening for signals broadcast from another world.

"When we reached a flat, sandy expanse, I declared that this was where we would camp for the night. We cut brush for our fires and pitched our tents; the men relaxed a little when the first fire was lit and they stood near its warmth and glow, smoking cigarettes and heating their food. They talked and even laughed once or twice, though they became quiet when they saw me.

"I felt benign and fatherly. My best men, and I had brought them this far, through terrible hardship, on the greatest quest of their lives. Of course it was not easy. Of course it was necessary to discipline them by whatever means I thought necessary. I took a walk through the camp, saying nothing, merely making my presence known; they knew and I knew that the gravel was still in my shoes. There was no need to speak. I retired to my tent, spreading my bedroll on the rocky ground. I lay down without taking off my boots; my feet throbbed gently with every beat of my heart. I watched a tiny patch of black starry night sky through the open ceiling flap and thought about the infinite universe. I did not feel small looking at all those stars; I felt huge, as big as the world, and full of purpose. My sleep was light and fitful, like the sleep of an overexcited child on the eve of a great adventure. I woke at dawn, stiff and tired but full of impatience to get moving again, only to be told by my first officer that the men were in bad shape, that none of them had slept at all.

"Something had kept them awake, and they could not agree on what it was or even what direction it had come from: Some of them swore it was a baby crying, some said it was a woman singing, others declared that it was music, a flute or an oboe, and one man said that it had been the whine of heavy machinery—agonized, like a saw cutting through metal. He was in the worst shape of all of them— taut, jumpy, bug-eyed, flinching at the slightest scrape of metal against metal as we broke camp. The men argued about what they had heard until I ordered them to desist. There will be no more discussion, I said. Whatever you heard was distorted by winds and echoes, not to mention the power of suggestion and your overwrought imaginations.

"We broke camp. I had put away my compass the day before, but as we were about to begin our march I had an inspiration. I drew the instrument stealthily out of my pocket. The needle spun in a random way at first, but I held the compass calmly in my hand and waited. Sure enough, the spinning eventually settled into a rhythmic pulsation. Like a heartbeat. Like something alive.

"Like something alive. I smiled a slow smile as the revelation bloomed in my mind. You *are* alive, aren't you? I said. Pretending to be mere dumb matter, opaque, inert, and blind. Patiently enduring. Watching, listening, waiting. But I see you. I see you!

"And the needle pulsed in response, perceptibly excited. Yes, it said. Yes. I am alive. I was waiting for you to discover that I am alive. And I will tell you which way to go. You are almost there.

"There it was. The final clue. Still smiling, I looked up from the compass. The men were standing in ragged formation, packs on their backs, rifles on their shoulders, watching me intently, waiting. Fatigue and unease were plain on their faces. I wanted to comfort them. I felt as if they were my children. I kept my smile. We are almost there, I said. Almost there.

"We marched all day, following the course indicated by my compass: If I held it calmly and patiently in my hand, the needle eventually settled into a lazy but definite one-hundred-eighty-degree swing. My strategy was simple: We walked in the direction that lay midway in the needle's swing, the apex of the arc. I knew that this was what it wanted me to do. After a while I put the compass away. I did not need to look at it anymore. Instead, I allowed myself to be guided by a more subtle indicator: I could sense its satisfaction and approval when I went in the right direction. I tested it. If I turned slightly to the left or to the right, I felt a tangible little wave of annoyance emanating from the instrument in my pocket, exactly the way a husband feels in his viscera what his wife is thinking, whether she is angry or pleased with him, with no words spoken. I could barely contain my glee at this discovery.

"In fact, I did not contain it. I laughed and shook my head as we walked. Then I thought that this must look peculiar indeed to the men. I turned, smiled, pulled the compass from my pocket, and was about to explain to them what I had discovered, but I changed my mind when I saw the expressions on their faces. At the same time I felt a small warning tingle from the compass. I put it back in my pocket. Never mind. They would know everything soon enough.

"After another hour or two we began to see vegetation. Nothing much at first—a tuft of grass here, a spindly weed there. I was elated. Farther on, water trickled down the rocks, with occasional flowers growing from clefts in the sheer walls. The air became sweet, and gradually the vegetation increased until there was a carpet of soft green grass under our feet and clouds of newly hatched insects in the slanting shaft of sunlight reaching us on the canyon floor. We found a pool about the size of a bathtub at the base of a small waterfall. The men looked at it with such pathetic longing that I took pity on them and declared that this was where we would camp tonight.

"It was a mild, clear evening. The men bathed, built their fires, ate, smoked, and relaxed. They were not quite so wary of me, and they seemed to have forgotten the unpleasantness of the night before. An animal, no doubt. You could hear anything you wanted to hear in the cry of animals, I thought, settling into my tent. I relaxed my grip on the compass in my pocket for the first time that day. I felt approval and satisfaction emanating from it. I also felt that it was giving me permission to take the rocks out of my shoes. I unlaced my boots, emptied the gravel onto the ground, and massaged my sore, wounded feet. Tomorrow I would bathe them in the icy water of the pool. I undid my belt buckle, unburdening myself of the weight of my pistol. I stopped then, and took the pistol from its holster. It gleamed in the lantern light, but I felt such sadness radiating from it that I laid it gently on my bedroll.

"Poor, poor pistol. The things I have made you do, I thought, and my eyes blurred with tears. I stroked the mute, dignified barrel. You have no choice but to serve me, I whispered, and you do it well, with never a complaint. But of course, until now, I never considered your feelings.

"I straightened up. I am becoming a new man, I thought. The closer I get to the hidden land, the more I am changing.

"I decided to take my bedding outside and sleep under the stars. I took my compass, gun, and torch with me—and of course, the skull goblet in its soft wrappings—settled comfortably, smoked a cigarette, and drifted off into disorganized dreams.

"I had been asleep for several hours. I was caught in a sticky and disagreeable dream in which I was reluctantly digging up a grave; I knew it was a dream, and struggled to wake up. When I did, I found myself paralyzed and surrounded by greenish light. A buzzing, crackling noise filled my ears, like the sound of high-tension wires humming and sparking. Through the buzzing I heard faraway shouts, gunshots, and terrible cries from the direction of the men's campsite, but my limbs and head weighed thousands of pounds and I could not lift them.

"The cries receded in the distance as the buzzing grew louder and I felt my consciousness being sucked away from any thought of the men or anything else in the world and directed upward to the cliff wall over my head. There, clinging like an enormous insect to the vertical stone, glowing with its own light, was the rocket launcher that we had left behind a hundred miles ago.

"It shimmered and buzzed, drawing every shred of my attention toward it like an undertow and commanding all my senses. I lay pinned and helpless, an infant swaddled in my sleeping bag, nauseated with dread. It wasn't that I thought the piece of machinery was going to fire at me or tumble down and crush me; it was much worse than that: It was that the thing was in the *wrong place*. And that this was what I was *meant to notice*. I knew it was a riddle, profound and sinister, but I did not know who was asking it, or why, or even in what language it was being asked. Look at me, look at me, look at me, it said; and all I could do was lie there in a state of animal fear.

"Eventually its light faded, and I felt my will flowing back into my limbs, agonizingly, the way sensation returns to a numb arm or leg after you have slept on it. The buzzing died away, and I was aware again of the melee coming from the men's camp. I lay in total darkness on the hard ground in my bag. I struggled to my feet. My body felt bruised and my legs weak and rubbery from fear and adrenaline, as if I had just been in an automobile wreck. I found my gun and my torch in the bedding and moved in the direction of the noise.

"The men's camp was in pandemonium. Torch beams swept this way and that, revealing glimpses of frightened, angry faces. There was shouting and arguing, and one soldier was on the ground weeping hysterically. I found my aide and demanded to know what had happened.

"There was an animal in the camp, he said. A wounded animal. That is, an animal that had once been wounded horribly but had survived. It walked on its forepaws and dragged its useless hindquarters on the ground. What do you mean, an animal? I asked sharply. What kind of animal? A bear, I believe, sir, said my aide shakily, an old emaciated bear. It was no bear, you fool, said another man angrily. It was a leopard. Not a leopard, another cut in. Not a leopard at all. An ape. Some sort of ape. With scruffy hair and bald patches. Silence! I shouted. Never mind what it was. What happened?

"They had been asleep, the aide said. They had been sleeping so soundly that they had let the fire go out. The aide woke up and heard something snuffling and rooting. He shone his torch at the noise, saw the ghastly half-crippled creature in the beam of light, shouted, and fired his gun in the air, waking the whole camp. The creature opened its mouth, let out a piteous bray, and scuttled toward the aide, who fired again, backing up in panic. Other men were on their feet, torches shining. The creature moved this way and that in the confusion of torch beams. Shoot it, one man shouted. Kill it! Someone aimed a gun, but another man knocked his arm up as he fired. No. You will not kill it. You will not kill such a pathetic creature. I will kill you first.

"The noise it made, said my officer. It was dreadful. It was inconsolable sadness, yearning, despair, betrayal. The men dodged, tripped over rocks in the darkness, blundered into one another, and fired wildly into the night sky, their torch beams on the creature as it dragged its dead legs toward one man and then another, bleating, filling them with pity and revulsion. It finally disappeared into the darkness, moments before I arrived.

"The weeping man on the ground looked up then, eyes streaming, voice strangled with grief. It wanted our love, he said. It wanted our love! Several other men were crying now, too.

"You will all retire for the night, I said, my own voice shaking. There will be no more of this nonsense. We are tired. Our imaginations are rubbed raw. It was an animal looking for food. That is all. And I turned and walked back to my campsite, quickly, before the men could see the flood of tears rising behind my own eyes.

"I lay on my bag and wept, for my lost children, for the people I had displaced and killed, for my vanished youth, for the garden snake I crushed with a rock when I was seven, for every betrayed, trembling creature facing the butcher's block anywhere in the world. The images boiled up out of my brain without mercy, a processional of worldly sorrows which I could do nothing to stop. Nothing except this, I thought, reaching for my pistol and putting it to my aching head, but I couldn't do that, either, so intense was my pity for my own poor body. I dropped into an exhausted doze just before dawn, and woke to a gray morning. I was lying on my side, and the first thing I saw when I opened my eyes was my compass, crushed where I had stepped on it in the dark.

"My will was gone. I was dead and empty. The processional had passed, but the dust still rose. I forced myself to my feet. I tied the skull goblet to my back and gathered up my bedding.

"We marched. I put one foot in front of the other out of habit. The men were dazed and silent but for an occasional snuffle of grief. I had nothing to guide me, for I had killed my little compass, and the overcast sky hid the sun so that I could only proceed in a vague northeasterly direction. The vegetation dwindled, grew sparse, and vanished. The water trickling from the rocks dried up. We trudged on. I no longer felt purpose in our motion. What I knew, and what I didn't tell the men, was that we were as lost as it is possible to be lost.

"We began to see ruins. Roofless stone structures, half standing, half tumbled into piles of rocks, the remains of fireplaces. We walked for an hour or more through the remains of a dead, ancient little city, bleak and forlorn. Here was what must have been the marketplace, and here was the elaborate front of a temple carved into the rock wall of the canyon, windows like empty eye sockets staring out at nothing. You've found Paradise, a voice in my head mocked, but you're just a little bit late.

"Then, in the midst of this desolation, I smelled smoke. I drew my pistol and moved round a low butte, and saw a stone shack built into the canyon wall, inhabited in the midst of the ruins; smoke curled lazily up from a stone chimney and a tattered hide hung over the doorway.

"Before I could decide what to do, the hide was

pulled aside and a hermit stepped out. He was skinny and old, the way most hermits are, with the usual tangled hair and dirty rags. He went about his business as if I were not standing there in plain view twenty paces from him. I could see that he was not blind, for he shaded his eyes and glanced up at the sky as if assessing the weather and flipped aside small stones with his walking stick. The men were following me around the rock by now; they stood and gaped like schoolchildren. The hermit, unconcerned, relieved himself against the canyon wall.

"When he was finished, he shuffled in our direction, causing us to mill about like disturbed chickens. He stopped directly in our midst, raised his black eyes to mine, opened his mouth, and let out a noise a thousand times worse than the noise the animal had made and which scattered us in all directions. We covered our ears and ran and ran and ran, blindly, heedlessly, wanting only to get as far from the noise as we could. When I uncovered my ears hours later, lying on the ground, panting, exhausted, only two of the men were still with me. The sound the hermit had made was no longer reaching my ears, but I knew that I would be hearing it in my brain for the rest of my life: It was the sound of one hundred children screaming under torture. I also knew that my quest was over. I had found the hidden land.

"We wandered for weeks. I had been raised a Christian, and the twenty-third psalm became my marching litany: Though I walk through the valley of the shadow of death, I will fear no evil . . . We ate lizards and rabbits and drank rainwater when we could find it. Eventually we stumbled onto the Silk Road, where a band of brigands decided for some reason to spare our lives in exchange for the Potala skull goblet. They took us to an airstrip in Hotan in the

Sinkiang Region, and we eventually caught a plane back to China. As for the rest of the men lost in the canyon, I do not know their fate. Anything at all could have happened to them. For a while after my return I thought of organizing an expedition to search for them, but found myself to be a broken man, prone to tears and weakness and pathological indecision. I made my report to the Chairman, but that was the last official act of my life. Shambala exists, I found it, but no sane person would want to go there, I told anyone who would listen. That was when they started calling me crazy.

"My daughter found me, brought me to this godfor-saken village, and this is where we have been for forty years. She tells me that my son is alive, too, but she will not say where he is or why he is never coming back.

"I don't believe her. I think it is a tale she invented to comfort an old man."

~

One evening after my father had told his story and was asleep, the young scholar told me that he had interviewed another old man just before he came to our village. This old man lived in Peking and had once been a curator whose job it was to catalog the collections of the leaders after their deaths. He had been in charge of the collections of the Chairman himself and some of his high-ranking colleagues. The collections were the choicest *objets* and treasures that China had to offer—porcelains, paintings, furniture, statuary, skimmed off and hoarded in the Forbidden City, the Summer Palace, and the luxury retreats of Huangchou. It was pure acquisitiveness that motivated them, the curator had said, but thank God for their greed because it saved priceless treasures from the whims of the mob.

Among the Chairman's treasures, the old curator had said, was a most unusual piece—a mummified corpse, estimated by its clothing to be Tibetan and hundreds of years old. A revered rimpoche, no doubt. It had been found, according to available information, in a bricked-up chamber in the top floor of a nine-story monastery in Gyangtse, just before the ancient building was destroyed by General Zhang.

Close examination of the mummy revealed another secret: a dry flap of scalp lifted to reveal an inscription carved into the skull.

The inscription was translated, and they found that it was similar to the writings found in several of the ancient "books" of clues leading the anchorite to the legendary realm of Shambala. The skull inscription appeared to be the first of a series of clues for the devout searcher.

I believe that I kept my face composed when he spoke these words, that I maintained an expression of attentive interest. I know that I had a hard time concentrating on his next few sentences. He couldn't possibly know it, but he had just answered an old, old question of mine.

He went on to say that the curator had explained that the clues could be interpreted in different ways—as a metaphor for a spiritual journey to the Shambala within, or they could be interpreted literally: as an actual journey to a physical place. The clue carved in the skull strongly hinted at the latter.

A particularly fascinating discovery, the curator told the young scholar, was that the inscription had been carved while the man was still alive. It did not take much forensic skill to see that the inscribed bone had healed along the edges of the cuts. Quite possibly, it had been the dead man's own wish that his skull be so inscribed. Who knows? He might even have done it himself, the old man had suggested, to ensure that his knowledge would survive him for years— centuries, even—after his death.

The curator said that the mummy had been sent from Tibet to the Chairman by General Zhang. When the rumors got around that Zhang had found Shambala but had returned a broken and defeated man, one couldn't help but speculate.

What irony, the curator had said, that Shambala should turn out to be such a terrible place that Zhang barely made it home and was so afflicted by the journey. Unless . . .

Unless what? the young scholar had asked the curator. Unless Zhang never made it to the real Shambala. Unless the clues were a deliberate trick, a series of false leads meant to send an unworthy searcher as far from the real Shambala as possible. Perhaps, the young scholar said to me, his eyes alight with hope, your father was—excuse me for saying it—just such an unworthy, which would mean that the real Shambala, the true Paradise, is out there somewhere, and that the real clues are waiting to be found. . . .

I did not argue the point that my father might be unworthy of the hidden land. Certainly, I did not take offense. Well, I told our guest, I suppose it is possible that my father was following a deliberately laid set of misleading clues, but didn't he think it just a bit farfetched? And if there were a set of real clues, surely they had been destroyed along with the monasteries and sacred books of Tibet.

I watched the hope fade from his eyes as he shrugged and agreed, reluctantly letting go of the dream of Shambala. I suggested, as gently as I could, that if there were such a place, perhaps it would best be left unsearched for—unless a person could be quite sure he was worthy. And who among us, I asked, is truly worthy?

When the young scholar left, part of me regretted that I could not tell him the truth—he was so sincere and optimistic. Never mind, I told myself. There was always the possibility that someday he would receive an invitation.

The question he had answered for me was also an old, old question of my father's. I agonized over whether or not I should tell my father. In the end, I decided not to. He had told his story, and was at peace for the first time in years. Why risk stirring him up again?

When the old men in Peking sent their orders to my father to search for Shambala, they said that the dead priest had spoken to them. Now, all these long years later, I finally knew what they meant.

~

We bury my father today. It is just me and the villagers now. Though cremation is the law of the land, they say we are remote enough to ignore the law. They insist on tradition, assuring me that it would be best for his spirit. I would have preferred something more Tibetan for him. But we are in China, and who am I to argue?

The village women helped me, as they have with everything else. They provided me with the burial shroud and the proper mourning dress for a filial daughter. We will be in white and there will be a procession complete with banners and mourners and the wailing of funereal music. All the ancient ceremonials will be intact. They bathed the body and purified it according to their custom; they also helped me purify the house for the funeral with special incense. The village men prepared a coffin. These people are simple, but they are compassionate and efficient, and I appreciated their effort. The dead are dead. And although I believe that I long since ceased to love my father, I did have pity on him.

May we all have pity on his tormented soul!

~

There were times during the long uneventful years here with my father when I doubted my own memory. Did I have any proof, anything I could present to myself so that I could be assured that what I remembered was real?

I stood over my father's grave on the evening of his funeral. I was thinking that I would like at least to raise a toast to his memory, but there was nothing to be had in the village but beer and rice wine. Then I remembered. I had something better than beer or rice wine. Much, much better.

I had a bottle of brandy, hidden away for forty years. There was only a swallow or two left in the bottle: French brandy, purchased on the black market in Lhasa during the Cultural Revolution, my gift to Mr. Conway. The aromatic truth serum which had flowed warm in our veins that afternoon over forty years ago, unlocking our secrets. He and I had drunk only a little bit together, and then it was time for him to go. The bottle was nearly empty because I had tried, without success, to drown my sorrow after he was gone.

I returned to the house, rummaging through my memory. Where had I put it? I had carried it rolled up in blankets in a duffel bag from Tibet to Peking and then on to this distant place, the last part of the trip bouncing over rough terrain in Cousin Huang's exceedingly uncomfortable

Russian-built jeep. The bottle survived the last bone-jarring miles, and when we arrived at our new home, I had hastily hidden the bottle away, scarcely wanting to look at it.

It did not take me long to remember my hiding place. I went to my mother's dowry chest, a sandalwood trunk, one of the few things that had survived our personal wars and made it this far west. Inside were my mother's treasures that had belonged to her mother and before that to her grand-mother. It had been all her earthly wealth when she married my father over sixty years before—linens, rare silks, small pieces of jewelry, jade and gold hair ornaments.

The bottle was there underneath the shiny rustling fab-rics and tinkling bits of precious metal. It was wrapped in paper—the same paper it had been wrapped in when I bought it. Protected from light all these years, the paper had scarcely deteriorated; I put my nose to it and inhaled, imagining that I detected a faint scent of the Lhasa marketplace. The bottle was tightly corked. I held it up to the light and looked at the dark liquid rolling back and forth behind the brown-tinted glass. There was just enough left for two small toasts.

I returned to the general's grave site, on a hilltop not far from the quarry, carefully carrying the bottle in one hand, and in the other, a package that had arrived just that morning from England, sent by our young scholar. He had written URGENT! MANUSCRIPT! on the package in bold letters, hoping to avoid the ubiquitous delays of the Chinese postal bureau-cracy. It was addressed to my father and I suppose that if the post had been faster to our remote village, it might have reached him.

My intuition told me what was in the package before I even tore the paper. My poor father. It is probably just as well that he never saw it. I don't know what it would have done to him. But I took it with me when I set out for the grave site with the bottle of brandy.

I uncorked the bottle, closed my eyes, and inhaled the vapors, bringing back that long-ago time. Someone explained to me once why it was that odors evoked the past in such an immediate way. The olfactory nerve, I was told, is an elongation of the oldest part of the cerebrum; smell is our most ancient sense. With my nose to the bottle, the room in Lhasa, the time, the emotions—all were resurrected.

Here's to you, Father, I said, and tilted the bottle to my lips. The brandy burned my throat and filled my chest with fire, and made me lightheaded almost instantly. Then I raised the bottle and poured most of the remaining brandy onto the fresh earth of the grave. The amber liquid made tiny craters and seeped down into the dirt. So, Father, I said, now that you have had a taste of Mr. Conway's brandy, I can imagine that both saint and demon, lama and warrior, have drunk from the same bottle.

I knelt, resting my knees on the soft warm earth. For that brief instant I felt closer to him than I could remember feeling when he was alive. Demon. Why had I used that word? My father was human—no more, no less—with all the implied weaknesses. He had been a kindly and attentive father when my Brother and I were children. And even when we first arrived in Tibet, he was still a good father, trying to keep peace between Brother and me. No, Father, you were not an especially bad man, not an originator or innovator of evil. You were simply . . . an opportunist. And now I've raised a toast to you, the man who might well have sealed Conway's fate. You were, after all, my father. And I kept my promise to you.

I held the bottle up and let the last drops fall to my

lips. The tiny amount of liquid on my tongue sent up a ghost of a taste. I swallowed it. This last toast was to Conway and our final night together. Here's to more nights together, I whispered. Then I looked for a more comfortable place to sit, since I was going to be here for a while. There was a nice flat rock nearby; I sat down and took the young scholar's manuscript from the envelope. It was time to close a few remaining circles. For that was how I thought about life— as a series of circles, closed or left open.

I read the letter the scholar had enclosed. He said that the author of the manuscript had been an Englishman named Rutherford. The untitled manuscript was preceded by a frontispiece, a single crisp white sheet of paper on which was typed a three-word Latin phrase, a terse classical challenge to our beliefs: *Quia Impossibile Est.* Whether one decides to believe the contents of this manuscript or not, the long-ago author implied, there could be no better reason than *because it is impossible.*

The manuscript had been sent to him by Rutherford's daughter, the scholar said, in response to a query the scholar had put in the London *Times* asking for lore, information, letters, etc., pertaining to the Shambala legend. Her father, she said, had written the manuscript in the 1930s after a trip to China. In 1973, when he was seventy-seven years old and a widower in poor health, he announced abruptly that he was going on holiday to Italy and vanished, never to be seen or heard from again. The daughter had kept the manuscript all these years. Now she was an old woman herself, and thought she might as well pass it on to the scholar.

1973. Just a few years after I watched Mr. Conway's plane become a speck on the horizon. Had Mr. Rutherford received one of those discreet hand-lettered invitations from his old, old friend? My heart gave a small leap. I raised my eyes to the west. Are you alive, I whispered?

I started to read:

> Chapter One. May 1931.
>
> During that third week of May the situation in Baskul had become much worse and, on the 20th, Air Force machines arrived by arrangements from Peshawur to evacuate the white residents. . . . A few miscellaneous aircraft were also employed, among them being a cabin machine lent by the Maharajah of Chandapore. In this, about 10 A.M., four passengers embarked: Miss Roberta Brinklow, of the Eastern Mission; Henry D. Barnard, an American; Hugh Conway, H.M. Consul; and Captain Charles Mallinson, H.M. Vice-Consul. . . .

In the end, I read both manuscripts out loud in their entirety over my father's grave. It took me a few days to do it, going back to our house only to eat and sleep, and I felt every one of my sixty-five years in my stiff, sore limbs. There you have it, Father, I said, rising to my feet. Now you know.

Though I did not believe in ghosts, I imagined for a moment my father's angry spirit materializing in Shangri-La on a moonlit night. I'm sorry we had to trick you, Father, I added, but you gave us no choice. No choice. And what choice did you leave me but to take care of you?

~

I placed both manuscripts in the padded mailing envelope. My timing was perfect. The hydroelectric construction below the old quarry was nearly finished. For days now, the heavy earth-moving equipment had been silent. Teams of engineers in hard hats swarmed all over the dam itself, giving final minute inspection to the gates and locks and sluices and giant turbines. Tomorrow they would release the floodgates on billions of metric tons of water that had been held for centuries in glaciers and mountain streams. Tomorrow.

And because tomorrow is the last day for me to record these events, I call upon my final reflections and memories of Shangri-La. There was another circle that was closed a long time ago. Time, now, has made this event clear, too: The Ancient Greeks speak of a connection not only between truth and beauty but also between the terrible and the beautiful, the terrifying and the beautiful. I understand the meaning of this now.

In those moments before I beheld my first vision of Shangri-La, my anticipation was not unlike terror. What had awaited us from the moment our airplane touched down on that precarious plateau was truly terra incognita, and some part of me must have sensed it with a kind of dread long before we dropped over the last ridge in Mr. Bryant's gondola. I had tried to hide it; Brother, pale and frightened, was displaying enough emotion for both of us. If it wasn't for the sustained effort of conversing and hearing Mr. Barnard's jovial good-natured American accent, I think I might just have fainted on the metal floor. And that was just the first of my remembered feelings. The rest came in sequence like the erratic frames of an old motion picture. And then the moving picture froze on the first frame of Hugh Conway.

Maybe it was the aroma of the brandy that brought it all back with such power and immediacy. I don't know. But today I relived the intoxication, and a taste of the anxiety, as if I were approaching that valley for my first time and last time, over forty years ago.

My heart is beating fast today, high in my chest. Sometimes I feel as if my heart is a little animal, separate from me, with a life of its own, trapped inside my rib cage. A prescient little animal that senses the coming of floods, earthquakes, upheavals. Today it is agitated inside its cage. What does it know?

We have a long journey ahead of us, yes. An arduous journey which might end in a chasm of ice, or worse, at a dead end. An old woman standing in front of a wall of mountains, with nothing but silence greeting her. All of that might make a person's heart uneasy. But I know the true source of my trepidation, this peculiar mixture of dread and fierce joy: It's that I may actually find my way back to Shangri-La.

What will I find?

He said he would wait. I will be transformed in his eyes, like poor Lo-Tsen. Only it will be forty long, hard, and very real years which will have taken away my dewy skin and shining black hair. I looked in the mirror this morning as I was gathering what I will take with me. I am old, but I am handsome and sturdy. Will he still be able to love me? I believe that he will. I remember what he said about Lo-Tsen when she left him in the mission hospital: She was still beautiful, never mind how old she was.

Assuming, that is, that he is alive at all. I have not

forgotten that droning insect, so frail and infinitesimal, disappearing over the horizon.

And of course, there is someone else, too, that I have thought of so many times over the years, someone else sending little jolts of anxious electricity through my poor heart.

Brother. Poor, poor Brother. You were so unhappy when they led you away. What has become of you? Did you die in some stupid, impetuous attempt to escape, like young Mallinson? Do you lie encased in ice, forever young, at the bottom of a dizzying gorge, where even the Sherpas could not go? And if you did die, might it not have been the best thing? Because I have wondered about you for all these years. Either Paradise transformed you, or you transformed Paradise. Conway led Father astray with a false trail, but what if he himself was on a false trail by going after Father? We left you in Shangri-La. For all we know we left a deadly virus there. Were you the seed of the fruit that caused Adam and Eve to be tossed from the garden? Perhaps I will arrive there, forty years and thousands of miles later, and find nothing but an empty hole. Or maybe I will find you living in a cell, an ascetic of your own making. Or the commander of a youth platoon, marching and reciting. A drunk, a lunatic, or . . .

Or perhaps I will find you, alive and well, transformed into some being I can scarcely imagine. Maybe the lush gardens and magnificent pavilions, scented and still in their muted green light as if they were underwater, the soft breezes that pass through the branches, the serenading wind chimes, the eyes around you, so receptive and cheerful, the music that is practiced in the courtyards and plazas nearly every evening . . . perhaps it finally found its way into you. Were you moved by an ancient gavotte by Rameau or Couperin? Or an unlikely piece by Cage or Glass or Chu-yin? Did something at long last touch you? There are stories of hardhearted young Red Guard adolescents from the sixties and seventies who outgrew the madness, who have come forth to repudiate their past deeds with great remorse. I would like to believe that you are one of the repentant ones, but it is a hard leap for me to make. In your mind, what crimes were there to repent?

~

I have packed what I need. I am carrying a small rucksack on my shoulders; whatever else I am going to need I will find along the way. I will not be returning to this house. I walk the long way round the hill toward the saddle and the quarry, avoiding my father's grave. Today it is quiet at the quarry. No longer an immense canyon, a dark somber brooding pit mirroring my feelings for so many years, now it is fresh and expansive and full of hope. My heart, though not quiet, is happier; today it thrums against my breastbone like the wings of a bird about to be set free.

It is a new lake that glints at us, sparkling and winking between the hills, as the high rarefied sunlight reflects off its startling blue surface. And as if it had always been there, the water dances and plays in the shimmering light, the wind sending up little white horses. It is a bright and beautiful place now.

I am standing at the edge: a sheer cliff wall that plunges a hundred feet or more straight down to the water. The water is very clear and I can see perhaps another fifty or one hundred distorted feet down the gray-white walls of stone until they vanish in the depths. It is a dizzying height for me. I am terrified of such vertical drops. But I had best get used to it. There are other, grander heights awaiting me.

I remember Conway's terrace that leaned out a mile above the lush valley floor, surrounded on all sides by those crystalline heights. The scents of frangipani, wild roses, lilac, and honeysuckle. There is another fragrance that I have long associated with him. It had only taken that one precious day—those few hours, really—to burn the memory forever in my mind. The smell of moonlight is what he called it. I will not forget that, either. It is linked forever with him. He told me that was how the Chinese had referred to the miraculous fragrance of the tuberose. I remember clearly that they were cultivated along the perimeters of his high terrace, woven in among the balustrades, their stalks and clustered flowers etched in sharp relief against the pale cool hues of the mountains.

I've returned there ten thousand times in my mind. Thought transports you. It is like reading a book; your mind is in another land while the pages are open in front of you. But this is a harsh world; the body is where it is; transporting the poor body is another matter altogether. There is only one way for me to get back, and that is to move my breathing body and my beating heart every inch of a thousand miles and more until I am there. I leave tonight.

So I stand now, uncomfortably, on the cliff that plunges straight down into that perfectly clear water. Today I consider my unnerving exploration a purely literary sacrifice. Or, should I say, an unliterary sacrifice! I have bound the envelope containing the two manuscripts with strong twine and I have weighted the package with heavy stones. Earlier, I had thought of burning all of this. Much simpler, indeed. But then how much like my father's funeral this would seem.

I wanted this to be different. I did not want to just erase it all so brutally. Those green depths seemed, somehow, more appropriate to the task. Soon they will hide my secrets. Secrets I have shared only with my father's ghost.

I approach the edge and have a moment of indecision. But I take myself in hand. I have a promise to keep. I drop the package: It floats in slow motion, down, down, bouncing off outcroppings. I think for an instant that the weights will be torn free and pages will flutter down and scatter on the surface of the lake, to be recovered and read by the world for years to come. But that does not happen. The package strikes the water, a tight bundle of paper. For a moment it lingers on the surface, reluctant to die. But that is only an illusion. It is pulled under. I see a tiny circle of suction. Already the ink on the tissuelike paper must be dissolving, and with it the tales of a secret land, of a great man, and of my father's disgrace and misfortune. Down. Down. The rectangular package does not travel straight; I am surprised how even with the weight it sinks like a feather on the breeze, rocking from side to side. Smaller and fainter with each moment it ricochets off the protruding rockface some fifty feet below the surface, and slips down into the blackening abyss.

Cooney, Eleanor

Shangri-La

| DUE DATE | | | E641   25.00 |
|---|---|---|---|
|  |  |  |  |
|  |  |  |  |
|  |  |  |  |
|  |  |  |  |
|  |  |  |  |
|  |  |  |  |
|  |  |  |  |
|  |  |  |  |
|  |  |  |  |
|  |  |  |  |
|  |  |  |  |
|  |  |  |  |